The Last Freedom

The Last Freedom

✦

**A novel on the real-life adventure
of Dr. Viktor Frankl**

MICHAEL F. RYAN

iUniverse, Inc.
New York   Bloomington

The Last Freedom
A novel on the real-life adventure of Dr. Viktor Frankl

Copyright © 2008 by Michael F. Ryan

iUniverse books may be ordered through booksellers or by contacting:

iUniverse
1663 Liberty Drive
Bloomington, IN 47403
www.iuniverse.com
1-800-Authors (1-800-288-4677)

ISBN: 978-0-595-44068-9 (pbk)
ISBN: 978-0-595-88391-2 (ebk)

Printed in the United States of America

Acknowledgements

You know how people on a concert stage will sometimes dive into the "mosh pit" and surf on a sea of hands carrying them aloft? That's exactly what it's like writing a book. For one thing, it's a leap of faith. For another thing, you need an ocean of friends and caring strangers to make sure you don't fall.

I wouldn't have taken this leap were it not for four people in particular: Sharon Stone—the Topeka, Kan., massage therapist, not the actress—who first told me about Dr. Viktor Frankl, and who later mailed me his classic *Man's Search for Meaning* out of the blue; Sister Sally Savery, the Brazilian missionary from Wamego, Kan., who inspired me to visit her children's shelter in Jacundá, Brazil—where I finally read Frankl's masterpiece to pass the time (and what a meaningful setting to read it in!); Dr. Jay Levinson of Baltimore, a 20-year assistant of Dr. Frankl's who took an even bigger leap of faith than I did by not only accepting me and my crazy project over the phone, but who also convinced the widowed Mrs. Eleonore Frankl to take me in and pour her heart out to me. It will always rank as one of the great privileges of my life.

The fourth person, of course, is Mrs. Frankl herself, who was the First Lady, secretary and soul mate to one of the great thinkers and humanitarians of the 20th Century; she was his rock, his typist, his co-pilot in life and, today, a great lady in her own right.

To the Frankls' son-in-law and daughter, Professor Franz and Gaby Vesely, and their lovely grown children Katja and Alexander—Dr. Frankl's beloved grandchildren—thank you, too, for taking me in so warmly.

OK, they're the ones who helped me jump off the stage. Now for just some of the hands that caught me.

One of the smartest things I did early on was assemble a group of respected friends in Topeka to guide my writing. I called them the Frankl Society of Topeka: Roger Aeschliman, the best-read man I've ever known and my best friend and hero; Jim McHenry of the Topeka Library Foundation, who helped conceive the book's title; Maria Russo Wilson, an incredible friend and an honest critic I tried hard to please; Mark Hood, my mentor and a model of love and selflessness; and my dear friend and effervescent chairwoman of the Frankl Society, Norma Chase, who makes everyone and everything she touches better.

I landed on top of another circle of supportive hands when I moved to Augusta, Ga., including Pat Goodwin, who seemed to want this project's success more than I did; it's a real friend who adopts another's vision so completely. Beth Bradley and JoAnn Hoffman rounded out the Frankl Society of Augusta, not so much by holding me up with their hands but by propelling me forward with their boots.

The goofy and wonderful Brian Mulherin, one of Augusta's greatest treasures, kept me on task by slipping me a few dollars for future publication expenses every time I saw him. My webmaster, Kim Luciani, has done more for me than I could ever do for her. Others, such as Angie and Carter Morris, simply read the book and kept my spirits up through the long and difficult road to publication.

And then there's John Bock, a newspaper friend whom I followed to Augusta from Topeka and who, on a dimly lit Hilton Head beach, shared with me the closely held ancient secret of book writing that a clandestine Da Vinci Code-style cult has handed down through the centuries: "Get your teeth around it and get the (expletive deleted) done!" Sage advice.

Along the way, there's always an occasional hand from a stranger—like the Heathrow security officer who saw me melt down late one night in the lobby when the airline lost my bag and delivered me too late for the last hotel shuttle. He pulled out his own British coins and used a pay phone to get me a ride.

Of course, absolutely none of this would be possible without my rock and foundation: my wife Susan, whom I proposed to 25 years ago after knowing her but two weeks and two days. The best leap of faith I will ever make.

My heartfelt advice to anyone considering writing a book—well, beyond getting your teeth around it and getting the &%@$*! done:

Make sure you have a mosh pit populated by some of the most wonderful people in the world, and you'll be just fine.

A Word From The Author

Though this is a work of fiction, and Roger Murphy and all his associates are purely fictional, Viktor Frankl was quite real, as are all his relatives and associates. All of their interactions with Roger Murphy are, of course, fictional, but the experiences of Dr. Frankl and his family and friends described in this book are real.

Prologue

"My God, that was close!" Viktor thought. "I'm not ready to die!"

His right foot slipped a bit more, sending a scattering of rocks racing to the chasm below. He knew one wrong step, one miscalculation, could end both his rock climbing and his promising young life and medical practice.

The thing is, he knew full well that his Aryan guide, Hubert, was in even greater danger than he—even if they both made it safely up the sheer wall of Hohe Wand—simply for allowing Viktor Frankl, a Jew, the harmless joy of this little rock-climbing adventure. For in Hitler's Austria, those citizens forced to wear a yellow Star of David in public were not allowed such liberties. Too good for the soul.

It was certainly good for Viktor's. After all the tense buildup of Hitler's impending annexation of Austria, it had been far too long since Viktor's last climb.

"For a true climber," he told his guide after hoisting himself to the top, "it's amazing how claustrophobic even the widest expanse of flatland can feel." Hubert nodded agreement, swiveling his thick neck around, both to survey the world below and to instinctively make sure they were alone and safe.

While Hubert's stocky build was as solid as the high wall they had just scaled, and his face was nearly as weathered as the rock all around them, king of the mountain was the last thing one would have thought while looking at Viktor Frankl. A thin man built precariously on two spindly legs, he was denied height every bit as he was bulk.

Yet, a mountain climber's most important attributes are, it turns out, neither legs nor bulbous flesh nor the shadow he sculpts on the ground below. They are, rather, a fiery heart and a nimble intellect. And Dr. Frankl was possessed of a combustible mixture of both.

Indeed, Frankl's peers down in Vienna were beginning to acknowledge more and more the obvious truth: Under Frankl's combed-back wavy blanket of black hair was one of the most brilliant minds of his day. And as his many female admirers in the city, and at Rothschild Hospital, recognized, this 30-something neurologist and psychiatrist not only had the potential to step out of the shadows of famed Viennese psychiatrists Freud and Adler, but he also had the beginnings of a stature large enough to cast his own powerful outline on his homeland and beyond.

Even in that short, bespectacled frame.

For the moment, as he once again basked in the cool sunlight of his beloved Rax mountains, he allowed himself to forget that, however bright his future might be, it was now clouded by the fog of hatred and oppression rolling in from Berlin. And that he had allowed his one chance of escape to slip through his fingers.

It's not as if he hadn't seen it coming. Everyone had. Austria had reluctantly thrown down a red carpet for Adolf Hitler. But while many of the city's Jews had already taken flight, Viktor had stayed. In the face of who knows what, he had stayed. In a moment trapped between pure fear and uncertain self-transcendence, he had opened his palms and let fly his freedom to the wind.

Viktor's eyes shot open. His thoughts returned to that fateful moment in the church like a boomerang, and he didn't like it. Not up here. Not where he should be at peace.

Hubert saw the whole thing. He noticed Viktor's slide into pangs of bitter memory, and his sudden return to reality. Hubert quickly turned to the panorama before them, lest Viktor realize that Hubert had been watching his every thought.

"It's madness down there, my friend," Hubert drooped with uncharacteristic resignation. "Pure madness."

"And here we are, in the safest place in the world!" beamed the ever-optimistic Viktor.

Hubert first smiled, then threw his head back and bellowed, "Yes, my friend. Here we are. The last two sane people on the face of the Earth—having climbed to rise above the insanity!"

"And so now we know the difference between sanity and insanity," added Viktor. "About 200 meters!"

When you've had precious little to laugh about, you have a full store of it to let out at once. And that's what these two friends did at this moment. Neither Freud's psychoanalysis, nor Adler's individual psychology—not even Viktor Frankl's own logotheraphy, which was just taking shape in his mind and in his writings and lectures—could have offered up a more therapeutic relief than this laugh, which shook them like an earthquake.

There they lay, alone above the strife, for untold moments—the Jew and the Aryan. Tied together by a lifesaving rope, yet connected by an even stronger cord that reaches through the umbilicus and straight into the soul. Humanity itself bonded them. Raw, open, real and, in its respects, divine. At this moment, though without an earthly audience—and, in fact, in spite of the fact that it could have brought both men severe punishment at the hands of the Nazis, had anyone seen them—the two men were sending a message to the heavens: a short story about man's *humanity* to man. The irony was as rich and warm as the late Vienna summer. And every bit as fleeting.

The setting sun would do so eventually, anyway, so Hubert broke the moment. "What shall come of us, Viktor?"

"I don't know, my friend," Viktor whispered, keeping his eyes fixed on infinity. He thought for a few moments, and Hubert let him. "I have so much I want to do. Need to do. I will publish a book, if the Nazis don't stop me. I have a beautiful young wife—and I must provide for her, regardless of what the Nazis say. My parents are getting older and more frightened by the moment. But I worry most about my patients. They need me. Likewise, I need them."

Looking over at Hubert, reading the unabated worry in his downy brow, Viktor smiled.

"We must use our wits to survive, Hubert. Like when I was 12." Viktor propped himself up on his elbows for emphasis, and Hubert took notice. "I was crossing a bridge when I was approached by a gang of youths coming the other way. 'Are you a Jew?' they asked me in an angry tone. 'Yes,' I said proudly. 'But am I not also human?' And you know what, Hubert? They left me alone and walked away. How could they argue with me then? How could they violate the line I had just drawn for them—a line that separates humanity from inhumanity?"

Both men knew—and each one knew that the other one knew—that it was a line that, in Austria and elsewhere, was being erased at that very moment.

Viktor looked over at his Aryan friend wearing his German armed forces uniform, and realized that he was preaching to the choir. Imagining a more wanting audience on the horizon, Viktor jumped up, gesturing toward the vista with his right fist as high as his small frame could lift it.

"Did you hear that, Adolf? I am also human! *I am also human!*"

1

Lord, how he hated heights.

To be sure, Roger Murphy would never have ventured out on the Golden Gate Bridge himself. He didn't much care for crossing it in a car, much less on foot and, heaven knows, stopping for any amount of time. For any reason. Not even to save his life.

But as it happens, he wasn't pulling his car over and stopping on the bridge to save *his* life.

It all started with that phone call …

◆　　　◆　　　◆

"Is this Roger Murphy?" a sudden, nervous male voice insisted more than asked.

"Speaking. What can I do for you?" Roger was a little annoyed by both the stranger's intrusion so late in the afternoon, as well as the volume of the intrusion.

"*The* Roger Murphy?"

Roger shifted in his broken-down, outdated and nowhere-near-ergonomic 30-year-old newsroom chair and poked his wire rim glasses back up the gentle slope of his nose. "The one and only. Now what can I …?"

"You need to come interview me," the voice quivered, a little pleading and a lot agitated.

"Oh yes?" Roger was audibly unimpressed. "And pray tell, why should I do that?"

"Because," the man fired back insistently, "I'm about to kill myself and I want *you* to tell the world why."

Roger Murphy was never at a loss for words. But now he was speechless, and a captive audience, pressing the phone nearly inside his ear.

He sat up in his chair, leaned both his elbows on the piles of assorted papers on his desk, and ran his free hand through his thick black hair parted precisely in the middle.

"Hello?" the voice on the phone flailed.

"I'm here," Roger registered meekly, again breaking new ground for him.

"You're my hero. You're the best writer at the *Chronicle*—the best writer in the bay area, period. That column you did on Mayor Agnos last week was incredible."

"Uh, thanks. Thank you," Roger managed with genuine gratitude—especially genuine since the compliment came from an apparently dying man.

"I'd be extremely honored," the voice continued, "and—uh, eternally grateful—if you would tell my story. It's not the most exciting story you'll ever tell, I'm sure. But at least," a long pause, "it's short and to the point."

Roger was still trying to clear his head. He was used to dealing with nutty callers. You can't be a journalist of 20 years, and certainly not in San Francisco, without getting all kinds of off-the-wall calls. His favorite, of many years ago, was the lady who kept him on the phone for 20 minutes telling him her theory that thick carpet is a conspiracy against women. It seems thick carpet makes women dig their high heels into it, tripping them, causing them to fall and sustain brain damage. Though not necessarily a terribly patient man, Roger was seasoned by hard experience and pain, particularly in Vietnam, and had therefore developed a patient ear. Listening is also good for business when one is a journalist, he figured. So, he usually just listened the poor souls out until they were through and gently lied, "OK, we'll get a reporter right on it."

It was always a lie, of course—a white lie intended not just to shorten the occasion but also to leave the poor caller with the warm feeling that, indeed, the media were looking into the presence of aliens in area restaurants, the chance that the president could be sending radio signals through a caller's tooth filling, or the distinct possibility that insects are set to take over the Earth.

He never gave the fringe callers a second thought. But then, he never imagined a life might be riding on his promise to "get a reporter right on it."

So this time he made no such empty promise. Quickly processing the gravity of the call, and sensing the sincerity of the besieged voice on the other end, he made his decision. For the first time in two decades of crank calls, he would take this one seriously.

Even if it were a prank, he thought, it would get him out of the office sooner and closer to the A's-Giants game that evening. Huge day in the bay area. Game 3 of the 1989 World Series between the two bay teams.

"OK, where are you?"

The man on the phone seemed to catch his breath—or perhaps it was the bay area breeze whistling through the phone. "Guess!" the man yelped, suddenly playing it cool despite his circumstances.

"I really wouldn't know." Roger frantically tried to recall the ambient sounds he'd been hearing from the other end: Wind. Ocean. Traffic—and a lot of it.

"I hear it's the No. 1 place in the world for this sort of thing," the voice offered.

"Oh no," Roger thought, seemingly loud enough to be heard on the other side of the conversation.

"The bridge?"

"Yeah, the bridge," admitted the man.

Roger's elbows slid out, his hand-covered face descending into the fault line between stacks of papers.

The bridge.

2

"The Golden Gate Bridge," Roger finished in his head, as it emerged, shaking, out of the crevice of his desk's landslide.

Why, oh why, did it have to be the bridge? Living in San Francisco is tough enough on a guy with acrophobia. You could check the city's cable car poles and measure the scratch marks Roger had left during each inhumane plummet along Hyde Street between the Hallidie Plaza and Ghirardelli Square. Why does this guy have to be flirting with a flying leap off a famously high, windy suspension bridge? Why couldn't he just be in some ground floor apartment with a gun in his mouth?

"OK," Roger finally cleared his head. "And, uh, you won't do anything until I get there?"

"Not if you hurry your ass here!" The man's agitation grew more discernible.

"I'll do my best. You know how the traffic is in this city, though"

"Just hurry up!" the man finally shouted. "It's frickin' cold out here!"

Not as cold as where you're headed, Roger thought, remembering how callous he could be.

◆   ◆   ◆

Roger crushed the black receiver into its resting place, knowing he'd need every second to think. Journalists are supposed to be cool in crises, but, truth be known, they generally don't find themselves in the *middle* of emergencies—they're usually the ones to show up afterward and do all the second-guessing. Someone once observed of editorial writers in particular that all they ever do is come down off the hill after the battle is over and shoot the wounded. Roger knew that wasn't far off the mark.

Thus, even for a journalist of some 20 years, it can be a shock to the system to suddenly find oneself awash in a crisis. Roger yanked off his glasses, burying his face in his hands and inhaling like an empty Hoover.

Someone needs to call the cops, of course. Or suicide prevention. Or both. The boss needs to know what's going on.

He glanced over to Ed Miller's glass office; the executive editor's totem-pole face topped by bushy silver hair was immersed in the pixels of his computer screen, working hard on something, most likely another computer game.

"Excuse me, Ed," Roger burped just before entering the office, careful to give the executive editor time to clear the game off his computer screen. "Something huge has come up."

Miller, a tall, 60ish man with glasses, only the facade of a chin pasted on a flat transition to neck, and a shelf-like paunch, swung around in his chair. His leading columnist was a hard-to-handle creative type, given to flights of fancy and bouts of emotion. Roger Murphy, Miller knew, could be irascible, grumpy, ill-tempered and immature. And he loved him for it, in no small part because he was a brilliant writer, but also because he saw a lot of himself in Roger, 20 years removed. But he knew that Roger Murphy, despite all his shortcomings, was not the kind to exaggerate one bit. So when Roger used the word "huge," he instantly had Miller's full attention, and not just because he really wasn't engaged in anything else.

"Did you call 911?" Miller asked upon hearing about the caller.

"Not yet. You're the first person I've told." Not only was that true, it was also certain to be a meaty entrée for Miller's burly ego to eat up.

"I'll take care of the cops. You just get your ass out there and talk that guy down!"

"Right, Chief!"

Normally, Miller would playfully respond, "Don't call me Chief!", just like Clark Kent's boss, Perry White. But not even hardnosed newsmen joke at a time like this.

They do, however, think odd things for human beings.

"Murphy!" he called. Roger leaned back around the corner. "Should we send a photog?"

Roger paused, but only for a half-second. "I don't think so, Chief. It might spook him."

"Right. Get going!" Miller swung the phone to his ear. "I'll see if I can't get the cops to beat you there."

Roger had grabbed his jacket off the hall tree near his desk and had one foot around the corner to leave when that foot stopped in mid-air, swung around and landed in the other direction. There was one more thing that couldn't wait.

"Come on, come on," he ordered the phone. "Melody! Roger. I've got a slight problem. No time to explain. Can you meet me at the 'Stick? Great! I'll try to be there right before game time."

◆   ◆   ◆

He needn't have worried that he might not find the man from the phone call. Before Roger even got close to the bridge, he could see the blinking lights of two police cars. He passed the cars and pulled his tired green Volvo to the right side in front of them, scraping the orange metal guardrail jutting up knee-high in front of the curb. Flipping on his hazard lights, he slipped from the car, sidestepped over the guardrail and strode gingerly toward who-knew-what.

Cars continued to zoom by, occasionally honking their displeasure that this group had closed off part of a coveted rush-hour lane. They didn't know what was going on, and didn't care. In contrast, the 10-foot-wide sidewalk, which normally featured its own rush-hour traffic, was nearly barren. Probably blocked off, Roger thought.

"Here he is," shouted one officer to another, instantly recognizing one of San Francisco's most recognizable faces. "Thanks for coming, Mr. Murphy. I'm Capt. Kincade, SFPD, and this is Lt. Stewart, California Highway Patrol. And this," he turned, nodding to the right over the bridge railing, "is the guest of honor."

Roger looked over the four-foot rail with trepidation, to see a much younger man than he expected—a slight, scraggly young man of maybe 20, wearing a San Francisco Giants baseball cap, white long-sleeve T-shirt and gray sweatpants and sneakers, standing on the narrow walkway just a few feet below and about 30 feet down the way.

Roger pulled back quickly, shaking off early feelings of vertigo. The more attentive officer, Capt. Kincade, noticed and grabbed Roger's elbow.

"They really need to put a higher rail on this thing," the captain excused Roger's fright. "It'd make my life easier."

"I imagine so," Roger quickly agreed.

"They tried to do it a few years ago," the officer continued, "but the politicians on the bridge board wouldn't hear of it. Aesthetics and all …"

"I know," Roger added meekly. "I wrote a column trashing the idea." The two of them just looked at each other for a long moment.

Just then, a lone passerby walked up and politely but brazenly stuck his nose in.

"Hi, officers, my name is Ron Pauley," declared the 50ish man with pull-over hair and a pocket-protector air about him, shaking the officers' hands. He glanced briefly at Roger, perhaps thinking it was *he* who was about to jump off the bridge. "I'm a retired crisis prevention counselor from the

Oakland side, and just happened to be driving by. Can you use my services, by any chance?"

"Actually, yes!" Roger piped up before the troopers could speak.

"Mr. Pauley, this is Roger Murphy with the *Chronicle*," the captain announced, as if introducing a rock act.

"Oh, *yes*," erupted the professorial Pauley, extending his hand to Roger. "You're that conservative fellow!" Roger nodded impatiently, wanting to skip the small talk.

The captain continued. "Our subject over here requested Mr. Murphy's presence, and he was kind enough to come down."

"Good for *you*, Mr. Murphy," Pauley percolated, suddenly leading Roger by the arm down the sidewalk, toward the nearly-forgotten jumper, and taking a subtle lead over the situation. "Would you mind if I gave you a quick briefing on what to do?"

Roger was suddenly thrilled to welcome this interloper's interloping. "Mind? Are you kidding? I wouldn't know the first thing ..."

"Of course. All right, then. We only have a few seconds, so I'll just give you the bare essentials.

"First, get his attention. I suppose his having summoned you, and you being a celebrity and all, that won't be a problem, yes? Well, then, the next thing you need to know is that you should make some expression of caring—and hope. Let him know in some compassionate way that the future is unknown and yet to be written, and that things can get better, and will. Fair?"

Roger thought this situation akin to being thrown without warning aboard a plane on D-Day and being told what to do when he lands on French soil and the shooting starts. But he nodded his head slightly and let Pauley finish.

"Lastly, search for something good in him, in his life that is, and remind him of it."

With that, Roger was led by Pauley on one side and the unfriendly-looking trooper Stewart to the railing, about 10 feet down from the young man on the walkway.

"Oh," Pauley stopped short. "One more thing. Help him find meaning."

Roger, being gripped on each elbow as if he were a danger to fly away, gave Pauley a quick look as if to say, "Is that all?"

The two helped Roger over the railing and onto the perilously narrow metal walkway sunken below the sidewalk—where, with nothing between him and a dive into the bay, Roger now had a totally unfettered view of the cold water below. He looked down, and for some odd reason focused on a group of sea lions swimming below.

Before letting go of Roger's arm, Lt. Stewart bent over the rail to speak his first words about six inches from Roger's face.

"Murphy!" he growled through clenched teeth. "Not on my shift." The officer wagged his finger nearly up Roger's nose, and lowered his voice noticeably. "Not on my shift."

"Does he know that, officer? Cause, hey, I can just shimmy over there and tell him to wait until next shift."

Stewart held onto Roger briefly, then let go and backed off.

For the highway patrol, this had to be a matter of some routine. There are dozens, if not hundreds, of suicides or false starts each year on this magnificent, awe-inspiring bridge. Eleven men perished building it in the 1930s; since then, something approaching 1,000 desperate souls followed them into the bay purposely. And that's just the ones we know about. After a certain amount of time presiding over, and often failing to prevent, this quiet carnage, if you're a cop you just do what you can. You follow protocol, and if you can save someone's life and go home and pop open a beer, great. If not, you've done your best, you feel sorry for the poor bastard for a minute or two, and go on. Not because you don't care—quite the contrary, because you *do* care, or you wouldn't be in this line of work. But the simple fact is, you've got to spread your caring out sparingly, if only to spare yourself. It's simply professional detachment—and a veteran of the force will tell you it's as essential to a law enforcement officer's well-being as a gun on the hip. Besides, a philosopher once argued that if you feel another's pain too well, all you've done is double the misery.

So, just looking at the police officers at the scene of this impending suicide, it might have appeared for all the world that they were gathering to calmly lure a catatonic cat out of a tree. But for Roger Murphy, this was a disaster waiting to happen, for several reasons. And *he* wasn't even the one going to jump.

Still a few feet out of earshot from the likely jumper, Roger edged carefully toward him on the narrow walkway. The young man appeared less nervous than he had over the phone. Perhaps he'd simply had time to calm down. The officers, knowing how to approach him, had made certain he remained as calm as possible; the last thing you want, they figure, is to make a jumper, well, jumpy. And at this point, their non-threatening presence seemed to give him the comfort and attention he'd been craving even without knowing it.

Nearby was an emergency phone placed there by the suicide prevention crowd for the express purpose of giving jumpers one more chance at a lifeline.

The kind of lifeline now being thrown to this desperate young man in the form of columnist Roger Murphy.

"Mr. Murphy, thanks for coming," the young man offered plaintively, having finally turned his head and seeing Roger. "Come on over," he added, as comfortably as if he were inviting Roger into his living room. When close enough, he extended his hand to shake Roger's.

Roger's heart was racing faster than the current below him as he walked like a man on a tightrope over to the young man whose party this was. The life-and-death uncertainty of the young man's predicament wasn't the only thing depriving Roger from oxygen.

Lord, how he hated heights.

◆   ◆   ◆

Now close enough to the walkway's edge to step casually over it, Roger told himself not to look down. He didn't listen. He should have.

Suddenly, like an eager fan rather than a despondent man contemplating ending it all, the young man grabbed and vigorously shook Roger's hand. Between that and the wisp of vertigo clouding his eyes, Roger was nearly tossed over.

"Easy there!" the young man flinched, reaching out with his free hand on Roger's shoulder to steady the dizzy writer—as if *he* were there to save *Roger's* life. The young man, now fully focused on calming Roger's nerves, was more at ease than ever. Reaching in his sweatpants' pockets, he pulled something out and extended it to Roger. "Want some gum?"

Roger looked at it and back at the young man's earnest face. "No, thanks."

"Really. I won't need it. No sense it going to waste, you know?"

It was still being presented to him. Roger looked at the gum, smiling slightly at the name—Carefree. "Thanks."

The young man watched Roger's every movement, from unwrapping the gum to putting it in his mouth and chewing, to fumbling with what to do with the wrapper. "Here," the man said, offering his palm. "I'll throw it away for you." Roger paused, gave him the wrapper and watched the man stash it in his hip pocket. Looking down at the bay water, Roger thought, "I guess that's what they mean by throwing something 'away.'"

A few awkward seconds blew silently between them. Roger had been concentrating so much on fighting the traffic and ignoring the hills that he hadn't really formed a game plan. Pauley's pep talk was lost on him for the moment. Oh, yes. Show caring.

"Why do this?"

Roger was struck, for once, by his own bluntness. And he was somewhat certain Mr. Counselor up on the sidewalk wouldn't recommend such an opening.

The young man looked out onto the horizon, then down as he recalled why he was there. "What do you do when there's nothing left to live for? Where do you go?" He looked over at Roger, and then away again. "Life sucks. Love sucks. Work sucks. No one cares. No one gives you a chance. And then you wake up one day and realize what a piece of crap you've become."

"Yeah, a disappointment not only to others, but mainly to yourself," Roger finished, looking over the water—and wondering who it was he was talking about.

The young man looked at Roger briefly as if to say, "Hey, this is my monologue!", then continued with a tone that, though it started as angry, had relaxed to mere resignation.

"Nothing really lasts anyway. Not your childhood, not you, not your work. Not your relationships. Nothing. We're here today and gone tomorrow." He looked at Roger. "Even *your* stuff is old news in 24 hours, right?"

"Or less, sometimes," Roger half smiled.

"I didn't get admitted to Cal this fall. I guess I just wasn't cut out for it. I suppose my drug habit hasn't helped. And now my girlfriend left me yesterday. For the fifth time, but she means it this time. I can tell. And you know what? I don't blame her. I'd leave me, too." He thought for a second and chortled. "I guess that's what I'm here to do. I'm here so *I* can leave me like *she* did."

"She's not worth this. No woman is." Roger knew a lame platitude when he heard himself spew it.

The young man dismissed it instantly, as Roger knew he would.

"It's not her. It's me." He looked around, turning the back of his head to Roger so he could barely hear the young man repeat, "It's me."

"No one tells you about this." Quickly he spun and looked at Roger. "That's what I want you to write. No one warns you when you're a kid. They make you read all those fairy tales and watch all those happy movies and they tell you not to worry about anything—that Mom and Dad, or one or the other, have it all under control. They don't tell you that they don't, that they're just as clueless as you are, except they've got facial hair and bank accounts and jobs and cars and apartments and bills with their name on them, but they don't have anymore of an idea than you which end is up or what it's all about.

"You're an investigative journalist," he pointed at Roger. "You tell me! What's all this for? How could it be any worse than this? What meaning could this life possibly have?"

Roger searched for answers. After a long pause, he ineptly offered, "I don't know. I'm sorry. I don't know." He glanced over his shoulder to check for the disapproving counselor's face, but couldn't find it.

The man persisted. "You've got it pretty good, no? Big-time newspaper guy, successful, relatively good-looking …"

"Relatively?" Roger burst out in semi-serious indignation, hoping a bit of humor might help. It did. For two seconds.

"What's the meaning in *your* life, Mr. Murphy?"

It was Roger's turn to scan the late-afternoon horizon. As the sun prepared to take a hard turn over their shoulders, fixing a spotlight on the textured city and bay water before them, Roger's thoughts turned to his own past—a relatively care-free childhood on the surface, but one haunted by his parents' angry and alcohol-spiked divorce and his own doubt that he'd ever be good at anything or loved by anyone. Then, his high school in a small Kansas town, where he was lost in the shuffle between the jocks, which he wasn't, and the druggies, which he wasn't either, but whom he both pitied and appreciated for their acceptance of life's losers. Then came Vietnam, a blur of pain and terror and sorrow and pride and then isolation, as he returned to an ambivalent homeland and a nonexistent homecoming.

The ensuing years were less of a memory, a bland mixture of professional accomplishment and personal gratification—certainly lots of that—but nothing in the way of anything that might constitute a deep meaning or any notion that might lure a man back from the abyss. The hope of mere creature comforts, which consumed Roger and, frankly, most people around him, didn't seem at all adequate to offer up to a man contemplating ending his life and looking for a compelling reason to change his mind. Roger replayed the young man's summation of Roger's life—"big-time newspaper guy, successful, relatively good-looking …" An hour ago, that might have satisfied him. And why not? But now, the big-time newspaperman was asking himself, "Is that all there is?"

As the sea breeze cooled him, Roger felt the chill of midlife, and all its taunts and tortures knifing into him.

He looked back at this young man, probing his eyes for signs that he would buy a ton of baloney at that instant. Of course, he would not. And so, Roger would not lie.

"I honestly have no idea. I'm sorry."

What they say is undeniably true: Misery does indeed love company. The two men simply stood on the fringe of the Golden Gate Bridge for the next few moments, taking in a small amount of comfort from the discovery of their shared ignorance, while still vainly hoping the answer might sweep in on the northern California ocean winds. Only the cold did.

Well, and one other mammoth, unexpected thing.

◆   ◆   ◆

Roger was startled by something that floated into view overhead, having soared without a sound over their right shoulders and over the bay. It looked like a huge baked potato rolled up in foil and riding in the sky.

It was the Goodyear blimp.

Roger knew instantly where it was headed and why. And it gave him a beautiful thought, at the moment he most needed it.

It was a thought that gave him pause at first. His eyes bounced back and forth like a pinball from the blimp's flight path to the young man next to him. He couldn't be sure if this was a good idea. But faced with the circumstances, he knew he could do nothing else, now that he'd thought of it. Still, it was a sacrifice on his part, and the pain of it shot through him and exited through a sigh.

He reached into his pocket. "I tell you what." He brightened up, looking over at the city for a brief moment, then back at the young man. "This is no place to look for the meaning of life. But *this*," he declared, waving the contents of his hands, *"this is!"*

The young man looked over and saw that his favorite columnist, while maybe not working from a full deck himself, had played the trump card.

World Series tickets.

The abridged smile that shimmied over the young man's face told the tale. Roger might not have known what to say, but in a crunch he had known exactly what to do. The young man was despondent, depressed and hopeless, even suicidal. But he clearly wasn't crazy. World Series tickets? Are you kidding?

Now *that* is to die for.

"You'd do that for me?" he asked, not accounting for how cheaply his life was being bought back. "You'd take me to the World Series?"

Roger realized he was finally following Pauley's prescription: to show caring. Sure, it was a guy's way of showing it. But, after all, he was dealing with a guy.

He wouldn't, of course, have seriously considered rescinding the offer now, but it still hurt. He would be standing up Melody Vasquez, one of the most beautiful women in San Francisco, and might never see her again; he'd somehow managed to finagle this date out of her *after* her going-away party. How could he give that up? Such self-sacrifice wasn't his forte, and it didn't feel all that good, even in the face of saving another man's life. But he knew it was the right thing to do. And he knew it would get him off that bridge in one piece.

"Well, sure. Yeah," he finally answered, sounding not totally convinced himself.

The young man looked out over the bay and back. "That's not fair." He turned back to look at Roger and the right corner of his mouth crept up as if to drag the rest of his mouth toward a smile. "That's not fair."

Roger smiled. "Tell me about it," he shot right back. "It's ruining a perfectly good suicide column!"

The young man couldn't help but smile now. Wiping at the corners of his eyes, he embraced Roger without warning. Stunned, and fighting dizziness, Roger patted him on the back. Pulling away, he used his head to briefly point up at the sidewalk above. "Let's go, shall we?"

The two were being hoisted over the railing by the officers simultaneously—and both Roger and the young man had luckily shifted their weight to the safe side of the railing at the very second that the bridge started belching and kicking and trying to throw them all off.

As every one of the men was thrown violently to the concrete, no words were necessary between them. Lying prone and wide-eyed, and well familiar with the cruel vagaries of San Francisco life, they knew instantly.

It was the The Big One.

3

Roger always figured that if he was about to die and needed to see his life flash before his eyes, his memory wouldn't make deadline and he'd be screwed.

Turns out, he was right. As the world rattled and seemed ready to swallow him up on that bridge, his memory missed deadline, big time. All it could flash before his eyes was the previous day's relative calm.

◆   ◆   ◆

Monday, Oct. 16, 1989, had started with a lazy morning in the Marina District, a morning of confident joggers with dogs and seagulls without agendas, and an old man strolling around the Palace of Fine Arts wrestling a squirrel over a nut for five minutes, only to crack it open with his shoe and hand it over to the confused little furball. Later, there were absolutely no problems at the Chronicle—a rarity for *any* writer at San Francisco's leading newspaper, much less for Roger Murphy.

Weather-wise, Monday had been a true city-by-the-bay trademark: a crisp-at-times but near-perfect fall day. Not everyone enjoys this city's ping-pong temperatures and irascible thermostat, most often set low enough to chill wine to perfection. Someone once cracked, Roger liked to recount, that the worst winter he ever experienced was the summer he spent in San Francisco. Roger Murphy knew that was absolutely true. It can be 80 in one neighborhood and seemingly 50 in another. In San Francisco, you have to live life in layers—a shirt over a shirt under a jacket, maybe chased by a parka. Too bad, he once opined, that one's eyes don't come in layers as well, to adjust to the bay's rolling waves of light and dark, compliments of clouds and fog and sun all battling for preeminence from dawn to dusk.

But for all its variances, San Francisco weather is the best on Earth, as a growing retirement class has set out to prove. It is eternal fall on the bay, and fall is a wistful, introspective emotion disguised smartly as a season of the year. There's also something reassuring about having to make use of a wrap that's available at any time.

Monday was like most days on the bay—only more so, as Roger's favorite *Casablanca* movie character might say. Evening blew in with a special cooling trend just for Roger: a smallish gathering in the Pacific Heights apartment of copy editor Sunny McHenry, who gave Roger a chill every time he saw her.

Sunny was pretty much everything Roger despised: a white-wine-drinking, humans-are-ruining-the-world, granola-gnawing liberal who never considered the possibility she might be wrong about anything or that a Republican might bleed red instead of—lord only knows what they might bleed. Her appearance also bugged the hell out of him: She looked like the result of an unfortunately successful experiment to turn mice into people—big, beady spectacled eyes, a nose and chin jutting out like a rodent's, pillar-sized front teeth and, he thought he'd seen more than once, whiskers and a tail.

But this was, after all, a going-away party for one of his favorite copy editors, Melody Vasquez. Melody, suffering an apparent midlife crisis at the ripe old age of 28, had abruptly announced her resignation to don a pair of tattered green jeans and travel the countryside for no obvious reason and to no certain end and with no apparent means. Roger knew a copy editing gig—a night shift, no less—was more than a little sedentary for someone so young and active as Melody. But he thought it inane and, frankly, unpatriotic to voluntarily transform oneself into a leech on the body politic. Still, he liked her, a lot, and she had a killer body.

So, at the very real risk of ruining a perfectly lovely day, Roger thumbed his glasses back up his nearly nonexistent nose, stole a quick nervous glance over his shoulder and down at the sloping street flowing toward the bay, mindlessly screwed the wrinkled brown paper bag tighter onto the neck of the wine bottle he was toting, and rang Sunny McHenry's bell with a mostly indiscernible scowl.

"Hello all," he disclosed meekly to the crowd after handing the wine without looking to McHenry, which she accepted without looking back.

At work, Roger Murphy was social, funny, confident and, when need be, sharp with his many critics. His co-workers would be astounded, he often thought at times such as these, at how truly shy he felt inside. But his reputation demanded working a room, and few could work a room like he could.

"Did you see what your Danny-Boy said today?" a voice in the crowd moaned.

The inevitable liberal challenge to the Bush-Quayle administration—which his liberal colleagues and readers naturally held him personally responsible for—took precisely 17 and one-half seconds to emerge, this time in the form of education reporter Tara Simpson.

"Tara," Roger replied matter-of-factly while accepting a beer and twisting off the cap and handing it to her, which she instinctively accepted. "You simply have to get out and meet more Republicans. You can't always depend on me to be your conduit to the fires of Hell.

"Tell you what," he continued. "There's a Satan-worshipping GOP campfire tomorrow night in Lincoln Park. Why don't you be my date? And, oh, by the way, do you know where I can get some virgin's blood?" Looking earnestly around, he added, "Oops, not here. Nope, don't think so."

As usual, he had prevented a nauseating liberal tirade with a blitz of quick, biting humor. All the chubby-cheeked Tara could do was growl as he mingled off—then, realizing Roger had left her with his bottle cap, she retreated quietly to the kitchen to find the trash and let her steam out the open window.

Roger tried to do some slithering himself, undetected, around the usual group chattering about earthquakes. The subject, truth be known, made him extremely nervous. It didn't help that his beloved Marina District, a coveted location in one of the flattest areas in all of northern California, had actually been man-made to begin with. In this posh neighborhood sandwiched by the Presidio on the west and Fisherman's Wharf on the east, sat row upon row of Spanish mission-style earth-toned and Victorian-colored apartments and houses—looking for all the world like giant Legos snapped together shortsightedly.

Shortsighted, because all of this was placed smack-dab on a bed of bay mud scooped together to make more room for the 1915 Panama-Pacific International Exposition. Roger was not a spiritual man, but he did think that if there were a God, the Marina District had to be one of His least favorite things. After all, at a time when God was toying with erasing California like an Etch-a-Sketch drawing and starting over, here was mankind actually trying to *add* to the state! Hubris, thy name is San Francisco, and thy middle name is Marina District!

"Murphy!" His slithering had failed, and the jig was up. Gay city hall reporter Mark Wasserstein roped him in. "*You* live in the Marina District." Roger looked at each of the five in the group and gave a "Yes, so?" smile back at Wasserstein with a commensurate and noncommittal "Hmm …"

"Don't you find that a bit unsettling? You know, earthquakes and all?"

"Well," they were expecting a snappy response, and Roger didn't disappoint, "if anyone knows about living on shaky ground, that would be you, Mark, wouldn't it?"

Partly to break the tension that might rise, one of the women in the group spouted, "Roger hates hills! Don't you, Roger?"

Before Roger could answer, Wasserstein interjected, "Well, now, he doesn't like hills. And he's not liberal. He doesn't ever eat seafood or ethnic food. And from what I hear, he's a flaming heterosexual." Roger seized the opportunity to appear triumphant at the last charge.

"You forgot the fact that I'm deathly afraid of the water and can't roller blade," Roger generously offered.

"Ah, and he's afraid of the water and roller skates."

"Blades. Roller *blades*," Roger clarified.

"So just why does a corn-fed Kansas boy come to live in the land of earth-quakes, hills, sushi bars, gays and roller blades by the sea, Murphy?"

Again briefly scanning the group, Roger softly explained, "I came here for the heat and the cows."

Wasserstein, a humorless fellow, was caught flatfooted. "What? Heat and cows? We've got neither."

"I was misinformed," Roger said wryly.

Even Wasserstein was disarmed and admitted defeat with a smile, as the laughter made for a successful exit on Murphy's way to a more engaging conversation.

◆   ◆   ◆

Melody was, of course, the center of attention around Sunny's baby grand piano, and not just because it was her going-away party, or because she played piano. She was young and pretty and sported a tanned body that not only was what nature aspired to, but didn't rely on heredity or luck to accomplish it. She lived just off the District, and took full advantage of the Marina Green's siren call for fitness buffs. There, one can weave one's way between soccer players and joggers and bicyclists galore, watch windsurfers and kite fliers fight their colorful battles for the foot of the Golden Gate, and join in a less-heated competition: go head-to-head with a 4-year-old to see who can keep whose foot the longest in the cold waters of the bay.

You could tell just by looking at Melody's not-an-inch-of-wasted-skin form that she ran with the Marina's fast set, one of a great and growing number of bay-area young women who enjoyed not only the atmosphere along Marina Boulevard, but also the climate of security in which to jog and skate.

"Roger!" she shrieked, parting her small assembled court of admirers like an ebullient young princess and flipping the right-side curtain of her shoulder-length medium-brown hair to the back of her neck to grasp him with such vigor he couldn't enjoy the moment, for fear of spilling beer on her back. "Thank you for coming!"

"Are you kidding? Couldn't wait to see you off!" he joked, realizing she knew otherwise.

When the hug had ended and she was still grasping him around the waist, forcing him to explore her walnut eyes up close for the very first time, he was suddenly struck with an aching desire to get to know his co-worker better—just in time to let her slip out of his life. As usual, his timing was purely awful, and he smiled, partly at her and partly at cruel fate, and swallowed the knowledge that his epiphany had come much, much too late.

And they wondered why this handsome, successful, heterosexual in the streets of San Francisco was so often alone.

Still, as the small talk evaporated into the brisk bay night, it became apparent to each of the two that they would be leaving the party together. The mutual longing had quietly crossed over the void between them, and she, too, seemed to be mourning the lost opportunity they would be trying to, at once, taste and forget in one night.

◆   ◆   ◆

He coerced the key into the apartment door, freezing in place as it unlocked. He turned with a start toward his guest.

"I forgot to tell you about my dog," Roger apologized somewhat fearfully to Melody. "Bruno."

"Not a problem. I love animals," she chirped in her typical upbeat fashion.

Nonetheless, being but 5-foot-5, Melody would have to assume something of a defensive position just to stop from being French kissed by a Great Dane or German Shepherd. Yet, when the door swung open and Roger called out "Bruno!", nothing attacked or even tried to kiss Melody on the mouth.

She glanced around as she paused in the second-floor apartment's 6-by-10 hard-wood foyer and Roger lingered behind to close the door and turn on the light. Taking her light nylon jacket along with his leather coat, he trudged ahead, calling "Bruno! Bruno?"

Suddenly, there he was in the opening to the bedroom: a short, black toy poodle with his rear end up in the air, shrub of a tail whisking back and forth like a grandfather clock, head stretched out and down to the throw-rug with a rubber hamburger clenched between his teeth. And ready for war.

"This is Bruno? Oh my word, he's darling!" she laughed.

Returning from the living room, having deposited the jackets on a worn-out sofa, Roger saw the two struggling for supremacy over the squeaky fake food.

"Be careful!" Roger warned. "He's actually a pit-poodle. He'll snatch your face right off!"

"He's adorable," Melody sang, scooping him up on her lap as she slid from her knees to a seat on the floor. As if on cue, Bruno transformed from warrior to Romeo, delivering the wet kiss Melody had fully expected at the door.

"If you don't mind, I'll let you two lovers get acquainted while I just tidy up a bit …"

"Please!" she squealed. As Roger disappeared, she straightened athletically onto her feet without so much as a push from her hands, which were still tied up with Bruno.

She let Bruno take her on a short, guided tour of the apartment, starting with the living room. A small boom box, with assorted cassette tapes scattered about, and a television from the 1960s were the only burdens borne by a length of wood plank that spanned four concrete blocks, two stacked on one another on each end.

"How do you like my home entertainment center?" Roger called from somewhere, seemingly sensing her every move. "Feel free to put on some music if you like." She decided she would pass on the offer, given it was after midnight, and the fact that on the way up to the apartment Roger had noted that the building superintendent lived just below. To convince herself, she shifted on her feet to make the wood floor creak. That right there was too much noise. She thumbed through the musical selections nonetheless: mostly jazz cassettes that he appeared to have taped himself.

Turning around, she noted two things instantly: a decided lack of items on the floor and a dizzying surplus of items on the wall. Looking at the room too long, she thought, would be sure to induce a bad case of vertigo; if you didn't know better, you'd think you were lying on the floor and looking at the room sideways.

Making up for the lack of furniture on the hard wood were the walls that spilled over with Ansel Adams prints, other color photographs and old movie posters. She noted, among the 10 or so movie posters, four from *Casablanca* alone. She looked down the hall, not seeing anything. Roger Murphy had a gruff exterior, she whispered to herself, but a guy who likes old movies can't be all bad. And a poodle named Bruno? This guy has secrets he's never shared with the newsroom. In only a minute of observation inside his apartment, Melody had learned more about the *Chronicle's* famous conservative columnist than she had in reading his stuff or working in the same office for the past five years. In truth, she realized upon a moment's reflection, Roger Murphy could talk the day away and never reveal much of himself. Why, oh, why, she thought, did she only begin to explore him on the eve of her departure?

"OK," he startled her, having flanked her by entering from the kitchen behind her with a glass of wine. "So, you're leaving tomorrow?"

"Yes," she confirmed, nodding a thanks for the drink. "Taking a Greyhound out of town."

"What a shame." Roger shook his head in mock disgust. "I was hoping…" he reached in his back pocket and pulled out a pair of tickets, "you'd come to the World Series with me."

Even in the dimness of the living room, lit only by a faint light from the foyer and leftover light from the kitchen around the corner, he could see her eyes light up. "I suppose I could be persuaded to stick around one more day…"

"Good," Roger smiled slightly, masking his glee. "It's a date then. So the day after that—Wednesday—where exactly are you going and what will you be doing?"

As she sipped her wine and mulled an answer, he noticed how, despite the bronze tone, Melody's facial features mirrored the Nordic beauty of Ingrid Bergman on the wall just over her shoulder.

"I really don't know," she finally allowed, plopping down right on the jackets on the sofa and not caring a whit. "First I plan to go stay with my sister in Montana for a few months. After that, who knows? Maybe go somewhere and help someone somehow."

He joined her on the couch. "You're giving up a great job."

"I can always get another job. I can't get another today."

Like a chess master whose attack was blunted, he tried a different front. "Won't you feel like you're not contributing anything?"

Rather than being annoyed or angry, she actually welcomed the intellectual challenge and the interest behind it. "Do you really think that you need money or a business card to contribute? Look at all the retirees and what they do."

"So you're retiring—at age 30?"

"Twenty-eight!" It was mock anger mixed with a jealous desire to hold onto those last two 20-something years. "Why not? Why wait until I have an artificial hip?"

He shifted on the cheap sofa. "Well, there's a fine line between a free spirit and a lost soul."

Now, that got her attention. Melody shifted to an upright and confrontational stance, twisting to face him even though they shared the same sofa. Yet, she spoke softly and patiently. "Roger." An hour seemed to crawl between her words. "Maybe I *am* a lost soul. I'll admit that. I don't know where I'm headed, and I sure don't know how I'll get there. And yes, it's scary. But it's also exciting.

"Besides. I think you're fooling yourself if you think a good job and a decent apartment…" She looked around and reconsidered her characterization of the place. "OK, an *apartment*," she smiled. "What I'm trying to say is, a good job and an apartment and an occasional warm bath and a soothing glass of wine isn't what life is all about."

He looked around the dim room. "You mean there's more than this?"

"Having a warm place, an address, even in the posh Marina District of San Francisco, doesn't somehow make your lost soul 'found,' Roger. It takes a little more than that."

"Oh? You seem to know all about my soul."

"Not as much as I'd like. I've often wondered what made you tick."

"Is this the part where I lie on the couch? Cause you're going to have to scoot down a bit …"

"You never answered Wasserstein's question at the party. I heard all about it. Why *did* you come to San Francisco? No one in the newsroom seems to know your story." Looking up at one of the *Casablanca* posters, she added, "How does it go again? 'Did you abscond with the church funds? Run off with a senator's wife? I like to think you killed a man! It's the romantic in me …'"

Roger smiled and brushed his floppy hair back. "I'm impressed. Anyone who can quote *Casablanca* like that is OK in my book." Lifting his wine glass, he added, "Here's looking at you, kid."

"Well? You still haven't answered."

Roger harrumphed. "I suppose I can't get by with claiming I came here for the waters." Melody's look, combined with her folded arms, gave him his answer.

Roger swiveled, putting his back against the sofa and turning away from her a bit. He was looking at his own lap now, considering how much to reveal. He certainly hadn't expected such an inquisition. Normally, he'd brush it off. But the fact that she was leaving in two days made him more inclined to open up.

Still, it wouldn't come.

"There was nothing for me in Kansas," he finally let drip out.

"Now, there's a breakthrough! A real dam buster!"

Roger got up, walked across the room and turned off the light in the kitchen, leaving the living room illuminated only by a halfhearted streetlight through the large picture window. He walked over to it and looked out to the row of mostly darkened apartments for a few awkward moments.

"You probably know I was in Vietnam."

"You've mentioned it in some of your columns …"

He kept looking out, but she could see his profile nod gently, the tip of his face illuminated by the streetlight outside.

"There's nothing like killing or being killed. I recommend the former, of course. But that ain't much of a choice, let me tell you. But at least I figured I had a life to come back to if I kept my head down and my aim straight. That's what I thought. Do what your country tells you to do. Live by the rules. Then come back and try to stop your hands from shaking as you try your best to put your life back together. Only, do it without all the pieces. Ever try to put half a puzzle together? It's not a pretty picture."

"What was her name?" Melody asked, without skipping a beat.

Roger turned slightly, and Melody thought she saw the corner of his mouth twitch upward.

"I always thought it had to be a woman," she pre-empted his unspoken question, "the way you never let one near for very long …"

"Ann Marie," he surprised her while staring out the window. "Nice small-town Kansas name, don't you think? Geez, haven't uttered that name for years. Ann Marie. Let me try it again: Ann Marie. That'll probably do for the rest of my life. You ought to charge me for this. It's good therapy."

Melody wormed an inch forward on the sofa. "So what happened?" She thought about adding "Or is it too personal?", but decided not to give him an escape route.

"We were engaged when I left Mac—McPherson, a town a little north of Wichita. When I came back two years later, we were—disengaged, I guess." He turned, putting his backside against the window sill and facing Melody, though now as a complete silhouette whose expression hid behind a shroud, if it existed at all. His voice revealed little more.

"She'd taken up with a guy I thought was our friend. I hadn't told anyone I was coming home—wanted it to be a surprise. It was. For me, anyway. They'd moved down to Moundridge, just a bit to the south. Hell, she was eight months pregnant when I finally found them."

"What did they say?"

"He wasn't there. Was off managing the Piggly-Wiggly or whatever. Never did see him again. She just babbled some lukewarm apology neither one of us believed. I didn't stay but about 10 seconds. Was on a Greyhound bus for Salina the next day."

"Kansas? What was in Salina?"

"No one I knew at the time, which stood tall in the town's favor. I couldn't stay in Mac. No one there had the guts to tell me what had been going on."

"Not even your family? What about your parents?"

Finally, a morsel of emotion fell from his voice. "My parents died in a car accident when I was five. I was raised by my uncle and aunt. He died while I was in Vietnam. Aunt Betty never had much of a heart for anything after that, certainly not for telling me my life was hemorrhaging while I was being shot at."

"So how does the road lead from Salina to here?"

Roger snorted, walking over to join her on the sofa.

"Rice-A-Roni."

"What?"

"I went to college at Marymount, a little Catholic school in Salina. Don't think it's even there anymore. Found out I liked writing, but didn't much want to stay in Kansas. It's a small state, people-wise. Probably more cows than people. It's surprisingly difficult to avoid people you don't want to see. And there were a lot of those people for me. So when I got out of school, I just wanted to leave. Felt like I was too close to—the past, I suppose.

"Well, here I am in the Kansas City airport—not sure where I want to go, just knowing I want to be somewhere else. While I'm having a beer in the lounge, thinking about where I might end up, I see a Rice-A-Roni commercial on the television. I liked the look of the cable cars. So I came here."

"For the rice?"

"Well, maybe for *Jerry* Rice. It sure as hell wasn't for the hills. I had no idea how—uh, hilly they are."

"You just came here not knowing anyone?"

"Well, at that point San Francisco had that distinct advantage over Salina."

"This is a fairly odd profession to get into, not being thrilled with people and all."

"Not really, when you think about it," Roger retorted, not exactly denying the premise of her statement. "Think about it: Sure, we meet a lot of people and we even take down their names. But our job is not to get involved. To be objective, stay detached."

"Not to let anyone close," she finished for him.

"I guess so. Never really thought about it before. But yeah, I guess that's one of the benefits."

"Some benefit! So that's it?"

"What's it?"

"Congratulations!"

"Hmm? For what?"

"You've become just like your hero, Bogart. Why did you come here? Why didn't you just move to Casablanca and open a café?" She was sounding angry now.

Roger was dumbfounded. "I don't ..."

"You're just like Bogart's Rick. One woman has thrown you over, so you blame the world. You escape into a profession where you think it's OK not to feel. Where it's not just OK, but, in your mind, encouraged, to not care about others. I suppose you're the only cause you're fighting for ..."

"I've seen first-hand what fighting for others gets you, babe," he said dryly.

Melody rose up, while pulling her jacket out from under her. "Sorry, Roger. I've always liked you, and I was hoping something could happen for us. But this just isn't me." As Roger turned on a lamp, Melody pointed up at a movie poster. "I don't even think you're as much of a sentimentalist as Rick."

Following her to the door, he argued, "I wasn't aware it was a crime to look out for No. 1."

Melody stopped in the doorway and turned to him. "It's not, Roger. The crime is not looking any farther than that. Get some new glasses. They make some now that reach past your own nose."

He unconsciously punched his glasses up his nose, and as she walked off down the hall, he called after her, "Does this mean we're not going to the game?"

At the top of the stairs, she stopped for a moment to think, then turned toward him. "Are you kidding? Of course it doesn't! I'm not *stupid*, you know."

As she disappeared down the stairs, Roger smiled. Looking back into the dark and empty apartment, he stopped smiling.

◆   ◆   ◆

"Morning!" Building superintendent Sherman Case's booming voice never ceased to startle Roger, even after his morning caffeine, and even after allowing half the morning to evaporate.

"Morning, Sherm."

"Nice night last night?"

Sherman Case never made small talk without having a point, and despite not having been awake very long, Roger instantly got it. "Oh, that. Sorry about that, Sherm. I know the rules. Quiet after 11."

Sherman, who had been talking to a workman who quickly decided to give up and move on, moved closer to Roger on the sidewalk, blocking Roger from getting past and taking his morning walk to the Palace of Fine Arts and the Marina. Sherman smiled slyly. "Look, I never begrudge a man that. Don't worry. I'm not complaining by any means. And besides, the wife was dead. Never heard a thing. Me, I couldn't shut down my racing mind …"

"Well, don't let your mind race too far, Sherm. It wasn't what either of us wanted."

Roger was past his comfort point, talking about his love life with his building super. But he was infinitely patient with Sherman Case. If you had to live above anybody, especially your super, it couldn't be a better man than Sherman. A self-described East Coast Jew with a yardlong resume and a suitcase that has seen more than CNN, Sherman Case was in hog heaven. He had found Nirvana on the Marina: a great job holding down the fort in a close-knit apartment complex in his favorite city in the world—all while he studied law pursuant to entering what seemed like the 23rd career in his 58 years.

Roger simply couldn't help but respect a man who was so intellectually alive, so well-read and so well-traveled. And it didn't hurt that Sherman was Roger's biggest fan. A columnist can have a few of those, but Sherman, in a very dignified way, seemed to really romanticize Roger and his importance. Sherman was genuinely proud of the fact that this local celebrity was actually in his building! When someone feels that way about you—even a 58-year-old toupeed man—it can't do anything but endear him to you.

Still, Roger wanted to be alone, so he bid his goodbye and strolled with his morning newspaper the two blocks to the Palace of Fine Arts—an inspiring structure built for the 1915 exposition and which still moves busloads of tourists to disembark and take photos and walk the pastoral grounds. It was quite simply Roger's favorite place in the world. And he could walk to it in minutes. Yet another reason for him to brave the hills and sushi of San Francisco.

◆   ◆   ◆

But he was wishing he never had, as the world seemed to be caving in around him …

4

Satan arrived in the bay area at four minutes and 34 seconds after 5 p.m. on Oct. 17, 1989.

As hell opened up, the earth, and everything on it, rolled and crashed like hot grease in a shaken pan. Only for 15 seconds, to be sure—but long enough for the buildings and bridges and humans to be tossed about like ants.

The opening to hell swallowed up people and cars whole, spewing gas and fire long after the initial shock. Buildings, along with the hopes and dreams of souls within, were knocked off their foundations. It was as if the planet itself had flirted with jumping off the Golden Gate Bridge and ending it all—then, 15 seconds later, decided against it.

When Roger Murphy and the men thrown with him to the surface of the Golden Gate had finally pulled up to their hands and knees—momentarily staying on all fours before standing erect, in order to make certain Earth had gone dormant again—they already heard the sounds of emergency sirens wafting in from the city. Smoke was beginning to blossom over the cityscape. And, like the stunned group on the bridge, people across the bay area were coming to the unreal conclusion that The Big One had finally hit.

"This can't be good," Roger deadpanned, looking over his shoulder briefly to see the police scurrying to their cars and completely forgetting the previous scene on the bridge.

"You think they'll cancel the game?" asked the young man, in all sincerity. A second's glance at Roger's incredulous face, and the man answered himself. "Yeah, I suppose."

"Oh my heavens!" Pauley screeched. "Look at the Marina District!"

Roger's ears pricked slightly and his gaze was transfixed on his neighborhood across the distance. The entirety of the district appeared ablaze.

There seemed to be two dozen or more fires raging over the city within seconds, but none more serious, proximate or relevant than the one in the Marina District.

Satan not only came calling this day, but he seemed to have Roger Murphy's address.

"That's my apartment over there," Roger nearly shouted to the young man, pointing over the bridge railing to the Marina fire. He turned to the man. "Will you be all right?"

"Yes! Please, go!"

Pauley jumped in. "I'll take him anywhere he needs to go, Mr. Murphy. You go home!"

Roger didn't need to be told twice. He took off running the other way, down the now-nearly-barren lane toward his Volvo, which didn't need an earthquake to look the way it did. As he ran on, he heard the young man yell; maintaining his gait, Roger turned his head and saw the man waving calmly. He figured the man was shouting some sort of thanks.

He might have saved the young man that day. But he couldn't save his car.

"Whoo, whoo, whoo." That's the sound a dead Volvo makes, after using its last bits of energy to power the hazard lights.

Roger banged both hands on the steering wheel and cursed it. As he jumped out, he turned to the San Francisco side of the bridge and saw Pauley and the young man driving off. He tried hailing them, but to no avail. He tried stopping the only other car he saw, but no one is going to pick up a hitchhiker at a time like this.

So he ran. And he ran. And he ran. With each step down the bridge and the roads and paths beneath, he was surprised and grateful that solid ground came up to meet his aching penny loafers. Past Fort Point, through the Golden Gate National Recreation Area and Promenade and Crissy Field he went, in and out of The Presidio, on the longest run of his civilian life. He wished that he had been running with those leggy women he always saw during all those days he strolled along Marina Boulevard. At least then he would feel somewhat in shape for something like this. Suddenly he realized he felt naked without his Army rifle and equipment—an experience he hadn't felt outside of his nightmares for years. He felt as if he were running toward a firefight in the Vietnamese jungle again.

This time, though, the war was at home. The enemy was even more treacherous and elusive.

Running down Marina Boulevard, it appeared indeed as if someone had declared war on his neighborhood. The Legos had been unsnapped, smoke was rushing out and people were streaming into the streets, screaming for others, screaming for help. Mark Twain once described a San Francisco earthquake by noting that "every door of every house, as far as the eye could reach, was vomiting a stream of human beings." Roger now knew what Twain had meant.

Finally, panting like a dog, his jacket now secured around his waist, he slowed to a walk on the greenway of the Palace of Fine Arts—which, he suddenly realized, was still standing. Within a couple blocks lay his apartment house at Beach and Divisadero. But he couldn't see it. Nor would he make it there just yet.

Earthquakes and tornadoes play with the human mind like no other disasters, natural or otherwise. They leave bizarre configurations in their wake. They depart as quickly as they come. And they leave some things standing erect and utterly surprised, right next to the unfortunate items they choose to flatten mercilessly.

It is, therefore, quite probable that not even Twain, Roger Murphy's favorite author, could have found the words to describe the sight of the second story of a Lego apartment having stretched out across the street. It was as if the neighborhood had developed an overbite.

Roger couldn't get through. So he continued running west toward Cervantes Street, where he figured he would turn and flank the disaster and thereby get to his apartment. But between local emergencies and other obstructions, before he knew it he had run far past Beach and had arrived at Cervantes and Fillmore, where all hell was breaking loose, even compared to the hell going on all around.

Fire Engine Co. 16 and Rescue Unit No. 2 were swarming a collapsed building, working feverishly amid the debris to get someone out.

Suddenly, either through a reporter's curiosity or the dumbfounded puzzlement of the shaken, Roger had gravitated too close to the scene. At first, he thought the firefighter barking at him was angry. But of course, the situation called out for yelling.

"I said take him!" shouted the firefighter, standing knee-high in debris and shoving something at Roger. He took it.

It was a baby.

Roger instinctively cradled the infant, which he guessed to be about 3 months old, as well as any mother could have. He stood there holding the little life for what seemed an hour, but what really was only seconds. His thoughts were swirling like the scene around him, but in a vacuum of silence compared to the mayhem about him. He looked into the child's face. The boy's face was bloodied (though he couldn't be sure if it was the baby's blood or someone else's), and smudged with dirt. It struck Roger how peaceful the child looked when everything around him was so chaotic. He imagined himself at that stage, wondering how one gets from that to the stage he was in. He thought about how fragile this little life was. He wondered how he ever made it as far as he had.

"I'll take him!" Another firefighter grabbed the boy just as Roger was getting comfortable with him. It had only been a few seconds, but when one's mind is racing it can outpace the second-hand.

Roger stumbled backward and watched as rescuers worked to help the baby. In the brief moment he had held the boy, Roger had no sense of the urgency of the situation. Watching paramedics surround the child with such dispatch made him understand. The boy was in grave danger.

Just feet away over to the left, uniformed rescuers and tattered civilians were carrying a woman out of the debris. Roger wondered if perhaps it was the baby's mother. His head was swimming more than ever now, but he managed to focus on the similar attempt to save the woman's life. Seemingly within seconds, the crew had the woman on an ambulance and on the way to the hospital.

Back to the right, the paramedics had finished working on the baby. They rose deliberately, and one of the rescuers carried the boy to a waiting ambulance. Roger was relieved—until he recognized the slow pace and ashen faces of the rescuers. Even if the mother survives, he knew, she had lost her son just months after giving birth to him.

Still, life was going on. Chaotically, painfully, perilously, life was going on.

"Roger!" It shocked him to hear his name in the middle of such bedlam. He turned back to the left.

"Melody!" he yelled, running the 30 feet to her. After a quick hug, he held her by the shoulders and stood back. "What are you doing here? Are you all right?"

She was beautiful and earthy, even at a time when the earth itself wasn't. "Yes, I'm fine. I was waiting for the bus to Candlestick when it hit. Where were you? Are you OK?"

"It's a long story, but I'm OK."

"And Bruno? Is he OK?"

He felt awful for having forgotten about his dog, even for the past few insane minutes. "I don't know. I was on the way there …"

"Go on," she yelped. "I'll help out here!"

Roger looked over his right shoulder to see firefighters and civilians teaming up to move debris from the building where the mother and son had just been carried out. The pace of work seemed to say there were more people trapped.

"No, I can't leave yet."

"OK, let's get to work, then," she urged.

Joining the assembly line, the two helped carry debris from the collapsed building just in time to be knocked off their feet.

He should have expected an aftershock after such a powerful first quake. But it took Roger by complete surprise. It had seemed like hours since the first one hit, but only because each second felt like a minute. In truth, it had been only 37 minutes.

The tremors and screams made it quite apparent that the aftershock was nearly as violent as the initial earthquake had been.

Roger and Melody picked themselves up again and surveyed the scene. The air was thick with escaping gas, and the collapsed building had shifted. The situation inside was even more intense than before. Firefighters had come within a breath of freeing a man and a woman near the rear of the building when the aftershock hit. Now, even with chainsaws and other tools of desperation, the victims seemed impossibly trapped.

The human conveyor belt continued its mission to move the rubble as firefighters worked to save the couple. Melody more than held her own, moving concrete and rock faster and with less effort than most of the men.

But once reached, the man and woman were gone. The earth had failed to swallow their bodies up, but the heavens had claimed their spirits.

Exhausted and frustrated and blackened by the soot on the ground and in the air, Roger and Melody collapsed to sit on the debris. Besides being all those things, the two were dispirited, having worked so hard to free someone in vain. Not a word escaped either of them. It didn't have to. There's nothing to say at such a moment.

For a few moments they simply sat and watched firefighters continue on as best they could. Firefighters are paid to do this sort of thing, certainly. But they're human, too. Roger admired how they could work so hard to save a life, lose the battle and yet continue on through the hurt and disappointment. Firefighters are resilient people in general; the ones in Engine 16 and Rescue 2 were giants among men this day.

Roger surveyed the city—at least what he could see from his little pile of rearranged Marina—and thought that the city must be full of giants just then.

He sat up suddenly.

"Bruno!" he barked to no one in particular.

"Oh my gosh!" cried Melody, now feeling free to leave with him. "Let's go!"

Renewed in strength, the two leaped up and took off running, from Alhambra to Mallorca Way to Capra Way to Scott and back north to Beach and over to …

Another disaster. This time, one that had hit home.

At Beach and Divisadero, Roger's two-story apartment had become a one-story building spilling out onto Beach Street. If the sight was incomprehensible, the scene was all-too-familiar: People were scurrying about like frightened children, having been spit out by their apartments, while firefighters were attempting to extricate more life from the deathly destruction.

The difference here: Just across the street was a raging apartment fire so intense that it was causing Roger's collapsed apartment building to sporadically catch on fire. Despite being equipped for such matters, firefighters searching the collapsed structure were having to take turns, in order to escape the heat from the fire across the street.

Just then, the burning building erupted like a volcano, spewing fire and small explosions, and partially collapsing.

"Get out! Evacuate the building now!" a ranking firefighter yelled to a colleague searching the remnants of Roger's building. The firefighter seemed to turn slightly as if to comply, but then stopped with a jolt.

"Wait! I hear something!" he called. Another few seconds. "Someone's banging on a pipe!"

The structure seemed to move a little.

"Jerry, get the hell out of there *now*!" the other firefighter shouted with more force than before. That thing's gonna fall any second!"

The firefighter inside ignored the command and followed the sound of a pipe banging. Shedding his protective gear and helmet, he climbed through what appeared to be a small open window—but in truth, could have been any kind of opening in a twisted mess like that. He stopped halfway through, as if becoming stuck, then backed out.

"I've got a live one here! Bring me some jaws!"

While waiting for the equipment, the firefighter stuffed his turnout coat through the opening, presumably for whomever was trapped inside. A man's voice could be heard from the opening, and shortly the firefighter was passing down a flashlight.

"Oh my God," declared Roger.

"What?" asked Melody, wondering what could be worse than the present situation.

Roger turned to her. "That guy who's trapped. It has to be Sherman. My building super."

"How in the world can you know that?"

"Only Sherman would be trying to tell the firefighters how to do their job." The two smiled at each other, realizing how odd, but also how easy, a smile can be at such a moment. "He probably asked for the flashlight because he saw something that needed fixing."

Sure enough, after what felt like about two hours of sawing and digging, and racing both fire and imminent collapse, they were pulling a bedraggled but talkative and fully functional Sherman Case from the wreckage of his building. As they escorted him down the pile of rubble to the street, Sherman appeared to be asking the firefighters detailed questions about the equipment they used to free him. Roger smiled—that would be just like Sherman, always curious, even in a crisis.

Melody had thought ahead enough to have grabbed a blanket from a Red Cross van nearby, but Sherman—who fancied himself a man's man—declined.

"You," Case roared, pointing menacingly at Roger, "really have too much crap in your apartment, Murphy."

Roger smiled and nodded, while wondering how it was that Sherman's toupee had stayed in place through all that mayhem. Then Sherman's words jogged him.

"My apartment!" Roger howled. "Have you seen Bruno?"

"No, I'm afraid not, son." Sherman laid a hand on Roger's shoulder. "There's no way he could have made it through that."

Speechless twice in one day. It had never happened to Roger Murphy before, not in all his 40 years. But what a day it had been.

Now, the full weight of the day began to push on his shoulders and tug on his clothes. He had been heaved into the middle of an attempted suicide, threatened by a cop, shaken and stirred by not one, but two, earthquakes, made to hold a dying infant, forced to witness death and destruction even a writer could not have imagined—and after all that, had returned home to find no home to return to, and no four-legged roommate to greet him there.

Roger collapsed slowly onto the sidewalk like a building whose foundation had been swallowed up by the omnivorous earth. He didn't feel sad. He didn't feel self-pity. Lord knows everyone had problems that night. Nor did he feel anger rising up within him.

He just didn't feel.

◆   ◆   ◆

The cold bay water lapped at his face as he struggled to stay afloat. "I don't want to die," Roger thought. "Not now. Not like this." But the more he chopped and kicked and flailed at it, the more the water took him into its cold embrace.

As he suspended his fight and sank slightly, he saw the young man from the bridge in the water next to him. He, too, was fully immersed, yet appeared perfectly dry. Stranger still, he looked peaceful, and simply smiled at Roger's panicky and pointless attempts to survive.

As Roger surfaced for one more attempt to breathe the air, he was greeted by the threatening cop, who leaned out over the edge of a row boat and grabbed Roger's lapels. Pulling Roger's face up to his, the cop snarled, "Not on my shift, Murphy! Not on my shift!"

Just then the cop started licking Roger's face …

◆   ◆   ◆

Roger Murphy hid behind his forearms as the black dog was licking him awake.

"Bruno!" Roger cried, shooting up to a sitting position and grabbing the black dog by its front legs. It took a few seconds for him to realize that, in fact, it was a stray Labrador, and not Bruno after all.

Disappointedly, Roger let go of the dog and let it go on sniffing about. As his eyes followed the animal for a few feet, they started registering the rest of the scene.

He wasn't in his bed or in his apartment, but he was on familiar ground: the palatial terrace surrounding the Palace of Fine Arts, the place he came to read each day.

The mind is accountable to no one but itself, and thus is free to create the most absurd realities with absolute impunity. So, for a moment, Roger wondered why he had fallen asleep on the cold Marina District ground. At almost the same instant, his eyes were darting about for the nut-crushing old man and the squirrel.

For a few more seconds he had all the directional sense of a gnat in an orchard. When he noticed the others sleeping or waking elsewhere on the grounds, and turned to see the intermittent destruction over his shoulder, he remembered the other nightmare—the one he had lived the day before.

Rubbing his aching neck, he began to take notice of the aching muscles now reporting in to the brain from all sectors of his body. Roger uprighted his 6-foot frame like an exhausted rock climber at a peak. He tightened the black and gold 49ers blanket around him and stiffly strode down to the bench by the palace pond. There, he sat and missed what he always called his four-legged roommate. And he tried to collect and recollect—and to decide what in the world he would do now.

He thought about the night before—the chaos, the order brought to it by firefighters and civilian volunteers. The frantic people—and those who had drawn their last breaths shortly after 5:04 and a half p.m. Melody, who'd run off and enlisted in a bucket brigade to help fight the Marina District fires. And about his own search for Bruno without any luck. He thought about the raging fire and the dozens of buildings that looked like victims of the Blitzkrieg.

At that moment, an elderly woman walking across the grounds stopped and handed Roger some change and walked off. Stunned, he looked down at the coins in his palm and back at the lady walking off. Then he visualized himself and understood: He must look like a chronic homeless person, of which there were untold thousands in the city even before the earthquake. "I'm new at this," he thought.

Then, the sound of the ordinary hit his ears: the reliable blare of the Golden Gate fog horn, a trumpet he had learned not to hear, since its blasts could be heard every few seconds around the clock, even from inside his bedroom.

The horn's burst jogged his frazzled memory.

"My car!" his mouth said to itself.

Checking his wallet and finding several fares, he rose up more determinedly this time and trudged the block or so toward the bus stop—not even considering the possibility that in all this mayhem, they might not be running. When the Golden Gate bus rolled up the largely desolate street, it hit him what an amazing feat it was. He felt that his one-dollar fare was an embarrassingly meager reward for such intrepidness by the folks at Muny, but he gladly fed the beast and twirled into the first seat.

The bus had long gone by the time Roger had walked up to the bridge's threshold. He hadn't walked far out onto the structure before he could see there was nothing to see. Either emergency crews had bothered to tow his car, or some entrepreneur without a conscience had somehow found a way to make it run. Either way, he was now officially homeless *and* carless.

He counted his change.

◆   ◆   ◆

It occurred to Roger as he approached the *Chronicle* offices that he'd encountered homeless people nearly every day of his life in this city—but had never given them much thought, nor certainly any of his change.

"You can't come in here, sir!" commanded the sweet-looking but firm female guard when the slovenly man in the 49ers blanket approached.

"It's me, Audrey. Roger Murphy."

She stepped off her thigh-high stool and leaned over the guard station. "Oh, my heavens, Mr. Murphy! I'm so sorry. I didn't …"

"It's all right, Audrey. Just had a rough night and all."

"Yeah, you and the entire northern coast."

He wasn't in the mood for chat, and luckily, wasn't forced by proximity to exchange it with anyone else on the way to his desk—despite the fact that the newsroom was as much of an active hive as he'd ever seen.

Nor was Roger Murphy much of an organized man. But he liked being comfortable, and so he kept a spare toothbrush and toothpaste in his desk's top drawer, and an unopened new white dress shirt in his bottom drawer. In the bathroom, he freshened up as best he could and put on the new shirt—a nice contrast, he thought, with khaki pants that had been through war and then slept in, and looked very much the part.

Back at his computer, his pants hidden under the desk, he began his column.

> "I confess to never having given much thought to the homeless problem.
> "Until, that is, I became a part of it …"

"Geez, Murphy," slurped Sunny McHenry as she waltzed by, "*you* look good!"

A small comfort, this: The earthquake hadn't put a crack in Sunny McHenry's perfectly rotten disposition. Roger smiled as if he'd really been complimented. When the earth moves out from under your feet, you grab ahold of anything you can.

◆   ◆   ◆

Normally, newspaper editors assemble for their daily meetings as if they were being led down a hall by a priest giving last rites. Why their jobs—basically documenting the most interesting stories about life each day—would ever be regarded as drudgery, Roger Murphy never knew. Passionless editors, he often thought, may be the industry's biggest problem.

But today was as far from drudgery that anyone in that newsroom had seen in a long time. Even the zombies were alive.

As key editors gathered in Ed Miller's taut office for inventory on the morning after the city's biggest earthquake since 1906, you could have cut the adrenalin with a knife. Roger took a few minutes to stand in the doorway and listen in. The assemblage was too hyped to notice either his presence or presentability.

"OK," began Miller, a master organizer. "Let's start with the worst damage areas."

"Biggest loss of life seems to be over at the Cypress Freeway," one editor chimed without emotion.

"The Marina District has the worst property loss—not a surprise when you consider it's built on landfill," added another.

"The Embarcadero is a mess," another joined in.

"So is south of Market," said another.

After a few more minutes of inventorying what they knew, Miller was ready to give the chaos some coherent form for the next day's newspaper.

"OK," he began. "I want breakouts on all the major damage areas. I want a rundown of past quakes and what the experts are saying about future risk. Give me a graphic on that. I want a compilation of the heroes and tragedies starting to emerge from this. I want a rundown of every city service and whether it's been interrupted. Marge, give me a story on all the cultural events that were postponed or interrupted. Of course, we'll be counting on sports to get us the effect on the World Series. And there's plenty of human interest stories in Candlestick alone.

"And Harrison, I want a reporter and photographer with the vice president when he arrives to tour the Marina District."

The requisite liberal groan at the mention of Dan Quayle signaled the end of the meeting. Roger let the others pass by on their way out, then entered Miller's office.

"Cripes, Murph, what happened to you?" Miller was genuinely concerned. Then he remembered the damage in the Marina District. "Don't tell me your …"

"Yeah, not only am I a disenfranchised conservative in the most liberal city in the world, I just joined the ranks of the homeless."

Miller fished in his pocket. "Tell you what. Run over to my house. Ellen just happens to be in Encino seeing her Aunt Dorothy for the week, so you can move in with us for awhile."

Roger caught the key and looked at it. "Thanks, Chief. I owe you more than usual."

"I know," Miller deadpanned. "Besides, I can't have my people looking rode-hard-and-put-away-wet."

◆   ◆   ◆

Everyone else in the Marina District hit the roof, if they had one, when Mayor Agnos decreed a few days after the earthquake that the residents of some 60 buildings had all of 15 minutes to get their belongings out before demolition.

Roger wasn't exercised, though. He figured it would take him about five minutes anyway. For one thing, his Spartan apartment didn't have that much to begin with. For another thing, he couldn't imagine that very much remained intact. Plus, he really didn't want to chance running across his little roommate's lifeless body.

Still, it was a more forlorn duty than he had ever anticipated. Poking around the ruins of one's own life is a chore he wouldn't have wished on anyone. He managed to retrieve some clothes that would survive with some cleaning, a pair of shoes, a microwave, the all-important corkscrew for California wine, and his most cherished *Casablanca* poster, which was scratched but surprisingly presentable.

The earthquake had nearly taken everything he had—including, it seems, his ability to feel much of anything. But now, stepping out of the rubble and placing his few possessions in the back of a borrowed pickup for a ride to his temporary quarters in his boss' house, Roger did feel something after all.

He felt like hell.

◆   ◆   ◆

It was a feeling that was more pressing than the San Francisco chill. For months it went on. He wasn't alone, of course, and he knew it. The *Chronicle's* own poll showed three out of four Bay area residents had been in a funk in the weeks and months since the quake. But it's one thing to be depressed while working on an assembly line or picking up trash or driving a bus. When a high-profile columnist is out to lunch in a big way, it has an embarrassing habit of showing up on people's driveways.

Ed Miller was glad to get rid of his house guest when Roger found his own apartment—again, above Sherman Case. But he didn't like the idea of losing his favorite columnist. And approaching springtime, it wasn't looking good. The higher-ups had always been unexcited about what they saw as Murphy's conservative rantings. In Roger's current nosedive, Miller had already had two or three conversations with the folks upstairs about the column's future.

And looking out his glass office, Miller could almost see the sharks circling. It was an open secret that Sunny McHenry had aspirations of taking over Roger's Monday-Wednesday-Friday-Sunday column spot. The column's slot was every bit the prime real estate that the Marina District had been. And, like the Marina District, the earthquake had shaken things up at the paper. Roger Murphy's standing was shaky, pure and simple. And his melancholia was playing right into his enemy's hands.

Miller's eyes stopped on an attractive figure floating about the newsroom. Melody Vasquez not only had decided to stay in town after the earthquake, she was welcomed back as a day-side reporter rather than a night-side copy editor. It had suited her interests and the newspaper's considerable post-earthquake news gathering needs.

Miller grabbed his suit jacket and overcoat and headed out. "Melody!" Miller was fond of calling men by their last names and women by their first— a quirk not unnoticed by the gals, yet chalked up to affectionate paternalism rather than sexism. "Grab your jacket and come with me!"

Editors like Miller either have an exaggerated sense of self-importance, or it's never entered their mind that their reporters might have something else going on whenever a whim arrives to pull them away. But as an eager new reporter, Melody was anxious to please and complied happily. She bounced to the sidewalk, eager to know where he'd lead.

"Where's the nearest coffee?" he stopped abruptly.

"Right over there, Chief," she pointed, amazed he didn't know. Maybe he's never had a cup outside the office, where others find it for him.

At the coffee shop, Miller seemed to hyperventilate at the counter. "Cripes, these places have too many doggone kinds of coffee. Don't they just make plain old coffee anymore?" Giving up finding what he wanted on the sign above, he turned to the poor clerk behind the counter and barked, "Can I just get a frickin' coffee? Please? Or is that too involved?" Then, turning back to Melody, he added, "If I wanted a milkshake, for Pete's sake, I'd go to Baskin-Frickin'-Robbins!"

Once seated, Miller became much more sedate. "I guess you're wondering why I grabbed you just now." He twirled his black coffee into a waterspout.

"I didn't think you needed my help to find coffee. Then again," she laughed, looking at his cup, "maybe you did!"

Miller looked up from his cup. "What? Oh, yeah. I only drink it when I've got stress, which doesn't happen but five or seven days a week. And I *never* go out for it.

"I'll tell you what's giving me stress right now is Murphy. I'm worried about him, Melody. He hasn't been the same since the earthquake and everything else that happened. I'll cut to the chase. He's not cutting it anymore. Don't get me wrong, I think he's our best when he's on. But he hasn't been on for an awful long time, and it shows no signs of changing.

"And you know, he's never been the golden boy here. He's always been sort of tolerated." He rose his glance to look Melody in the eyes. "I'm under a lot of pressure to do something about him."

Melody was stunned. She'd never been included in this kind of inside baseball, and she sure didn't think Murphy was on the bubble like that.

"I've latched onto you because I know you two are friends, and I was hoping you might be able to help."

Mature beyond her years, Melody simply looked out the store window to the bustle outside and turned back to her boss. "I'll see what I can come up with, Chief."

◆   ◆   ◆

Sure enough, the next morning Miller saw that he'd been visited by the good idea fairy.

"Chief," the note on his desk read, "I think this might help. It's made a huge difference in my life. I also think you might want to assign him to interview the author. He's quite an international phenomenon, and might not only help Roger, but all of our readers struggling with the uncertainty of life after the earthquake.—Melody"

The "it" the note referred to, he learned as he put down the notepaper and picked up a well-worn paperback, was the book, *Man's Search for Meaning.*

Miller thumbed through it ever-so-quickly. A newspaper editor doesn't waste much time with something he doesn't have to read. But it looked readable, and he took Melody's word for it that it was a good and helpful book.

Early the next day, Roger Murphy stopped by Miller's office. "You wanted to see me, Chief?"

"Sit down, Murph." As he did so, in a chair across from Miller that had an annoying habit of threatening to fly backward, Miller edged up to his desk and leaned in Roger's direction. "Roger"—uh, oh, Roger thought; he never calls me that!—"I think you know that for the past few months—hell, the whole winter—you've been pretty much in a funk."

"We all have."

"Well, maybe so, but you're a special case. You've been worse than most. And let's face it, Murph—when a star columnist has a bad day, that gets noticed. When he has a bad six months, it raises eyebrows—and questions."

Roger sat up, though throwing his feet to the ground for balance when the chair seemed to tip back. "Are you firing me? Am I being fired?"

"No, you're not being fired, Roger. Not yet, anyway."

That got Roger's attention.

"I don't mind telling you, you have a lot of enemies in this town—and in this building. You've got some pretty powerful people that would like nothing better than to see you go down in flames. And, well, I hesitate to tell you this–"

"Go ahead. I can take it," Roger lied.

"Well, the jockeying out there for your job has already started."

Roger glanced out to the newsroom. "You've got to be kidding. What a bunch of vultures." He thought a second more. "Are you talking about Sunny McHenry? Tell me you're not talking about Sunny McHenry! Ed, you know she's got no talent, no fire. She couldn't write her way out of a one-round spelling bee!"

"I'm just telling you you're on the bubble, Roger. Something has to change, drastically, and soon."

Roger sat back, again jerking his body to prevent tipping backward. "What are you suggesting?"

"Well," Miller said, reaching in his top drawer, "I'm glad you asked. I'm sending you on assignment—to Vienna!"

Roger took the plane ticket from Miller. "Italy?"

"Not Venice, Roger. Vienna. Vienna, Austria."

"What the hell is in Vienna, other than sauerkraut and snow?"

"This man." Miller tossed Roger the book.

By now, Roger was standing, preparing for departure—but not to Austria or Italy or wherever Miller had in mind. He glanced at the title of the book he had been handed, *Man's Search for Meaning*, and tossed it down on Miller's desk.

"Thanks, but no thanks." The plane tickets made a hard landing on the desk now. "I appreciate the sentiment, Ed, but I don't need an intervention, if that's what this is."

"Roger!" Miller caught him just as he was about to leave the office. "I'm not asking."

Roger stopped. Miller walked over and handed him the book and tickets again. Roger skimmed the back of the book.

"This guy's a head doctor, *isn't* he?"

"I think so."

"I thought so."

"Melody thought …"

"Ahhh," Roger purred., glancing toward the dimly lit newsroom. "I might have figured she had something to do with this. Look, Ed, why do I need some shrink on the other side of the planet, when I've got a perfectly good bartender right here in the city by the bay?"

With that, Roger walked out.

The book and tickets had found their way back to Miller's hand almost without his notice.

◆   ◆   ◆

It was dark, Roger had been dozing, and he was disoriented, not recalling he was living in a new, smaller apartment, when the knock came at the door. The window also was open, and the chill inspired him to be brisk with whomever was there.

"Hi, Roger," a sheepish Melody murmured, quickly sizing up that he wanted to be left alone. "Look, I won't stay. I just wanted to bring you this…" She held out the same book that Miller had that morning. "Even if you don't do the story, I wish you'd read it." She shook the book slightly, which was still in the limbo between offer and acceptance.

Reluctantly, and only out of guilt for having caused Melody this special trip, he took the book.

She turned and sped off down the dark brown, poorly lit hallway toward the stairs. He watched her all the way out, looked down at the book, then closed his door.

He had no sooner closed the window and grabbed a sweatshirt and sat back on the sheet-covered couch when the knock was back. More annoyed than he should have been, he opened the door expecting Melody. Instead, it was the suicide prevention guy, Pauly.

"Mr. Murphy, hi," the visitor intoned politely, hat in hand. "I don't suppose you remember me—Ron Pauly? From the bridge?"

How could Roger forget the worst day of his life? "Yes, I remember. How can I…?"

"I hate to intrude on you like this at home, especially in the evening," Pauly continued. "But you've been awfully difficult to reach at the office recently. They told me—actually," Pauly pointed his nose over his right shoulder down the hall, "the young lady who just left here—told me I might be able to find you here."

"Oh she *did*, did she?" Roger asked, more curious than angry. A short, awkward pause told Roger he was being unnecessarily standoffish now. "Won't you come in?"

"Thank you. I won't intrude long."

Turning on a dim light to show a poorly appointed dive, Roger pointed to the couch. "Can I get you something? A Coke? A cockroach?"

"Nothing, really. But you *do* make it sound enticing." Pauly plunked down, awkwardly fiddling with his hat over his knees. "I'm here about the young man at the bridge …"

Roger sat down in the room's only chair. "He sent you? Why didn't he call me? Surely he knows the number."

"Actually, I'm sorry to bring you the news that he's dead, Mr. Murphy."

Roger leaned back and exhaled.

"All I know is that the Coast Guard found him—let's see, this is Friday—three days ago."

Again, Roger could only breathe in and out.

Pauly fidgeted with his hat, found no more words, then arose, straightened his overcoat and covered his head with his hat. "I'm sorry to have to bring you the news, but I thought you'd want to know." Roger kept sitting and listening, looking straight ahead rather than at Pauly, who had taken three steps toward the door. "I worked in this field many years, Mr. Murphy. I can tell you that we—you—did everything possible under the circumstances. Please don't feel bad."

Pauly stopped and put his hand on Roger's shoulder. "I can let myself out. Thank you for your time, and for doing your best. It doesn't always work out, and I'm sorry."

◆   ◆   ◆

Roger had never known the young man's name. He wondered whether, if he'd gotten to know his name, he might have saved him.

The thing is, even after the earthquake's indignities had been visited upon him and the Marina District he loved, and he had lost Bruno, and had become a refugee in his own land, and had been threatened with unemployment—even after all this, Roger hadn't shed a tear.

Now, upon learning of the death of the young man he tried to save on the Golden Gate Bridge, he did. He cried quietly yet bitterly for half an hour in that begrimed little apartment—not so much for the life lost, but for everything that had come to pass.

It was after midnight on the cool northern California coast when Roger woke up in the chair with the dull light still blazing. He took a few moments to gather himself before rising for bed.

He had contacted the knob of the lamp when his eyes stopped on it. Roger leaned forward and picked it up off the dingy garage sale coffee table. He stared at it absent-mindedly. He put it to his forehead and felt its edge against his skin.

He pulled it back and looked at it again. *"Man's Search for Meaning,"* it seemed to say out loud. Maybe Melody and Miller were right. Maybe it was time he got to know the guy who supposedly wrote the book on the meaning of life.

First thing tomorrow, he thought, I'll call this Viktor Frankl guy.

5

Snap!

Roger didn't know what the sound was, but he knew it couldn't be good.

Not where Dr. Mike Mahoney was concerned. Or where he was currently positioned.

And not while Roger's white cheeks were exposed by the hospital gown. He turned and saw the worst: Dr. Mahoney was wearing The Glove.

"Come on, Roger. You've been putting this off long enough."

Roger scooted farther onto the exam table paper. "Not from where I sit!"

Mahoney smiled. "You asked for a physical. Well, come and get it while it's hot!"

"*I* didn't ask for anything," Roger corrected him. "The insurance company did. They won't cover me abroad without it." Mahoney just stood there, smiling. "Look, Mike, I'm anal retentive. That means I want to hang onto my a …"

Mahoney cleared his throat. He was ready to get it over with, even if his patient was not.

"This could be the only bad thing about being a guy," Roger grimaced.

"You could be right!" the doctor blared, not at all comforting his patient.

Seeing the resolve in the doctor's eyes, Roger relented. But not without some horror. He had always admired Mike Mahoney's thick fingers and wondered how such massive hands could work a suture. Now he was about to see how they worked in *really* tight situations. In the dark. At his expense.

Roger decided to be brave—but it didn't take.

The nurses and patients outside the exam room must have thought Dr. Mahoney had started treating dogs.

"Good grief, Roger! What would you have sounded like if I'd run into something unexpected?"

"Then I'm clean?" Mahoney gave him a sardonic stare. Roger cut him off at the pass. "OK, I mean, there's nothing unusual?"

"Nope. Fit as a fiddle, you are. We'll do the usual blood work and such. You didn't howl when they took your blood, did you?"

"Very funny. Listen, I don't suppose you had your hands surgically enhanced, did you—knuckle implants for your patients' comfort?"

"No one's complained before." Now it was Roger's turn to stare. "OK, maybe one or two other dog howls. I couldn't play the violin with these, so I went into medicine." Mahoney paused before peeling off his gloves. "How does it feel being on the other end of some probing, Mr. Journalist?"

"I'm thinking of doing an expose on sadistic pigs who buy fraudulent medical licenses."

Ignoring the threat, Mahoney changed the subject while dropping the gloves in the waste can. "You certainly look svelte. Have you been dieting? Working out?"

"No—neither." Pushing up his glasses, Roger added, "I *have* been—well, under a lot of strain. Stressed."

"Depressed?" the doctor asked. Roger just looked back and forth between him and the floor. "It's OK, Roger. It's nothing to be ashamed of. It's not unmanly."

"Yeah, I guess so. A lot of things came together this past fall that kind of threw me for a loop."

The doctor made a few notes in the file. "Anything else out of the ordinary?"

"Not really. Just the usual winter stuff—fevers, colds."

Mahoney kept making notes, but shifted fronts. "So where are they sending you again?"

"Vienna."

Mahoney was genuinely excited, pausing from his writing. "Really! Wonderful! One of my favorite cities. You'll love it. See all the buildings. Kiss the pretty women. Try the pastry. But not too much of it. What's in Vienna, anyway?"

"Some supposedly famous shrink—guy named Frankl I'm supposed to see."

"You're kidding! You don't mean *Viktor* Frankl, do you?" Roger had never seen Mike Mahoney so interested in anything, not even invasive surgery. Mahoney, whose stiff, wiry red-brown hair might have been taken for dyed if it weren't for the boot-sized sideburns of the same color, was of an odd build—large, round cheeks that were red year-round, but a much thinner body than the face would suggest. Still, the 6-foot-3 frame was big-boned and imposing.

"Yes, that's the guy. Know him?"

"Are you kidding? *Man's Search for Meaning?* Maybe the best book ever written! I did papers on it in high school *and* college. The guy's a genuine hero. You're not telling me you're going to *interview* him?"

Roger was starting to wonder if he was the last person on Earth to have heard of this Frankl fellow. "That's the idea, although they didn't exactly say yes to the interview—only that he'd be 'in town' while I'm there. I'm impressed, Mike. I didn't figure you for the intellectual type. Then again, you *did* pass medical school, didn't you?"

"Careful, Roger. As your doctor, I can suggest you're not getting enough rectal exams."

"Gotcha, Doc. I'm declaring *both* orifices closed for the day, starting with the one on my face."

Mahoney ripped a small note off a pad and handed it to Roger.

"What's this?"

"A prescription."

The note read:

> *"Take two weeks in Vienna and call me with all the details."*

Roger folded it and put it in his pocket. "I guess it's doctor's orders!"

◆   ◆   ◆

On his connecting flight out of New York, Roger could tell immediately he was leaving the country: The European woman across the aisle who appeared to be speaking French and was juggling two toddlers and a baby wasted no time in offering her breast to her restless infant—and to anyone who wanted to gawk, which Roger felt himself doing. The woman smiled at Roger blithely, as if he were admiring a book she was reading rather than her exposed breast. He tried to be nonchalant about it, but one doesn't see a woman's breast offered up in public every day, not even in San Francisco. She repeated the scene three times before they'd attained cruising altitude, convincing Roger he was in for a very long transatlantic flight. But he preferred breasts to crying babies. And, truthfully, after holding the dying infant briefly in the rubble of the earthquake, Roger had more empathy for the little creatures now. Even if the kid screamed the entire flight, he thought he'd be fine with it.

He shook his head just listening to his thoughts. They sure didn't sound like him anymore.

Finally, the stewardess was about. "Excuse me," he told her. "The young gentleman across the aisle has received beverage service three times already…"

She was not amused, and thankfully the mother didn't appear to understand English. She just smiled at him politely.

Roger fumbled through his carry-on for something to read. He picked out Frankl's book—but it seemed like work, and he tried never to work after 6 p.m., ever since leaving the night-side reporting desk. So, being as how it was an overnight flight, he put the book down on the vacant seat next to him and chose his pocket guide to Vienna. It prompted him to think the trip wasn't such a bad thing after all. He suddenly liked the sound of Vienna, especially in spring.

He realized he felt warm now, and peeled off his outer jacket. Living in layers has its benefits, he thought.

The book was full of touristy information. Vienna seemed to be a living memorial to the Renaissance and its aftermath, with all the fancy palaces and baroque touches. But the Gothic spires and Romanesque arches, the book noted, are dramatic reminders that Vienna—strategically situated between the Carpathians and the Alps, notably near a vital gap in the former mountain range—has been a pivotal crossroads for Western and Eastern Europe for centuries.

And, Roger thought, obviously not built on as shaky a ground as the Marina District.

Roger hadn't been expecting to be impressed, but when one city can lay claim to Mozart, Beethoven, Brahms and Strauss, it's doing something right.

Roger looked slyly across the aisle for the breastfeeder. Three drinks and the kid was out for the night. "The kid can't hold his breast milk," Roger thought.

Looking back at the map of Vienna, he thought that San Francisco—or just about any North American city—would be laid out perfectly in comparison. Vienna looked like a spilled drink on a merry-go-round. Except for one beltway in the center, around the older part of the city—a boulevard known as the *Ringstrasse*—there seemed to be no rhyme or reason to the lines on the map except for their messy emanations from the core. No wonder the public transportation there—which includes streetcars, buses, trams and a subway system—is so developed. It's the only way you're going to find your way around the place: have someone else do it for you.

"This is what happens," he mumbled, "when you let medieval artists and musicians lay out a city!"

But he was already beginning to like it—and he had no idea why.

It wasn't the history. That wasn't his thing. Nor was it the music—pleasant enough, certainly, and cultured and all that. But Roger would take Stan Getz's jazz saxophone any day. Nor was it the artwork or the ornate architecture. He would enjoy seeing it all, and would appreciate it—but rather like one appreciates a good mashed potato: without a great deal of passion.

Maybe it was just the notion of Vienna as a crossroads. It's been that for nearly all of human history, all of modern Western civilization's history, certainly. And it sure had the feel of a crossroads to Roger this night.

Roger caught himself staring blankly across the aisle and quickly looked away; if he was going to be caught gawking, he wanted it to be actual gawking and not the blank gape of daydreaming.

When he dove back into the Vienna guidebook, he was thumbing through the index and stopped at "F."

Fashion

Ferris Wheel.

"Ferris wheel?" he asked out loud.

Franz-Ferdinand, Archduke. Wasn't he the guy who started World War I?

Freud, Sigmund. Now, there's a familiar name.

"No Frankl," he muttered. "If this guy is such a hotshot, why isn't he listed?"

"The father of modern psychoanalysis," is how the book described Freud, whose old apartment is now a museum.

"And here's the bathroom where he first developed his theories about sex," Roger thought out loud. He looked around him, just in case someone heard.

Closing the book, Roger wondered why all the fuss about Freud and not a whisper about Frankl. Maybe it's that it's hard to be appreciated when you're alive. That's one possibility. Maybe Freud had a better PR firm.

The other possibility, he considered as he looked out at the moonlight ocean, was more telling. Freud was all the time writing and talking about sex. The fellow was one sex-crazed guy. That kind of subject matter tends to get attention. Frankl—well, he wasn't sure, since he hadn't cracked the book yet, but the title and all, *Man's Search for Meaning*, doesn't raise the eyebrows, or anything else for that matter. Sex sells. An intellectual pursuit for life's meaning? What fun is that?

In fact, Roger felt himself dozing at that very second. With the rare good fortune of a vacant seat next to him on this transatlantic flight, he stretched out a bit and stopped thinking.

As Roger slipped into unconsciousness and slunk into the seat cushion for the night, the Vienna guidebook dropped to the floor, while Viktor Frankl's bespectacled blue face slid silently between the seat and the airplane hull.

◆   ◆   ◆

It never occurred to Roger, not once—not until he stepped foot out into the brisk Viennese morning air—that the folks here speak something other than English.

Not all of them, mind you. Young Europeans find it easy to pick up English, and difficult to negotiate their American culture-saturated lives without it. And plenty of older Austrians, especially shopkeepers, have worked hard to earn a working knowledge of English.

But you find large pockets in even cosmopolitan Vienna in which a question in English will only get you head scratches and shoulder hunches.

Roger found himself there right away.

Somehow, he managed to get some dollars converted to schillings—he had absolutely no idea if the pretty brunette in the exchange booth cheated him or not, but she did whatever she did with a remarkable smile. And he found the red bus that would take him to the taxi station for the ride to the apartment that the newspaper had made available for him. It would be cheaper, he was told, than taking a taxi all the way from the airport east of town.

Once he got off the bus, though, he made no headway trying to communicate his desires to a stationary herd of taxi drivers. He did his best to ask how much a ride would be—careful to speak louder English when they couldn't understand. They seemed to be snickering among themselves when one finally held a door open and stuffed his oversized duffle bag in. Roger figured his goose was cooked; when they figured out he was totally lost and couldn't speak German, he knew he'd be ripped off.

Indeed, either the taxi driver had just arrived from another country too, or he was taking the longest way there. After numerous concentric circles, the driver finally pulled part way over and stopped, blocking the right lane on a busy one-way street—another ploy to rush him into paying too much, Roger thought. He paid what the meter seemed to say, plus a bit more. Either unimpressed or wanting to make a quick getaway, the driver zoomed off, this time infinitely more certain of where he was going.

Roger stood there, tired, confused and feeling violated, and not altogether sure where to go. He fumbled in his jeans pocket for the address.

"Mr. Murphy!" Roger looked up to the fourth floor of windows, where a man was leaning out. "Come to the door and come in when it buzzes. Take the elevator to the fourth floor, 420."

Roger crossed the street and pushed on a gate that seemed to lead to an open-air parking garage. It stood firm. Suddenly it buzzed and he pushed through. In a door to the right and to the elevator he dragged his green bag.

"Welcome to Vienna, Mr. Murphy," greeted the 50ish man with a Turkish accent. "I'm afraid the last guest didn't clean up too well, and I didn't realize it …"

Roger stepped into the enamel-floored apartment, dropping the duffle behind the door. To the left, a small sitting room with an odd mix of traditional and futuristic furniture, with thin blankets thrown over the chairs and couch. Straight ahead, a long hallway for such a small apartment, leading to the bath. Off to the left, a kitchen—and the mess that the man was talking about: Wine bottles, water bottles, dirty dishes and assorted foodstuffs crowded the counter. The man had stuffed what he could into a paper sack on the floor.

"This is fine," Roger said earnestly. "I'm a bachelor. This is actually an upgrade."

The man was grateful he could quit his work and leave without guilt. "Let me show you a few things. Down the hall here, on the right side of the hallway, next to the closet, is a water closet. Please note that you must leave your hand here for a few seconds to flush. OK? OK.

"Over here is your bedroom." A bed with no sheet, very nearly on the floor. "You will find sheets in the main closet. And in the laboratory, there is a washing machine." Laboratory? Well, Roger knew what he meant, looking into the bathroom. He was impressed, not having expected laundry facilities. "It does not work. Do not try to make it work or it will flood the apartment below. OK? OK. You may wash your clothes in the sink and dry them here," he more or less insisted, touching a waist-high contraption with thin painted rods for hanging things. "All we ask is that you are quiet after 10 p.m. at night, OK? OK. And that you leave the apartment at least as good as you find it. OK?" The man looked about him. "That won't be a problem, I can see! OK."

With that, the man gave Roger a key, shook his hand and left.

"OK," Roger told the door.

◆　　◆　　◆

"Dr. Frankl is busy with correspondence and writing until lunch," the German-accented woman pronounced kindly but assertively on the phone. "After that, he takes a nap and again works on his books and papers and letters—he gets several dozen letters from all over the world each and every day, and he answers each one! You will come at four tomorrow. This is acceptable, yes?"

Roger recognized the difference between a question and a command. "Yes, thank you, that will be fine."

Hanging up the phone, Roger looked at his watch. It was close to noon. He emptied out his duffle bag and put his clothes away for the week. He inventoried the contents of the refrigerator—half a liter of sparkling water, quite possibly having lost its sparkle, some old fruit that appeared to be plums collapsing on themselves, various sauces and some sort of alcohol he had no interest in.

Tonight or tomorrow he would read up on Frankl. For now, it was a good time to check out the town.

◆   ◆   ◆

A chill blew lightly by as Roger stepped into the soothing midday sun. The small park just a couple blocks away was teeming with folks sitting on long benches, chatting, feeding pigeons, eating ice cream or just enjoying the arrival of spring. Everywhere, there were working-age people strutting confidently to or from something that appeared to be important. Roger made a mental note of the Italian ice cream store across the street; he would join the squatters later and do some serious people-watching.

Tucked in the middle of the park was an entrance to the Vienna subway system, known affectionately as the U-Bahn. A descent into the mouth of the U-Bahn, and a check of the map on the wall, seemed to indicate Roger was at the southern terminus of the red line, station *Reumannplatz*. Approaching the ticket counter, he felt his lack of German rising up in him, along with the feeling a leech might have before doing what a leech does. Still, he had little choice but to rely on the natives to speak his language. It isn't much to ask of subway ticket-sellers, who see lots of Americans who don't bother to learn the local language. But Roger knew he would be swimming upstream in other social settings, and he wasn't looking forward to it.

It never occurred to him that Viktor Frankl might not speak English— and the notion startled Roger momentarily. But then, his assistant did well enough on the phone, so the worst that might happen is that she would have to translate for him.

The U-Bahn was waiting for him down some more stairs. He jumped in just as the doors whooshed shut, and grabbed a seat, checking the map on the wall again to chart his destination: *Stephansplatz*, which seemed to be not only in the city's center, but also to be a favorite tourist destination. Roger looked at his ticket, good for a week. He realized in retrospect that no one had checked it before he entered, and there had been no turnstile. It appeared to be the honor system. Still, he slipped the ticket into his wallet, just in case some subway cop wanted to verify his honor. This was a Germanic-feeling place, after all. While some formalities, such as checking everyone's ticket, were dispensed with, there was a chill of formality as tangible as the early-April Vienna air. People are wary of each other in any big-city subway, but Roger could actually feel his fellow subway passengers avoiding eye contact. He began to find himself doing it, too, in case the others would think he was mental for staring at them.

If you do it right—that is, with a child's eye and a romantic's heart—emerging from the U-Bahn at Stephansplatz is a little like being born. You glide up the escalator from the large, dark hole in the ground and burst into being. All around you is life. People shopping, eating, talking and walking throughout the outdoor pavilion. This must be the dizzying effect a newborn suffers. What should one try to see or hear? The man in the Mozart costume hawking tickets to the crowd? The Gothic, baroque and Romanesque buildings seemingly in every direction? The street performers entertaining passersby? The ice cream?

Ah, the ice cream! Like tracking a river to its headwaters, Roger followed a trail of people with cones and cups until he found the source. The girls next to him in line shouted out something very close to "chocolate" and "vanilla." So when it was his turn, he simply pointed at their concoction. He felt pretty sly—until he handed the girl behind the counter what he thought was a reasonable amount of shillings. She looked at him like he was nuts, then smiled at him as if he were a child.

"Too much!" she chanted with an accent thick as ice. She handed him back three-quarters of what he'd given her. A small, money-back lesson in humility.

Turning back to the crowd, he now appreciated why the place was called *Stephansplatz*. Roger's eyes crawled spider-like up the tall spires of St. Stephens Cathedral, the Gothic heart of all the activity around him. It looked like the sort of place a hunchback would live, or a princess would be trapped.

Roger made his way down the outdoor mall toward a crowd assembled around a puppeteer.

"You shake my nerves and you rattle my brain!" sang the puppet, doing its best Jerry Lee Lewis at a tiny puppet-sized grand piano. A boy of about four years of age broke from the crowd and approached the performers gingerly. As the boy got very near a hat on the ground in front of the piano, the music stopped abruptly. The boy froze in sheer panic. Jerry Lee's strings led him to lean slowly and intently over the top of the piano and toward the young patron. Payday! Even a puppet can smell it. When the puppet got too close for comfort, the boy screamed, dropped a coin on the ground near the hat and ran for dear life, disappearing back into the delighted crowd and, presumably, into the arms of safety.

Roger couldn't resist. Feeling like a child, he took one of his coins and, squeezing through two layers of people, broke from the crowd. Now, nothing separated him from the menacing musician, which was back to wailing on the faux piano. Roger crept toward the hat as if it were a sleeping baby. As soon as he got close, the music stopped again and the puppet pianist was leaning over his piano to see a coin drop in the hat. Roger froze. The puppet moved an inch closer. Roger moved an inch closer. The puppet lunged.

"Aaaaaaaaah!" Roger yelled, dropping his coin on the ground, missing the hat, and plunging back into the crowd.

The crowd applauded Roger's performance. And he felt better than he had in months, if not years.

It was money well-spent.

6

The sun had done its best to announce the day, but Roger wouldn't hear of it. Not, that is, until the unlatched bedroom window blew gently open and the crisp morning air overwhelmed his thin blanket.

He fought his way up and over to close the window, lingering there to scan the patchwork of apartments across the street, which were in various stages of life, all the while unmindful of the spectacle his unadorned body was presenting to those he was watching. On several terraces, laundry flapped in the mild wind. Several people were scurrying about in their apartments, apparently rushing to leave for work. One man, in no hurry, was eating breakfast on his porch—in a T-shirt, and in what had to be 40-degree weather. Roger couldn't see anyone worth watching very long, but it wasn't for a lack of looking.

Then he remembered what happened to Jimmy Stewart in the movie *Rear Window*—and simultaneously became aware of his own nakedness. He promptly drew the curtains and headed for the bathroom.

After showering and dressing, he poked around the kitchen for edible food. There was none, at least what he would consider edible. Roger remembered Mahoney telling him to eat the pastry. Doctor's orders and all. But that didn't seem substantial enough. He recalled seeing a McDonald's on the walk to and from the U-Bahn station, so he headed there.

As he bit into it, he knew he should be dining on something more exotic or indigenous than an Egg McMuffin. But it was his favorite breakfast, especially on the road. And in a strange world, where the newspaper on the table in front of him was written in an inexplicable language, this was comfort food. A taste of the ordinary can be extraordinary when one is out of one's element.

Three bites from finishing, he froze in horror. He replayed things in his mind. He mentally looked under every rock. He gestured with his hands and mouthed instructions to himself. All to no avail.

He crammed the rest of his sandwich in his mouth, tossed in the rest of his orange juice to make it chewable, and ran out and up the entire four blocks to the apartment.

He turned the bedroom upside down. He did the same with each successive room. And for good measure, he repeated the feat.

No Frankl book anywhere.

Roger sunk into the cheap cloth-covered chair in the living room as the realization began to sink in on him: He'd left *Man's Search for Meaning* on the airplane.

It was 10 a.m. The interview was at 4. But all was not lost.

Roger jumped up and rifled through the German-language yellow pages until he'd stumbled onto the entry for books, and had written down the addresses of four apparent book stores and what appeared to be a public library. When, a few hours later, the store search came up empty, he struggled for half an hour to find the library; his initial reaction to the map of Vienna had proved accurate: He found the city to be, while charming, nearly impossible to figure out.

"I need this book, desperately," he told the first English-speaking librarian he could corral.

"Yes, we have that," the man whispered louder than some people yell. Roger sat down and waited with relief. The man returned a few minutes later with the book, a hard-cover version.

In German.

It was nearly time for the interview.

He'd have to go in blind.

◆   ◆   ◆

Roger left plenty of time to get to Mariannengasse 1. And, as it turned out, he needed every minute of it.

He thought he had memorized the directions Frankl's assistant had given him over the phone. But after taking the U-Bahn to *Schottentor* station, following a switch from U-Bahn 1 to U-Bahn 2 at *Karlsplatz* station, he was more than a little hazy on which direction to proceed. He took the first streetcar he could find—not needing to dig into the handrail on these flat streets, as he did on the hills of San Francisco—but soon got a sinking feeling he was headed the wrong way.

He jumped off. He ran into a store and asked a clerk for directions. She sent him to a streetcar going the opposite direction, but after a few minutes he could not spot any streets that sounded like Mariannengasse.

Finally, with 4 o'clock approaching, and Roger running down a narrow street of apartments, he found a man who professed to speak a little English. The man pointed the way.

At precisely 4 o'clock, Roger was upon the apartment of Mariannengasse 1. What a relief, too: He knew he was arriving pitifully unprepared, which was totally unlike him. He was confident in his ability to finesse the interview; few journalists asked better off-the-cuff questions than Roger Murphy. Still, he certainly didn't want to compound the error of being unprepared by also showing up late.

He quickly scanned the apartment buttons until he found the name. "Frankl," it spelled. As he waited for a response to his buzz, he straightened his white shirt under his leather jacket and tucked it into his jeans. And he began to feel as if this journey had better be worth it, as difficult as it was becoming.

"Yes?"

He leaned into the speaker. "Roger Murphy to see Viktor Frankl."

A slight pause. "*Dr.* Frankl is expecting you." The woman's voice was assertive, yet formal and polite. But the emphasis on "Dr." was unmistakable; Roger knew that he had committed his first *faux pas* by referring to Dr. Frankl by his first name rather than his hard-earned title. Roger had been forewarned that the Viennese were quite a bit more formal than your average San Franciscan. Roger respected that; his Catholic school upbringing made him quite comfortable with formalities, especially where elders were concerned. It was just a difficult transition from everyday American life.

He glanced down at his jeans and thought them too American for the particular occasion. Another *faux pas.*

"Please come through the door when you hear it unlock."

Into the vestibule and down a dim marble hallway he walked, and up several flights of stairs to where a gated door was opening. A short gray-haired woman, simply dressed with a white blouse and brown pants and a kind smile, beckoned him in.

"Hi, I'm Roger Murphy, from the *Chronicle* in San Francisco. You must be Dr. Frankl's assistant."

He got the "Dr." part right this time. He got the assistant part all wrong.

"I am Elly Frankl. Dr. Frankl's wife."

Faux pas No. 3 was now in the book, and he had only now walked in.

"May I take your wrap?" Mrs. Frankl asked adamantly. Her English, powered by a forceful voice, especially coming from such a short source, managed to cut easily through her thick Viennese accent.

"Yes, thank you. I'm sorry for assuming you were his assistant …"

"Oh!" she chirped with a high-pitched giggle. "Many people make that mistake. They think that, 'Here is this world-renowned Dr. Frankl, who everybody wants to see and to touch and to listen to; he must have a large staff to protect him and do his letters and his books and phone calls, and to cook his meals and take care of his home and—no, no, I am all he needs. I do all these things for him.

"But you know? One patient leaving Dr. Frankl's office gave me a tip—like you give a waitress, yes? He, too, thought me a lowly assistant! Well, what was I to do? To give it back would have embarrassed him, or worse, offended him. So I kept it!"

She giggled some more as she hung the coat in the large closet in the entryway presided over by a chandelier that looked like a disco ball exploding into crystal shards.

"But that's not all!" she continued. "The people, people on the street, they think I know it all too, yes? They think I am a logotherapist like him. Well, you know how it is. You are a writer, yes? Well, you know how it is when you are typing something that someone else has written—you are only typing the words, yes? You don't listen to their meaning! And so it is with me and Dr. Frankl's books.

"But I go to get milk and people stop me and say, 'Frau Frankl! Can you help me?' And they tell me all their problems, and they say, 'Now, Frau Frankl, what should I do?' At first, I tried to tell them, 'Listen, I am only his wife. I take care of him and help him. I am not the doctor; *he* is.' But after so much of this, I just listen and give my advice."

Roger was instantly in love with this woman. "And Dr. Frankl—does he worry about the competition you give him?"

Mrs. Frankl laughed briefly, then her eyes opened wide and she pointed at Roger. "*This* is what he says. When I take three hours to go to the market, he asks me and laughs, 'Elly! What street corner has been your office today?' So I suppose one could say, as you do, that I am his assistant. But this is not what I wish! I want only to be his wife. That is enough for me. But," she shrugged, "this is not what life asks of me. So do you know what I do? I do what life asks me to do. It is this way with everyone, of course."

That caught Roger off guard. "Yes, I suppose so."

"You are from San Francisco, did you say?"

"Yes. Are you familiar with it?"

"Oh, yes. Please, we will sit down."

She ushered him down a short hallway to a living room, where a tile-covered wood stove occupied one corner, a large tropical plant another and a third corner hosted the large room's only furniture—two simple lime-green crushed-velvet chairs and a matching sofa. The fourth corner of the room was quietly commanded by an impressionistic portrait of a dignified-looking Viktor Frankl. Along the large row of curtained windows was a thigh-high wood-surfaced cabinet with books piled in its open front and just a few items—they appeared to be awards—on its top. On either side of the room were white double doors leading to other rooms: The one on the right, which he could see into through one open door, appeared to be a storage area; the one on the left was obviously Dr. Frankl's office, for the doors were closed and Roger could hear Dr. Frankl talking animatedly to someone.

To say the furnishings were spartan, especially for a doctor of apparent world renown, would be to compliment the Spartans on their frugality.

The small round glass coffee table was set with some kind of fritters and juice. In the corner by the portrait was a modest three-level mobile glass serving tray with a pitcher, probably of coffee.

"Please, eat and drink whatever you like, yes? Dr. Frankl no longer sees patients, but they occasionally see *him*, you know? I apologize, but it will be a few minutes. Is there another thing I can bring you?"

Roger, pouring the pitcher of yellow-orange juice into a small clear glass, was beginning to be overwhelmed with her hospitality. "No, thank you very much."

She was sitting in the other green chair now. "I will take some juice too, I think." In a display of old-fashioned European manners, she made it plain through body language that she would allow him to fill her glass for her.

"A woman from San Francisco once called me," Mrs. Frankl continued, taking a drink.

"Yes?" Roger had learned the hard way during his career when to just listen.

"Dr. Frankl was in the hospital, and I was with him there until midnight. I came home and the phone was ringing. It was a woman from San Francisco—your city! She commanded of me, 'I want to talk to Dr. Frankl!' I told her he was in the hospital. She screamed, 'I don't care! I need to talk to Dr. Frankl. I have a gun to my head and I am going to kill myself.'"

A few months ago, Roger could not have related to that. He was rapt now.

"Well, what should I do? Tell her to call back when Dr. Frankl is better? She might not be alive then! Well, I was very tired from being at the hospital. But I talked to this woman on the telephone for two hours. I simply told her what I thought Dr. Frankl would tell her, and what I tell people who stop me from going to market or going home from it, yes?

"A few weeks later, the telephone rings, and a woman, a different woman, says, 'Mrs. Frankl?' And I say, 'Yes, this is she.' And she says, 'Go down to your door in 10 minutes.' Well, I went down, and there was a package. I took it upstairs and we opened it. It was a mink coat! With a note: 'Thank you for saving my daughter's life.'"

Roger set his glass down. "That must feel wonderful," he sighed, with a twinge of sadness—remembering his own failed attempt to do the same for the man on the bridge.

"All I did was show her some of the things Dr. Frankl shows people."

"What did he think of your gift?"

Mrs. Frankl laughed and swatted the air dismissively. "He says to me, 'Elly! All these years I have seen patients and no one ever gets *me* such a thing!'" She laughed harder now, stopping suddenly and widening her eyes again. "And you know, six months later, I got another call. 'Mrs. Frankl? Go down to your door; there will be a package for you.' It was *another* mink coat—a different color! So now I have *two* mink coats and Dr. Frankl has *none*!" She delighted herself with that.

"They must come in handy here in winter."

"Heavens!" she scowled. "I have never worn them. Not once! What do *I* want with such things?"

A booming laughter came from behind the office door, and a slightly built white-haired man with glasses exploded out. One arm around the shoulders of his guest, he led the guest down the hall toward the foyer, not even noticing his wife and the reporter in the living room.

Mrs. Frankl turned back to Roger. "You know, this is very unusual."

"What?"

"Dr. Frankl does not give many interviews. Not many at all. He's a very busy man. And he …"

"Yes?"

"I'm sorry to say this, but he doesn't trust reporters. They ask many silly questions, and waste Dr. Frankl's time—and then they write things you just don't believe! Ugh!" She shook her head with disgust and swung at the air again. "Why is this so?"

"I don't really know, Frau Frankl."

She was astounded. "Frau Frankl? But you don't speak German! Hmm. I thought not. But you learn quickly—calling me Frau so quickly. You need to learn German! It is a very useful language. And you really must learn German to appreciate Dr. Frankl's writings.

"You know, we have been told that people in Eastern Europe learn German *just so they can read Dr. Frankl's writings!*"

Roger was dutifully impressed. He glanced over toward the foyer to see this man she spoke of, where the conversation with his guest continued. "Frau, why do you suppose Dr. Frankl agreed to be interviewed by me? You told me he most often says no."

"Yes! Yes! Nearly all the time!" She rested her hand on Roger's forearm. "I don't know why he said yes to you. Perhaps it was the young lady from your newspaper who called and talked to him."

Roger was puzzled. "Lady?"

"Yes. Oh, I don't remember her name. It was ... something to do with music."

"Melody?"

"Yes! Melody! She must be a very persuasive young lady to get you in to see Dr. Frankl."

"I'll have to thank her." Mrs. Frankl appeared not to smell the subtle scent of sarcasm in the remark.

"Come. Dr. Frankl is nearly ready for you. Come wait in his office."

Roger walked in ahead of her, through the double doors, and was jolted when the doors closed behind him and he found himself alone.

He put his satchel on a lonely chair in the corner between the doors he just entered and another set of doors that led to a bedroom. Above the chair were crossed fencing foils mounted on the wall, and a couple of certificates—one of them declaring Dr. Frankl an honorary citizen of Austin, Texas, of all things.

Roger turned and scanned the rest of the large office—or maybe it just seemed big due to the sparse contents: two tall bookshelves in opposite corners, a narrow day bed, a portrait of a woman, and a television that seemed much too modern for the rest of the room.

The room's command center was a utilitarian black-surfaced desk—containing only one book, a small calendar and a few papers—and the tan leather executive chair behind it. The chair had its back right up against the center of a set of bay windows that looked out onto the urban setting below.

Looking toward the desk from the room's opposite corner, with an elegant chandelier in-between, one almost got the feeling this was the Oval Office. But it wasn't opulence that conveyed that message. Far from it, in fact: There was little of visual consequence in the room. Clearly, Dr. Frankl felt about furniture and other niceties the same as Mrs. Frankl felt about mink coats. Neither had any use for any of it.

No, what gave this room its dignity had to be the nature of the work that went on here—and the man doing it.

Roger's eyes were drawn to something rather quickly, however: In a small display case cut into one of the bookshelves was what appeared to be a small wooden statue of Jesus reaching skyward with both hands, with flames licking at his side. Roger felt guilty for thinking it, but the statue's pose reminded him of Jerry Rice catching a football.

"I've been watching too many 49ers' games," he mumbled to himself.

◆   ◆   ◆

"Suffering man!"

Roger was startled not just by the suddenness of the words, but by the cannon that must have fired them across the room. He turned around.

There stood Dr. Viktor Frankl.

By now, from everything he'd heard, and everything he'd *almost* read, Roger was ready to be impressed by Dr. Frankl. And perhaps he yet might be. But here before him was a short, skinny man with combed-back white hair, an impish, toothy smile and broad, black-rimmed eyeglasses large enough that one would have supposed they needed more of a foundation than they had on his frame.

"Pardon?" was all Roger could think of to say.

"Suffering man. I call him 'Suffering Man.'" The doctor moved over to where Roger was and continued talking, while looking at the statue. "I saw it at a sale one day and had to have it."

Roger glanced back to it. Considering the Frankls' ambivalence for material things, it spoke volumes that Dr. Frankl wanted this little thing so badly.

"You must be Mr. Murphy. I am Dr. Frankl." With a wide grin, Dr. Frankl extended a hand. His handshake would have been firm and vibrant for a 40-year-old, much less a man who was in his 80s.

"Yes, doctor. Pleased to meet you."

Carrying the chair with Roger's satchel from the far corner of the room to the front of his desk, Dr. Frankl directed, "Come, sit down and we will talk. You write for an American newspaper, yes?" Dr. Frankl shimmied around the desk and into his chair, which seemed to swallow him whole.

Roger placed his satchel on the throw rug, grabbing a tape recorder and notebook and pen out of it with one swoop. "Yes, the *San Francisco Chronicle*."

Dr. Frankl beamed. "San Francisco! I truly believe this is one of your most interesting cities! Also one of the most beautiful in the world. I especially like your hills and cable cars!"

"I could do without the hills myself."

"Oh, but life is nothing without hills to climb, you see? Now, how far is it from your city to Disneyland?"

Roger was stunned by the odd question. "Well, that's in southern California, and …"

"I love your Disneyland! The rides, the popcorn—Magic Mountain! What a wonderful place!"

Roger nearly laughed out loud. Here was one of the pre-eminent psychiatrists of the time, a man in the land of Freud, and he's talking about Mickey Mouse! "Me too." And Roger wasn't lying a bit.

"Well, then. You have questions of me, no?" Dr. Frankl's voice was unusually powerful for such an unimposing man.

"Well," Roger stammered uncharacteristically, "I suppose you could say I've been sent here to find out the meaning of life."

Dr. Frankl seemed to levitate in his chair as he became as vertical as a pillar.

"Oh you have, have you?" The smile was gone now. "And you believe you will find it here, do you?"

Dr. Frankl was smiling, but Roger could feel the steam slowly building in the man.

"Call Dr. Frankl, fly to Vienna, turn on a tape recorder and the meaning of life will just escape his lips and land on your tape and off you go, back to your newspaper office to solve the question of the meaning of life for everyone!"

Roger knew he was in trouble now. The kindly man who entered the room had suddenly been replaced by an angry professor—angry because the student before him had posed an absolutely inane question.

The volume of Dr. Frankl's voice was flowing like lava now.

"Which of my writings have you studied before coming here, young man? You know, I have on occasion put pen to paper on such matters as that which you have so boldly asked me about! Have you not read my most widely published work, which in your language is entitled *Man's Search for Meaning*?

"They tell me I am responsible for nearly 30 such works, and I can tell you that my dear wife, Elly, with whom you have made an acquaintance, has not only personally typed all these books, but also 700 articles for journals in the world's scientific journals, many of which I believe, until this very day, have been printed in the language we are both speaking here at this moment!

"My dear journalist, I am a modest man. The world has given much to me, and I contemplate each and every day, without fail, what it is that life requires of me to give back, you see? I do not ask for much in return. Only to live and to breathe and to have my family and to share my work in the hope that it means something to the world.

"But I ask also this little thing: I ask that a reporter who comes to consume my time, that he comes only after reading a pittance of my writing—so that he may ask questions of me that a child on the street would not have been able to construct because the child on the street has not read my words and has not considered even the questions of life, much less the answers! If you had done this simple little thing, you would not come to me and say, 'Dr. Frankl, tell me the meaning of life!'

"How can I tell you such a thing? How can anyone? Who am I to walk out there," he pointed out the large bay windows over his shoulders, "who I am to walk up to a shoemaker and tell him what the meaning of his life should be? What do I know of shoemaking? What do I know of his life? What do I know of yours?"

Roger thought at that moment that he had no need of the tape recorder; he was certain the entire apartment building was getting this down.

"Imagine for a moment that I am a grand master of chess! Will you come to me to ask, 'Grand Master, what is the best move in the game?' The question has no relevance whatsoever, do you see? What is a good move at one point in one game is not at all a good move in another, you see?

"It is the same with life! What gives meaning to my life at this moment may not give meaning to me tomorrow—or any day to yours. I may live to work in a garden; for you, it may be drudgery of the worst sort.

"Just as there is no best move in chess, there can be no abstract meaning in life. These things I have made very clear in my writings and lectures!"

Suddenly, the doctor fell silent and simply stared at his steamrolled interviewer.

"I do not wish to be rude, my dear guest. But you see, you are wasting both our time. There is nothing worse in all of creation than a minute that is spent foolishly."

Dr. Frankl opened a book on his desk and, without looking up, ended the interview as loudly as it had begun. "Go and come back when you are ready to ask questions worthy of being asked, and worthy of my time and yours! Good day, Herr Murphy."

Roger wasted no time gathering his things and walking meekly out, quietly closing the office door behind him. Not even the nuns back in grade school had made him feel this small.

He zipped up his satchel and started toward the hallway leading out. Out of the corner of his eye, he noticed movement coming from the opposite storage room. Mrs. Frankl emerged, closing the door behind her.

She scurried over to Roger, handing him a book.

Man's Search for Meaning. In English.

"Dr. Frankl dictated this book in nine days," she whispered, as if gossiping. "But it can be read in much less time, yes?"

Roger could only say "thank you" with his eyes, and the sensitive little woman before him read his face instantly. She opened the door to the flat, and before he was all the way through, she stopped him with a hand on his right arm.

"This book has helped a lot of people," she beamed. He smiled another thank you and left.

"Elly!" Even through the closed office doors, the professor's voice boomed down the hall.

"Coming, Viktor!" she boomed right back. She threw open the doors to the office, where Dr. Frankl, still behind his desk, drew off his glasses.

"Do you think I was too harsh with him?"

Mrs. Frankl simply shook her head and shrugged her shoulders noncommittally. "We are loud people, Viktor. Some people don't understand that. He may think you were more angry than you were."

Dr. Frankl swiveled around and looked down to the sidewalk below.

"He'll be back," he deduced, putting his glasses back on. "If he is serious about his search, he will be back." He swiveled back around to face his wife, still standing in the threshold. "We might want to keep the next week fairly open, Elly."

Across the busy street, and through a breezeway leading to a tree-covered park, the American journalist walked down a narrow asphalt walking trail, one of several crisscrossing the park, and found the lonely wooden bench where he would begin the journey of his life.

7

Roger snapped awake and to full attention. He had almost forgotten what a phone sounded like.

Running down the hall in the mid-morning light, still not acclimated to the time change, he reached the phone in his apartment's sitting area just as it finished its fifth ring.

"Mr. Murphy!" He instantly recognized the kindly voice as Mrs. Frankl. "Dr. Frankl would very much like for you to join him at Hohe Wand tomorrow at 11 in the morning."

"OK …" Roger's voice was threaded with both surprise and wonder—most particularly, wonder about where and what Hohe Wand was.

Mrs. Frankl either anticipated his question or read the question in his short answer. "Anyone in Vienna can tell you how to get there."

"OK." There was a definitive conclusion to Roger's "OK" this time, signaling no further question—although he had many.

"I must say," added Mrs. Frankl, becoming her animated self now, "I have never known Dr. Frankl to invite a reporter to Hohe Wand. This is quite unprecedented."

"Well …" Roger was still a bit foggy from sleep and surprised by the quick turnaround in Dr. Frankl's receptiveness. "Uh, tell Dr. Frankl I accept his gracious invitation and will see him promptly at 11 tomorrow."

◆　　◆　　◆

"Excuse me," Roger smiled to the Turkish-looking woman named Fatma behind the counter. "Do you know where Hohe Wand is?"

Fatma gave him his Egg McMuffin and orange juice, along with his change. "What? No, I'm sorry, I don't." Without another word, she turned and barked something in another language—Roger wasn't sure which—to a man working behind her.

"Yes, sir." The man had the most helpful air about him Roger had ever breathed in. "You were asking Fatma about the Hohe Wand?"

"Yes." Roger couldn't believe how much trouble the McDonald's crew was going to for him.

"You are a rock climber, then?"

Roger had been holding his tray. Now he dropped it on the counter. "A what?"

"Climber? Mountain climber? Rock climber?" When Roger simply returned a stunned stare, the 30-something man, who also appeared Turkish, began to smile broadly. "Ah, you are not! But you want to go there, yes?"

Roger took a few seconds to gather himself. What was Dr. Frankl up to?

"I have an appointment there tomorrow at 11."

"You are from out of town, yes? American?"

"Yes."

"The Hohe Wand is about an hour from here, to the south more or less. Do you have a car?"

Frankl's plans were beginning to sound like hazing to Roger. "No, no car."

The man stared at Roger like a grinning statue for the longest time. Finally, he spoke, even more animatedly than before.

"I will take you!"

Roger, who'd picked his tray up again, dropped it again on the counter. "You what?"

"Yes! I will take you. Tomorrow is my day off. I have no other ideas of what to do, you know? And I love the Hohe Wand."

"I can't …"

"But I insist! Please! It will be my pleasure."

The man introduced himself as Abdul, McDonald's daytime shift supervisor and part-time nightclub guitarist—and weekend rock climber. Roger motioned to a seat, indicating a desire to get on with his late breakfast. "Tell me," Roger swallowed loudly, "about Hohe Wand."

"Ah, I sense some fear in you. Am I right?"

"I'm not a big fan of hills."

Abdul threw his head back and laughed heartily. "Then let me ask you: How do you feel about hills 200 meters high with sheer cliffs and loose rocks?"

Roger just stared at him, prompting Abdul to laugh again. "This describes Hohe Wand, friend. But rest easy. There are many paths to climb, some easier than others. And I will be there with you, so nothing to worry about. Why are you summoned there, may I ask?"

"I've been invited by Dr. Viktor Frankl."

"Hmm. Don't know of him. But it is wise to be climbing with a doctor!" Again Abdul laughed.

"He's not that kind of doctor. He's a psychiatrist. Although I guess he's a neurologist too."

"And what does he want with you? Are you crazy? If so, maybe I don't attach my rope to you!"

Roger smiled a sarcastic smile. "Actually, it's me that wants something from him. I guess I'm going there to interview him for the newspaper I work for."

"Excellent. You will write about me, too. Please take care to write my name correctly. So will you interview him on the way up or at the top?"

"Whoa, fella. I have no intention of climbing the least little boulder."

Abdul arose to return to work. "Then it is clear you must choose."

"Choose? Choose what?"

"Choose whether or not you will fulfill your mission."

Well, Roger thought, when you put it that way …

◆   ◆   ◆

When Roger arrived back at his apartment, it was dark and the phone was ringing. He slammed the door shut and hit the wall to his right several times with his palm, looking for the light, and came up empty. He felt on the left for the door to the living room and couldn't find the knob quickly. The phone kept calling him. He scurried down the hall to the kitchen, where an outside light gave him some bearings. He scuttled through the kitchen and around to the left to the small sitting room where he hit his shin on the glass coffee table before knocking the headset off the phone.

"Yeah, hey there," Roger said warmly. "How'd you know where to find me? Oh, right. OK. You bet. I'll see what I can do."

"OK, yes, I'm sitting down," he lied. Then he listened in silence for the longest time. "Yes, I'm here." He could barely hear himself. "Yes, I understand. No. No questions. OK, I'll see you as soon as I can."

His friend on the phone was right. He needed to sit down.

He did all night long.

8

Roger awoke with the strangest sensation he'd ever awakened with. Someone was wagging his foot.

"Mr. Murphy, wake up! Wake up!" It was Abdul. Roger was still in the sitting-room chair; it was light out now, and Abdul was in his apartment.

"How'd you get in?"

Seeing Roger was awake, Abdul let go of Roger's foot and raised up out of his baseball-catcher crouch.

"Sorry for being so bold, my friend. Your door was unlocked, and thank goodness it was. It is time to leave for Hohe Wand, and you are most difficult to wake up!"

Roger sat up straighter, though still in a slouch. Added to the fact that he had just awakened, he also had a hard time caring about his appointment or even that anyone could have entered his apartment while he slept. He had a hard time caring about anything. And he felt hung over, though he had not consumed near enough alcohol the night before for that to be the case.

Oh yes. The phone call.

"If your friend the doctor is a stickler about time—and most Viennese are—I suggest you get moving immediately. If you hurry, we can still be on time, but if you continue to sit …"

Roger waved his hand and nodded yes. It was all he could muster. It might have been a blessing that Abdul was forced to barge in and wake him up. If Roger had been awake ahead of time, and had had time to think things over in his current state of mind, he would have begged off the trip to the mountains—or just left the apartment and not allowed himself to be found.

As it was, he struggled to the bathroom and threw water on his face and slicked back his hair and agreed to leave primarily to get his insistent guest out of his face. Roger was in no mood to go rock climbing or to spend time with an intense, demanding psychiatrist—but he was in even less of a mood to argue. So he was simply going to comply with whatever he was asked to do, perhaps to the point of scaling a mountain ledge.

He grabbed his coat, and just like that he was on his way to the Rax Mountains.

◆   ◆   ◆

An hour later, Abdul pulled up close to a small open-air food stand with outdoor tables and seats, about half-occupied with snackers and even early beer-drinkers. Following Abdul's lead, Roger walked over and took an unoccupied table farthest from the stand. He looked around and saw that they were now basically at the foot of the cliffs that he might be called upon to climb. He was about to turn to Abdul and decline the opportunity when something near the hut's kitchen caught his attention. It was the waiter. The elderly man could have been Dr. Frankl's twin brother.

"Old Austrian guys all look alike," Roger muttered to Abdul, nodding slightly toward the waiter. "That guy could be Frankl."

Abdul smiled. "I know that man. He is a climber, just like your friend you are meeting here today."

Roger checked his watch, though he knew it didn't really matter; wherever the clock's hands pointed, his mood pointed to a beer. "Waiter! Beer here!" Roger shouted without thinking. Realizing his mistake, he turned to Abdul. "How do you say 'waiter' in German?"

"*Kellner*!" Abdul yelled for him.

The old man had picked up a tray of mugs on his way to the kitchen, and had his back to Roger and Abdul. He stopped on a dime and turned slowly.

It *was* Dr. Frankl.

Roger swallowed hard as his eyes opened wide. He'd lost count of his faux pas since he arrived, but the volume didn't matter. This felt like the worst.

"What is it?" Abdul asked when he saw the look on Roger's face.

Without moving a facial muscle, Roger exhaled, "It's him!"

"It's him who?" Abdul looked back at the man, who was now walking over. Abdul looked back to Roger. "You mean *him* him?"

"Yes! *Him* him!"

Dr. Frankl looked stern. "Herr Murphy! I suppose you realize your mistake!"

Roger sat up in his chair. "Yes, sir. I'm sorry. I didn't realize it was …"

"You did not indicate what type of beer you wished! We have many here, you know."

Roger was too shocked to feel relief. But when he saw Dr. Frankl's smile, he couldn't help but smile back. "I'll have whatever the locals have, Herr Doctor." Dr. Frankl nodded and walked off. Roger shouted after him, "I mean, *Herr Kellner!*" The distinguished waiter turned just enough to shoot a smile back.

As Dr. Frankl disappeared, Roger melted onto the table, shaking his head in his hands. "I can't believe it. A world-renowned psychiatrist and Holocaust survivor tells me to meet him in the mountains, and it turns out to be his weekend job!"

"I have seen him here many times, though never waiting tables before," Abdul offered. "He's a very well-recognized climber in the Rax Mountains. Out here, he is just another climber. But a very popular one. Here," Abdul continued, reaching into a bag he'd brought with him. "I had to assume that you were not prepared for rock climbing. So I brought you some things— extra things of mine."

Roger looked down at the bag in horror, as if Abdul had instead just unzipped the foul-smelling innards of a dead animal. There was a pair of polyester long underwear, leather climbing boots, gloves, over mitts, socks, a hat, a rain parka, a knife, first-aid supplies, granola bars, bottles of water, sunscreen and more.

"And of course," Abdul declared, "we will go nowhere without this!" He pulled out a bundle of ropes and jangling metal clips of some sort.

And that was enough for Roger. "Abdul," he said, standing up and sending his chair toppling behind him. "I don't think ..."

"You didn't think," interrupted Dr. Frankl, "that we were actually going to climb today, Herr Murphy. Did you?"

Roger and Abdul just looked at him.

"Are you a climber, then?"

"Well," Roger stammered.

"By all means, climb!"

"I didn't ..."

"I am sorry to tell you that I may no longer do such things. My last climb was when I was 80. That was five years ago. I miss it very much, you know." Dr. Frankl put two beers on the table and sat down, followed by a still-stunned Roger Murphy. "I had climbed since I was in high school. Other than logotherapy, and my wife and family, *alpinism* is my great passion."

"Actually, Dr. Frankl," Roger finally managed, "I'm not a climber. In fact, I'm something of a clinger."

"A clinger, Herr Murphy?"

"Yes. One who clings to the ground for dear life."

Dr. Frankl burst out laughing. "A clinger! Well, I suppose I have become one myself, Herr Murphy. But may I suggest that men of your age ..." Dr. Frankl shot back and forth between the two men.

"Sorry, doctor. Dr. Viktor Frankl, this is my friend Abdul."

The two men shook hands. "I am honored to meet you, Herr Doctor. I am quite familiar with you up here, but did not realize you were the great Dr. Frankl." Abdul expertly exaggerated his familiarity with Frankl, which suited Roger fine.

"Now, *he*," Roger chimed in, "is a climber, doctor."

"Well, good man! Herr Murphy, I absolutely implore you to give it a try. You will find that there is nothing quite like it in the world. While climbing, all the problems of your existence fall off your shoulders. You forget everything but the task in front of you. Face to face with the rock, battling gravity for your very life, you must live completely in the moment. It is the only way I have ever been able to forget about my books, my lectures, my correspondence and all my other obligations."

He pointed up to the plateau above them, where a cable railway led up the mountain. "I believe it is up there that I have made my most important decisions. It is there that I can truly think."

Roger looked up, then back down at Abdul's equipment. "It sounds wonderful. I hope I don't offend you gentlemen, though, if I put that day off …"

Abdul, who was always smiling, laughed heartily. "I am not at all offended, Mr. Murphy. I have some climbing friends meeting us here soon. We will go on without you. After all, one must be in the right frame of mind to climb. Isn't that correct, doctor?"

"Absolutely! In alpine climbing, the challenge to the mind is even greater than that to the body. You must be ready and willing. Herr Murphy, you and I will take the tramway to the top—or perhaps you would prefer to hike the trail?"

Roger smiled. "The tram sounds better. But Herr Doctor …" Roger paused and looked at him in a most serious manner. "What time do you get off work?"

Dr. Frankl looked down at the green apron he had on, chuckled, and took it off, folding it neatly. "I am quitting as of this moment! The pay here is worse than atrocious!

"In truth, this hut is run by a climbing friend of ours. For many years now, Elly and I have helped him occasionally so that he could get done with work and come climb with us. Now, I miss the climbing—but I need not miss helping him!

"Actually, Herr Murphy, you are not the first person to mistake me for hired help. On an occasion or two, someone has seen me clearing tables and asked me to retrieve them a beer or something to eat. When I did that, happily, they left me a tip! I tried to give it back, but they insisted, and do you know why?"

Roger smiled broadly. "No. Why?"

"Because they said I had a nice smile!" Dr. Frankl laughed and slapped his knee.

"Herr Doctor, it's just like some of your patients have tipped Mrs. Frankl."

"Yes. Perhaps we both missed our calling!"

"I rather doubt that. So, doctor, how much was the tip and what did you spend it on?"

"As I recall, my first tip was 35 cents. I donated it to the Institute of Logotherapy." He thought for a moment. "I have to believe it was the best investment that diner ever made!"

◆   ◆   ◆

At the top, as Roger stood and surveyed the scene below, he came back to reality—remembering the phone call and how it was already changing his life. His mind drifted back to the young man on the Golden Gate Bridge. He felt a kinship with the man that he'd never felt before. He began to feel like the young man. He began to question everything—his life, his past, his future, life itself—all in the span of seconds. He leaned a little. He looked down and imagined falling down the sheer cliff. He wondered how quickly consciousness, and then life, would be stripped from him.

Back inside his head, he succumbed to vertigo and fell back gently to sit down.

"You seem preoccupied, Herr Murphy," Dr. Frankl nearly hollered, coming over and sitting next to him, an amazingly agile man of 85.

"I suppose I am, doctor."

"Do you care to elaborate?"

Roger turned and looked at Dr. Frankl. Here was one of the world's great psychiatrists—who, despite his initial anger with Roger for being so bold as to enter an interview unprepared, was now willing to just listen to his problems. Roger was somewhat overwhelmed. "It's nothing, really. Thanks for your interest, though, doctor."

Dr. Frankl also surveyed the view, and let it speak for itself for the longest time. "You know, I have been here many times in my life. There may be no better place on Earth for me. And certainly no better place to clear one's mind. Climbing this rock and enjoying a few moments of peace up here is the only time I can free my mind. It's the only time I have been able to not think about my next lecture, the paper I am working on, the book I have yet to finish. It is a place where I am at peace. Isn't it paradoxical—that the best time for one to think is when one has nothing on his mind to think about?" Roger nodded his head and simply listened. Dr. Frankl smiled slyly. "This place can be such a place for more than I."

Again, Roger nodded and didn't speak. Trying another tack, Dr. Frankl continued, "I remember once, the people at *Who's Who in America* sent me a questionnaire in which they asked me to express, in one simple sentence, the meaning of my life.

"I mentioned this questionnaire to a group of American professors, psychiatrists and students who were in Vienna to perform research. I asked them how they would guess that I might have replied to the questionnaire. One student, from Berkeley as a matter of fact, said, 'The meaning of your life is to help others find the meaning of theirs.' His answer absolutely jolted me, and do you know why? Because these were the very words I had used in responding to the questionnaire!"

Finally, Roger gave in. When the man who wrote the book on the meaning of life offers, at several different points and in several different ways, to help you with your problems, you don't turn him down, ultimately.

Roger picked up his hands, which had been propping him up, and wrapped them around his knees. He looked down for a moment or two and finally spoke. "I know it doesn't compare to your own situation, doctor …"

"Of course not! Why, no one's situation is like anyone else's! But that does not make anyone's suffering any greater or lesser than another's! Suffering is suffering!"

Roger nodded his appreciation and went on. "I received a phone call from San Francisco last night." He paused and breathed out heavily. "It looks like I have cancer."

Dr. Frankl rubbed his chin and thought for a moment. "I see. Well, that's some news, indeed. I understand your preoccupation now. What type, if you don't mind me asking?"

"They're thinking it's a low-grade lymphoma."

"Any idea of the stage?"

"No. They won't know until I get back and they take the lymph node out and take a look at it."

"Well, that's certainly a serious matter. But you can take heart in the fact that it's a very survivable disease, especially when caught in the early stages." Roger just nodded, more out of politeness than solace. "Well," Dr. Frankl continued, "let me just say from the outset that you must not diminish your situation by comparing it to some romantic vision of mine. At least I had the luxury of knowing and facing my tormentors. You, on the other hand, have engaged in a battle with a silent, unknown enemy."

Again Roger nodded, this time with even less enthusiasm. Dr. Frankl moved as if he were about to rise. "You have several more days in Vienna, however?" Another nod. "Well, I had already decided this, and now what you say gives it more urgency. You will come to my office tomorrow and the day after that and the day after that until I have answered all your questions, yes?" Roger had been looking down. By now, Dr. Frankl was standing, and as Roger looked up to him, he understood for the first time that the man before him was truly a giant—and why.

"Yes," Roger smiled slightly. "Thank you, doctor."

Dr. Frankl, despite being all of 85, put a hand out to help Roger up. The two men were standing face to face. "Now we will go down as we came up—the easy way!" Dr. Frankl smiled, patting Roger on the shoulder. "The difficult part is over.

"For now, at least."

9

"Let's just start at the beginning," bid Dr. Frankl, swiveling slightly in his tan-colored leather executive chair so he could reach his coffee.

Roger hadn't even asked a question this time, and the interview was on. And that was fine with him. He crossed his right leg over his left and reached over to Dr. Frankl's black shiny desktop to turn the mini-recorder on. Over his right shoulder, he saw the double doors being quietly shut by Mrs. Frankl. He turned around, where Dr. Frankl was framed by the bay windows looking out onto the busy Vienna day.

"Did you know that my birthday—March 26, 1905—coincided with the death of the great composer Ludwig von Beethoven? It is because of this that a classmate told me that seldom does one mishap come alone.

"I am told that I was a pest as a child, although why this was thought I don't know. But I will tell you that I insisted that my mother sing me the bedtime song, *Long, Long Ago*, else I would not attempt to sleep. Much later, my dear, kindhearted mother acknowledged to me that she often sang it with the words:

'Keep quiet, you little pest,
'Long, long ago, long ago …'

"Well, at least the melody was soothing.

"I was very attached emotionally to my home and parents. And when we had been deported to Theresienstadt concentration camp, and my father, Gabriel, had died there, I made certain to always kiss mother upon meeting or leaving her. This way, we would always part in peace."

Dr. Frankl paused momentarily, as if lost in the long, long ago.

"If you don't mind me saying so," Roger interjected, "what you are saying is indicative of a level of emotion—passion—that might be regarded as surprising in a man of such great intellect."

"You simply don't know the wisdom of what you say, young man! I may be a perfect blend of my parents—my father's stoicism and sense of duty, and my mother's heart and piousness. Do you know the Rorschach test, the one using ink blots? I was once tested by a psychologist in Innsbruck, who proclaimed that he had never seen such a range between rationality and emotion.

"But we are getting ahead of ourselves."

"That's not a problem," Roger reassured him. "I'll piece this together. You just say whatever comes to mind."

"That is *my* line to say! Who is the doctor here?" Dr. Frankl exclaimed in mock anger. "Anyway, a common misperception is that I created my theories—which I came to call logotherapy, 'logos' from the Greek word for 'meaning'—while I was in the concentration camps, or certainly after. Well, I tell you, this is not the case. Indeed, I had written my first draft of my book *The Doctor and the Soul* before my deportation to the camps. My intention was to get my theories of logotherapy down in writing so they could survive me.

"Still, they almost did *not* survive me! The manuscript was sewn into my overcoat before my deportation, and it was lost when the Nazis forced us all to throw everything we had on the ground and leave it. I ultimately was able to reconstruct it in the camps—we shall come to that in a moment—but there was no reconstructing my badge from the Donauland Alpine Club, which I had to leave behind. It was my pride and joy!

"Again, I am ahead of both of us. You should know that since the age of 3—3!—I had wanted to be a doctor. And I did become a practicing neurologist. This is something many people forget, or do not know. I was director of the Neurological Department of Rothschild Hospital in Vienna before the camps, and performed a similar function at the *Poliklinik* here afterward. You know, I had flirted in my mind with dermatology, and even obstetrics. But one day another medical student used a quote by Kierkegaard to change my direction. He—meaning Kierkegaard—said, 'Don't despair at wanting to become your authentic self.' What a grand idea of his! And how utterly true. So many of us fight our destiny, or our inner voices. This other student felt I was gifted in and interested in psychiatry—and he knew better than I that it was the truth.

"Isn't that amazing, how one offhand comment from one being can alter forever the course of another?" Remembering the chain of events that led him to Dr. Frankl's desk, Roger couldn't help but agree. "Well, from that moment on I knew I would be a psychiatrist too—and the link between neurology and psychiatry is a close one, you see.

"I am satiating your curiosity slowly, but surely, I trust." Dr. Frankl took a rare break from speaking and sipped his coffee.

"You're doing fine," Roger nodded with a sense of humble irony; he knew Dr. Frankl needed no assurance from him.

"I have long felt that a talent for psychiatry is somewhat like a cartoonist's abilities. Both can spot the weakness in a person. This is all that a caricature artist does, is spot the visual weaknesses of someone and exploit them for comic effect. I do this all the time, including to myself. But as a psychiatrist, you can go beyond the appearance of weakness and go to the cause, or at least find some ways that the weakness can be overcome. One can see beyond the misery and find some meaning in it, if one knows how and where to look. By doing this—and this is the essence of logotherapy—you can turn suffering into an achievement. I truly believe there is no situation from which meaning cannot be extracted."

"With all due respect, doctor," Roger interjected, "I've long felt that your field—psychiatry, I mean—is pretty much just an ego trip for a lot of psychiatrists."

"Oh, my goodness yes! It is one thing to have a talent for psychiatry; it is quite another to have the correct motivation for applying that talent. So many people go into the business for the purpose of obtaining power over others. I confess to have tasted such power, in my early use of hypnosis. I was once asked to hypnotize a woman at Rothschild Hospital who could not take a narcotic for her surgery. I don't remember why, but apparently a local anesthetic wasn't available, either. So I was asked to keep the woman comfortable through hypnosis.

"Well, it worked—but all too well: The nurse handling the surgical tools complained bitterly afterward that I nearly put *her* to sleep as well!"

Roger had a hard time believing this man could put anyone to sleep; just five minutes into the interview, Roger had concluded that Dr. Frankl was the most fascinating figure he'd ever met—or perhaps ever would. "You grew up in the shadow of Freud, did you not?" Roger sensed immediately this was a hot-button issue.

"Yes!"

"Did you meet often?"

"This is what is so strange: only once! But before that, in my youth, I would often mail Dr. Freud something I had written, or something that someone else had written that I thought was especially pertinent or exciting. And do you know, he would always respond to me—a teenager—with a handwritten postcard within just a few days. Always."

"Do you have this correspondence? May I view it?"

"No, no. This is a terrible thing. The Gestapo took all of it, every bit, when I was deported. It is all gone. This you must know, however: When I was 17, Dr. Freud wrote back to me about one paper I had authored and sent to him, and he said, 'I have sent your paper on to the *International Journal of*

Psychoanalysis. I hope you have no objection.' The paper was published two years later. Here, this giant was publishing the paper of young Viktor Frankl, a nobody!"

"But you did meet at some point."

"That is a wonderful story in itself. One day I was leaving the university to take a streetcar home from *Schottentor*—this is a station you yourself know, yes? Well, I saw walking toward the park an old man with a silver cane and worn hat. I thought it couldn't be him, but the man was headed toward Bergasse—Freud's street—so I decided to walk behind him. Up the street we walked, and down the hill, until we came to Bergasse 19.

"So you might say that on this day, I became a follower of Freud!"

Dr. Frankl's hearty laugh was interrupted by the phone. "Frankl!" he barked into the receiver. Whoever called might have been startled by the yap—or that a world-renowned psychiatrist would answer his own phone; regardless, Frankl had to momentarily argue with the caller about the fact that he was, indeed, Viktor Frankl. The caller, it became clear, was affiliated with some other country's ambassador to Austria.

"Another social reception," he scoffed after hanging up. "This is all very nice, but why do I want to go to a party when there is so much to be done? Now, where was I?"

"Meeting Freud," Roger offered.

"Yes! I caught up to him at his residence. Do you know, I told him my name and he interrupted, 'Wait! Czerningasse 6, Apartment 25?' He knew my address from our correspondence. Amazing."

"Not really," Roger said. "Not for a pest."

Frankl roared with delight. "Yes, even at the university level I was a pest! But I assure you, I did not ask Dr. Freud to sing me a lullaby." Another roar. "You must know, too, that even at that brief meeting outside his residence, I was already becoming disenchanted with his psychoanalysis. In that way, in retrospect I can say it was as much a goodbye as a hello. You see, Mr. Murphy, it is not that psychoanalysts are altogether wrong. But one simply cannot reduce every part of what it is to be human to sex, or unconscious impulses. That is a dim view of humanity, don't you think?

"Plus, when I was under the spell of psychoanalysis, and was even encouraged by Dr. Freud himself to seek membership in the Vienna Psychoanalytic Society, it seemed one had to be *indoctrinated* into it. I wondered what kind of science would require such indoctrination. I still wonder to this day. So, I gravitated, you might say, to Adler's individual psychology."

Roger didn't want to interrupt, but …

"I'm sorry. You'll have to explain that."

"Forgive me. Dr. Alfred Adler is credited, quite rightly, with having formed the second school of Viennese psychiatry, after Dr. Freud. I am often accused of creating the third, and to this I gratefully plead guilty. Regardless, for Dr. Adler, the primary motivating force in the human animal was a will to power, in various forms. Status. Dominance. You understand? I never had the pleasure of walking to Dr. Adler's residence behind him, as I did with Freud, but I was a follower nonetheless! Until one night when two courageous mentors of mine, Rudolph Allers and Oswald Schwarz, publicly broke with Adler in front of his society meeting. Allers and Schwarz believed, as I did, that it was wrong to reduce the human being to one animalistic drive only. It was the same mistake that had driven Adler away from Freud—and here *he* was, making the same error, and driving us away in turn.

"Well, when they made their break, I stood with them. I believed Adler's individual psychology could be saved—but sadly, not from its creator. Dr. Adler rebuked me bitterly and, in truth, I don't believe ever uttered the slightest word to me ever again. Not even would he return my greetings on the many evenings I would approach his table at the Café Siller! Dr. Adler had saved me from psychoanalysis—but ended up pushing me away when I was hopeful of, shall we say, re-humanizing his approach. So be it."

"So you started logotherapy …"

"You make it sound so easy—like turning on a light! Well, perhaps this analogy is not so bad; discovering hidden truths is always as if a light is being turned on. But mind you, I traveled many dark hallways alone! I was young—questioning! I even had what you might call an atheistic, or at least agnostic, phase. I followed the dark light of nihilism and the existentialism of the day, which preached against religion, faith, traditional values—and exalted a meaninglessness to life. What a trap! It was, and still is, a trap from which so many young people never escape. In many ways, what I call the 'existential vacuum'—a collective meaninglessness to life—is worse today than ever!

"And I don't mean to insult your wonderful country, which I love and know so well …"

"It's OK. I can take it."

"… but the existential vacuum seems to be worse there than in many places. Yet, you see, I understand this phenomenon quite well because I, too, have suffered through it. Meaning does not simply present itself to you, my fellow. Else the title of my book would not include the key word, which is 'search.'" He paused and gazed at Roger. "You, yourself, are on something of a search, no?"

Roger was trying not to inject himself into the interview, but to keep it going—and to be intellectually honest with himself and his interviewee—he had to nod in agreement. "But," Roger quickly added, throwing the ball back in the doctor's court, "why is it you say the so-called existential vacuum is worse today?"

"Why, the evidence is all around you!" the doctor nearly screamed, waving his hand toward the bay windows behind him. "There is empirical evidence! Industrial society has set out to fulfill every need there is, and some there aren't—some needs that they must first *create* before they can fulfill! You know this to be true!

"Yet, all along, the greatest need there is—a need for a meaning in one's life—goes largely ignored. And industrial societies have only aggravated the problem. Consider: Unlike animals—and in contrast to the teachings of some—man is not a slave to his instincts and drives. Nor is he, today, bound by tradition as he used to be. In other words, man need not be a slave to what his instincts tell him he *must* do, nor is society always telling him what he *should* do. He is, therefore, at a loss for what he might *wish* to do. The result is the existential vacuum I speak of. And it is most acute among the young.

"I was once in America to speak at a university in Atlanta, and the title they gave me for my lecture was, 'Is the New Generation Mad?' I hated that title, but I was stuck. I asked my taxi driver on the way to the university what he thought—whether youth were indeed crazy. He instantly said yes, that they *were* mad. I asked why. He said, 'They kill themselves, they kill each other and they take dope!'

"Well, a short psychiatrist from Vienna with whom you have recently made acquaintance could not have put it better, could not have identified the symptoms of the existential vacuum any more precisely than that taxi driver in Atlanta. These three things he identified, I call the 'mass neurotic triad': depression, aggression and addiction.

"It is because of this that I say modern man has the means for a good life, but lacks the *meaning*. And in the *mean*-time," he paused to enjoy his pun, "we are told to worship at the shrine of self-interpretation and self-actualization.

"Well, of course, everyone should be allowed to actualize themselves. It is certainly what I did when urged on by Kierkegaard's admonition to not despair at wanting to become my actual self. But if you set out precisely for self-actualization—your own happiness, to the exclusion of others, which most often must be the case when you pursue your own interests—then more often than not you will miss it entirely.

"It is like a boomerang. Our prevailing view of a boomerang is that it is designed to fly back to the thrower. Right?"

"Yes."

"Ah, but this happens *only* if the hunter has missed his target! It is the same with man. The essence of a human is his ability to transcend himself—to care for, to work for, something other than himself. It is only if that mission is frustrated, or simply missed, that an obsession with self returns to him—like a boomerang that has missed its prey!

"The essence of logotherapy, you might say, is that self-actualization is not the goal—that the 'boomerang' of man's internal drive is, rather, aimed at something other than himself.

"The only path to self-actualization is not to strive for it at all; instead, you must aim for man's true target: self-transcendence. The ability to devote yourself to things, ideals, causes—people—other than yourself. Do you know the name Abraham Maslow?"

Roger thought for a second while turning the tape over in his machine. "Maslow. Wasn't he the man behind the hierarchy of needs?"

"Yes! And what else is the hierarchy of needs about than self-actualization? Do you know that even Maslow, before he died, acknowledged that what I am saying is true? That the goal of self-actualization is a mistake?

"Your own Constitution—or rather your Declaration of Independence, yes?—refers to the 'pursuit of happiness.' No, no, no! Do not *pursue* happiness! It cannot be pursued like some hapless prey."

Roger challenged him. "What *should* you do, then, if you want to be happy?"

"Many, many things, except to pursue it! You must simply do the right things and trust that happiness will ensue as a result of it. And do you know what? It *will* ensue. It will."

At the last syllable, his left hand finished stabbing at the air and settled on his cup of coffee. He leaned back in his chair, partly to sip his drink and take a rare breath, but mostly to let the point find its leisurely way to his listener's brain.

"So, spell it out for me: Am I to conclude that to seek meaning in life through self-actualization is a mistake?"

"Yes, for the most part. This is not to say you should not work on your talents or your fitness, your intellect or any other aspect of your being. No, no. This is not what I am saying. Rather, while working on yourself, you cannot expect that *you* can be the source of meaning. This is the fatal error made by our unfortunate friend Narcissus."

Roger started asking a question and stopped short.

"What?" Dr. Frankl spouted. "Speak up! Do not be shy."

"Well, considering my transgression of a few days ago, I hesitate to ask this. But you do, in your writing, suggest other ways of finding meaning in life."

"Aha! Now, I hope you don't mind me saying, this is a much superior question to that which you posed to me at the beginning of our friendship!"

Roger was stunned—not by the compliment for his question, but by the word "friendship." Did he mean it? Does this man who, a couple of days ago nearly tossed him out the bay windows, consider the possibility that this unmatched pair could be friends? No, of course not. It must merely be a slip by a man for whom English is a second language. Still, Roger liked the sound of it.

"I don't mind telling you, as I have maintained again, and again and again, and have yet to be proven wrong, there are three main ways in which a human being can find meaning: 1) creating a work or doing a deed—in other words, having some sort of work or activity out there to accomplish; 2) experiencing your values, especially by loving another person; and 3) suffering."

Roger shifted in his chair. "I understand the first two, Dr. Frankl, but the third escapes me. How can suffering *ever* be good?"

"This is key: First, it must be unavoidable. Inviting *avoidable* suffering upon oneself isn't noble, nor is it a path to any sort of meaning; it's simply stupid or, worse, sick.

"But when faced with *unavoidable* suffering, one often finds opportunities for great meaning—most prominent among them, the opportunity to face up to your suffering with dignity and with a sense of purpose."

"Purpose?"

"Yes. The chance to turn a tragic circumstance into a great achievement. We see this quite often in patients who are faced with an incurable disease…"

Dr. Frankl froze for a second, realizing the awkwardness. "Please forgive me, Herr Murphy. I do not wish to appear insensitive to your own precarious situation. I mean merely to share what I have learned."

Roger was clearly bothered, but only by his having to face cancer—not by Dr. Frankl's inadvertently calling attention to it. "Please, no apology necessary, Dr. Frankl. But surely you can appreciate how difficult it is for someone in my position to understand what you're getting at."

"And surely, Herr Murphy," Dr. Frankl turned up the volume for emphasis, "you can appreciate the fact that a survivor of Nazi death camps knows a little something about suffering."

Roger had quit counting his *faux pas* since landing in Vienna. "Forgive me."

"Ah, but you inspire me to make an important point. I do not mean to hold my experience over your head, or to insinuate some sort of moral superiority due to the nature and extent of the conditions in the camps. Not at all! Suffering is suffering. It matters not whether your torment arrives in the form of the hellish environment of a death camp or from as simple a thing as a lost love. Pain is still pain. What matters is how you deal with it, you see.

"Nor did suffering flow for the first time from that horrible invention of the Nazis, the death camps. Suffering has always been a part of the human obligation."

"So, doctor, the point is, you suffered before your deportation."

"Of course! No man or woman can escape suffering, nor should he or she always try. I earlier mentioned to you my agnostic phase, and the influence of the existentialists. This was not an easy time for me. Believe, me, I went through complete and utter hell long before the Nazis ever laid a single railroad tie in the netherworld's direction. I wrestled with meaninglessness like Jacob with the angel. Ultimately, I was able to say yes to life, in spite of everything."

"But how?"

"I wish I could say it was easy or overnight, but I cannot. Gradually, I began to reject the pessimism and narrow views of the darker existentialists. I read the works of more optimistic writers and philosophers—Martin Heidegger, Gabriel Marcel, Karl Jaspers, Martin Buber. And I learned not to simply assimilate the views of others, but to think for myself.

"For example, when I began my internship at the University of Vienna School of Medicine, and then my residencies at Schlossl neurological hospital and Steinhof psychiatric hospital—oh, my goodness what a place—I determined to forget what I had learned from Freud and Adler and to learn from my patients."

"How?"

"By listening, of course! How simple, yes? But all too rare in my profession, sadly, especially at that time. You see, a doctor or a university professor simply was not considered to be on the patients' or students' levels. But how can you listen if you are on different levels? How can you learn if you don't listen?

"I'm sure my colleagues thought it quite impertinent for me to allow patients to call me by my first name. And I imagine my fellow doctors and nurses thought me quite mad when, at a dance at one of the pavilions at

Steinhof, I in my white medical coat was there dancing with a woman in a straitjacket! Can you imagine doing the tango in that circumstance?"

Roger noticed an uncharacteristic lack of animation in Dr. Frankl's voice in retelling what the doctor clearly thought was a delightful and revealing anecdote. Roger reached over and clicked off the recorder.

"Doctor, we've been at it awhile. Would you like to break for a few hours?"

"Yes! I must have a small lunch, a short nap and then dictate some letters. Come back in three hours, Herr Murphy, and we shall continue."

Roger stood up, turning around and bending to place his pad, pen and recorder in his bag. But in the middle of doing so, he was startled upright by a loud sound behind him.

"Elly!" Dr. Frankl boomed. Roger hadn't realized an 85-year-old man could make such a noise. As if on cue, the white double doors whisked inward and in popped Mrs. Frankl.

"Viktor," she barked right back. "Time for lunch."

"Yes, Elly, Herr Murphy will return in three hours, when we will continue with our work."

Roger noticed, and appreciated, how Dr. Frankl's words—"we will continue with *our* work"—seemed to signal that he had taken ownership of Roger's intrusive work.

Maybe he *was* becoming a friend.

◆   ◆   ◆

As Dr. Frankl arrived in his study to a waiting Roger Murphy, he found his guest admiring the haunting portrait of a woman over the doctor's day bed. Roger, who had been in a bit of a trance, was jostled out of it by the closing of the double doors.

"If you don't mind me asking, who is she?" asked Roger.

"A beautiful young woman, no? You have discovered my first wife, Tilly," the doctor responded, sidling up to the opposite side of the day bed, so that the two men now flanked it.

"Yes, I remember you writing about her. Do you mind telling me about her?"

"Not at all!"

"She *is* very beautiful," Roger interrupted. "You were quite the ladies' man!"

Dr. Frankl barked, partly a laugh and partly a denial. But he was clearly flattered. "Well, unfortunately, this would be not much of a trick. You see, a young man with a promising future—any future at all, really—was very much in demand in those days in Vienna. And I admit, with some amount of shame, that I was quite comfortable with that!"

"Doctor!" Roger protested.

"Yes, I am afraid it is true, my son. I confess that I stand before you today as a man who did not always live up to his high-minded principles!" Roger thought he saw a baby grin emerge from the doctor's face. "Let me tell you of one incident in which I was especially demonic!

"Each year in February, there was something called the *Fasching Ball*, a party in which girls in search of suitors would congregate and we would dance and such. And each year, one could attach oneself to two or three girls to date throughout the year.

"Well, this one particular girl that I had my eyes on was playing hard to get, so I said to her, 'Do you want to come to a lecture with me in the evening to hear a magnificent speaker, one who will captivate you like no other?' And she said yes, that she would. So we went there, and we sat at the end of the row waiting to hear this brilliant speaker I told her about. I said, 'Be alert, now. He's about to begin.' She looked around with wonder, and as she did so, I arose and strode to the lectern and began my lecture. Well, she was very impressed, indeed—and the speaker was marvelous, as advertised!"

Roger smiled broadly, extending a handshake. "You are a man's man, Dr. Frankl."

Dr. Frankl chuckled and shook Roger's hand. "Your congratulations are dubious, but accepted, my good man. Come, let us sit."

As they sat, Roger pulled out his recorder and placed it back on the table. The late-afternoon light from the bay windows was softer now, and it was easier to see Dr. Frankl's expressions.

"You were going to tell me about your first wife, doctor."

Dr. Frankl gazed back up at the portrait, which he could barely see from the side. "You were quite correct, Herr Murphy. She was lovely indeed." Dr. Frankl turned back toward Roger. "But this is not why I decided to make her my wife.

"Though she trained as a tailor, and was very skilled in it, there was a need for nurses at that time, and she acted as an untrained one, a station nurse—splendidly, I might add. When we began to date—this was before the deportations, of course—she was actually out for revenge: I had broken up with, and in Tilly's mind had done wrong to, her best friend. I surmised this, and confronted her about it, and that seemed to impress her.

"But what impressed me most with Tilly Grosser was not her beauty or intelligence, but her strength and character. Let me explain.

"After the arrival of Hitler, and when things were becoming difficult for Jews, her mother was protected from deportation due to Tilly's position as a station nurse. But at one point that protection was set to expire. The night before, we were at her mother's apartment and there was a knock at the door. How we were all frightened! This was not a good time to hear unexpected knocks on the doors of Jewish flats, you understand.

"It was a messenger, who told us Tilly's mother would have to report in the morning—to a job, rather than a camp. She was to begin working to clear out the furniture of Jews who had been deported. Moreover, there was an order in writing that extended the deportation protection for Tilly's mother!

"We were all relieved, as you can imagine. But Tilly said the most remarkable thing, something that both captured the moment and put into just a few words what theologians might spend a lifetime saying. After the door closed behind the messenger, she looked at her mother and me and said, 'Well, isn't God *something*!' Remarkable.

"Then, what truly made me decide to marry her was an incident in my parents' flat. Tilly was preparing our lunch when there was a telephone call, an emergency waiting for me at the hospital. It involved a woman who had been brought in after a suicide attempt. I threw a few coffee beans in my mouth and ran out without having eaten.

"I fully expected, when I arrived two hours later, that the group would have eaten, and in fact my parents had. I further expected Tilly to express some feelings of frustration with my being gone so long and interrupting her fine meal. What she said, though, was, 'How did it go? How is the patient?' How can you not love *that*?"

"A dream woman," Roger concurred. "If she liked football, even better!" Roger thought better of joking about the man's deceased wife and offered a meek, "Sorry."

"No, you are right! Of course, I have no idea her stance on football. But she truly was remarkable. Do you know that, when we were married, we were among the last two couples in Vienna to do so—the other was my high school history professor and his bride—before the Jewish registrar was closed? Unofficially, the National Socialists forbade Jews to have children. And, at that time anyway, one was expected to marry before having children. They also didn't have legislation against Jews getting married, but a notice was sent out warning that Jews who applied to get married would be sent to concentration camps." He paused for a moment, looking back up at Tilly's face. "There was nothing, of course, that the Nazis could do to prevent a Jewish woman from becoming pregnant—which Tilly did. Pregnant Jewish women were routinely deported to the camps, you know. We were in a dilemma—with only one way out."

Dr. Frankl picked up a book from within his desk and placed it gingerly on his desk. "This book of mine—*The Unheard Cry for Meaning*—I dedicated to our unborn child. The child we had to abort to keep Tilly alive."

He handed Roger the book. Indeed, the inscription read:

"To Harry or Marion, an unborn child."

Roger looked at the publication date of the book: 1978. His jaw nearly dropped to his knees. "So many years later, doctor." Roger looked up at Dr. Frankl, who had turned and was staring blankly out the window. "So many years later, the unborn child was still on your mind."

Dr. Frankl's head nodded slightly. He took his glasses off and seemed to wipe his eyes. "It is a terrible thing, Herr Murphy, to be required to choose between certain death for your wife, and death for a son or daughter unseen, unheld, but not unloved. I do not wish this choice upon anyone. Not anyone."

A few moments passed in silence. Roger breathed heavy and swallowed hard. He folded the book up and placed it carefully on Dr. Frankl's desk.

"I'm so sorry, sir." Roger's voice was quiet enough that he wondered whether the old man heard. He got his answer when Dr. Frankl's head, still aimed at the horizon, nodded again, either to thank Roger or to say that, even these many years later, he, too, was sorry.

After a few more moments, Dr. Frankl leaped back into the discussion, swinging around in his chair and nearly making Roger jump.

"It was a terrible, frightening time to be Jewish and to live in Vienna. I remember the night of the *Anschluss*—Hitler's so-called annexation of Austria. It was March 1938. I was lecturing for a colleague, substituting for him. And what do you think of this? The title of my lecture was, 'Nervousness as a Phenomenon of Our Time.' How deliciously ironic, don't you think?

"As I was lecturing, the doors to the hall flew open. There stood a man in a Nazi uniform. I remember thinking at that precise moment that I couldn't believe the chancellor of Austria would allow such a thing! The young SA man was clearly there to shut down my lecture. But do you know, I braced myself as never before and did something the young man could not have ever expected! I faced him straight on and continued my lecture as confidently and forcefully as I could. He appeared stunned, and simply stood there in silence! Even today, I consider this to be the moment of my highest rhetorical courage.

"But the die was cast, as we say. When I returned to my parents' apartment, making my way through perhaps a hundred-thousand manic people in the streets, I found my strong, kind mother reduced to desperate tears. She had just heard Chancellor Schuschnigg give his farewell on the radio. She was now in bed, crying to the sad music that followed the startling announcement."

Roger spied to see that his recorder had captured the drama. "So that was it," Roger prompted him. "Hitler was in Austria."

"He arrived in Vienna on Tuesday, March 15, 1938—after my lecture, which was the Friday evening prior. But that was not quite 'it,' as you say. Such ends are never so sudden as you imply.

"Certainly there were many Austrians who greeted the Third Reich with cheers and flowers and open arms and chants of 'Heil Hitler!' Hitler was greeted as a conquering hero! Can you believe that? Of course, Adolf Hitler was born in Austria, and he and his people were selling this event as a glorious unification of German-speaking nations. But, you know, those of us required to wear yellow stars to exhibit our Jewishness for all to see, we understood it was, instead, an invasion by a hostile force. And we knew our lives might go on for a time, and that we would be working and playing and living and loving—for as long as they would allow it—but never as before. Still, you should have seen the throng that came to welcome the mustached mad-man in front of the chancellor's office that day!"

"You had a glimpse of what was coming—when the Nazi came to stop your lecture. Why didn't you get out of Austria?"

"Believe, me, I applied for a visa eventually. But it was very difficult to get one, especially for a Jew. My word, Jews weren't even allowed to use the trams, although in my position as head of neurology at Rothschild Hospital, a position I obtained in 1940, I had a pass. Even so, there was a belligerent conductor who would not let me board one day.

"And those of us who weren't yet deported, we sometimes had our homes taken. My sister Stella and her husband had their flat taken when their apartment was 'Aryanized'—such a nice, clean, word for eliminating a race, don't you think?"

"I can't imagine, frankly," Roger admitted.

"No, because such things are unimaginable. If you took the things that man has done to his fellow man and suggested them as a novel, the publisher would be incredulous. 'No such story is even possible,' he might say. But it is. Just take, as an example, the *Kristallnacht*."

Roger didn't wait for an explanation. "The what?"

"In English you would call it the 'Crystal Night.' It is the night in 1938 when anti-Semitic fever reached a pitch. It is called that because of all the broken windows that accompanied the violence against Jews and their properties. It was actually more than one night. No doubt the SS was behind it all, but people get into a mob mentality, and these things tend to take on a life of their own, you know? Dozens were killed, and many synagogues were destroyed or vandalized. Not even the police bothered to help, or to protect the city's Jews. In fact, it only got worse: Public parks were made off-limits to Jews. Violence and repression became more abusive and open all the time.

"So, you see, it does not happen all at once. The water comes slowly to a boil."

"What were you doing during all this?"

"Surviving—and helping others survive. After my schooling, my year of internship at the University of Vienna School of Medicine, two years' residency at Maria Theresien-Schlossl Neurological Hospital and four years as a resident at Am Steinhof Psychiatric Hospital, I had started my private practice in the living room of my sister Stella, and, of course, married Tilly Grosser. Ultimately, when Stella's flat was taken, I moved my practice to my parents' flat. But even there I was only allowed to see Jewish patients.

"As it turned out, there were plenty of Jewish problems to attend to! This I did—especially after becoming head of neurology at Rothschild. You see, we played a little game—some of my colleagues and I, with the help of Dr. Otto Potzl, my mentor and friend at the university school of medicine. Dr. Potzl and I knew that if we diagnosed a Jew with schizophrenia or some other mental illness, the patient would be deported to certain death. So we found other, more 'acceptable' diagnoses to keep them from the Nazis. I called schizophrenia 'aphasia,' which is a form of brain damage, and melancholia I diagnosed as fever delirium. We found some beds at the old Jewish home that had protective bars. It worked beautifully, and helped my patients avoid being euthanized for having a mental illness."

"That sounds awfully dangerous for you, though."

"Absolutely! But I ask you: more dangerous for me if I do it, or more dangerous for the patients if I do not?"

Roger nodded his understanding.

"You can see, I think, that there are some life-and-death decisions that ultimately require no decision at all. Once we happened upon this little scheme, how could we not have carried it out?"

"What about your family? We haven't talked much about them. You mentioned that your sister, Stella, and her husband had lost their apartment. What happened to them?"

"Stella and Walter—Bondy; their last name was Bondy—eventually left Austria for Australia. He went there to start a business, and she followed."

"Your other siblings?"

"My older brother—his name, too, was Walter—left with his wife, Else, for what they hoped would be safety and security in Italy."

"Why do you suppose it was that you never got a visa?"

Dr. Frankl leaned forward. "You assume too much, my journalist friend."

"You mean you *did* have a visa?"

"Quite!"

"To where?"

"To the very country which you have the good fortune to have been born in!"

"But they got you before you could get out?"

"No. Nothing 'got' me. Imagine my feeling when the notice arrived from the American embassy that I was now able to come and pick up my visa. Can you imagine? Just think if I told you right here, right now, today, that as you sit here you may die or suffer greatly if you stay here—but that I have a document here in the desk ..." Dr. Frankl fished out a piece of paper, "that will save you, deliver you to safety. What would you say to that?"

Roger waited for the answer, then realized Dr. Frankl was waiting for him to supply it. "Well, I'd say yes. I'd be foolish not to."

"Precisely!"

"But you did not?"

"No. And here's why."

"Imagine that everything I have told you is true—that you will die or suffer greatly if you stay, and that this piece of paper could deliver you to safety and a full and long life abroad. But also imagine that I tell you, just before you pluck this paper from my fist, that in the next room are your parents. And if you leave, they most certainly will endure the fate that this paper relieves you from! *Now* what do you do?"

Roger nodded slowly.

"I am sure, as I sit before you today, that I knew in my heart that I could not go. But the song of this piece of paper," the doctor said, waving an imaginary visa in the air, "is a beautiful, alluring sound. It is the sound of life. And remember, I was now of the opinion that life had unconditional meaning. That it was worth everything. That one must say yes to life, in spite of everything!

"Now, you must also remember that at this point I had devised the beginnings of my logotherapy, and had begun my first manuscript for *The Doctor and the Soul*. Do you see the importance? This is my life's work I am thinking of. Consider that, if I stay and get deported and die in the concentration camps, my work will die with me. Unlike Freud and Adler, my work had not yet been disseminated. And not being the promoters that Freud and Adler were, I had not a cadre of supporters—disciples, as it were—to see that my work and my writings and my thoughts would live on.

"All these things are swimming in my head, you see. And surely you see, now, how difficult it is to say no to this?" Again he waved the *faux* visa.

"Yes, sir. I do." Dr. Frankl already had Roger's respect, but now it was overflowing.

"As for my parents, though, the choice was much clearer. They were thrilled that I could save myself, as my sister and brother had done. What parent would not feel that way about his or her child? Well, despite that, as I mentioned, I am certain that I knew the answer. But I was tortured nonetheless. And I don't mind saying, I was hoping for some sort of hint from heaven.

"Just then, I was walking by *Stephansdom*—St. Stephen's Cathedral. You have been there by now, surely. Well, there was organ music from within. So I went inside and thought and prayed. And, again, I knew in my heart that my responsibility would lie in looking after my parents rather than my own self-actualization, my own work.

"But do you know? Tilly was right: God really *is* something! For, strangely, even after an hour inside that beloved cathedral, my hint from heaven didn't arrive until I myself arrived home.

"When I got home, my father showed me a broken piece of stone. I asked him what it was, and he told me it was a piece he had retrieved from our synagogue, which had been destroyed—that it appeared to be a remnant of a tablet containing the Ten Commandments. He showed it to me, and do you know what it was? It was a portion of the Fifth Commandment."

Roger gave him a blank stare. "I'm sorry, I'm not much of a religious scholar, and I was a pretty bad Catholic …"

"It's all right, my friend. The commandments are numbered differently in the Jewish faith, anyway. It was the Fifth Commandment: 'Honor thy father and thy mother, that thy days may be long upon the land which the Lord thy God giveth thee.'"

Roger was not only silent, he was dumbfounded.

"A hint from heaven, no?" Dr. Frankl's question showed in his face. Roger nodded. "So, I knew at that moment what I should do—what I always knew I had to do. I stayed and looked after my parents. And I let the visa expire. I let the bird of freedom fly off to the horizon."

Dr. Frankl swiveled slightly and looked out the bay windows, to where the sun had set.

"As it turns out, I didn't see that bird again for many, many months—and, very nearly, never again."

10

Roger was standing alone behind the Frankls' elephantine split-leaf philodendron in the corner of their living room, awaiting another audience with Dr. Frankl and holding open the white curtains to gaze out the window, when the doorbell rang. He turned around, and was able to see down the dim hallway where, within seconds, a video camera was barging through the Frankls' front door and into the large foyer.

"Who the hell is horning in on my interview?" Roger wondered in a whisper.

Just then, the cameraman, escorted by what appeared to be a lovely young reporter, stopped and brought the camera down to his hip—and promptly kissed Mrs. Frankl.

Roger was wondering what kind of ethics these Viennese journalists had—but was pondering whether such tactics might lead to better interviews—when it began to dawn on him that this was the doctor's family come to call.

"Herr Murphy," roared Mrs. Frankl when the group had reached the living room, "permit me to introduce my pride and joy: my grandson, Alexander, and my granddaughter, Katharina."

They were two dark-haired, strikingly handsome youth with luminous smiles and convivial eyes. As he accepted their firm handshakes, he wondered why Viktor Frankl's grandchildren would be so welcoming to a journalistic interloper from another land. But he appreciated it. Roger learned only that Katharina—whom Mrs. Frankl and the others called Katja—was 20 and Alexander all of 15, before the bell rang again and there was another scramble to answer the door. As Mrs. Frankl scooted down the hall toward the insistent bell, Roger and the Frankl grandchildren—a sort of Viennese Donnie and Marie Osmond—sat down on the green velour furniture.

"Grandmother tells us you're from San Francisco," Katja said.

"Yes, that's right."

"Grandfather goes there sometimes. There was a World Congress of Logotherapy there five or six years ago—1984, I think."

Roger was genuinely impressed. "Really! I need to research that."

"Montana!" spurted Alexander, as if he'd just planted a flag and named the state.

Roger's brow wrinkled and he pushed up his glasses. "Excuse me?"

"I was trying to recall the gentleman's name. Joe Montana. Isn't he from San Francisco?"

Roger smiled and his throat grunted acknowledgement, while his ears noted how clearly these two young Viennese spoke English. "Yes. You're a football fan?"

"No. We just hear about him."

"What's with the video camera?"

Katja answered for him. "This is his first love. Alex wants to be the next George Lucas."

Alexander smiled shyly. "Well, my first love was space. I wanted to be an astronaut. But a few years ago, I got dizzy on a carnival ride and chipped a tooth. I figured my equilibrium wasn't what it should be for space travel."

"I still think," Katja advised Alexander, "that you should sing. You should hear him sing, Mr. Murphy. He and grandfather both are very musically inclined."

Roger had never seen such complimentary siblings, and he thought it was devastatingly charming. Just as appealing was their modesty; Alexander quickly sought to change the subject from his apparently many talents.

"Grandfather can compose wonderful songs, even though he has never been trained in it and can't even read music. When an orchestra comes on the radio or TV, he likes to get up and act as if he is conducting it. And he does quite well. He once told me that he always has a melody in his ear—sometimes something he's heard, other times something that his mind is apparently composing on the spot."

Roger shook his head. Is there nothing this man can't do? "That's certainly the sign of a genius."

"So," Alexander changed the subject yet again, "San Francisco. You must like hills to live there."

Roger managed just to get out an equivocating "Well," just as another couple of men emerged from the hall with Mrs. Frankl in tow.

"You must be Mr. Murphy, the writer from America?" Roger stood and shook hands with another dark-haired man of Roger's approximate height and age. A soft voice and narrow eyes that seemed to have no whites made the man appear both kind and professorial. "I am Franz Vesely, Dr. Frankl's son-in-law. Welcome to Vienna."

Glancing back over his right shoulder, he continued, "I see you have already made the acquaintance of my children." The dots were being connected now.

But the other man's identity remained a mystery. "Let me also introduce to you Dr. Harald Mori, a friend of the family."

Mori, a full-faced man in his 30s with a short haircut and narrow wire-rimmed glasses, had the build of a rugby player and the thick fingers and firm handshake to boot. "Very good to meet you," he bellowed. Roger noticed that the accent became slightly more noticeable the further you got from Katja and Alexander.

As the group sat down, the three Veselys on the couch and Mori and Roger in the two chairs, it felt for all the world as if the family had assembled on Roger's behalf—that maybe they were staging some sort of intervention or, at the least, a grassroots interview.

Mori, the family friend, seemed to be in the lead. "So, you are in the process of writing an article about Viktor Frankl?" He was cordial, but firm.

"Yes. That's the idea. He's been quite kind in granting me access."

"You perhaps do not realize how much of a privilege it is," Mori quickly replied. "Many people, including many writers, wish to be granted such access. Of course, we cannot oblige very many of them."

Roger thought Mori's use of the word "we" strange for a "friend of the family." Perhaps this man, as soft-spoken as Franz Vesely, was more. Right now, he had all the appearances of a family bouncer who was sizing up the guest and his motivations.

"You have read *Man's Search for Meaning*?" Mori asked abruptly.

"Yes. Very recently."

Mori looked over at Vesely and back at Roger. "You understand, of course, that Viktor Frankl is 85 years of age." Roger looked blankly at Mori, not getting the point and in no hurry to prod it out of him. Mori let a moment pass, then continued. "He was in the concentration camps for, what, three years? You see my point?"

Roger shifted in his chair. "I think so."

"You cannot summarize Viktor Frankl's life in an article, or even a book, by looking only at his experiences in the camps. He has done many things in his life, both before and after. He has written something like 30 books, and they have been translated into nearly as many languages. He has lectured all over the world, in …" Mori turned to Vesely and said something in German.

"More than 200," Vesely finished, both to Mori and Roger.

"More than 200 universities, on all continents," Mori repeated.

"He's not counting those continents that chiefly boast penguins, you understand," Vesely added. "One supposes that if there were an institution of higher learning for penguins, Dr. Frankl would add another continent to his collection." Vesely sported a sly smile with his dry wit, and it made Roger feel a little more comfortable.

Mori went on as if uninterrupted. "He has been awarded honorary degrees from almost 30 universities around the world. We just learned he will get one from the University of Pretoria, South Africa, this year." Roger raised his left eyebrow and nodded, but said nothing in order to let Mori finish his point. "In that room," Mori pointed over Roger's shoulder to the Spirit Room, "are more awards and degrees and certificates and letters from the elite of the world than you will ever see."

"Although he doesn't care about such things," clarified Mrs. Frankl, who had been walking in and out of the room and caught Mori's monologue.

"No, he does not," Mori continued after she left. "He is a very humble man. And I am not saying these things to impress you or to promote him. Dr. Frankl does not wish to be 'promoted.' I merely mean that the man is so much more than his experiences in the camps. That is all."

Roger could feel Mori's shell softening. "I understand," Roger assured him.

This was obviously someone who cared very deeply for the Frankls. But now it was time for Roger to go on the offensive and take over the interview. "If you don't mind my asking," addressing both Mori and Vesely, "how did you two gentlemen become acquainted with Dr. Frankl?"

"Well," Vesely was the first to offer, "I was first interested in Dr. Frankl's daughter." Another sly grin. "I was working in the summer to earn money for college, at an agency involved in conference management, as was Gabriele. I really didn't know of Dr. Frankl's work and the extent of his fame. He was never mentioned at my high school philosophy or even psychology classes, which today I cannot fathom. But I had a great interest in those subjects, even though my dissertation would be in physics.

"When I came here as a suitor, I was a bit put off—stunned, really—at the volume of voices at the Frankl flat. I come from a quiet family, as you might guess from hearing me speak. And as a professor of physics, I am not what one might term 'excitable.' It appeared to me, initially, that the Frankls were mad at each other, or just rude. And, frankly, it shocked me to see Gaby participate in the noisy reparte.

"But Dr. Frankl seemed to take a liking to me, and gave me a copy of his book *The Doctor and the Soul* for me to borrow. Well, I was so engrossed in it that I missed my station on the way home and had to switch cars to go back. I was a young man at the time, 22, and was obviously very eager to impress the father of my girlfriend. But I felt he looked through me—he has a way of doing that, you know?"

"Yes," Roger swallowed, "I know."

"But it is very gratifying to think that he did look through me and still accepted me."

"I think I understand what you mean," Roger grinned.

"But to add to what Harald has said," Vesely continued, "Dr. Frankl has never wanted to be known as a victim of the Nazis. He is a psychiatrist, a doctor—a neurologist—and a philosopher. He wants to be remembered as someone who is a doer. Not someone who has suffered something. I must tell you, he is sometimes impatient when someone sees him only as the author of *Man's Search for Meaning*."

"So noted," Roger pledged. Turning to Mori, Roger asked, "and you?"

Mori smiled for the first time since the initial handshake. "I was in school, and had no shower in my student's apartment, so I paid to use one nearby. I met Dr. Frankl in a sauna there, after a friend of mine who owned the place told me I should get to know him because I was studying medicine. So I say that when I met Viktor Frankl, we were both nearly naked."

Roger couldn't help laughing, as did everyone in the room, including Mori. "Dr. Frankl doesn't seem like the country club type," Roger said.

"I think you are perceptive," Mori nodded. "I do not think he goes to the sauna because it is a luxury, or for status, or even relaxation. I think he goes there because it is good for him—although …" Mrs. Frankl was now standing off Mori's shoulder. "He wouldn't take the time to dry off. He would walk home wet, even in winter. Isn't that right, Frau?"

"Ugh!" Mrs. Frankl scrunched her face, and with the wave of her hand was off to the kitchen again.

"It had taken me a year to approach him after being told about him," Mori began again. "And even more time before I realized how famous he was—how many other medical students and such would love to have been in that sauna! I began taking logotherapy classes at school, and Viktor would invite me to pepper him with questions, even during his massages! Here I was, taking classes in logotherapy—and enjoying a weekly Friday sauna and massage with its founder! It was my little secret.

"In truth, I learned more about psychotherapy from riding in the ambulance, which I did as a volunteer, and talking to Viktor Frankl and working with patients in my own practice, than I ever did in school."

"What's so great about Viktor Frankl?" Roger asked provocatively.

"Everything," Mori retorted, pausing to think. "He's got very young skin!" Again, everyone laughed.

"Too much information!" Roger objected.

"I became a friend almost before realizing his fame, so it was unique for me. He's more of a friend and mentor than a hero, which he is to many people. But what I like about Viktor, and what I think is so special about him, is the way that he is completely present in the moment. If he thinks you are sincere and interested, he will give you his full attention, his everything."

Roger could see all the others nodding their heads.

"It can be a very intense experience, speaking with Dr. Frankl," agreed Vesely.

Roger looked at him slyly. "Spoken like a true intimidated boyfriend!"

Vesely laughed. "Precisely. That has never left me!"

"Speaking of intimidating," Roger accosted Mori, "I was starting to think you were going to bounce me out of here!"

Mori's eyes nearly disappeared as he chuckled. "I apologize. We must be very protective of Viktor. I sometimes must be a bit rough, or abrupt."

"He was trained as a body guard," agreed Vesely.

"What he means," Mori said, "is that I was a rower in school."

"I knew it was either that or lifting defenseless city buses," Roger added. "Anyway, you make it sound as if Dr. Frankl were a rock star."

"That is not a bad analogy," Vesely granted.

"American women are especially aggressive," Mori said. "It took me years to get close to Viktor Frankl. These women want to be intimate with him instantly!"

Mrs. Frankl had again appeared and couldn't resist the topic. "I got used to people kissing me. Viktor never has! Whenever it happens, he runs to the bathroom and washes!"

"It is true he doesn't like to be pawed at," Mori confirmed. Turning to Mrs. Frankl, he asked, "Do you remember your trip to South America, when they tore at your clothes?"

She put her hand to her forehead and nodded. "It was so frightening. They loved us, but too much! Such passionate people! They wanted to tear a piece of clothing for a souvenir!"

At this, Katja spoke up. "It is strange sometimes, that people want to simply touch me or hug me because I come from Viktor Frankl's family."

"So what's it like having a grandfather like that?"

Katja paused, then answered, "Like having a grandfather! It is maybe not normal, but it's the only normal I've ever known. I know he's very famous among people who have read his books. But there is a real human being behind all those books and apart from the scientist and the person who survived the concentration camps. I know he did these things, and it seems surreal that the survivor in *Man's Search for Meaning*, the person who experienced all those things, is someone I know and love.

"But he is, after all, my grandfather. To me, he is not the great Viktor Frankl, author and world lecturer—although I think he's great! To me, he is the loving, white-haired, funny man who would take us to the *Prater*—the big amusement park with the famous Ferris wheel—so many weekends. He loves that place! It's very near the *Leopoldstadt* district where he grew up."

"As a child, Katja wanted to marry him!" chimed in Mrs. Frankl with great enthusiasm. "I would put my red bedspread around her when she was just a little thing and pin brooches on her and she would parade up and down the hall, up and down the hall, with Viktor in hand, and I would be humming the wedding march. You know, 'Dah dah dum-dum, dah DAH dum-dum …"

Katja wasn't the least bit embarrassed by the revelation—rather, she seemed proud, and even added to it. "And grandmother, do you remember how he would give a show with his feet?"

"Excuse me?" Roger wondered.

"Sometimes when he was lying in bed, he would pretend his two feet under the covers were characters named 'Bof' and 'Nebof,' and they would give a show—one in a low voice and one in a high voice."

"And now that you're older?"

"Well," Katja said, looking around at the group, "now that I'm no longer a teenager, I can say he always was able to see through me, as my father told you. He always seemed to know when I was love sick or something, even when I wouldn't say anything. I never talked much about such things with my parents—sorry, Dad." Vesely smiled and shrugged a father's futile shrug. "Not with grandfather, either. But he always knew. And I knew that he knew. He asked me once, 'Is there something you can't do anything about?' He was—still is—the greatest grandfather ever."

Katja paused, putting a cloth shopping bag from the floor onto her lap.

"So, you see, Mr. Murphy," she went on, "this is somebody who is quite normal, who never wanted to be a guru of any kind. To me, that is the most important part of that person."

Roger just nodded his head. Not only was her point well-taken, but Roger was quite enamored with the articulate young woman, and simply basked in her radiance. Suddenly, Alexander was reaching for his camera—and the double doors to the study were being flung open.

"What kind of conference have I stumbled upon?" the doctor shouted in mock surprise.

With Alexander's camera rolling, each member of the group greeted Dr. Frankl as a returning hero from the study. Katja was last, with a bear hug and the shopping bag she'd brought. "Grandfather, I have something for you!"

"My calamari!" he exclaimed, taking a can from Katja. "Katzl, you have made an old man deliriously happy!"

Just then, he gazed at Roger.

"Herr Murphy. Do you mind terribly?"

Somehow, Roger knew exactly what he was asking. "No, sir, not at all. If I had calamari waiting for me, I wouldn't let anything get in the way of me." He thought for a moment and added, "If I at all liked the stuff."

The group enjoyed that, then squeezed into the hall toward the kitchen.

◆   ◆   ◆

By the time the group had broken up and shared their goodbyes, Roger had enjoyed a few moments of solitude. As Dr. Frankl was escorting Roger into the study for their interview, Mrs. Frankl interrupted.

"Viktor, who was it that called earlier?"

"The university that called yesterday. I told them no again," he said matter-of-factly.

Mrs. Frankl looked at Roger. "They want Viktor to come and speak, all the way to Asia. How much were they offering?"

"Ten thousand American dollars." Turning to Roger and closing the doors behind them, he added, "What do I want with $10,000? Do you see anything around here that needs $10,000? Is my roof leaking? Are my windows bombed out?" The two sat down, Roger in front and Dr. Frankl behind his desk. The doctor sighed. "Herr Murphy, what I want, $10,000 cannot buy."

"What's that, doctor?"

"Time."

11

Roger held the recorder in his hands, and paused before turning it on.

"We've gotten to a pretty intense point, here, Dr. Frankl." He spoke as warily as if there were a hairy insect crawling on the doctor's shoulder. "The point where you are deported to the camps. I can't imagine it's too much fun for you to go back there."

"It's not a problem, Herr Murphy. You know, when I returned from the camps, I dictated *Man's Search for Meaning* in nine days. I cried shamelessly on the shoulder of my good friend, Paul Polak. And I talked with Elly about my experiences at the start of our courtship. Since then, I have not talked about what occurred, except to answer the inevitable questions at my lectures and appearances around the world.

"So what I am saying is, so much time has elapsed, and I have been questioned about it enough, that your inquiries, as long as they are pertinent, will not be overly bothersome to me. OK?"

"OK. Thank you."

"Now, I expect you want to know how it was that I and my family members came to be deported to the camps, yes?"

"Yes. Whatever you'd like to share."

"Well, as you can imagine, the noose around Jews in Vienna was tightening and tightening all the time after the *Anschluss* in 1938. All along, even though the restrictions and threats were many, there were various non-Jewish angels sprinkled throughout the city, who would risk everything to help us even a little bit. My friend Hubert Gsur, an Aryan, is a shining example. Hubert, even though I learned much later that he was a member of the resistance against the Nazis, was a member of the *Wehrmacht*, the German military. But whatever he was, Hubert was a friend, first and foremost. So, when he could tell that the prohibition against mountain climbing by Jews was breaking my heart and giving me wistful dreams, he risked his life to dress up in military uniform and take me climbing for one day. This is true friendship.

"Poor Hubert got into trouble in other ways, as a Nazi resister, and was eventually arrested and actually beheaded in *Landesgericht* prison for so-called crimes against Hitler's Third Reich. But I am encouraged that his wife, Erna, was able to smuggle in a copy of my earliest *The Doctor and the Soul* manuscript—and his friends have told me it gave him great strength and comfort in his final days.

"So, you see, amid the horror of what the Nazis were doing, there were little stories of great heroism and friendship. Such acts must be recorded for all time as great human achievements!"

"So noted."

Dr. Frankl straightened in his chair. He looked straight ahead, but was clearly looking back. "It was September. Nineteen-hundred and forty-two. The phone rang.

"It was our turn."

The words haunted Roger as if they had been spoken about *him*.

"'Be ready to report tomorrow,' the man said, as lightly as he might have arranged a lunch. Escorts would take us to the *Sperlgymnasium*—our old high school. There, we would wait for several days before being put on crowded trains for Theresienstadt.

"Before we left my parents' apartment for the final time, we all packed what we could, of course. But father was 81, and could not carry much. So we put a few of his prized possessions in a round ladies' hatbox, including a cigar given to him by his boss.

"'Wait!' my father said with a jolt. And he produced a small bottle of whiskey he had kept for years. 'This,' he told us, 'is for the day Hitler dies.' So we packed that, too, hoping we would be able to use it someday.

"Of course, we heard rumors about the camps. But we could not have known that so many Jews would fail to survive those places. What chance did a celebratory bottle of whiskey have? Yet, what a beautiful sentiment! I do not drink—but this memory sometimes makes me wish I did!

"At the Sperlgymnasium, we received the first taste of camp life, believe it or not. They shaved my head completely, as well as father's head and flowing beard and mustache. He looked so old, so different. I could hardly recognize him. You must understand, I had never seen him without a beard and mustache my entire life. He had this since all the way back in his own youth! And, I don't mind saying, he looked dashing. Though he had been a bureaucrat in his working life—having risen to the level of director of the Ministry of Social Service—his distinguished beard and mustache made him look every bit the stereotypical Viennese psychiatrist!

"This is why I say, you can't imagine that moment, how degrading it was—shorn like animals, shaved like criminals. It was not a good sign, and we knew it in our hearts, though no one would utter a word of gloom.

"Eventually, we were herded onto trucks and taken the two miles to Aspang Station. In the three years ending with that one, 1942, according to the sign that is there at Aspang today, 10,000 Jews were loaded onto trains for deportation to the camps. 'Never forget,' the sign says. I do not. And now, you will not."

"No, sir, I will not." Roger jumped in. "Did your standing—as a psychiatrist, head of neurology at Rothschild—help you at all?"

"Yes! No doubt that it did! Because of my status as a doctor, we avoided the most crowded train cars. They put us on a train car with separate rooms, with a number of Jews with psychoses and other mental problems. The Gestapo decided—wisely, I might add—that it would be my job to supervise and come to the aid of the patients during the trip. Unfortunately, this arrangement was not completely understood by all the Germans in charge, because at one point as I was making my way along the outside platform to inspect the patients in their 'rooms,' I was nearly shot for trying to escape!"

"What was the mood?"

"Excellent question! One of my most vivid memories of our endless march into Theresienstadt was of my father's cheerfulness. He suddenly said to me, *'Immer nur heiter, Gott hilft schon weiter.'"*

"What does that mean?"

Dr. Frankl stared for the longest moment at Roger before answering. "You know, I believe I will have you find that out yourself!"

Roger smiled. "Homework."

"Yes. Homework."

"Please go on. You were entering Theresienstadt."

"Which, I perhaps neglected to mention, is north of Prague a bit. Theresienstadt was billed as Hitler's gift city to the Jews, a place that was largely governed by Jews—and which was cleaned up very nicely for a visit by the Red Cross. In truth, it was a filthy ghetto in which, certainly, some favored Jews—called 'capos'—had a limited amount of authority over the rest of us. And not far away there was a compound of buildings known as the 'Small Fortress.' Such—what is the word in English when one wants to pretend something is nicer than it is?"

Roger thought a second. "Euphemism?"

"Yes! Euphemism! For every foot of mud in these places, there was a foot and a half of euphemism!

"This Small Fortress was a place far worse than the ghetto of Theresienstadt. It was where they would send you for punishment, or just to provide entertainment for the sadistic men there. I was taken there not too long after arriving at Theresienstadt. For what reason, I was never told.

"A friend of mine had warned me. He said, 'If they ever try to take you to the Small Fortress, pretend to faint. Don't let them take you!' Well, foolish Viktor was too prideful to feign a faint, so to speak. So they took me there.

"A brutish man had me performing the most unnecessary acts, running with a bucket of water in the rain to splash on a pile of compost taller than me! Of course, I had trouble doing it to his satisfaction, so he hit me, unprovoked, with a very forceful uppercut. I went flying, as did my glasses, which broke. There we lay—my glasses and I—in the rain, in the mud, in the indignity of being brutishly punished for nothing more than being the 'wrong' ethnicity. Up to that point, I had never been hungrier, more in pain, more humiliated or more acutely aware of the cruel whims of fate.

"When I was taken back to the ghetto, I carried back something that I had not taken with me to the Small Fortress: 32 injuries!

"Well, when Tilly saw me, she said, 'For heaven's sake, Viktor! What have they done to you?' She naturally nursed me—bandaged me as much as she could in the barracks. What felt even better, however, was what happened that night.

"As a way of taking my mind off my suffering, she took me to another barracks where a jazz band from Prague was actually playing. Can you imagine? Well, I don't think it was officially permitted, but there it was. And how grand it was! And what a contrast to the bitterness and the blood of the day. I remember they played a song which became for us the 'national anthem' of the Jews in Theresienstadt: *Bei mir bist du schön*—'To me, you are beautiful.'"

Dr. Frankl took a moment to sip his coffee, which he never seemed to be without, and to ponder where he was in his tale.

"That's amazing to me," Roger interjected, "the contrast of the day and night in Theresienstadt that you just described."

"Yes. Like day and night."

Roger also marveled at this man's love of humor and his ability to make jokes about what were the most harrowing experiences anyone could ever have. "So there was culture, even in the camps?"

"Yes. It's an amazing ability of the human spirit, don't you think, to seek out song and art and philosophy under even the worst of circumstances. We largely had one man to thank for that in Theresienstadt: Rabbi Leo Baeck. What a fine man! Why, even the SS had to respect him. He could have escaped Berlin to London, but chose to stay with his people and even to go with them to Theresienstadt. And while there—until the camp's liberation in 1945—he made certain there was culture.

"The good rabbi even drafted me to give a series of lectures. A much better use of my time than to throw water on a pile of compost, don't you think?"

"Yes, I'd say so. What did you talk about?"

"A number of things I thought might be of use in the camp. Sleep disturbances; how one could keep his nerves healthy; 'life weariness' and 'life courage'; and some purely fun things, such as the psychology of mountain climbing.

"Wait! What am I thinking?"

Dr. Frankl rooted in his desk for something, then produced a photocopy of something.

"Here. You may have this. This is a copy of the announcement of my lectures in Theresienstadt, if you can believe it!"

Roger scanned it quickly. "Did you write this off to the side?" he asked, waving it so Dr. Frankl could see.

"Yes."

"Do you mind me asking what it says?"

"Oh, forgive me! I keep forgetting you do not speak or read German. It says, simply:

"'There is nothing in the world that can so much enable a person to overcome outer difficulties and inner troubles as the awareness of having a mission in life.'"

Roger absorbed it, then asked, "And you wrote that in the camp?"

"Yes. But, of course, in later camp experiences, my words would be tested on me in ways I could not have imagined."

"I assume," offered Roger, "that not every day and night was like the one you described."

"No, no. At night we had our occasional joys together; in the day, we worked and saw our family when we could. Men and women were put in separate barracks. I lived with a handful of other doctors, and we ran a clinic. We also took care of each other, I should mention, in that we took turns allowing each other private visits with our wives in the barracks.

"I also helped set up emergency teams to prevent suicides, especially among the new arrivals. We knew what desperation they were going through, because we had been there ourselves. We made sure they knew there was hope, and that things would get better. But there were also disease and hunger and depression, enough to keep us fully occupied.

"I was privileged to attend to my father when he became very ill with pulmonary edema …" Dr. Frankl noticed the quizzical look on Roger's face. "He was dying of double-pneumonia."

"I'm so sorry."

"I was just thankful to be there—and to be of minimal help. You see, one of the few things I was able to sneak into Theresienstadt was a vial of morphine. As he clearly neared death, I gave it to him, injected it. I asked him if he still had any pain. He said no. I also asked him if he wanted anything or wished to say anything to me, which he no doubt realized was an invitation to a last request. He just said 'No,' and I left him alone to die.

"I am very thankful for that moment, and the opportunity to, in effect, say goodbye. As a doctor, I also am thankful I could escort him to the threshold of the other side. Do you know how few people in my situation were granted such a privilege?"

"Or anyone in life," added Roger.

"Yes. Or anyone."

◆   ◆   ◆

Roger stood at the round, chest-high counter of the Schottentor station pizzeria and bit into a slice of cheese pizza while he watched the serious Viennese bustle about. The small cubbyhole of shops and restaurants was underground, but open-air at one end, where covered escalators took people up to the street cars above while subway cars circled beneath.

An elderly man in a grimy brown overcoat was eating popcorn on a bench facing the incoming subway cars. Suddenly the man rose up, hunched, and started following a pigeon around the floor, offering him a kernel of corn. Other pigeons seemed perfectly willing to take it, but the man had his heart set on this particular bird, which was clearly wary of his would-be benefactor. Finally, the man dropped the kernel near where the bird might get it on his own, but one of the less timid birds snatched it up immediately. The old man sat down, shaking his head as if to say, "I can't help you if you won't let me."

Roger thought of his old man at the Palace of Fine Arts who took so much trouble to help a squirrel with a nut. These kinds of small struggles with helping other creatures must go on by the millions each day, he thought.

Roger checked his watch and realized it was time for him to return to the Frankl flat. He stuffed the rest of his pizza in his mouth and chased it with orange soda, then grabbed his bag off the floor behind him and took the escalator up to the streetcar for Mariannengasse.

◆　　◆　　◆

"Dr. Frankl," Roger began as the conversation continued anew, "even through the death of your father, you seem to have taken much solace in your work."

"Between the lectures, the physical problems and the psychological matters to attend to, we doctors did indeed have much to occupy ourselves. This, of course, has to do with one of the three methods of finding meaning in any situation—that is, by doing work."

"Those you were attending to weren't as lucky. They must have felt awfully useless."

"I am glad you said that. That was very much a problem. A feeling of uselessness can be fatal in many cases, if the person also has no hope of that feeling ending, or a sense that something or someone is out there waiting for him in the future, you see?"

Roger couldn't help remembering the young man on the Golden Gate Bridge—or his own feelings of emptiness after the earthquake and, again, at Hohe Wand after hearing his diagnosis of cancer.

"There was a great woman, Regina Jonas, the first woman rabbi, who was in Theresienstadt with us. I asked her to share some of her wisdom with us, and she told a wonderful and meaningful story about Moses, and how he had destroyed the tablets of the Ten Commandments in anger at the idol-worshipping he saw. Then, after he had obtained new tablets, not only they, but the broken tablets too, were carried in the Ark of the Covenant.

"You see, by this story she was trying to tell us that no one is useless—that we all retain a use and a dignity even in times when our bodies are broken or unwilling."

"Like the broken parts of the tablets …"

"Yes. Even they were worthy of carrying those 40 years …"

Roger knew he'd never looked at life that way, and was instantly humbled.

"You must know, Dr. Frankl, that my country, especially, is very—well, it almost worships at the golden calf of the physical …"

"We are very aware of this in Europe. I heard one European say—or maybe I read it—that you Americans, with your vanity and adoration of athleticism, seem to carry on as if death were optional!" Dr. Frankl chuckled lightly. "But at the same time, you lead the world in compassion for the infirm. What was the law you most recently passed for people who are handicapped?"

"The Americans with Disabilities Act," Roger answered, not bothering to add that he had opposed it.

"Yes! What a beautiful thing to reduce to your country's code of law. This law has the spirit of Rabbi Jonas! You know, Herr Murphy, we cannot expect perfect health or functioning of our bodies throughout our entire lives. Assorted things go wrong—this is the work of a neurologist, of course. So, the point is, an investment in caring for the infirmities in others is, necessarily, an investment in your own well-being.

"But as true as this principle is with regard to the physical, it is more true with the metaphysical. The more you tend to others' needs, the more your own seem to be met."

"I may have sidetracked you …"

"No need to bother. I do that very well on my own. So, where were we?"

"Life after your father …"

"Yes. Well, life went on for months and months—amazingly, with difficulty, with very little food, hardly any information about the wider war, with constant rumors of death or freedom, with various stages of hope and hopelessness. Then, in May of 1944, Tilly's mother, Emmy, was ordered for transport—to where, we were not told. As it turns out, it was for Birkenau—a part of the infamous Auschwitz camp."

"I remember that Tilly was somewhat younger than you …" Roger prompted.

"You are about to conclude that her mother was not very old at all. And you would be right. She was 49. That is all."

"And you? What were your ages?"

"I was 39. Tilly was all of 24."

Roger nodded, glancing up at Tilly's portrait. "Twenty-four. She hadn't yet lived."

"No. But she had already experienced much, just the same. The abortion of our only child. Difficult work in hospitals and, in Theresienstadt, at a—I don't know the word in English, a place where one manufactures ammunition. And, of course, she, along with all the others, had to experience the degradation of the camp."

Dr. Frankl also glanced up at Tilly's haunting image on the wall.

"In October of that year, 1944, it was my turn to be listed for 'Transport East.' We were told this was for a ghetto that would be better than Theresienstadt. But in my heart, I knew better. It, indeed, was Birkenau."

"And did you go alone?"

"I wish that it were so. I argued with Tilly to stay. In Theresienstadt, with her work at the factory, she was safer. And anytime you volunteered for transport, and it appeared you were trying to get out of work or somehow sabotage the German war effort, you risked the considerable wrath of the SS. But she insisted on going with me, and was approved for some reason I shall never know.

"I once wished for her only that she would be true to herself. On the transport to Birkenau, she was. At one moment she was afraid, saying, 'You'll see: We are headed for Birkenau.' But soon, she was peaceful and was sorting out the passengers' cluttered luggage and even enlisting others to help her."

Here, again, Dr. Frankl became subdued.

"We were separated at Birkenau. All the men and women were. But before we were, I told her this as forcefully as I could, because it was of the utmost importance to me: 'Tilly, stay alive at any price. Do you hear me? At any price!' As a man, Herr Murphy, you might understand my meaning to her at that moment."

Roger paused, awkwardly. "I think I might …"

"I simply meant to say that she should not hold onto her wifely loyalty to me at the price of her life, you understand."

Roger simply nodded and looked down. A few seconds of silence passed between them.

"For some reason unknown to any of us, my mother was left behind. But I believed then that she would be safer in Theresienstadt. Before the transport to Birkenau, thankfully, I was able to say a quick goodbye to my mother, Elsa. I remember it as if it occurred yesterday. 'Please give me your blessing,' I begged her with great zeal. 'Yes, yes, I give you my blessing!' she told me. And it seemed to come from the depths of her very soul. As I carried that mother's blessing with me to Birkenau, so I have carried it with me each day of my life until this very day!"

Dr. Frankl thought for a moment. He rose up from his chair and stepped around his desk and past Roger, across the study to the bookcase where Suffering Man's moment of torment was frozen in time. He gazed silently at the little statue for the longest time. Then, stepping back a bit, he seemed to be taking in the entirety of the bookcase. He turned like a cat toward Roger.

"I made a plan that day. I knew that when I was reunited with my mother, I knew exactly what I would do. As one does to royalty, a queen, when meeting her, I would kiss the hem of her coat.

"This plan, this dream, helped sustain me."

Dr. Frankl brushed back his white hair and took his seat again. He seemed at peace for a few seconds, then leaned forward and spoke again.

"That blessing was not the only thing I carried inside me the day I arrived at Birkenau. Inside the lining of my overcoat I had sewn the manuscript to *The Doctor and the Soul*. It, and my badge from the Donauland Alpine Club, were my most prized possessions.

"I was forced to hand them both over to the cold ground upon entering Birkenau. I never saw either again. My pride and joy—the badge from the Donauland Alpine Club—and, in effect, my spiritual child—my manuscript—were gone. To no useful end, I might add, for who among the world's population at the time could have cared about those things the way I did?"

"That manuscript had indeed become your child—you meant it all along to be your legacy, should you die in the camps, didn't you?"

"Exactly! And now it was gone. Completely and forever. I had to wrestle with whether the meaning in my life was also not gone. Of course, as we sit here today, it is easy to understand that a life that is wholly dependent on even the finest prose one could write isn't much of a life after all, do you agree? But I also found hope in the most unexpected place!

"After being divorced of all my possessions—Tilly and I even threw away our wedding bands to avoid having to hand them over to the SS; and she took great delight in smashing a gilded clock of hers rather than let them have it—I put on the rags of a poor soul who no doubt had gone on to the gas chambers before me. And in the pocket I found a bit of paper with the main Jewish prayer *Shema Yisrael*. It contains the command to 'Love thy God with all thy heart, and with all thy soul, and with all thy might.'

"How else could I take this? As a pure coincidence, I suppose, but that seems highly unlikely. And at a moment such as this, as you are grasping for hope, hoping for meaning, you take any morsel thrown to you.

"Well, I took it as a message that I should say yes to life—yes!—in spite of everything. I decided, in that moment, to dedicate my life to living my thoughts and theories, rather than merely putting them down on paper."

Roger leaned forward and turned over the tape in the recorder. "I got the distinct impression that in your camp experiences, there were many queues—many times in which you were asked to line up and you didn't know what you were being selected for."

"Yes! And this is why I wrote that you had to let fate decide for you. You just never knew if a specific line of inmates or a particular transport would take you to a better circumstance or to a certain death.

"I can give you a very vivid example of that, Herr Murphy—an incident involving my entering Birkenau. In all my writings, I have never until now mentioned this particular story, partly because it seems so far-fetched and imagined. But I now realize it to be a true recollection of what happened to me.

"Dr. Joseph Mengele himself was directing incoming prisoners either to the left or to the right. He directed me to the left line. But recognizing no one, and now being behind his back, I switched over to the right line, where some of my colleagues were. The right line, which I switched to, was destined for labor. The left, which I avoided, included old people and the infirm, and I have no doubt was headed directly for the gas chambers.

"I do not know where I found the wherewithal to make that brazen move. But I believe it saved my life."

"Were there other times you believed you had narrowly escaped execution?"

"Oh, most certainly. Quite likely many more times than I even know. But there was one time that a particular Viennese man, who I always considered a scoundrel, took matters into his own hands. I was in a line for transport to somewhere and this man, who was working with the Nazis, began to beat and curse another man who was not in line with us. He threw the man in line, all the while using swear words and hitting him and acting as if the man had tried to get out of line. Then, the scoundrel pulled me out of line.

"I believe the group was headed for doom, and that for some reason that man had decided to rescue me from that fate."

Roger nodded. "But you never knew when the next threat would come…"

"Or from where! Exactly. Just a few days after arriving at Birkenau, I was on a transport with several thousand others; I still recall the sickly feeling of believing we were headed for Mauthausen, just west of Vienna—one of the worst camps. Many of us were convinced we were being taken to our deaths.

"So, you can imagine my feeling as the train slowed and finally stopped at a station in Vienna—and took us by the street and house I was born and lived until the day of my deportation to Theresienstadt.

"The train car was so crowded there was only room enough for some people to stand while others squatted. There were two small peepholes with bars on them. As we began to pull out of the station, I begged those in front of the peepholes to let me have one last look at my city, my neighborhood, my street. I felt like a ghost wishing to look down on an existence I once lived but no longer lived.

"But at such times, people are rarely at their best, and the men in front of the peepholes refused me rudely, saying, 'If you lived here that long, you have seen it enough already!'"

"So, by now," Roger summarized, "you've left your parents and wife and all your possessions behind, including the manuscript you've worked so hard on and which you thought might be your legacy. And now you've left your city for the second time...."

"And what I thought would be the final time. Yes. But even at such moments, one can find things to hold onto. For example, when the men monitoring the peepholes saw that we had continued west, even after passing the turn north to Mauthausen, we were overjoyed. We were happy to be going to Dachau! Can you imagine that?

"And when we arrived at Dachau's Kaufering III camp, you would have thought we'd just been liberated. You see, there was no chimney in sight, no gas. The group was laughing and joking."

"I can't imagine such a moment," Roger confessed.

"It is difficult now, even for me! But I remember that the sense of relief we felt was able to survive even the first cold, wet night—during which, the entire night, we were made to stand as a punishment for some reason known only to the Nazis.

"Of course, our sense of relief and even joy was short. The work at Kaufering was long and difficult and regimented. We reported each morning at 5 a.m. for roll call, then marched to the railway station where we were loaded onto trucks and driven some 10 kilometers to a site where we were laying more rail line. I, and another inmate, had to lift heavy steel rails ..."

"Had you a breakfast to work on?"

Dr. Frankl barked a chortle. "Only watery liquid they told us was coffee."

"How in the world did you keep going?"

"Well, the truth is, only through what you might call mind over matter. Our bodies, you know, had already been abused—worked, deprived of sleep and comfort, diseased, cold, and, most cruel of all, nearly starved. We did this work on probably less than 850 calories a day.

"The other answer to your question is that many of us did not 'keep going,' as you put it. Many of my colleagues simply died there. It seems so sanitary to sit here in this comfortable apartment, with all the food one would wish for, and to talk of such things. But truly, we toiled each day at the gates of hell itself. I remember hearing some colleague of mine or another experiencing nightmares in the dark and reaching over to wake them up. But just before doing so, it occurred to me that whatever horrible experience they were dreaming up in their sleep could not be as terrible as the reality that I would be waking them up to face. So I let them sleep, as I would have wanted them to let me."

"You also wrote of the dilemma of how to—well, ration your rations."

"Yes! First, you need to understand that under such dire circumstances, one is working on very few calories anyway; one cannot afford to waste even the energy in one's brain to think of things that do not advance one's survival, you see? And one of the things most important to your survival was how you dealt with the meager pieces of bread and watery soup that was afforded you each day."

Dr. Frankl trained his piercing eyes on Roger and leaned forward, putting his elbows on the desk and clasping his hands tightly.

"Herr Murphy, I do not wish to be seen as complaining in the least bit. I have had a good life. And since the experiences we talk of today, though they have never been out of my consciousness for even one day, I have not spoken of them very often. Not much at all, do you understand?"

Roger wasn't sure if he was being taken to task or not—but was nonetheless more than a little uncomfortable that a man who went through what this man went through would begin to ask leave to "complain."

"Dr. Frankl, you needn't …"

"Yes! I need!" the doctor interrupted. "You need to understand. I do not tell you the things I am about to tell you because I hold myself up as any kind of hero or martyr. I am simply a man—a very blessed man, I should say."

"Understood."

"I also want to make it clear that my suffering does not eclipse that of any other person there; far from it, in fact. So many died, and so many suffered in ways that I did not. And, due to my professional education and experience, in many ways I was spared a much worse fate."

Roger nodded.

"What is more, I do not hold up my suffering as being any greater than yours or anybody else's out there," the doctor said, pointing back toward the bay windows and the crowds on the street. "Suffering is suffering, whether it be of the body or of the soul. Do you understand?"

"Yes, doctor. Though I would like to go into that a little further …"

"And we shall. But first, let me tell you this: While our suffering at Kaufering and the other camps I would not place above yours, I will say that someone who has not lived through such things cannot begin to imagine the effect on a human being.

"By now, as you can imagine, the last layers of subcutaneous fat on our bodies were a forgotten memory!" He swiveled slightly and reached his right hand over his left shoulder to pinch the leather on his chair's head rest. The material groaned a low groan between his forefinger and thumb. "We were upholstered skeletons—with skin such as this chair, but without the cushion underneath. You see?

"So, you see, as the body is working more than it dreamed possible, the mind's energy is expended primarily on the wish for food. Whenever we were working, and there were no guards closely watching us, we talked incessantly about food. One man would ask another what his favorite dishes were, and so on. In this way, the man doing the asking would be living—eating—vicariously through his comrade—who, likewise, could only live the experience through his thoughts.

"Two men—enjoying a sumptuous feast through nothing more than the conjured images of their own imaginations!

"It seems laughable for me today to sit here and tell you that, while we men worked all day doing heavy labor in ditches, we often would exchange recipes! This is the extent to which food filled our thoughts and conversations.

"Then, the word would come down through the men that a guard was coming, and the conversation would stop. But not the thoughts. They would go on and on and on. And all the while, our bodies—worked to the bone and starved of the flesh—would be devouring themselves before our very eyes."

"As a doctor, what did you think of that obsession with food?"

"Well, I succumbed to it myself, so I am not speaking to you here as a disinterested observer. But I always considered it a dangerous escapade, to stand in such grave states of malnutrition yet wallowing in imagined buffets of plenty. The constant dreams and talks about food were seductive and psychologically pleasing, but I was truly concerned about the physiological effects it might be having. We were mentally programming our bodies, after all, to prepare to gorge themselves, while we could only offer our pitiful stomachs small portions of once-daily bread and watery soup. An 'extra allowance,' as our captors called it, might consist of a bit of margarine, a meager portion of cheese, indigestible sausage or synthetic honey or watery jam.

"Such a diet could hardly sustain an inactive person, much less one who was made to perform manual labor from sun up to sun down. And the sick among us—why, the lack of sustenance left them in even worse shape than they would otherwise be. The paradox was that our captors were relying on the very muscle they were allowing to disintegrate!

"Man by man, those in my little hut began to die. And with each passing day and hour, we could see it coming, slowly, slowly. We could look at a man, and with fairly precise accuracy determine when that person's time would come. 'He won't last long,' we would whisper, one to another. And, generally, our prognosis was right.

"We saw it in others, yes, but we were forced to see it in ourselves, too. Can you imagine? Put yourself there. At the end of a day's work, you are checking yourself for lice, as you must. Parenthetically, I ask you: Isn't it amazing that a louse would find it worthwhile to attach itself to such sorry creatures as we were? Pity the poor parasite left with such a meager meal. I have to believe those lice unfortunate enough to stumble upon me faced starvation for their trouble. Anyway, as you check your body for these bloodsuckers, though, you are struck with the fact that you, yourself, Herr Murphy, are a walking corpse. Can you imagine it?"

"No, sir, I can't."

"Nor can I. It is only through the living of such a thing that it can be believed.

"But I was about to explain the dilemma of eating. As you feel yourself evolving into a cadaver before your very eyes, each morsel of food is seen as the thread by which you cling to life, do you see? And so the dilemma: How should one approach his daily rations?

"This must seem such a trivial consideration to you, Herr Murphy. But to a man who is slowly starving and being worked to death, it is the most fundamental question of his day."

Roger spoke slowly and uncertainly, given the mood of the moment. "So, what did you do, Herr Doctor?" Roger hadn't even noticed he'd used the German courtesy title to address Dr. Frankl. It was now second-nature.

"Well, as I pointed out, this was a matter of great deliberation. So there developed in the camp two schools of thought. One was to devour the food immediately. In this school of thought, the worst hunger pangs were dispatched with great speed. And—not at all a small consideration—this also prevented one from losing the food or having it stolen, as frequently happened, I am sad to say.

"The other school held that it was wiser to divide up your rations and eat a little at a time during the day. I ultimately decided this was the better course. Occasionally, one would do that and forget that one had done that, and you would find an unexpected and forgotten fragment of food in your pocket. What a delight—if a fleeting one."

Dr. Frankl leaned back and seemed to be debating with himself.

"There were other fleeting delights we engaged in that, perhaps ironically, are not pleasurable delights, in the strictest sense. You must understand that we were constantly cold—working in the cold air in inadequate dress, then sleeping at night on the cold ground in our half-underground huts. So, I remember taking odd pleasure in the temporary warmth created by urinating right there as I worked in the ditch, or even in the soup line."

Roger shifted in his chair uneasily. Not to change the subject, but out of urgent curiosity, Roger asked, "What pleasures dominated your own thoughts and dreams?"

"What I wouldn't have given for a warm bath and a *schaumschnitten*!"

"Shawn—what?"

"You don't know *schaumschnitten*? My goodness! Only the best pastry in the world."

"Forgive my unbridled ignorance, doctor," Roger smiled.

"Only if you pledge to strike at your ignorance with a bit of this heaven on Earth before you leave this city."

"Promise. Now, food, of course, was not your only concern—even from a purely physical standpoint."

"No, you are right. Remember that we were inadequately dressed for the weather—in rags given up by souls who had gone on before us. And shoes! What a precious commodity, to have shoes that actually enclosed the entire foot, toes and all.

"Of all the hours of the day and night in Kaufering, morning was the worst. It was still dark out when those three short whistles would signal that it was time to arise. And you are rudely kidnapped from the peace of sleep— even the relative safe harbor of your worst nightmares—and forced to awaken to the realization that your reality was worse than any nightmare. And that it was time to live that reality one more long, cold, hungry, uncomfortable and desperate day.

"Perhaps the worst part of that worst part of the day were the shoes: still wet, still not up to the task of holding in our swollen, aching feet or holding out the cold and wet. And in the dark and cold and the fog of having just been awakened, one must try to tie two pieces of wire together as laces.

"But even that was better than the alternative: I recall that, one morning, a fellow prisoner whom we all regarded as brave and dignified woke up and simply cried like a baby because his wet shoes had become too small for his swollen feet. He knew the guards would have no sympathy for him whatsoever, and that on that day he would be proceeding to work on the snowy grounds in his bare feet.

"Of course, you know about frostbite. I don't know what you may know about trench foot …"

"Very little. Only that it was a problem in World War I."

"A terrible problem! Especially for the Allies. The Germans inspired the practice of trench warfare, but were spared many of the effects of trench foot because they chose higher ground for their trenches. Allies' trenches were dug in lower, wetter ground—the perfect, muddy mix for trench foot. The constant exposure to cold and wet would numb, then redden and then blacken the foot. Left untreated, it would cause gangrene and the need for amputation—or, in the extreme, bring on death itself.

"Well, we in the camps knew enough to know it was a potential death sentence. Seeing that man dress for work that day unable to put on his shoes was like seeing him open the notice of his impending execution. We all knew it.

"Not only did I feel relatively fortunate at that point to have any sort of footwear, but I also gave myself another treat: As I reached into my pocket that morning, I found a bit of bread that I had saved and had forgotten about.

"You take any little joy you can …"

◆   ◆   ◆

After a brief break in which Dr. Frankl returned phone calls and letters, he opened another session before waiting for a question from Roger.

"I want to make something clear before we go on further," Dr. Frankl directed. "While everything I told you about our thoughts of food was true and not exaggerated, you need to know, too, that there were other things that occupied our minds, particularly as we marched along the road to the work site—all along dodging stones and puddles and the butts of rifles urging us on.

"We thought of our loved ones.

"One man lamented, 'If our wives could see us now! I hope they are better off than we, and that they don't know what has befallen us.' I thought very often of Tilly and my mother—especially my wife. I saw her distinctly in my mind, and as I walked in the early morning and saw the pink sunrise begin to take hold, I thought that, in my mind, she was more luminous than the sun at that moment."

"With all due respect, Herr Doctor," Roger interrupted, more forcefully than usual. "You said and wrote that, with regard to thoughts, in particular, of sex—well, let me quote you …" Roger pulled open *Man's Search for Meaning* to Page 52 and read from it: "'With the majority of the prisoners, the primitive life and the effort of having to concentrate on just saving one's skin led to a total disregard of anything not serving that purpose, and explained the prisoners' complete lack of sentiment.'"

"So I did. An apparent contradiction, Herr Murphy," Dr. Frankl acknowledged, in a somewhat defeated tone. "But this is not quite the paradox it seems, you see.

"It is true enough that the prisoners exhibited a near-total lack of sentiment for the things going on around them. But, quite opposite of that, when going through the unbelievable, unbearable experiences of such camps, a quiet sentiment within one's soul can even grow and flourish—and, in fact, can be a chief stimulant to keeping you alive.

"Indeed, this apparent paradox almost took flesh and blood form. Let me explain.

"I observed, for example, that some of the more intellectual and spiritual prisoners took the physical rigors of the camps most hard. After all, it was these types of men who were most often the most delicate. But whereas the more physically adept men could handle the physical demands placed upon them, they fell behind their peers in terms of emotional strength. Meanwhile, the more spiritual of the men often exhibited a stronger spiritual core, even as their bodies withered.

"As to my sentiments about Tilly, they helped me realize how critical it was for me, and others in my situation, to have an orientation toward the future. For me, this meant the day I would once again be reunited with my bride.

"Of all places, it was in the camps that it came upon me, this overwhelming sentiment. I believed then, as I do now, that for the first time in my life I had stumbled upon the truth discovered by so many and written down in words and put into song by so many poets and artists before me: that love—love!— is the highest goal to which a human being can aspire.

"May I?" Dr. Frankl held his hand out for Roger's copy of *Man's Search for Meaning*. He took it, and quickly thumbed to the page he wanted and began reading:

> *The salvation of man is through love and in love. I understood how a man who has nothing left in this world still may know bliss, be it only for a brief moment, in the contemplation of his beloved. In a position of utter desolation, when man cannot express himself in positive action, when his only achievement may consist in enduring his sufferings in the right way—an honorable way—in such a position man can, through loving contemplation of the image he carries of his beloved, achieve fulfillment. For the first time in my life I was able to understand the meaning of the words, "The angels are lost in perpetual contemplation of an infinite glory."*

Dr. Frankl folded the book closed and held it out for Roger.

Roger was still stunned. The picture of this historical figure reading his writing to Roger—and out of Roger's copy of his book—was a moment to let soak in. "You didn't know, as you were thinking these things," Roger finally managed, "whether your wife was alive."

"No, I did not. Of course, I had no way of knowing, not since those moments in Auschwitz when we were separated and I told her to save herself at any cost. And do you know, it was nearly irrelevant to me, at least in terms of how I felt. Love does have a magical power to transcend the physical. The important dimension of love is the spiritual one.

"I did have a strange occurrence come upon me during my second night in Auschwitz, if I may digress there for a moment. I was exhausted and sleeping deeply, but awoke with a start to the sound of music coming from the senior warden's room nearby. There were drunken voices and very poor singing—to this day, I have no idea what the occasion there was.

"But suddenly the noise stopped and was replaced by the singular voice of a remarkably sad-sounding violin. It was a melancholy melody that cried out in the night—and I remember realizing just then that Tilly had turned 24 that very day. And though she was living in a barracks unreachable by me, I could feel her presence. I could feel it, as sharply as the air against my skin."

"Forgive me, doctor," Roger butted in. "But I still don't understand how you were able to stay above the despair."

"We shall talk about that more in detail later. But for now, let me just say the short answer to your curiosity is that I did not always do so. In our normal lives, it usually takes no conscious thought to maintain our living; we simply do it without question. Our minds are otherwise occupied with the details of that living, or with dreams yet unrealized. Moreover, we normally have no incentive to think of discontinuing that life.

"But there are exceptions to that rule, in and out of the camps. I confess to you that I was not always able to live by the principles I had begun to set out in my logotherapy. There was one particular time in Kaufering when I apparently was sounding particularly despondent. A fellow prisoner—a man known as Benscher, who later became a television celebrity in Munich—implored me to abandon the pessimism I was giving into at the time. I realized in my heart, even then, that chronic gloom, under such dire circumstances, could and would be fatal.

"I truly believe Benscher saved my life that night."

"Wait a minute," Roger interjected. "Let me get this straight. You're saying being depressed in the camps was potentially fatal, in and of itself?"

"Yes, this is in effect what I am saying. All else being equal, one's attitude could be the straw that broke the camel's back. I once saw the importance of one's faith in the future dramatically demonstrated. My senior block warden told me one day about a dream in which a voice told him he could ask any question at all. Do you know what he wished to know? On what date he would be liberated.

"The voice told him March 30th, 1945. As the day drew near, and news of the war seemed to indicate that the liberation would not take place, he suddenly fell ill—on March 29th. By the 31st, he was dead.

"One might have thought it was typhus. And certainly that was the overt cause of death. But those who knew him, and had seen this sort of giving up in other prisoners, knew the signs of letting go of life. In a way, he was indeed liberated—by death.

"One can understand, especially if you've been through it yourself, how someone would give up on life under such circumstances. Whatever you were in your previous life, you were a number, and were beneath both your captors and the capos—people from among your ranks who were 'promoted' above you. And the awful conditions—the cold, hunger, work, lack of adequate clothing, the vermin and filth.

"But do you know the worst part of camp life? Worse than anything else? It was the indeterminate nature of our captivity: We simply had no idea how long this 'provisional existence' was going to last. So, you can see why my friend, given any question he could pose in his dream, asked when it would all end."

"How did you think yourself through it?" asked Roger.

Dr. Frankl thought.

"Barely," he said. "Barely.

"One device I used, particularly if the cold was bitter or my feet especially exposed or swollen, would be to imagine my sufferings as something I was looking back on in a clinical way. I saw myself in a warm lecture room giving a rapt audience a speech about the very things I was going through at the moment. This helped me see my suffering as having some sort of meaning, and as something that was already in the past!

"Not only did that mental exercise provide me a little added layer against the wind, but it also gave me something more interesting, and high-minded, to ponder—instead of the incessant wondering if I would have enough food, or if I should trade my cigarettes, or curry favor with the capo ..."

"And it kept you off the slippery slope toward giving up."

"Precisely. Well stated! I must have known this from the start, for at the very beginning of my captivity, I made a conscious decision never to 'run into the wire'—it was the most popular form of suicide, this running into the electrically charged barbed wire fence."

Dr. Frankl contemplated something for a moment.

"The irony, of course, is that even those who wished fervently to live on might make the wrong decision, or be in the wrong line at the wrong time. Whenever there was a transport to another camp, you always took a chance—by either going on the transport or by staying behind! Can you see how this constant dilemma, over which you have no control, might be maddening?

"It is in this way that I was approved for a transport to Turkheim, which was another part of the Dachau system.

"The chief doctor at Kaufering, a Hungarian who was very kind to me, told me of this transport to a 'rest camp.' He told me he could arrange for me to be on the transport the next day, as the rest camp's medical doctor. But you know, he advised me against it. He knew, as well as I, that it could have been a trip to the gas ovens.

"Or, as happened earlier, it could have been a ruse. What the guards did, sadistically in my opinion, was announce a transport to a rest camp. The consensus was that it was to the ovens. So, when the guards announced that anyone who volunteered to work the dreaded night shift would be taken off the transport, 82 men volunteered.

"In the end, the transport was canceled—it probably never was going to happen to begin with. And those men who did their best to avoid death by volunteering to work the night shift, most of them were dead from the extra work within two weeks."

"And you knew this as your transport was being arranged? That you might be headed for the ovens or, if you beg off, might be worked to death there in Kaufering?"

"Yes. Also, there was a chance that the transport might be back to awful Auschwitz. But for me, getting on that transport was an easy decision. For one thing, I told the chief doctor that I had learned not to try to outmaneuver the gods—to try to outguess fate. I was simply going to let it take its course. I also felt it was wiser to go with my friends on the transport and to have the chance, if even a slight chance, to work as a doctor in a rest camp. Even if the transport meant death, it meant a meaningful death—one in which I either acted as, or intended to act as, a medical doctor taking care of the others. I felt the alternative, to stay in Kaufering, was—relative to the fate at the rest camp—simply meaningless suffering."

"So you went."

"The chief doctor did his best to prevent it. He urgently told me that he had made it clear to those responsible that I could have my name taken off the transport list until 10 o'clock. I simply told him that that was not my way. With a look of pity, he shook my hand as if I were a condemned man."

"For all you knew, you were!"

"Yes. And my friend back at my hut, Otto, believed it. It was I who had to comfort *him*. And at that time, also, I made my will, verbally, to Otto.

"Of course, normally a will involves prescribing where your worldly goods will end up. This was not an issue for prisoners of the Third Reich, you see.

"What I told Otto was simply this: If you see my wife, tell her I talked about her day and night. Tell her I have loved her more than anyone or anything in the world. And lastly, tell her that the short few years I have been married to her, and the even shorter time that we spent together, outweighs all the suffering and misery I have experienced here. Tell her it outweighs everything."

Dr. Frankl looked up at Tilly's portrait, took off his glasses and dabbed at his eyes with a handkerchief. Quickly, he stuffed it away and replaced his glasses.

"I always wondered what became of Otto. Given the fact that I have been somewhat accessible over the years …"

"You mean famous?" smiled Roger.

"More important that my *ideas* be known, don't you think? But I have to assume Otto, had he lived, would have been able to find me. I am not optimistic that he did survive, and let me tell you why. Months after my liberation, I met a man whom I had known in Kaufering, and he told me that he, as camp policeman, had once been given the disgusting task of finding a piece of flesh that had been stolen from the corpses in the camp.

"You see, shortly after I had left, it appears cannibalism had broken out in Kaufering."

Roger just swallowed loudly.

"If I had stayed, as appeared at the time to be the way of self-preservation, surely I would have died. I left just in time."

Roger pondered that momentarily. "So, in your effort to help others as a doctor in the next camp, you actually ended up saving yourself."

"Yes. Is it not often the case that one helps oneself best by setting out to help another? This also shows us how fickle fate can be. It reminds me of the story of 'Death in Teheran.' Do you know it?"

"No, I'm afraid I don't."

"A rich man of Persia had a servant who was frantic, saying that he had just encountered Death itself in the garden. He begged his master for his fastest horse, so that he could ride to Teheran that very minute in order to avoid Death. The master agreed, but soon he also came upon Death inside the palace. 'Why did you frighten my servant this way?' the rich man asked Death. 'I did not mean to frighten him,' Death replied. 'I only acted surprised to see him here, when I had planned to meet him tonight in Teheran!'

"It was very much like this in the camps. You could try to out-think death, but not always succeed.

"This realization came upon most of us, and kept us afraid of making any decisions that might change our fate. One never knew if it was for the better or for the worse."

"Such as with the transports," Roger added.

"Yes, but in other ways, too. The decision of whether to make an escape attempt was often before us. I had one such opportunity, one such decision, I would like to tell you of.

"Of course, there were many rumors about the war, and we had largely decided to discount all of them. But it was clear to us that the battle front was approaching. And it was a very hopeful, enticing thought, as you might imagine. Well, it so happened that a colleague who had occasion to be outside the camp on his medical duties told me he would mount an escape attempt—and wanted me to come with him.

"I decided to do it.

"We took turns breaking into a hut that had been used for women prisoners, and we gathered some provisions in rucksacks. I went back to my hut to get my few things—my food bowl, some mittens and the few scraps of paper on which I had started to rewrite my lost manuscript.

"Then I made one last, quick round with my patients—typhus was ravaging the camp at that point—who were lying on the sides of the hut on top of rotten pieces of wood. One of them was a fellow Austrian who seemed to sense that something was afoot. 'You are getting out too?' he asked me. I denied it, and continued on my rounds.

"After my rounds, I returned to him. This time, without words and with only a hopeless look in his cavernous eyes, he seemed to be accusing me.

"The guilt that had been planted since the moment I agreed to escape grew into a tall oak at that very moment. I rushed outside and, with some amount of arguing, convinced my colleague that I was staying. I instantly felt relief. I felt an inner peace and contentment that I'd never before felt, and perhaps never have again."

"Like the moment you knew you would stay with your parents in Vienna, rather than use your visa to America?"

"Yes—similar. But this feeling may have been deeper. The feeling in Vienna was mixed with more dread—and the meaning of staying hadn't been made totally clear to me at that point. In contrast, in Turkheim, having lived through what I had already, and knowing the end was coming soon—either through death or liberation—and knowing my vast responsibilities to my patients, this feeling of peace was more complete and satisfying."

Dr. Frankl paused only briefly, and continued with a start.

"Do not, however, think that I was content enough to wish to stay a moment longer than absolutely necessary. Far from it. While I felt serene about my decision to stay with my patients rather than abandon them in an escape attempt, I longed all the more for freedom and rescue. Perhaps knowing that a colleague might be experiencing these things while I was still captive made the desire for liberation more intense.

"But, ironically, conditions in the camp became more perilous than ever as the battle front drew near. For one thing, after being surrounded by it and treating so many patients for it, I succumbed to typhus, which was spread by lice and flea-infested rats.

"Having seen the progression of the disease—its high fever and the night delirium that so often brought about death—I had the knowledge, and made the conscious decision, to avoid this. I waged war against nocturnal deliria by fighting back sleep with every ounce of my strength left.

"I did this, in large part, by using my intense, excited state—induced by the fever, no doubt—to reconstruct the manuscript that had been taken from me upon entering the camps. In this way, I made an achievement out of my suffering!

"But while one has mastery over many aspects of his life, he is not the master of it. And so, there was only so much one could do to save oneself.

"Indeed, the last day presented perhaps the greatest threat to our survival."

12

There was some sort of commotion at the entrance to the Frankls' apartment building as Roger Murphy rounded the corner on the way to his morning session with the doctor.

On the narrow street that was Mariannengasse, there was a bus parked directly in front of the door. A Japanese woman was scanning the menu of buttons before finding the one by the "Frankl" name. She buzzed it, twice.

Roger recognized Mrs. Frankl's voice. "Good morning! Herr Murphy?"

The woman didn't even try to decipher what Mrs. Frankl was talking about, or to put the name with Roger's face as he stood watching her.

"Good morning!" the woman said in a silky, accented voice. "We are a group of Japanese tourists, and we respectfully ask an audience with Dr. Viktor Frankl please."

There was a brief pause.

"Oh my, Dr. Frankl is busy!" Mrs. Frankl's voice was an odd mix of apology and irritation. "He has an appointment with a journalist from America all day—tomorrow, too. Please call back for an appointment. We are so sorry!" And you could tell Mrs. Frankl really was.

By now, the tourists, about two dozen of them, were out on the sidewalk and street snapping photos of the building and their tour leader at the entrance. She glanced back at them, appearing a bit upset that they had spilled out of the bus before being summoned. Then she looked over at Roger, looked down at his bag, and put two and two together. She politely bowed her head slightly, though Roger could sense frustration mixed with jealousy. He imagined she was wondering who the hell this guy thought he was, jumping ahead of her and hoarding such a great man—and tourist draw—all to himself.

Roger did feel a little guilty as he watched the woman bark some Japanese to get the group back on the bus. He felt like he'd kicked all the other kids out of Disneyland so he could have all the fun himself. He didn't have the heart to buzz the Frankls until the bus had disappeared around the corner. The magnitude of Roger's access and the extent of the privilege being extended to him this week was brought home to him in that moment.

"This guy *is* a rock star," he mumbled to himself.

◆   ◆   ◆

"Dr. Frankl," Roger began, "I can't believe how generous you've been with your time. I will try to be a good steward of it today, and perhaps you will be finished with me finally."

"Yes, we should finish today. I hope I have helped you in some way. But I should tell you that this time with you, and talking to you about these things, has been therapeutic for me. I have not visited these things in such detail for a very long time."

Roger bowed like the Japanese tour guide and turned on the recorder. "You were about to tell me about the danger of the last day at Turkheim."

"It very well could have been our last day of life!

"The front was near, and the camp was being emptied quickly with mass transports of prisoners and patients. There were orders that even the sickest patients would be evacuated, and that the camp would be set on fire in the evening.

"But do you know, the trucks never came for the sick. And even as the rest of the camp had become vacant, the gates were closed and the fences guarded carefully—so it seemed that the sick had been consigned to burn with the camp!

"Well, with this becoming plain, there was no reason not to consider again taking fate into our own hands and escaping. Even if we were allowed to escape the coming inferno, surely our captors would wish us dead and unable to testify as to their atrocities. And so, we devised a plan.

"Two of us had been ordered to bury three corpses just outside the camp. We were the only prisoners left who were physically able to carry out the task!

"Thus, our plan: On the trip to bury the first body, we would hide my friend's rucksack in the coffin. On the second, we would hide mine. And on the third trip, we would simply make our escape.

"As we prepared for the third trip, my colleague went looking for a piece of bread to sustain us after our escape. He was gone for the longest time, and I became impatient. I was beginning to recognize the taste of freedom that had so long eluded my tongue. But he did not return, and did not return.

"Finally, at the very second my friend returned, the gates were thrown open. In came a car with red crosses all over it. The International Red Cross had arrived—this time not to be fooled by the Nazis, but to provide a bridge back to civilization.

"The delegate provided boxes of medicine and cigarettes and a promise that an agreement had been signed, and that the camp was not to be evacuated after all. Just like that, it was over.

"Or so we thought.

"We had forgotten about the third body, so we proceeded to bury it—and one of the guards even prayed with us over it. Obviously, the writing was on the wall, and this guard hoped that when the tables were turned, and the captors became the captive, that we would look kindly on him. Anyway, you can't imagine the fervor with which we prayed over that body, knowing that peace and freedom and salvation were at hand. Our joy was premature.

"The Red Cross delegate had arranged to stay in a nearby farmhouse. And that night, the SS showed up with trucks, and orders that the remaining prisoners were to be transported to another camp—from which they would be taken to Switzerland within 48 hours to be traded for prisoners of war.

"These SS were also friendlier than before, as was the guard at the burial. Rather than fear and whips and clubs, they used encouragement and verbal persuasion to convince us to get on the trucks. Those who could jump on under their own power did so; the others were lifted onto the truck.

"Thirteen of us would be on the next-to-last truck. But when the chief doctor was done counting out the 13, my friend and I—brazenly holding our rucksacks now—had been left out, and the truck left.

"We were angry; the doctor apologized, saying he thought we'd been planning to escape anyway. And he explained that he was tired and distracted.

"Well, we sat and waited for the last truck to freedom. It never appeared.

"Finally, exhausted and depressed from the emotional roller-coaster we'd been on, we invaded the vacant guard room and slept soundly on their mattresses.

"I awoke to the sounds and flashes of a fierce gun battle raging outside the hut and in the camp. The front had arrived!

"The head doctor stormed in and yelled to take cover on the floor. As I did, a patient from the bunk above me landed on my stomach, ensuring that the battle had now earned my full attention!

"When the day dawned, and the battle had waned, we looked out and saw a most peculiar sight: waving in the morning breeze on the camp's flagpole was a white flag."

Dr. Frankl leaned forward.

"And do you know, we had no idea how fate had toyed with us that night. Many weeks later, I saw photographs of a camp not too far from ours in which prisoners had been locked in a small hut that was then set on fire.

"The corpses were not so badly burned that I couldn't tell they were the men who left on that second-to-last truck my friend and I had so badly wanted to be on that night.

"Again, we had narrowly escaped death—while thinking all along that it was life and freedom that had eluded us!"

Roger shook his head in amazement. "Pure luck."

"Perhaps," Dr. Frankl added. "Or perhaps only *mostly* pure."

"What do you mean?"

"I mean, remember when the second-to-last truck was being loaded with prisoners and patients, and my friend and I wanted desperately to be among them? But the chief doctor had counted us out."

Roger's eyes widened, his eyebrows raising slightly. "What are you saying? That the chief doctor left you out on purpose? That he knew it was an ill-fated trip?"

"I am not saying this at all. Only suggesting the possibility. To say it would be pretentious of me—and would make one wonder why, if he thought it was a doomed cargo he was loading, that he would have participated in it to begin with. But that wouldn't be fair to him, because I know—having been there—that he had no choice but to go along with the guards. And, after all, there was always the possibility that it was as the guards described, that we were being traded with the Allies for prisoners of war.

"I merely suggest that if the chief doctor was the least bit suspicious of the truck's true destination, that he may have purposely left my friend and I out of it. But it's a moot point; either way, he saved my life."

"Yes, but Herr Doctor, if you will allow the impertinence …"

"Whatever it is, Herr Murphy."

"You have talked often about other people having saved your life. I fear you are being overly modest. Can it not be argued that you saved many a life yourself?"

Dr. Frankl smiled slightly. "If this is an argument to be made, then I shall leave it to others, such as yourself, to make this argument. It is certainly not for me to say.

"You do remind me, however, of one of the shining moments earlier in my captivity—a moment in which, as you suggest, I may have made a difference in the survival of some around me.

"It had been a particularly bad day all around. Our captors had cracked down on prisoners for such trivial matters as tearing small portions of our blankets in order to use them as ankle supports. They threatened us with hanging for such high crimes! Can you believe it? And, due to the theft of some potatoes some days previously, they withheld food from all of us for the day. You can imagine how irritable and despondent a starving man might feel when told that the insufficient crumbs of food he had been looking so forward to would be withheld!

"Add to that the fact that in the hut that night the electric light went out. So there we were, a herd of miserable, starving and hopeless beasts.

"Well, the senior block warden called upon me to lift the men's spirits. What pressure! I was certainly no better off than they were, either physically or emotionally. I was in no mood to save the world. I had my own problems, my own struggles with mere survival. But I also realized that, once called upon to help, it was my solemn obligation. So I spoke to the men huddled in our earthen hut, as best I could.

"Now, I may have told you that the prisoners who ran about spreading blind and chronic optimism were, in my opinion, the toughest ones to be around. I preferred the occasional kick or blunt blow to the head from a capo or SS to the constant ramblings of mindless positiveness. So I would never have served that up, and certainly not that evening.

"Yet, I started my talk by telling the men an absolute truth that was next to impossible to believe at that particular moment: that things could, indeed, have been much worse. Even in abject poverty, and having suffered immensely, I reminded the men that they, in truth, had not lost much that was irreplaceable. Material things, positions, relationships—most of what the men had been deprived of could someday be restored. This was inarguable.

"And, after all, whoever was still alive still had hope. Further, I quoted from Nietzsche: *'Was mich nicht umbringt, macht mich stärker'*—'That which does not kill me, makes me stronger.'

"I also talked to them about the future, which I did honestly and plainly. I told them my own chances of survival were probably no better than 1 in 20—so I was neither trying to fool them, nor myself. But I made clear I had no intention of giving up. I reminded them there was no telling what the future might bring, even one hour from now.

"I then talked to them about the past. I assured them that their suffering had not been in vain. Not one thing that we had endured had been for nothing. And everything we had experienced—including everything that we had thought or dreamed of—was created by us, brought into being by us alone. No one else could have created the great thoughts or endured the monumental suffering that we had. Every man's suffering, every man's every thought, was unique.

"What was more, I told them, was that all these experiences and thoughts, once we created or endured them, were safely locked away into the past. I quoted a poet who wrote, '*Was Du erlebst, kann keine Macht der Welt Dir rauben*'—'What you have experienced, no power on Earth can take from you.'"

Dr. Frankl paused, fixing his gaze on Roger.

"Herr Murphy, take special note of this phenomenon, for I believe it to have very important application in today's fast-paced world, when everything seems to go by so quickly, even time itself. I can't tell you how many times I have had patients tell me, 'But Dr. Frankl, everything is over so quickly—what meaning could it have?' Well, I have just told you: Having done something, or experienced something, you have safely delivered it into the past, where it is forever unalterable." Dr. Frankl was nearly shouting now. "This is the opposite of transitory, Herr Murphy! This is forever I am talking about!

"But I digress. Finally, I spoke to the men of two things.

"First, the many opportunities one has, even in such a setting, to find meaning. I believe it is this particular point which brought you to my acquaintance, yes?"

Roger nodded and smiled.

"I told my fellow prisoners that the hopelessness of our situation had nothing—*nothing*, I told them!—nothing to do with the *meaningfulness* of it. Our struggle, as with all human endeavors and every human life, had not only meaning but dignity. And no one could attend to that dignity and meaning, or preserve it for posterity, except us. Only we could do this.

"I reminded them that someone right now looked down on us and our difficulties—be it a loved one or God—and that we should not disappoint them! They would hope, no doubt, that we would not only suffer proudly and with dignity uncharacteristic of our surroundings, but—if need be—also die in the same way.

"Secondly, I talked of our sacrifice and the meaning of it. And I recalled how one new arrival had made a deal with Heaven to take him, and not a loved one. He asked to sacrifice his life to save someone he loved. What more meaning could a human being ask for than that?"

Seeing that Dr. Frankl was finished recounting his speech, Roger spoke up. "How was your speech received, doctor?"

Dr. Frankl's small smile disappeared.

"Herr Murphy, when the light came on, my comrades arose and limped toward me in tears to thank me. I cannot imagine a more moving moment."

How ironic, Roger thought. A man who has given lectures all over the world, and been in the spotlight for decades, may have spent his finest hour, may have given his most shining performance, in the dark to a group of desperate concentration camp prisoners.

"Herr Doctor," Roger finally asked, "tell me about your liberation."

Dr. Frankl sighed and rubbed his face. He pulled his glasses off and rubbed his eyes, which seemed to be aching. He put his glasses back on and ran his palm over his hair from front to back.

"Herr Murphy." Another pause. The suspense was about to kill Roger. He had no idea what would come out of Dr. Frankl's mouth next. "Suppose for a moment that you have a wish. A very fervent wish. Suppose that your wish is to have …" Another pause. "Suppose that your wish is to have this desk. You want it more than anything in the world. For years you see it in a window, and for years you wish it to be your own, in your own study.

"After a number of years, you begin to believe that your wish will never come true. So much so, that as you pass the store with the desk each day, you begin to not notice it. You forget that it's there. You even forget what it looked like.

"Then, one day, when you least expect it, it simply appears in the middle of your room. What are you to think?"

Roger blinked, looked at the desk, blinked again and looked back up at the former prisoner.

"I will tell you. You don't believe it. You look at it for hours on end. You walk all around it, surveying it from every possible angle. You caress it—carefully, though, because you are not quite sure it's real.

"Once you have accepted its reality, you expect it to be taken from you. When there is no knock at the door, by men coming to take it from you, you accept that it's here.

"Then your dilemma is simple. You have to remember what it's for.

"You might guess that we dashed with mad joy into the fields, once the gates to the camp had opened wide. That we were delirious at our newfound freedom. In truth, we stepped gingerly into that new world, a world that had been denied us so long that we had forgotten its texture. We walked out a few steps from the camp and looked at each other in wonderment. No shouts. No blows or kicks. In fact, the guards were there—but they were now in civilian clothes, offering us cigarettes. Can you imagine?

"We walked and walked and walked, even though our legs rebelled openly against us. We saw fields of flowers, we heard birds. But we had the strangest sense that we no longer belonged to this world. And we had oddly few feelings about it.

"Once back at our hut for the evening, one prisoner asked another, 'Tell me, were you pleased with what we experienced today?' The other prisoner replied, 'Truthfully, no.' And he spoke for us all.

"You see, we were suffering from what I call the psychological equivalent of the bends. As a deep-sea diver is under much pressure from the water, we, too, had been under the most intense mental and emotional pressure bearable for several years. And now, for that pressure to be released so suddenly—well, we were frankly in great danger!

"Certainly the body was much more adaptable to the overnight change. After years of starvation, it eagerly and immediately began to devour enormous amounts of food—really, you would be amazed!"

Roger held up his hand to signify an interruption. "Doctor, just what was your physical condition at that point?"

Dr. Frankl smiled. "At the time of liberation, I had put on significant weight! I moved the needle on the scale all the way to 38 kilograms—in your measurement system, 84 pounds!

"Newly arrived medicine helped get my fever down. I had an irregular heart rhythm, hunger-induced edema and frostbite on three fingers. All these things were treatable, with time. And the body is more resilient than we know.

"But the mind is more wary and distrustful—and disbelieving. The tongue certainly had no inhibitions, and no difficulty learning to taste again. But the apprehensive mind was not so trusting.

"You must remember that the mind had had its hopes dashed so often. Sometimes by external circumstances—such as unfounded rumors of liberation—and sometimes by internal factors: the incessant night dreams of liberation and post-liberation banquets and conversations. Then, to have those dreams shattered by the shrill blare of the camp's morning whistle—well, you can see how the mind is programmed not to believe what the body is seeing, tasting, smelling and touching. So, it took time for our new reality to be accepted by the mind.

"And you might be surprised to hear that once accepted, the new reality wasn't necessarily one that brought great joy. I will never forget how one of my fellow prisoners—a good man, absolutely—rolled up his sleeves and shoved his hand near my chin and yelled, 'May this hand be cut off if I don't stain it with blood on the day when I get home!'

"Likewise, one could see that some personalities among the prisoners were susceptible to repeating the kinds of brutal behavior, once liberated, that they themselves had endured. They, in effect, were going to lash out at life for what it had done to them.

"A friend of mine and I were walking toward the camp when we came to a field of lush, cultivated oats. I made an almost unconscious reflex to avoid the field, but my friend grabbed my arm and whisked us both through it, saying, 'After what has been done to us, and my wife and child have been gassed, you would prohibit me from walking over a few stalks of oats?'

"I realized at that moment that we had much to re-learn about being human. As our souring experience the first day after liberation revealed, we had forgotten how to be pleased. As my friend proved in the field of oats, we had to be reminded that no one has a right to do wrong—even if the most horrible wrongs had been done to him.

"We needed time for introspection. Time to come to grips not only with what had happened to us, but with the fact that it was mercifully, but quite suddenly, in the past. And not all of us took that time.

"Not too long after liberation, and before our transfer toward home, I was walking toward the nearest town, past those fields of flowers and the birds. And I walked and walked. And when I stopped, I looked around me. And I looked into the sky. And I fell on my knees. And I struggled with the fact that I really didn't know myself anymore, or how I, myself, would be changed by what had occurred.

"But I had one phrase in mind, and as I knelt there for many moments, I repeated the phrase again and again.

"'*I called to the Lord from my narrow prison and He answered me in the freedom of space.*'"

Dr. Frankl leaned back ever so slightly. "As I sit here today, I can tell you, Herr Murphy, that in that hour, on my knees in the meadow, I began my new life. Where it would take me, I had no idea. But in those moments, I began my long march back to Vienna.

"And to becoming human again."

"It doesn't sound easy, doctor."

"No. It was like learning to walk again. And I wish I could tell you there weren't stumbles along the way. But there were."

The white doors swung open, signaling that it was time for a break. Mrs. Frankl was very protective of her husband.

Without the need for words, Roger packed his things into his bag and made for the door and Mrs. Frankl, who was waiting with a smile to escort him out. He turned around briefly, to see Dr. Frankl standing, staring out the bay window, and to the long, long ago.

13

The Frankls' door swept open and the sight nearly knocked Roger off his feet.

"Good afternoon, Herr Murphy," greeted Dr. Frankl, opening his own front door. "I thought for this afternoon, we would enjoy a bit of the Vienna spring by taking a walk. Do you mind?"

"I'd be delighted." Roger breathed in a whiff of the privilege just offered him.

As Dr. Frankl gathered himself and grabbed a jacket and they ambled to the elevator down, Roger thought of the historic nature of the man next to him. And he wondered why there was such a disparity in reputations. After all, were he to have had this honor with Sigmund Freud, his friends would have been impressed indeed. But were he to return and share this story about the time spent with Dr. Frankl, perhaps only Dr. Mike Mahoney would raise an eyebrow.

Roger wasn't about to confront Dr. Frankl with this question about his reputation. It might seem impertinent. And it's probably a question best left to someone else to answer, he thought. Sure, among the initiated, Dr. Frankl was a celebrity—even a human tourist attraction, as Roger saw when the Japanese tourists showed up unannounced. But while famous to a point, even a rock star to some, Roger thought, Dr. Frankl was still oddly obscure, sadly unknown.

He was beginning to become convinced that that was a crime against humanity.

"This pathway," Dr. Frankl pointed to the tree-lined walk across the street where Roger had first gone to read *Man's Search for Meaning*, "they have named after me." Indeed, Roger saw a plaque on the wall of the archway leading from the street to the large public courtyard within. "It shows you what can happen when you grow old enough and stay in the same place long enough," Dr. Frankl laughed.

Now, there's one key to Dr. Frankl's underperforming reputation, Roger thought: his modesty, which often showed up in self-deprecating humor.

As they walked toward a bench, and the warm spring breeze made the many tree shadows dance on the green grass, Roger pulled out his tape recorder.

"Doctor, would you mind telling me about the adjustment to life after the camps?"

They stopped at a wooden bench and sat down. Dr. Frankl put his hands on his thighs and let out a sigh.

"There were three primary emotional challenges, I would say.

"First is how one felt about one's captors. There is no denying that among the guards were what I would call 'true sadists.' They truly did take pleasure in inflicting pain—not just in brutal beatings, but also in little things—such as overturning a warming fire and extinguishing it in the snow for no reason other than to hurt us. And then to smile! It boggles the mind.

"But one cannot separate men into groups of guards and prisoners and say these men are evil and these men are good. Not at all! One of our own prisoners, who acted as senior camp warden, was tougher on us than any of the guards! In contrast, the camp commander, an SS, never touched us, to my knowledge.

"And this camp commander—Hoffman was his name—when we entered Turkheim, he was absolutely appalled at the condition in which we had been sent from Kaufering. He thought it a scandal. Well, after liberation, remarkably, we prisoners hid this SS commander in the woods, away from the Americans until they would promise that no harm would come to him. They eventually agreed and, in fact, he was given some authority to oversee a collection of clothes for us prisoners from surrounding villages.

"Years later, when we organized a reunion of prisoners, I had wanted to invite him. But, sadly, he had died shortly before. And a priest told me that he had always been tortured by having participated in the camp. Yet, I could have told him he was a decent man.

"So, you see, human kindness does not wear a particular form of dress or speak a particular language with a particular accent. It comes in all uniforms, all shapes, sizes and colors and voices of human beings."

"And the other two emotional challenges?"

"Bitterness and disillusionment—and I speak not of the prisoner's experiences in the camps, but of the conditions surrounding his new life back home.

"Bitterness would set in when one came across a—how shall I put it?— lackadaisical attitude of people toward his sufferings. Here he comes, with all this emotional baggage he carries home, and the best the townspeople can offer is, 'We did not know!', or 'Believe me, we have suffered, too!' This was wholly inadequate to the situation, you understand. Not at all in keeping with the unexplainable weight of the former prisoners' agony and distress.

"At that point, seeing how unimpressed, unmoved and unsympathetic the people were toward his ordeal, it was natural for a bitterness to set in. 'Why had I even gone through this, if it didn't matter?' That sort of feeling. It was very pervasive.

"Disillusionment reared its head, perhaps in large part out of the bitterness I talked about. But this feeling is different. Rather than being aimed at people, the disillusionment I speak of was toward fate itself: After suffering so much, they were disillusioned by the fact that they would have to suffer even more.

"And let's not forget that, despite my encouragement to the men in that dark hut that they needed to hang on for somebody or something that waited for them in the future, many men found this to be tragically not the case, at least on the surface. In some cases, the loved ones they kept in mind during their suffering had, themselves, perished or could not be found.

"Can you picture boarding a trolley and stopping at a home where you expect a loved one to be waiting for you, only to have a stranger answer the door? Our hopes, our dreams, upon exiting the camps were not, I think, unreasonable: a return to a life that somewhat resembled the one we had been torn from. We didn't even hope for, or expect, happiness! This was not a goal. Just a life that we considered normal. That is all.

"But while prepared not to ask for happiness, I am sad to say many men were not at all prepared for what awaited them: *un*happiness. This is why I talk of disillusionment."

Dr. Frankl stopped and sighed heavily.

"It seems so unreal, sitting here," Roger said.

"I lived through it, Herr Murphy, and it seems unreal to me. For many prisoners, the day comes when it all seems to them just a nightmare. But we lived it. And many died it."

Roger let the next moment pass in silence. Dr. Frankl finally spoke again.

"But, perhaps outweighing all these dangers and negative feelings, is the realization that after all he has suffered, the concentration camp survivor has nothing left to fear, except his God.

"Many days since then, if something bad has happened to me during the day, I fall on my knees and thank God—yes, actually thank God—that nothing worse has happened to me that day. Living through Hell gives you a certain perspective about Heaven and Earth, my friend."

Roger nodded. "What awaited *you*, doctor?"

"What awaited me?" Dr. Frankl smiled slightly. "I could not get back to Vienna immediately. Though I was liberated by troops from your country, Eastern Austria was under Russian control, and the borders were sealed for months.

"For a time, I was assigned by the Americans to work in a hospital not far from Turkheim. The hospital had been taken over for what your soldiers called 'DPs'—displaced persons. It was fulfilling work, but I was absolutely mad with wanting to know the whereabouts of Tilly and Mother. And there was simply no word.

"Finally, I gave up and left the hospital—in good hands, I assured my American friends—and moved in with a nurse's family in Munich. It was closer to home, and afforded me the opportunity to pursue news of my loved ones. I spent the summer there, waiting for some news, seeing horrible images in news reels at the cinema, and working on my writing. I also was asked to give radio talks on Radio Munich about the psychology of post-war Europe. I enjoyed that immensely, and wondered—if things didn't feel right when I returned to Vienna—if I might just return there someday.

"It was on my last day in Munich—before I was able to finally leave for Vienna—that the long-awaited word came about Mother. She had perished in the gas 'shower' at Birkenau, immediately upon her transfer there only a few days after I myself had arrived. She and a thousand other men, women and children. All stripped naked and together."

Again, the doctor was lost in the long, long ago.

"I'm sorry," Roger feebly offered.

"Life did not afford me the opportunity I so wished for, to kiss the hem of her coat. But I had her blessing to take with me, to this day. And that is something."

He looked up at the trees dancing to the wind's beat. Without looking down, he continued. "Hearing of my mother's horrible death brought me again to the depths of what the human being can bear in its soul and in its heart. How ironic that, upon liberation, I felt as if I could not go on. But on I went, nonetheless—on a crowded open-air truck made for troops, headed for Vienna and an uncertain, frightening future.

"We arrived at the *Rathausplatz*, outside the City Hall of Vienna, and I jumped out, having no clue where to go or what to do. Someone suggested the *Altersheim*—the Jewish nursing home and hospital to which we had sent mental patients to save them from deportation.

"Of course, Vienna was nearly in rubble after the war. Many of our most cherished buildings had been decimated by bombing. And the only way for me to get from Rathausplatz to Altersheim was to walk a very long way. The people running the nursing home were very kind to me, offering me a meal and a bed. But the bed was rife with bedbugs, and though it was preferable to camp life, I simply could not stay there.

"Before I left the following morning, however, word came of my wife. She had survived the liberation of Bergen-Belsen camp.

"Only to die shortly thereafter."

Roger didn't even offer his "sorry" this time. His silence seemed to offer more substance.

"Your British allies were the ones to liberate Bergen-Belsen. They appear to have encountered some 60,000 prisoners alive, living amid many—perhaps thousands—of rotting corpses. Many of those still alive could not survive the liberation. They died of malnutrition, disease or both. My Tilly was among them."

Finally, Dr. Frankl's head lowered.

"The ironic thing is, she was so much younger—and had expressed to a friend her fear that I, being older and frail, would not survive the camps. All the while, I was certain that her youth and her usefulness to the Third Reich's war effort would sustain her, given the great deal of luck and providence that all camp survivors required."

Roger hesitated to inject himself, but had to. He made sure he did so delicately and respectfully, though. "Herr Doctor, I have to imagine that hearing the news of the death of your mother and your wife in such rapid succession was as much a test of you as anything the Germans threw at you in the camps."

"I think that you may be right, Herr Murphy. It was a test of my will to survive, a test that not even the worst physical conditions in the camps could have brought about. I now knew that the two lives that had sustained my own during my captivity had been taken.

"I will confess to you, Herr Murphy, that at that point I simply wished not to exist. This was a frightening feeling that, for the most part, had evaded me during my captivity. Thankfully, my good friends in Vienna saw this and did what they could to protect me. They were as worried for my life then—seeing the vacuum in my soul—as they might have been when I was gone for all those months and years.

"Professor Potzl was as kind and as concerned for me as anyone—but had lost his job that very day as chief of psychiatry at the University Clinic, for having been a former member of the Nazi party.

"Dr. Tuchmann took me to see Dr. Bruno Pitterman, whom I had known before. Dr. Pitterman set me up with a typewriter and nearly forced me to apply to the neurological department of the Poliklinik Hospital. I got the job and was head there until 1970!

"Otherwise, I poured my feelings out to my friend Paul Polak. As we stepped out onto his balcony alone, my emotions exploded. I cried and cried, and talked it out. He was so understanding. And it meant so much for him to listen. I needed that desperately.

"Having no one, and questioning my own existence, I buried myself in my work. I hired stenographers—three of them working in shifts. The words exploded out of my mouth until, every now and then, I would tumble into a chair and weep.

"I had made a conscious decision to live—if only to get this book out of my system before I died.

"But despite my despondency, there was something in me that spoke of life, not death. Even as I despaired and released my despair on my friend, Paul Polak, I told him that my suffering had to have some meaning. I just felt there was something waiting for me—that I was destined for some task I could not yet see.

"I clung to this feeling, because that, and my book, were the only things keeping me alive."

"Your writing got you through …"

"I suppose you can say that it did. That and my friends. You see, it was awhile before Pitterman had me sign a blank piece of paper and use that signature as an application for a job for me. As it turned out, I got a choice of heading Steinhof mental hospital, where I worked before the war, or being chief of neurology at the Poliklinik—which was a city clinic not far from where we sit right here. I chose the Poliklinik because of the frustrating bureaucracy of Steinhof. I didn't need such troubles!

"But I didn't start at the Poliklinik until February 1946. It was the publication of my first book, *Ärztliche Seelsorge*—which became *The Doctor and the Soul* in English—that I focused on in late 1945. And when my friends asked for more writing on the experiences in the camps than I had included in the first book, I set out to write *Man's Search for Meaning*. I dictated it in only nine days!

"It was my belief that the book should be published anonymously. I did not believe it should win the author notoriety or literary fame—only that it demonstrate, through the very graphic experiences of one anonymous soul in a concentration camp, the concept that life has unconditional meaning even under the worst of circumstances.

"Well, my friends insisted, I relented, and later editions had my name on the cover—but the first edition, in German, only contains my name on the title page. We did that at the last minute!

"Its first printing was only about 3,000. Its second printing of 1,000 did not sell well at all. But then, I was comforted by the fact that Dr. Freud's great work on psychoanalysis—1,000 copies in its first printing—did not sell out for 10 years!"

"And now," Roger added, "your book—just one of many that you've written—has sold millions, and brought you tourist buses from Japan. How ironic, doctor, that a book that you sincerely intended to be anonymous has become your most famous—and, by all accounts, one of the most influential books of our time."

"The irony is *not* lost on me, but thank you for pointing it out, Herr Murphy. Yet, this is not to, in any way, glorify my contribution. The point here is, simply, that one can attain success, and more, by *not aiming for it*. In fact, the more you *try* to be a success, the less likely it is that you *will* be. The best route to success is through forgetting about it—and simply giving yourself over to a cause or a person greater than yourself.

"Success, like happiness, cannot be your aim. If it is, you will miss it. Both must merely be side-effects of what you do for other ends."

The doctor sat silent and watched a child on roller skates fall, pick herself up, and fall again.

"By the way, let's be clear on what we define as success, Herr Murphy. I believe most people define it in financial or material terms. You can be quite assured that I do not. You have seen my apartment. It is the same apartment, the very same, that I obtained when I returned from the camps. Furthermore, its accoutrements are much the same. I simply do not care for material things. They are not important to me—except for a few things, such as Suffering Man and so on, that have special meaning to me. But they have meaning not because of their monetary value, or the price I had to pay for them.

"Rather, here is a true story illustrating what I consider to be a success: A man who was, for a time, wrongly imprisoned for murder—eventually the true culprit came forward—came to visit us one day. He said that when he was in jail, he was in total despair—until someone gave him *Man's Search for Meaning*. It was the only thing that gave him hope and determination, he said. I feel that was a great success!

"And I once read in *Newsweek* that an Asian politician imprisoned by the dictator he opposed also was sustained by the book. Moreover, not a week goes by without a letter from someone professing that the book had changed their life.

"Now *this*," he said, raising his index finger for emphasis, "*this* is success."

Dr. Frankl drew his jacket around himself as the late-afternoon breeze began to bring a chill with it.

"Herr Murphy, let us away, to ensconce ourselves back within the warmth of the Frankl flat, shall we?"

As they set off on the short walk back to the flat, Roger felt the time with Dr. Frankl melting away.

But he felt he'd never spent time any more wisely.

14

Mrs. Frankl stood in the doorway smiling at the two men.

"I thought perhaps I would be forced to get a date in order to have some company tonight!" she joked loudly.

As she took both the men's coats, Dr. Frankl put his arm around her.

"We have talked long about my adventures and my first wife and so on—too much! But Herr Murphy, you must write about the woman who has been my salvation since 1947!" Mrs. Frankl scoffed audibly, waving her free hand in the air and pulling away to hang up the coats in the foyer's closet across from the door. "She won't hear of it, of course! But I tell you the truth, Herr Murphy, I do believe that this woman's sacrifices have been greater than my own!

"Consider this: Since the second edition of *Man's Search for Meaning*, in 1946, it has been *my* name on all those books and papers. It is *I* who have stood in the light on the stage during all those lectures. It is *I* whom people write to and compliment and ask for advice.

"And I get so wrapped up in all of it—what else can I do? I am so absorbed during dictation, for instance, that one time I was lying in bed with the machine doing dictation and Elly came to remind me that we had to be at the train station in half an hour. Well, I panicked, and with the dictation microphone still in my hand, I actually said, 'Elly, comma, please get my bath ready, exclamation point.' How she laughed!

"But the point of all this is, despite the fact that I have been so absorbed by my work, it has not escaped my notice how much my wife has sacrificed for me. Famed philosopher Jacob Needleman called her 'the warmth that accompanies the light.' And it is absolutely true.

"Elly is in every one of those books, papers and lectures. She has typed her fingers to the bone. She has taken dictation endlessly. She has raised our only daughter, Gabriele—right under my nose, mind you, and I can't reconstruct how for the life of me. She has registered—how many miles, Elly?—following this scalawag all over the planet."

"This is a terrible thing!" Mrs. Frankl nearly shouted, turning back from the closet. "We used to keep a record of all the miles we traveled together. Every mile. But this book was stolen from us during a burglary some time ago. What use can that be to the person who took it? Anyway, all we can do now is guess. We think we have traveled close to 6 million miles. Viktor, do you remember the 1957 world tour? So many places, so many people!"

"We often used fictitious names in the hotels to maintain our privacy," Dr. Frankl divulged, "and occasionally I would slip up and sign my real name on a room service ticket. We imagined the hotel workers had quite a bit of fun at our expense—talking about the old guy who's having an affair with this young thing, but is so old he can't remember which fake name they're using."

The two seemed to be feeding off each other's energy. Roger could see how they could conquer the world and still have fuel left over.

"Do you know, Herr Murphy," Dr. Frankl picked up again excitedly, "that young East Europeans and Russians, even those too poor to justify doing so, used to take German classes just so they could understand my lectures when I came, or read my books that had yet to be translated! This is quite an honor, don't you think?" Roger just nodded and smiled, not wanting to interrupt the flow.

"My wish," added Mrs. Frankl, in mock resentment, "was never to marry a medical doctor and to type. This was not my fervent wish when I was a little girl! And what a scandal it was! A Jew and this little Catholic girl—more than that, we had the audacity to live together before marriage. Ah! This was unheard of at that time."

"Yes, we were a quiet scandal, I am sure," he confessed, "especially considering that, even though I knew that Tilly had died in the camps, I had not yet received *official* word—so, technically, I was not allowed to remarry just yet. This is why we chose the route of living together first."

"But we have been a good team," she added. "It has been a wonderful, fulfilling, interesting life. I have met the greatest people of the 20th century—including Pope Paul VI. As a Catholic, that was very meaningful to me."

"And meaningful to this Jewish neurologist from Vienna!" the doctor shouted, adding, "What was especially meaningful to me was what the pontiff stated just before we left: 'Please pray for me.' Can you believe that? What a statement!"

"Come," invited Mrs. Frankl, eagerly. "Let me show you something else."

She churned down the hall and to the right, through the living room and into the room they called the "Spirit Room"—a place for the Frankls to store all their honorary degrees, plaques and other memorabilia, most of which were simply stacked on shelves. She pulled out a dedication to the Frankls written by Bishop Fulton Sheen.

"Viktor loved to watch Bishop Sheen. Just loved to! Look at what he wrote to us:

> '*To Dr. and Mrs. Frankl,*
>   *Who so long lived in shadows which were the shade of God's hand*
> *outstretched caressingly in love.*'

"To think of our troubles as only the shadows of God's hand that will someday touch us—what a lovely thought."

Roger agreed with her. "Doctor, you have so many awards and honorary degrees here—what are you proudest of?"

"Oh," interrupted Mrs. Frankl. "If he helped someone to overcome the urge to commit suicide, this satisfied him. He was happy about this. But proud? No, I wouldn't say. Viktor is not a proud man. He is a very modest man. About the only thing I know to tell you that he is proud of is that certificate he got for his first solo flight. Viktor learned late in life to fly a plane—he took lessons in California, actually."

"And did he make you take lessons too, like he made you climb mountains?" Roger asked.

"Good heavens, no! I would never do such a thing! But he does wake me up sometimes, at 3 in the morning, to tell me about a situation he might encounter in a plane and to discuss what he might do in such a situation. Why he asks me, I don't know. I don't know anything about flying. Maybe it's just that I'm the only one he can talk to about it at 3 in the morning."

"I shall tell you the greatest honor anyone could have," he returned to the original thought. "It is simply to help others, wherever and whenever we can."

"Ah!" a thought suddenly skipped out of the frisky Frankl. He motioned Roger toward the study. Across the living room, into the study and around the door to the left they went, until they were facing the narrow wall with the fencing foils and a certificate from the city of Austin, Texas. It had seemed totally out of place, and Roger had been meaning to ask about it.

"The U.S. soldiers who liberated us from Turkheim, some of them were from Austin, Texas. Once, when I was in the area, I was invited to visit the mayor of Austin, who made me an honorary citizen of that wonderful city. Of course, I accepted. And you can see, by its placement on my study wall—with not very much else—that it means very much to me.

"But I told the mayor at the time, rather than you make me an honorary citizen, it is I who should make you an honorary logotherapist. If not for your soldiers, who risked and even sacrificed their lives for us, there would be no Viktor Frankl, and there would be no logotherapy. The mayor was quite moved by that thought, although it was merely the truth."

Roger saw that Dr. Frankl was looking fatigued. And the day was late.

"You are tired, and I must leave you alone. But I wonder if you could spare just one more morning. I want to hear more about what you learned, and about the lessons of logotherapy you've been sharing with people all these years."

"Yes, I have tomorrow morning free for you, Herr Murphy."

Roger hesitated, glancing between the Frankls. "I am curious …"

"Yes?"

"… to hear about how you two met."

Dr. Frankl suddenly looked bushy-tailed and raring to go. "Come, let's sit for a moment in the living room and talk. Elly, let's have coffee!"

They settled in on the plain green furniture, Roger in a chair, the Frankls on the couch together. She poured coffee, which had been at the ready, and offered Roger some sort of fritters, which he sampled.

"What were your first impressions of each other?"

Dr. Frankl looked very stern. "Herr Murphy, it just so happens that I do very adequate impressions of many people, but alas, not my wife. But I will tell you what I first thought of her, if that will do."

Roger marveled at how such a great man could be so downright goofy. "Yes," Roger smiled. "That would do very nicely."

"I was working at the Poliklinik, the city hospital, as head of neurology, in 1946. But as 'Primarius'—my title as department head—I had no reason to know of Eleonore Schwindt, a 20-year-old nurse in dentistry."

"Oh, but I knew of Herr Dr. Primarius," she exclaimed with wide eyes. "I had not yet met him, but his reputation was widespread."

"You mean of a budding author, a famous doctor?"

"No, of a very difficult man!" Mrs. Frankl laughed heartily. "At this time, there were not that many men in Vienna—and many of the ones who *were* there were somehow disabled from the war. And here was this still rather young Dr. Frankl. Well, all the women had to be interested in marrying this kind of man: stable, with a good career—and breathing. And I am quite sure he got around …"

Dr. Frankl's impish smile was his guilty plea.

"But he also had this reputation of being difficult, so one day when we needed a bed for an oral surgery patient to recuperate in, the nurses and aides were debating whether to approach the fearful Primarius. I couldn't believe it. 'My goodness, how bad can it be? Let me do it.' And do you know, the others looked at me as if I had just agreed to be executed. And I remember thinking, after he instantly agreed to give me the bed, that he was really quite a nice man. A little odd, perhaps. But nice."

"Aha! Always respect your first impressions, Herr Murphy," Dr. Frankl joked.

"Well, my colleagues were shocked. Absolutely shocked," she continued. "They asked me, 'Did he shout? Was he upset?' I assured them that no, he was quite cordial about it. They thought that perhaps I had talked to the wrong man."

Roger turned to Dr. Frankl, who needed no cue.

"She was quite confident and assertive, which I liked, but not rough. She interrupted our rounds to ask me about the bed, but she did so with grace. I watched her walk back up the stairs toward her department, and remarked to a colleague, 'Did you see those *eyes*?' For me, it was love at first sight!"

"For me," she chuckled, "it was a bed for our patient. I thought nothing about it, until a few days later when I saw him again and he told me he had a terrible, terrible toothache."

Dr. Frankl explained: "It was blatant lie, I must admit! It was also the day I discovered a rich acting talent I never knew I had."

"Well, I believed him! And I told him it was a simple matter for our head of neurology to come up to our department and be seen by a dentist."

"But I told her I was deathly afraid of dentists," he continued, "and always had been. I told her that she would have to lasso me and drag me to the chair if a dentist were involved. I needed a capable nurse; only that would do."

"So the next day," she chortled, "just for fun I made a lasso out of gauze and went to his office and started to swing it as if I were going to put it around his neck. He smiled and agreed to come peacefully, without the noose."

"But on the way up, I told her the truth—that both my toothache and my supposed fear of dentists were only a ruse—that my real aim was to see her again."

"Well, of course, what else could I be but delighted?" she laughed. "I always loved a good prank, and here the Primarius was playing one on me—in order to flirt."

"I asked her to come see my apartment—the same one in which you are now sitting, although at that time I had many housemates here. I told her that I had killed the most poisonous snake in the country, and had preserved it in a jar."

"I didn't know if this, too, was a prank, but I thought it might be fun to find out."

"This part was true! I did indeed have a snake."

"Not too many days later, I was walking past his apartment on the way to the Poliklinik, and I looked up. In his window was the lasso I had made. Well, of course, it was hilarious, and very romantic of him to do that. He might as well have used it to lasso my heart."

"And why not?" he chimed in. "She had mine from the start. You know, there were other women at the Poliklinik, and they were—how may I put this?—a bit over-solicitous, always coming by. Elly was not this way at all."

"And I could not believe the way Viktor was."

"What do you mean?" asked Roger.

"Well, as our friendship grew, he began to talk more and more about his experiences in the concentration camps, the conditions there, his close calls with death and, of course, about the horrible deaths of his mother and first wife. And yet, I saw no bitterness in this man. None at all. When we talked about this—his experiences in the camps—he said, 'Now you know everything, and I think it's over. It's over.' This is when I knew I loved him.

"And then, the accident."

"The accident?" asked Roger.

Dr. Frankl answered for her. "Elly had been in a streetcar that was hit by a car, and she was suffering headaches and problems with her hands. I was worried, and admitted her to the Poliklinik. So now she was one of my patients."

"And sitting there among the other female patients," she continued for him, "I was amazed at how they were swimming around Viktor, in their minds, like sharks after prey. My! They did not know about my relationship with Viktor. So, right in front of me, how they would primp themselves before he arrived, and talk about catching him. One patient even admitted that the only reason she was in the hospital was not because she was sick, but because she wanted to marry Viktor."

"But only Elly had the lasso! At first, I was afraid she could never love me—I was old enough to be her father! Then, when it appeared she did, I was afraid her affections were more out of pity than anything else. Pity for what I had gone through, and all. But then, she wrote me the most beautiful little note. I still have it. It said, simply:

'It is not pity, but love.'

"I was alone when I read it, so there is no reason to confess this, as no one would know any better. But her note made me sob like a baby. We did not know each other before the war. And so there is no way either one of us could have expected the other. Yet, her note made it clear to me that, as I had promised the other prisoners, someone was indeed waiting for me."

15

"So," he intoned, pausing for a few seconds. "We have come to the nub of the question. The reason you are here."

"Yes sir, I guess we have." Roger was facing Dr. Frankl behind his desk for perhaps the last time. He had one morning in which to extract the rest of the gold from this rich mine. It was like being given a 15-second shopping spree at Fort Knox. There just wasn't enough time to do it justice. But the two men would simply have to do their best.

"I'd like to get to the very heart of logotherapy and what it means," Roger proposed, "but if you could ..."

"Yes. Just ask."

"I'm hazy on its relationship to psychotherapy."

"This is a good question. Do not be shy about asking it. Someone once described, in somewhat flippant terms, what psychoanalysis is. He said it was where a patient lies on a couch and says many things that are not pleasant to tell. I responded, also somewhat flippantly, that logotherapy is where a patient lies on a couch or sits in a chair—his choice—but must *hear* things that are not pleasant to *hear*.

"This is a joke, but not completely inaccurate. Psychoanalysis is very intro-spective, and, in my opinion, can have the unintended ill-effect of making a neurotic person chronically self-centered. Logotherapy is focused on the future, on self-transcendence, on the outer world—on meanings that could fulfill one's life—and, therefore, tends to act *against* self-centeredness. I will try to explain it as simply as I can.

"The Freudian school holds that the primary motivator in the human being is the will to *pleasure*; the Adlerian school holds that the will to *power* is controlling—a striving for dominance.

"I do not reject these arguments. In fact, I believe they are absolutely true—as far as they go. I only maintain that they are *not* the primary motivating force in human beings, and as a result, they too narrowly define what it is to be human. In fact, in many ways, they *ignore* what it is to be human. For, after all, these two things—the will to pleasure and the will to dominance—are true about all animals, are they not?

"Surely we are different from the animals. And our differences from the animals are the essence of what it means to be human.

"Logotherapy holds that the primary motivator among human beings is the will to *meaning*. You can see this anecdotally, but it is also scientifically recognizable; the evidence is all around us of man's search for meaning—and what happens when that search is fruitless, frustrated.

"The other two schools of thought miss this phenomenon because they fall short of looking in the right place: in the unique human dimension of existence, which includes spirituality, values, ideals, self-transcendence and sacrifice. They are, in effect, looking for humanity in the basement—where animal drives are stored—when, in fact, humanness is upstairs.

"Consider the rich and powerful. They have access to all the pleasures on Earth. And they have dominion over others. But so often, it is they who are the most troubled, the most unhappy. How can this be so, if pleasure and power is what drives them? I'll tell you why: Because these things are not the most important thing to a human being. The primary motivator in these people—the will to meaning—has, for whatever reason, been unfulfilled. One possible reason is self-centeredness. There is not much spiritual meaning in glorifying oneself.

"It is in these cases that I say that man has the means to a good life, but not the meaning.

"So, you see, the will to meaning can be identified and recognized not only in its presence, but in its absence—when it is frustrated. As I have noted before, I call the lack of meaning the 'existential vacuum.' And it is worse today than ever."

Dr. Frankl became excited now.

"And do you know what is so maddening? My psychoanalyst colleagues will tell their patients that their depression is an illness! Well, perhaps it *is* in a particular case. But in many cases, it is not a neurosis or illness at all. Quite to the contrary, it is a manifestation of man's will to meaning—something one can look to out there that is good or great to live for other than oneself. That phenomenon, far from being an illness, is really the *best* of what it means to be a human."

"Doctor, why does the existential vacuum, as you call it, seem worse today than ever?"

"There are two chief culprits, as I see it. First, as opposed to animals, man is not a slave to his drives and instincts—those things that tell him what he *must* do. Second, if there is a waning of traditions within a society, as we see today, man is no longer told what he *should* do. He is then left only with what he *wishes* to do—and he may not know! This is a particularly dangerous situation for the self-centered."

"I have to believe there was a huge existential vacuum in the camps," Roger conjectured. "How did you fight it?"

"Well, for one thing you had to nip it close to the bud. Once a man had started down the path of despair, it was difficult to bring him back—next to impossible to come back from it himself. And, I don't think I mentioned, there was actually a rule against cutting down a man who was hanging himself. So it was imperative to prevent him from trying in the first place.

"The typical argument in favor of suicide was that one had nothing more to expect from life. But we turned that argument on its head, so to speak, by suggesting that, just perhaps, *life had more to expect from them!*

"What could that something be that life expected? It could be living for, or simply loving, someone else; it could be creating a great work. Or, arguably, it could be the suffering itself. What greater accomplishment than to simply survive the kind of suffering in the concentration camps? While no one would ever rationally bring something like that on himself, living through such things with bravery and dignity—even dying the right way— was something to be extremely proud of. This alone has meaning.

"Why, our very individuality gives life meaning. No one else can do what you do. No one could possibly replace you; you are absolutely unique.

"Herr Murphy, this uniqueness carries with it a tremendous responsibility! Once you are aware of this responsibility—to someone else, to a cause, to your unfinished work, to things and people in the future that have yet to be revealed to you—you are persuaded not only that there is meaning, but that you have a *responsibility* to it.

"One problem that our young, especially, face, is impatience. If they cannot see it now, today, this very moment, it does not exist to them. Therefore, they lack the vision and patience to accept the fact that the various meanings in their lives may not be apparent yet. They need to understand that someone, or something, waits for them in the future—a task, for instance, that only they, as unique beings, can be responsible for.

"You asked me how to fill the existential vacuum. No one can do that for you, but they can help you. I have tried to do that, by identifying the three main ways one can find meaning in life: 1) through work and deed-doing; 2) through love; and 3) through suffering."

Roger crossed his legs and folded his arms. "Doctor, what you're talking about is a serious paradigm change in how we think of life. From what life owes us to what we owe life."

"Exactly! And yes, I understand how difficult this can be. I have attempted to make this shift in attitude, in myself and in those around me, in the most difficult of circumstances—at a time, in the concentration camps, in which it is nearly impossible to believe that anything has meaning. But what we learned was true: It doesn't matter what we expect out of life, but rather, what life expects of us. Thus, we need to stop demanding of life, and start paying attention to the demands that *life puts on us!*

"It is not for us to question life! It is for us only to answer the questions that life poses to *us*. You see?

"This is why your initial question to me a few days ago was not entertained, Herr Murphy. Life has no general, universal meaning—not one that we, as mere humans, can ascertain, anyway. In logotherapy, we refer to this as the 'supermeaning.' Rather, because each individual is unique, as we have seen here, and each situation, each moment, of that unique creature's life also is unique, life carries different meanings at different times for different people. Do you see?

"Only you can ascertain the various meanings in your life. No one else. It is not only your responsibility, it is your destiny!"

"Doctor, you must understand how difficult it is for someone who has not suffered as you have, and triumphed over it, to fathom how to focus on the bright side of it."

"Yes. Remember, one does not have to be in a concentration camp to suffer greatly. It is man's special burden to suffer, in all manners of the word. The question that life asks of you at such times, however, is how you will bear that burden. In the camps, I found that actions were more important than the best words. Say what you will about bravery, dignity, facing your suffering—the important thing was to put these things into action. Showing a right example, in any situation, is a very powerful way to make a statement without opening one's mouth.

"And I don't mean not to cry. Certainly, it was important in our circumstance to keep tears to a minimum. But tears were—and are today— nothing to be ashamed of. Quite the opposite, they demonstrate one of man's greatest acts of courage: the courage to face one's suffering.

"The principles and behaviors I am speaking of are all thought processes and acts that exist far above the animal world's primitive capabilities— thoughts and acts of self-transcendence, of sacrifice, of focusing on the future. Man is alone in his ability to exist in this dimension. All animals suffer. But man is capable of facing up to unavoidable suffering and, in fact, turning it into a triumph. This, an animal cannot do."

"Yes, doctor, but this, too, seems paradoxical."

"But Herr Murphy, you must not always run and hide from a paradox. Sometimes it is just the thing. We have not talked about my method of 'paradoxical intention,' have we?"

"No, sir."

"I began to use it well before the camps, in 1929, although it was not given a name until 1939. Let's take some irrational, or baseless, fear—say, of going outside. The real problem, as we know, is not the outside. Most of us go outside every day and turn out fine. The problem for the patient, then, is the fear itself, yes? So, we fight that by teaching the patient not to resist the thing they fear—and, in fact, to embrace it. Eventually, the focus comes off the fear, and it goes away.

"We had one patient with just such a fear. We told him to run outside and try to have a heart attack. We told him to pretend that yesterday he had two heart attacks, but that today it is still early and he has time for *three* heart attacks.

"Of course, he could not do that; one cannot will himself a heart attack. But in *trying* to do so, his fear of it lifted. The paradox is in telling the patients to actually *want* what they fear, to invite it on themselves. So, you see, paradoxes are not always bad.

"Now, to your question about suffering ever being 'good.' While work and love are the most advisable avenues toward meaning in life, suffering—when it is unavoidable—can actually bring the *most* meaning. Why? Because if you face it well, it can elicit in you the highest and most admirable characteristics of a human being. Moreover, I submit that the highest and best form of humanity may be our ability—unique among all living things—to actually turn our tragedies and sufferings into triumphs. I most often use the example of one who is stricken with an incurable disease, yet has the opportunity to face it nobly and with dignity and strength. Why, Elisabeth Kubler-Ross even called death 'The Final Stage of Growth.'

"When we can no longer change our circumstances, all that is left is to change ourselves, you see. We have a choice of whether to change ourselves for better or worse. I tell you, and I believe this with every cell of my being, Herr Murphy, life can have meaning under any circumstances, and up to your last breath. Think about this: You are being told by a man who may have seen the worst of what life has to offer that, even under its worst conditions, life had meaning. Does this not mean that the meaning of life is unconditional? That life holds unconditional meaning?"

Roger pondered the thought. He was way out of his league intellectually, and he knew he was only skimming the surface of this man's brain. But the doctor was putting things in easily explainable terms. And his logic was unassailable.

"Let me give you an example that does not involve me or my suffering," Dr. Frankl continued. "I have many such examples from patients over the years. But I am especially fond of this one. A fellow medical practitioner came to me with severe depression over the death of his wife. She had died two years earlier; she had been his world. Now, how should I have treated him, Herr Murphy? Do you think his despair was a 'disease' as such? Of course not. Was there any surgical procedure I could have performed to either erase the memory of her or bring her back? Of course not.

"Here's what I did. I asked him: 'What would have happened if you had died, instead of your wife?' He instantly said, 'Oh, she would have been wracked with grief as I am.' So, I said, 'Well, in living beyond her, you have saved her this suffering. Instead, you have taken it on yourself, and have saved her from it.'

"At that moment, his suffering had taken on a meaning that, previously, had been lost on him. He still suffered; I did not magically take that from him. What I *did* do was lessen that suffering by helping reveal its uplifting meaning for him. Now, not only was his suffering more understandable, but he saw it as an achievement: He could see that by bearing it, he saved his wife from the same fate."

Roger looked out the bay windows and his problems flashed by his eyes in a second. "So what you did was change his attitude toward his suffering."

"Precisely. You know, today's literature and clinicians have a terrible habit of informing you that, not only do you have a right to be happy—perhaps there are lawyers to make certain of this?—but you must avoid suffering at all costs. Clearly, my example with my medical colleague is evidence that not all suffering is avoidable—and that it's a mistake to attempt to run from it.

"Edith Weisskopf-Joelson, a professor of psychology at the University of Georgia, saw this mistake, and wrote about it, and the value of logotherapy, before her death. She wrote that the cult in which unhappiness is considered a disease, or a maladjustment, actually *increases* the amount of unhappiness by inducing people to be unhappy about their *unhappiness*. And she was right!

"Let me tell you of a time when I visited a group therapy session that involved a woman who was suicidal. Her 11-year-old boy was dead, and her only remaining child was crippled. She had taken steps toward killing herself and her crippled boy, but, notably, he stopped her. He was utterly resolute in his love for life, even in a wheelchair. Now, the question: how to give the woman a sense that her life had as much meaning as her crippled son's?

"Well, I challenged the group to imagine they were on their death beds in their old age. One woman imagined she had gone on to marry rich and have a pleasurable life—but a childless and, ultimately, meaningless existence. But when I asked the woman with the crippled son to look back on her own life, as if on her own death bed, she imagined a life having cared for her crippled son. She 'recalled' she had suffered much, but had done her best to make a good life for her son, and was proud for having done so. In this way, the woman foresaw a life that was difficult, but highly meaningful. And how she cried then!

"Too often we want meaning in our lives to only be easy and pleasurable. But some of the greatest meaning a human being can realize is through necessary suffering. Life questions each man. His best answer is simply to be responsible. In being responsible—to life, to others, to causes, to principles—we find the essence of being human.

"In fact," the doctor stopped, pausing to look at Roger for a moment, "I have long admired your country's emphasis on individual liberty. Your Statue of Liberty is a tremendous beacon to the world. But I have also long thought that you should have another statue, on your west coast, to go with your Statue of Liberty on your east coast. This statue would be the 'Statue of Responsibility,' a reminder that with rights come responsibilities. And what a grand monument to the very essence of humanness. Don't you agree?"

As Roger nodded, he saw Dr. Frankl's eyes sparkle behind his glasses.

◆   ◆   ◆

The morning was late, the time nigh to leave.

"It is nearly time for me to leave you," Roger almost grieved after a short break. "I can't thank you enough for all the time you've afforded me, doctor. But I have several more questions before I go."

"Fire away, young man. I shall help if I can."

"Well, we've talked a lot about the meaning that can be found in suffering—how you confirmed that the hard way. And you have obviously found much meaning in your work. But the third path to meaning—love."

"Yes."

"I'm interested in your thoughts on that, because—with all due respect, sir—I suspect you are nothing but a closet romantic."

Dr. Frankl nearly toppled his chair from laughing. "I suspect you are correct, Herr Murphy."

"It seems like," continued Roger, "love and sex are often confused."

"And what a tragedy! But logotherapy tries to turn this tragedy into a triumph, so to speak. Love is much more than the outgrowth of sexual urges and drives. Take, for example, our experiences in the concentration camps. Beyond the first experiences in Theresienstadt, where we doctors helped each other arrange clandestine conjugal visits with our wives, our very survival became tested. Between work and exhaustion and discomfort and starvation and the fear that any moment might be our last, the sexual urge had completely vanished.

"But thoughts of love? They never escaped us, not even in our darkest days. In fact, while the phenomenon of sex became irrelevant, for most of us the phenomenon of love became paramount to our existence. The thought of my loved one gave me the strength to live on. So when push comes to shove, as we say, the uniquely human experience of love triumphs over one's basement-level sexual drives.

"And thank the heavens! Love, after all, is the only path on which one soul can truly meet up with another. Loving another, truly loving another, involves accepting and understanding and embracing the other person's very essence. And not only that, but in loving another you see more than his or her essence: You see their *potential*. And by recognizing your loved one's potential, you bring it out in him or her—making them a better human being in the process. Just by loving!"

With a nod of the head, Roger shut off the recorder and began packing his things. In part to fill what he felt was an awkward silence, Roger glanced up at the portrait of Tilly Grosser Frankl and stood erect.

"Well, doctor, I was right about one thing all week. You *are* a closet romantic!"

Again, Dr. Frankl nearly convulsed with laughter while getting up and walking around his desk. "You have missed your calling, Herr Murphy. I do believe you have a future in psychology!" He shook Roger's hand, and the two men stood shoulder-to-shoulder and looked at the portrait of Tilly. "I have been very blessed, with two great loves. I suppose, even as I buried myself in my work, I always was a romantic at heart, all my life.

"Something that happened shortly after my liberation at Turkheim, though, may have set that romantic notion in concrete. Do you remember the walk I took in the meadow, when I fell on my knees and repeated a prayer of thanks over and over? Well, on that same walk, I encountered a man who had a little bauble in his hands. When I asked to see it, I saw that it was the same necklace that I had given Tilly and which had been taken from her— the *very same*! Only a very few of them had been made, to my knowledge. And I insisted on buying it from him, which I did.

"This bauble, hanging from a necklace, was a depiction of the Earth, with these words inscripted on it:

'The world turns on love'

"Well, my son," Dr. Frankl smiled, putting his hand on Roger's shoulder, "I can tell you from experience: It does!"

◆   ◆   ◆

Mrs. Frankl was magically awaiting the men in the foyer to bid Roger goodbye. Roger was touched that she would take the trouble. It seemed to be more than mere Austrian courtesy. He *knew* it was more, when Mrs. Frankl rejected his extended hand and held out for a hug.

"This is permitted, yes?" she intoned in her thick, high-pitched accent.

Even if he could ignore the surprising sentiment behind it, Roger could not resist the adorableness of this short, cute fireball. She gathered him up in an Austrian bear hug, with a warmth and acceptance that he suspected was reserved for only the very privileged.

"So, you will be writing about our little talk?" Dr. Frankl asked.

"Yes. I believe I will."

Mrs. Frankl piped up, "You will be able to send us what you write?"

Roger was amazed that this couple, which had seen so much written about them all over the world, would express an interest in his modest contribution. "Yes, of course."

Dr. Frankl extended his hand.

"Herr Murphy, it has been a great pleasure. Please do stay in touch, and we sincerely wish that you would visit our humble home again."

"Thank you," Roger said humbly. "I sure hope to." And he meant it.

Dr. Frankl kept ahold of Roger's hand. "I certainly hope that something I have shared with you over the course of the last few days has, in some way, helped you, Herr Murphy. I know your colleagues thought that you might benefit from making my acquaintance—and this was without their knowing of the newfound threat to your health."

As Mrs. Frankl pulled open the door to the flat, Dr. Frankl let loose of Roger's hand, but put his hand back on Roger's shoulder, walking him the few steps down the dim hallway toward the elevator cage. "Just remember the power of your attitude, Herr Murphy. Remember your spiritual freedom. Apathy can be overcome. Fear can be conquered. The best of you can surface at your most trying time.

"We in the camps saw this often, in the men who maintained their dignity in the face of death, and in those whose self-transcendence knew no bounds—starving men who would somehow give up their last scrap of food, or a word of encouragement, to the sick and despairing.

"These men, who seemingly had everything taken from them when they entered the camps, discovered the one thing that could never, by any means, be taken from them: the freedom to choose one's own attitude, no matter what the circumstances.

"This," he concluded, "is the last of the human freedoms."

As the gate shut, and the elevator took Roger down toward the lobby, he watched as Viktor Frankl ascended out of sight.

16

Sorrow crashed over Roger Murphy like a bay wave tossed by an earthquake.

He wasn't even sure why, really. Partly over the fact that his time with Dr. Frankl was over. In the short few days that he'd had the privilege to be near the man, Roger had begun to feel again. It had been so long, he couldn't remember the feeling of feeling. Like Frankl with his friend Paul Polak, the floodgates of feeling now seemed to open.

And there was something about the man that just made you feel good. About yourself. Things. The world. Roger felt diminished by leaving that.

He also felt his own suffering was dwarfed by that of the concentration camp survivor. Despite Dr. Frankl's sincere belief that his suffering could not be held up as anything greater than anyone else's, Roger knew this was not so. And so, sitting on the same bench in the courtyard he had shared with Dr. Frankl, Roger felt a great sense of guilt for not having faced up to his own suffering with more dignity and strength.

Dr. Frankl might have been a neurologist and psychiatrist, but he might as well have been an optometrist, Roger thought. He helps people see more clearly.

And, in retrospect, Roger realized that he had yet to have an emotional release of any kind after his diagnosis. So, for various reasons, he was overdue. And out it came.

Gathering himself, Roger turned his thoughts to his remaining hours in Vienna. It was now just after noon; he would be flying out late the next morning. Aside from digesting some of what the doctor had taught him—it was an awful lot to assimilate—Roger wanted to use those remaining hours to get a parting gift for the Frankls, and perhaps to find firm ground again.

Just as he was getting up to go, Roger saw a squirrel at the base of an oak tree nearby. Roger thought for a second and looked down.

He slipped off his shoe and hopped over on one foot to within about four feet of the puzzled little creature. He found an acorn, smashed it with his shoe and held the treat out for the squirrel—making that puckering noise that, for no particular reason, people make when trying to entice a timid animal. After a few moments, the squirrel zig-zagged over in spurts, and finally grabbed the offering and ran.

Roger knew it was totally inconsequential. But it made his afternoon.

17

Roger didn't recognize the voice answering the intercom at the Frankl apartment building.

"Dr. Frankl isn't here. Please call in a few days for an appointment, if you will," the voice buzzed.

Roger pressed the button. "This is Roger Murphy; I've been interviewing Dr. Frankl the past few days, and I just wanted to leave him a little something—a gift, actually—on the way out of town. I won't stay long."

There was the slightest pause, which seemed forever. Roger felt like he was trying to see the Wizard of Oz.

"Please forgive me. I didn't know. Come in. You know the way, then?"

"Yes, thank you."

Roger was surprised, and pleased, to see that the voice had been that of Harald Mori, the Frankls' young friend and sometimes-bouncer. Harald was subdued, but warm and welcoming.

"So good to see you again, Mr. Murphy. I'm sorry to have been a bit standoffish at the intercom, but, you see, there's been—an incident."

"I hope everybody's …" Roger was cut short by the sound of Mrs. Frankl's voice down the hall.

"Oh, Herr Murphy, good morning." Her bustle was bustling, but her spirit subdued, her tone muted. "You are leaving this morning, yes? I am sorry not to be able to see you at the moment. I'm on the way—has Harald told you?"

"No, ma'am. Told me what?"

"Viktor! He's in the hospital!"

"What? Whatever for?"

"He is blind!"

Roger's bag slid off his arm to the ground with a thud, as his shoulders wilted. "Blind? How? What happened?"

"It was last night. About 7:30. I was in the kitchen, and Viktor was in his study watching the news on television. All of a sudden he called to me, several times. I knew something was wrong. When I got there, he howled, 'Elly, I am blind!' Just like that! He could not see out of one eye. With the other, he had partial vision, but not good at all. I don't know the English word for it. He could only see a little out of the sides of that one eye."

Roger felt a pang of guilt immediately. "I'm sorry, Frau Frankl. Especially for monopolizing him so much the past few days."

"Oh, do not feel this way. Not at all. Dr. Frankl chose to use his time this way. He was glad to do it. Besides, you had nothing to do with it. But Viktor is at the hospital, and I was only here for a short time and must go back."

"I understand. Please send him my sympathies."

"I will, thank you. Now," she stopped. "Oh, wait. There is something for you, and I know that Viktor would want me to give it to you. Please …" She motioned him to follow her down the hall and to the left, into the dormant study. Harald followed the two in.

Out of the desk, she pulled two white sheets of paper. "I don't know if you know this or not, but Viktor is quite an artist. He drew this especially for you."

Roger immediately glowed like a Van Gogh. Harald looked over his shoulder. "You should be quite honored, Mr. Murphy. Dr. Frankl does not make caricatures of everyone. Only people he likes very much." Roger looked back at him and nodded, and turned back to the drawing. "It is an amazing likeness of you, don't you think?"

"Perfect."

The drawing featured Roger's ample black hair, parted in the middle and flowing backward, and his glasses larger than life. He was sitting at a typewriter. In the typewriter was a piece of paper. Typed on it were the words, "The meaning of life." The man's sense of humor seemed to have no bounds.

"That is not all," declared Mrs. Frankl. "Viktor wanted you to have this, too."

Roger took another piece of paper from her. It was a rather crude drawing. But Roger recognized it right away.

"The Statue of Responsibility," he whispered through his smile. It appeared to be an original drawing, not a copy. "You're sure he meant for *me* to have this?" he asked Mrs. Frankl.

"Yes, Herr Murphy. I am sure of it."

Mrs. Frankl looked at Roger's bag and realized she'd better make some other provisions. "Here. Allow me to …" She took the two drawings and put them in a worn blue folder, folding the edges and taping them shut to fashion a protective case. "There! Now the drawings will be safe in your bag."

Returning to a more harried state, Mrs. Frankl accompanied Roger downstairs and out of the building, where they exchanged a quick goodbye.

She went one way, toward the hospital, and he the other, toward the series of streetcars, subways and buses that would ferry him to the airport and his flight home.

He felt like a man returning from war in Europe. He felt like he had lived through one of his own before he came, and then through Viktor Frankl's. And he knew he faced several more wars back at home—the battle to retain his job, amid the doubts about him, and the scrambling in the newsroom to replace him.

And, of course, the quiet battle for his life raging inside him.

As the plane hit its lofty plateau, and Vienna fell away through the thin clouds, Roger pulled out a T-shirt he'd bought. He'd asked the shirt shop to print one of his favorite Frankl sayings on it:

What is to give light must endure burning.

Roger was contemplating the thought when another one hit him like a brick.

He put the T-shirt down and reached into his soft briefcase until he found his notes. Whisking through the pages, he finally came to the place he wanted: the part where Dr. Frankl had told him what his father exclaimed out of the blue during their march into Theresienstadt. It was the phrase that Dr. Frankl had uttered only in German, and had challenged Roger to find the translation of.

"Excuse me," Roger stopped the stewardess walking by. "Do you know German?"

"Yes, I do. How may I help you?"

"Can you tell me what this means?" He showed her his notes, which said, "*Immer nur heiter, Gott hilft schon weiter.*"

"Yes. It says, 'Be always cheerful, for God will help us.'"

18

Roger's apartment was cold and dark, and stayed that way even after he'd slapped at the wall to find the light switch. There was a card on the floor, which he took out to the hall to read under the dim light. He knew it was trouble when a bright red "NOTICE" was staring at him right away.

"Oops," he muttered to himself after reading his power had been cut off for nonpayment. "So that's how it works." He smiled to himself—mostly in amazement. More characteristically, he would have put his fist through a wall. But here he was making a joke of it and smiling. He might just take this in stride—even though it was Saturday night, and there would be no power until Monday at the earliest.

He leaned against the second-floor hallway wall and thought for a moment. What would Viktor do? "I know what he'd do," Roger mumbled. "He'd laugh, get on his knees and thank God nothing worse has happened today."

"Still," Roger mumbled, pushing himself off the wall, "doesn't mean I want to be here."

And just like that, he had a plan.

He brought his duffel bag back out to the hallway, dug out a couple packages and his shaving kit and took it into the dark bathroom, leaving the duffel propping the door open for what little light that provided. When he'd finished, he threw his duffel into the apartment, grabbed the packages and headed downstairs.

"Murphy!" The voice stopped him as he was curving around the stairway on the first floor headed to the lobby.

"Hey, Sherm!" Roger realized it was probably the first time he'd ever sounded enthusiastic about seeing his downstairs neighbor and building super. And the feeling was sincere.

It was also apparently mutual: Sherman Case came up without another word and gave Roger a bear hug. Ever since the earthquake—and since Roger had moved into a new Sherman-run building just a block from their old one—Sherman seemed afraid to let Roger out of his sight.

"Great to have you back! How was the trip? How'd the interview go? Where you headed? It's past nine, you know."

Roger chuckled. Sherman should be the journalist, he thought, he's so inquisitive. "It went well. Very well. No, actually, great. Thanks for asking. But I forgot to pay the light bill, so …"

"I'll bet it's cold. Stay with *us* tonight. I insist. Do you like bagels and cream cheese? How about real blackberry jam?"

Again, Roger chuckled. "I don't know. Can I let you know in a bit? I've got some friends to see."

"Oh, I get it," Case snapped, pretending to look angry. "You're going to choose a 20-something girl over me, right?"

"Might be."

"I'll never figure out your taste." Case turned and walked to his apartment and, before going in, turned and added, "We're up till midnight. I'll leave a key over the door and a blanket on the couch just in case she kicks your butt out!"

Roger smiled, shook his head in amazement and went out into the cool San Francisco night air—though it was actually warmer than in his apartment. And, at least outside, one expects cold air.

◆   ◆   ◆

Roger hesitated slightly before knocking. What he was about to do was crazy—which, despite what others might think, wasn't totally out of character for him. But this kind of crazy was.

"Hi, Sunny. How you doing? I was in the neighborhood and I …"

Sunny McHenry never looked at Roger nicely, but right now she was looking at him as if he were quite insane.

"I was wondering—could I come in for a minute?"

Too shocked to say no, even if she'd wanted to, Sunny backed up to let him through like a matador inviting in a bull, and closed the door behind him, still speechless.

Though he'd been to her apartment before, that was when it was full with partiers. So he looked around now as if it were the first time he'd set foot in the place. "Nice place you've got here," he said, realizing how trite it was, but actually meaning it. She still wasn't saying a thing. Picking up a photo of a 30ish man from a table, Roger asked, "Brother?" When he heard no response, he moved his gaze from the photo to Sunny, still standing just off the foyer and still speechless.

"No," she finally whispered. "My husband."

"Husband?" Roger was genuinely shocked. "I never knew you were married. Didn't take, huh?"

She walked around the end table now and sat on the sofa facing him. "No, actually it took quite nicely. He died in a plane crash eight years ago."

Roger guessed he might have to start keeping track of his social blunders in America now, too. "I'm so sorry," he grimaced, placing the photo on the table as gingerly as if it were the body itself. "I guess we've never really talked…"

"I guess not," she agreed, tucking her hair over her shoulder. "Is that why I've been so privileged tonight? So we can talk?"

"Actually, yes." Roger sat himself down on a comforter-covered loveseat facing her. "Mind if I sit? I realize we've never really been on good terms, and—well, I was hoping to change that."

Sunny stiffened and seemed to shift a foot taller in the sofa. "If this is about the column, Murphy, forget it. I don't want your job. I'm happy with what I'm doing. OK?"

Roger smiled and exhaled, partly a sigh and partly a chuckle. He didn't know whether to believe her or not, but he didn't care. "No, it's not about that at all. Nothing else but—mending fences, I suppose."

"I see. You got religion in Vienna?"

"No. Maybe. I don't know," he tottered, a bit thrown off balance by the suggestion. "But, I did get this."

Roger reached into his green Army-style coat and pulled out a small gift-wrapped package, and raised up enough from his seat to reach over the glass coffee table to hand it to her.

She took a moment to register the fact that he was offering her a gift, and raised up slightly to take it from him. She looked at him quizzically and put the gift to her ear. "Just checking to see if it's ticking," she smirked. She opened it, and inside a five-inch rectangular box was a baby grand piano.

She looked up at him, and he'd never seen her eyes so large, not even through those thick lenses of her big round glasses.

"Open the piano. Go ahead. Lift up the lid."

As she did, it began playing "Edelweiss" from *The Sound of Music*—which, as far as Americans are concerned, is the national anthem of Austria.

"Thank you," she nearly sobbed. "I love this song."

It was late, Roger had more he wanted to do, and he didn't want to spoil the moment by wallowing in it. So he got up to leave.

"I won't keep you. I just wanted to …"

Before he could finish, she'd wrapped him in a hug tighter than Sherman's. Stunned, his hands found her back slowly and softly. She held him for what felt like half an hour—and at one point, he thought he heard her sobbing.

Finally, she loosened her grip, composed herself and walked him to the door. She thanked him and, just before letting him by, she grabbed his arm. "You need to know something. Jake, my husband. He was a concert pianist." Roger nodded slightly, glancing at the real baby grand in her apartment, and smiled at her gently. "So you can see, this is pretty meaningful to me."

As the door closed behind him, Roger thought it amazing that such meaning could be found in the most unexpected gestures.

He also realized how much less the hills seemed to bother him now.

◆   ◆   ◆

"You still wanting to help the homeless?" Roger asked.

With a high-pitched squeal, Melody Vasquez leaped through her apartment's threshold to grab Roger. He felt like he was on a hugging tour of San Francisco.

"When did you get back? Come in!"

She was almost whispering, but with great force and enthusiasm. Roger had hoped Melody would be glad to see him. He had no idea she'd be *this* glad.

"Just about an hour ago."

Melody led him by hand over to the overstuffed couch, the only real furniture in her small apartment's living room.

"So you came to see me first thing?" She really was touched.

"Well, almost. I just came from Sunny McHenry's …"

Melody, dressed until now in green painter's pants and a pink tank top, now also wore a look of utter disbelief. "You what?"

"Yes. Melody, I'm here to tell you: Sunny and I are engaged."

She squealed, hit Roger on the shoulder hard and seemed to spurt a Spanish cuss word at him. She put her hand over her mouth and looked toward the bedroom. In a loud whisper, she blasted, "You really had me going for a minute!"

Roger whispered right back. "I really did go to see her. Why are we whispering?"

"I'm keeping a foster child for a few days. Luciana. She's 8 years old. Really bad family situation. They're trying to find an extended relative to take her."

Roger smiled and nodded, unsurprised. "Always thinking of others," he whispered.

"So what's this about you and Sunny McHenry?"

Roger scooted back from the edge of the couch, where the two had been facing each other. "I just stopped by to see her and extend an olive branch. I thought maybe it was time for a fresh start. Did you know she was a widow?"

"No! I had no idea! So you patched things up?"

"I think so. I just gave her a little gift and … Wait! What am I thinking?" Roger pulled out another package, this one much bigger and ill-defined. "This is for you."

Melody looked like a little girl as she took the soft package and opened it. Inside was a small stuffed bear dressed up in traditional Austrian clothes. She was about to speak when the bear interrupted her with a yodel. It delighted her, though it made them both worry about the noise.

"Sorry."

"It's fine. Wonderful, actually. Luciana is a heavy sleeper. We probably don't have to whisper. I *love* him!" she cuddled the bear, then the bearer. Breaking away, she wondered, "What was that line about the homeless?"

Roger pushed his glasses up his nose. "I forgot to pay my electricity bill, and there's no power. I was …"

"You're staying here."

"You're sure? I don't want to be a problem. Besides, there's a lovely little landlord with bagels and blackberry jam leaving a light on for me and a couch open …"

She looked at him slyly. "Your choice."

Roger looked down at the hardwood floor. "Your floor looks pretty plush…"

"And there's room for two," she grinned.

Roger smiled.

"… just in case your landlord wants to come over. As for me, I'm sleeping with Luciana."

Roger's smile disappeared. "Right. The couch looks good to me at this point." He also realized that whatever might happen between them, Melody was making it clear it would happen slowly.

"How was your trip? Did you meet with Dr. Frankl? Did you learn a lot?"

"Yes, I did." He suddenly felt tired from it all. "I did learn a lot—including some things I'd rather not have learned."

"Such as what?"

It wasn't the time, and he didn't have the energy for such talk right now. "Later. I wonder if we could go ahead and get turned in …"

"Sure," she said, standing up. He stood up with her. "I'll get you sheets and blankets and a pillow." Before walking off, she hugged him again and kissed him on the cheek. "It's so good to have you back. You were missed."

It's good to *be* back, he thought. Really back.

◆   ◆   ◆

Roger didn't understand why he was dreaming of getting an eye exam— until he actually opened his eyes and saw a giant eye looking at him.

"Are you dead, mister?" the eye's shrill voice said.

"I don't think so."

"Who are you?" the eye said.

"My name's Roger. Who are you?"

The eye hadn't moved an inch or even blinked. "Luciana. What are you doing on Melody's couch?"

Roger pulled his head back as far as the couch would let him, grabbed his glasses from the table over his head and, shoving them on, saw that the brown eye did, indeed, have a pretty little girl behind it. He wiped his eyes, checked for drool on his chin and pulled his blanket up over his shoulder as he raised up on his left elbow.

"I'm a homeless man she let stay here last night."

"You are?" she exploded. "Me too!"

Roger thought it sweet and sad at the same time. Luciana just thought it a wonderful coincidence that two homeless creatures would meet in Melody's apartment.

"She's a nice lady, isn't she?" he asked her.

"Yes. I want to live with her forever."

Roger ignored the impossibility of that, so as not to spoil her wish. "I could think of worse things," he assured her, truly coming to that conclusion only after saying it. "Where is she? What time is it?"

"It's time to get up, of course. She's in the shower."

"Oh."

"You don't need to do that, do you? Homeless men don't shower, do they?"

Roger smiled with his lips together in order to contain a laugh. "We do, just not as often as we'd like. But we're no different than you."

"Yes you are."

"How?"

"You've got a lot more hair," she poked his chest.

Roger felt himself falling in love, and before breakfast yet. "Have you eaten yet?" Roger amazed himself with the paternal sentiment.

"No."

"Well, maybe we can find something."

By the time Melody made her entrance, towel on head, Roger had cooked up a breakfast burrito for Luciana and was putting the finishing touches on one for Melody, who bowed to his culinary acuity and dug in.

"I see you two have gotten to know each other," she allowed after her first bite.

"How many other homeless people will live here?" asked Luciana.

Melody flashed a questioning look toward Roger, who shrugged his shoulders and returned to his cooking.

"It depends," she told Luciana. "If they can all cook like this …"

◆　　　◆　　　◆

The three eventually made their way to the grounds of the Palace of Fine Arts. Roger hadn't realized how much he'd missed it. He thought that perhaps he felt about this place the same way Viktor felt about the Prater amusement park in Vienna.

It was a Sunday morning in April, and it was a glorious one. He wasn't sure if it was the time away from home, the battle he was now facing, the things that Viktor had helped him see—or having Melody with him. But something seemed to give more bloom to the plants, more warmth to the sun, more joy to the skaters and strollers. It all painted beautiful colors on top of his underlying sense of dread.

As Luciana skipped off to watch the fowl in the water, Roger and Melody sat in the grass and watched. And Roger felt it was time to talk. He'd already talked volumes with her, on their walk to the Palace, about his interview of Dr. Frankl and some of what he'd learned. Melody had nearly walked sideways as they strolled toward the Palace grounds, soaking in every word about the Frankls and his experiences. He was excited to tell her, too, partly because he was so invigorated by the experience and partly because it was Melody who made it possible.

But now it was time for other topics, less inviting.

"Melody. I need you to tell Ed I won't be in to work tomorrow."

"OK." She warily awaited the why.

"Remember I told you that part of what I'd learned over there I would have rather not learned?"

"Yes."

"Well, it wasn't something I learned from Dr. Frankl. It was something I heard from Dr. Mahoney."

"He was in Vienna with you?"

Roger had been looking straight ahead, but turned to her, momentarily confused. "What? Oh, no. He called me from here."

"And?"

He looked forward again. "It looks like I've got cancer."

Melody managed a soft "Oh," leaving the rest unspoken.

"I don't know anything more than that. He wouldn't give me a prognosis until I could see him again tomorrow."

Melody had a million questions, but decided to let Roger share whatever information he wanted to. Sensing that, Roger went on.

"It's low-grade lymphoma. They're going to remove the lymph node tomorrow—I guess from that, and maybe a cat-scan, they'll be able to tell if it spread."

Roger felt her hand slip into his and squeeze. "Whatever you need. Whatever you need."

His smile conveyed his thanks, and she slid into an embrace.

◆　　◆　　◆

"This won't hurt a bit," Dr. Mahoney lied, wielding what appeared to be a fencing foil.

Roger suddenly felt more than one lump in his throat. "You're going to suck it out with that?"

"Nope. This is the local. Unless you want to be put all the way under. We can do that, but I can't promise what will happen."

"What do you mean?"

"Well, with your wallet and other valuables. This managed care situation forces us to do some pretty extreme things in order to get full reimbursement."

"Very funny, Doc. I'll take the local."

"OK, but you have to promise—no howling. Animal control's been getting complaints about you."

Roger looked up, in order to offer his neck, but looking at the needle out of the corner of his eye, he let out a quiet, "Woof?"

◆   ◆   ◆

"OK, here's the scoop." The doctor sat down behind his desk while his thick fingers fumbled with Roger's file. "The good news is that what we wanted to happen has happened—that it's a Stage 1 lymphoma."

"What's that mean?" He edged forward in his seat as if peering down a cliff.

"Stage 1 means it's likely contained in one place—the place we took from you already. The tests show it has not spread. And that's great news."

Roger sat back and put his chin on his chest in relief, saying a silent prayer.

"Wait. It could get even better. If the cancer cells have spread to the edges of the lymph node we removed, you'll have to undergo radiation treatment. But if not—if the pathologist finds in a few days that it's not around the edges—then you don't need any treatment at all."

Roger knew he couldn't have asked for that. But he was, quietly. "When will we know?"

"Monday."

"OK. But you said that was the good news."

"Yes."

"Let's have the bad news now."

"I'm not going to sugarcoat it for you, Roger. Even if we find out you need no treatment, you will live with this the rest of your life."

Roger sat up. "I don't get it. If I'm clean, and you've taken it out, how can I be living with it the rest of my life? That doesn't make sense, Doc."

"No, but that's cancer, Rog. Your prognosis, from everything we've seen so far, is excellent. Don't let me fool you. The combination of your age and the stage and other factors all indicate you can live a long, full life."

"But there's a catch …?"

"There simply is no cure, at this point, for lymphoma, Roger. You're not cured by the removal of the lymph node. Your cancer is merely in remission."

Roger sat back again, but didn't slump this time. "I see. So I have this cloud following me …"

"I wouldn't put it that way, Roger."

Roger instantly knew that Viktor wouldn't have, either. "Well, OK, I guess it means I'd better—appreciate every healthy day …"

"That's a much healthier way of looking at it. Like I told you, the chances are very good, depending on the pathology report Monday, that you could live a disease-free life."

Disease-free life. The words were supposed to comfort, but they were haunting. Only days ago, living a disease-free life was effortless, thoughtless. Now, it would take effort.

Perhaps a lot of effort.

"So what kind of regimen are we talking about? I assume, best-case scenario, that we're talking about a significant amount of monitoring, tests, through the years."

Mahoney eased back in his chair with a broad smile. "I guess that's why you're a journalist, Rog. Yes, there's a significant regimen of monitoring by you and physical exams and tests by us. The first three years—and remember, here, we're talking about if there's no other treatment indicated by pathology—you'll need to be seen every three months. Then, every six months or so after that."

"In-between?"

"In-between you watch for any out-of-place weight loss, intermittent fevers—we'll get you a list of things to watch for."

"And the goal?"

"What we talk about is long-term remission. What we want is for you to live out your dream—of becoming a dirty old man, or whatever your dream is. And I want you coming to me with your Medicare money, you no-good lout!"

Roger cracked a smile, but wasn't in the mood. "Let's talk about the worst-case."

Mahoney snapped back upright in his chair. "OK, let's. If pathology says it's to the edges of the lymph node, then it's a whole different ballgame. We have to fight quite a bit harder for long-term remission. The start is radiation therapy."

"You said mine was Stage 1. What's Stage 2, and 3—and how many stages are there?"

"Good question, as always. There are four stages—and yes, you're in Stage 1, and that's excellent news. Stage 2 is when the cancer is present in two locations above the diaphragm. Again, yours is not. I'm just answering your question …"

"Understood."

"Stage 3 is below the diaphragm. Stage 4 is in the bone marrow."

Roger cringed. "Let's not go there. Tell the pathologist we're not going there."

"I'll send her a memo."

"Strongly worded?"

"Scorching."

19

As Roger fumbled with his apartment key, he heard the phone ringing. Quickly he turned the key and then the knob, and proceeded to sail over the duffel bag he'd forgotten was right inside the door. He landed face first on the hardwood floor of his foyer. Of all the possible cancer treatment options he and Dr. Mahoney had discussed, throwing oneself onto a hard floor was not one of them.

As it happens, though, he landed right by the shelf with the phone. Without rising, Roger pulled the phone's cord until the receiver fell off the side—and onto his head.

"Good lord, Murphy, what the heck you doin' up there?" asked a genuinely concerned Sherman Case from the apartment below. "Wrestling an elephant?"

"Yes, and it's over. Guess who lost."

"Listen, sorry to interrupt, but I heard you get home—how could I *not*?—and there's a gentleman down here to see you. We're having bagels with cream cheese and real blackberry jam—not that stuff they pass off as blackberry jam in the stores. Why don't you freshen up and come on down?"

Roger rubbed his head where the phone hit him, now lying on his back. Sherman always has every detail worked out. "OK, be down in a minute. Did I have an appointment that …?"

"No, he admitted he's here unannounced. Just get down here. We'll fill you in, and feed you too."

The smell of warm bagels wafted all the way down Sherman Case's hallway. Roger knocked and heard pans crashing in the kitchen inside.

"Be right there!" Sherman yelled. Another crash.

"I take it you didn't need my couch the last couple of nights, lover boy," Sherman leered when he opened the door.

"No, thanks, though. I stayed—at a homeless shelter."

Sherman's eyes were hard to see anyway—his brow was forever furrowed, as if he were always squinting. But you could tell he was squinting now, not sure whether to believe Roger about the homeless shelter or not. Sherman decided to ignore it and move on.

"You have power now? I called first thing this morning."

"Yes, thanks. You sure put the 'super' in superintendent, Sherm."

"Nothing but the best for my star tenant and favorite newspaper writer. Now, come in. There's someone who is very anxious to meet you. Roger Murphy, meet Jerry Long."

Stepping into Sherman's small living room/dining room combination, Roger was greeted by a middle-aged man in a wheelchair with a gregarious air.

"Hello, Mr. Murphy. Jerry Long. So very glad to make your acquaintance."

"Likewise," Roger said, holding out his hand—before realizing the man was a quadriplegic. "From your accent, I'd say you're not from the Marina District …"

Long laughed, quickly adding, "A little south of San Jose, actually. Texas, to be fairly precise."

Roger sat on a chair opposite Long and crossed his legs. "I understand you came to see me. How is that?"

"See? What did I tell you?" Sherman thundered to Long. "These reporters, they don't waste a minute. They get right to the point."

Again, Long chuckled. "That's perfectly fine. He must be wondering why this quadriplegic middle-aged man is showing up at his apartment building without notice and while he's away at the doctor's."

Roger shot a glance and polite smile to Sherman, while wondering how much detail his building super had given to the guest. Sherman, aware of the liberty he'd taken, had armed himself and proceeded to change the subject. "Tea?"

"I believe—thank you, Mr. Case, but no—I believe we have an acquaintance in common, Mr. Murphy."

Roger was already sipping his tea, so he just let his eyebrows ask the question.

"A Dr. Viktor Frankl."

Roger's eyebrows shot up even more. He put the tea down on the coffee table and punched his glasses up his nose. "Yes. I just interviewed him."

"He told me."

"You're friends, then?"

"Of sorts. I'm his friend; he's my hero."

Sherman butted in. "That's a nice kind of friendship to have."

"I assure you, Mr. Case, Dr. Frankl is the best sort of friend one could hope for. Mr. Murphy, I hope you don't mind the impertinence of my coming to see you out of the Texas blue, as we say, but I was in the bay area and thought I'd make a courtesy call on you."

"I'm glad you did. How is it that you are acquainted with Dr. Frankl, and what brought you to town?"

"I am a logotherapist, and, I suppose you could say, one of the chief proponents of the science in the United States. There is a Viktor Frankl Institute at Berkeley …"

"I didn't know that," Roger interjected.

"Yes. I occasionally visit to speak there, as I did so this past weekend. Now, I am on my way out of town and hoped to meet you after Dr. Frankl mentioned he had been talking to you. I trust you found your time with him—well, I have to expect extraordinary."

"That's a good word for it," Roger smiled.

"Yes, I'd say so."

After a momentary visit by an awkward silence, it dawned on Roger what Mr. Long might be doing there.

"Did Dr. Frankl ask you to check up on me?" he asked politely, but accusingly.

Long chuckled. "Dr. Frankl warned me you might catch on rather quickly. Yes, he might have mentioned something about looking in on you. Said you're dealing with a lot about now. But you seem to be managing well enough."

"Thanks." Roger's sarcasm couldn't hide his gratitude.

"You asked how I was acquainted with Dr. Frankl. I'd like to share that story with you, if you have a few moments."

"Sure," Roger said keenly. "I'd love to know."

"It all started with a letter, just a simple little thank-you from a freshman in college to the author of *Man's Search for Meaning*. I had read it for Introduction to Psychology. I assume you have read it, too—and now, of course, you have had the great privilege of meeting its author and probing one of the great minds of the 20th century. This has had some sort of impact on you, I trust?"

"Yes—I'm still sorting that out, really."

"It takes time with such things. His words are very profound. But you see, it took very little time for me. At the time I read his book, it was nine months or so since I had become paralyzed from the neck down in a diving accident. You can't imagine, or maybe you can, what his book meant to me. Time and again I saw similarities in the emotions running through me and through his writing, his experiences. So I wrote to him and thanked him. And do you know, within 48 hours he was calling me!"

"Holy cow!" exclaimed Sherman.

"I expect Mr. Murphy is less surprised, having taken his measure of the man in question …"

"I wouldn't put it past him," Roger agreed. "But I also know he gets a lot of mail. He must have been quite moved by your letter. What did you write?"

"In his phone call to me, Dr. Frankl took note of the fact that I had explained in my letter that I was typing with the aid of a wooden stick between my teeth. And he became quite fond of what I told him was my life's credo at that point: 'I broke my neck; it didn't break me.' He asked my permission to repeat my story in his lectures, which he has quite often, I'm told.

"Dr. Frankl's message, as you well know by now, is that meaning can be found in any life, at any moment, under any circumstances. I didn't quite know that in my mind before reading his book, but I think I knew it in my heart. All I knew was that I wanted to become a clinical psychologist so that maybe I could help others through their suffering. I guess Dr. Frankl put that sentiment to work—within the framework of the science of logotherapy."

"As you certainly have. Mr. Long …"

"Jerry, please."

"Jerry. I hope you don't think this is a hopelessly naïve question, especially considering where I've just come from—but I wonder how you would define logotherapy."

"It's not naïve at all. I even asked Dr. Frankl that question myself. We were at the 1983 World Congress of Logotherapy in Regensburg, Germany. I was there to present a plenary session. We had a few moments alone, and I posed the question to him, as apologetically as you just did to me. He answered me with a little parable:

"A man came upon three stonecutters and asked the first one what they were doing. 'Cutting stone—what does it look like?' the first one sharply replied. He asked the second one, who answered, 'Making a cornerstone, of course!' He then asked the third stonecutter what he was doing. This one put down his tools, brushed off his hands and announced proudly, 'Making a cathedral.' Dr. Frankl felt this was a fine example of what logotherapy seeks to do—to concentrate on the cathedral rather than the stones."

Roger nodded. "He must have felt that you embodied what logotherapy is about, too."

"I risk immodesty in admitting it—but it is *his* claim, not mine. Yes, he often said that. And, in fact, now that you say that, it was at that 1983 World Congress that Dr. Frankl surprised me with an honorary membership in the Austrian Medical Society for Psychology. He shared I was only the third recipient of such an honor—the other two being relatives of Freud and Adler.

"It says, 'To Jerry L. Long Jr.—a living testimony to logotherapy lived and, more specifically, to the defiant power of the human spirit.' Of course, I didn't feel worthy of that then, and I still don't. I feel the best example of logotherapy lived is Dr. Frankl himself.

"But let me share one other anecdote that I think illustrates the value of logotherapy, albeit in an indirect way.

"I was once asked during a presentation how the medical profession could best serve people in my physical situation. I told the interviewer several things, including the following: If medical professionals treat only the physical and mental, and ignore the spiritual, then the only difference between them and veterinarians will be the clientele!

"This is what logotherapy is. And be careful not to confuse its spirituality with religiosity. I'm not talking about bringing God into psychology. I'm talking about, and Dr. Frankl is talking about, bringing human beings into psychology. Somehow or another, they got shoved out of it! Dr. Frankl talks often about the need to re-humanize both psychotherapy and psychology. And even re-humanizing humanity."

"Amen, brother," Sherman loudly concurred.

"Thank you, rabbi," Roger teased Sherman, who guffawed. "Jerry, don't you find it amazing that a man could live through what Dr. Frankl lived through and not be bitter? I find it so hard to believe."

"Because it *is* hard to believe," Long agreed. "But consider this, too: His trials didn't end with his liberation from the camps—and the slings and arrows came from all sides. Obviously, anti-Semitism survived World War II, and as a high-profile target, he's taken more than his share of hatred. But he also gets it from the Jewish quarters, some of whom hate him for not buying into collective guilt—the trendy belief that all Germans were to blame for the atrocities of the Holocaust. He just never bought into that. He always felt there were good and bad people of all races, as you probably learned while you were in Vienna.

"You can't imagine how angry this makes some Jews. He once was on a program—I think it was 1978—at the Institute of Adult Jewish Studies at Congregation B'nai Jeshurun in New York with people like Shimon Peres, Sammy Davis Jr. and Gerald Ford. But when Viktor spoke out against collective guilt, many in the audience rose up to shout him down and, given the opportunity by the host, to leave rather than listen to Viktor. I know it had to hurt him, because he told me about it. They even called him a Nazi pig. So wrong. So cruel."

"So he gets it from both sides."

"No," Long disagreed. "He gets it from *all* sides. For instance, the Freudians."

"I know he had a theoretical split with them early in his career," Roger recalled.

"It goes far beyond that, friend. You see, whereas a psychoanalyst might spend years probing unconscious motives in a patient that may or may not be there, and creating this sometimes sick dependency, a logotherapist often works much quicker—and, instead of creating neuroses where there may be none, creates an awareness of the healing of self-transcendence. As you might expect, this creates some animosity among our psychoanalyst friends." Long chuckled suddenly. "Did the Frankls tell you the story of what Gabriele said at the airport when she was just a little thing?"

"No." Roger turned to Sherman. "The Frankls' daughter."

"In the 1950s, Viktor was preparing to fly to some conference or lecture, and in those days Elly would often stay behind with Gabriele. They were seeing Viktor off at the airport when Gabriele cautioned him, 'Make sure your airplane is not shot down by your enemies, the psychoanalysts.'"

Roger and Sherman enjoyed the story, as Sherman refilled Roger's tea.

"Dr. Frankl doesn't speak like a man with so many scars," Roger suggested.

"No! Well put. He is so at ease with people—all types of people. He could talk to you and me right here like nothing—and turn around and rub elbows with the pope, you know? And he goes around quoting taxi drivers. The man is incredible."

"And yet goofy, in a way—in a good way."

"What a sense of humor! Did he tell you his bordello joke? One of his favorites. A man enters a Polish village with a large Jewish population. The man is looking for a brothel, but is embarrassed to ask. Finally, he stops an old Jew and asks, instead, where the rabbi lives. The old man points to a house nearby. 'What?' the visitor yells. 'Your rabbi lives in a brothel?' Shocked, the old man says, 'Of course not! The brothel is that one over there!'

"But my favorite aspect of his sense of humor, Mr. Murphy, is how self-deprecating it can be. He once joked that he was reluctant to let people know he had doctorates in both medicine and philosophy—he just knew that his hard-bitten colleagues in Vienna, instead of saying he was twice a doctor, would say he was only half a physician."

"The Rodney Dangerfield of psychiatry," Roger asserted.

"Exactly," Long agreed.

Looking over Roger's shoulder, Long suddenly barked, "Oh, my! I need to be going. I have a plane to catch. Well, Mr. Murphy, I appreciate your willingness to meet me on my impulse. I just wanted to let you know that you had stumbled onto perhaps the best-kept secret of the 20th century. Millions of us know about Dr. Frankl, but so many more do not. I hope you can, in your own modest way, help change that."

"I appreciate that. I'll do what I can." Roger jerked to a halt. "By the way, when did you last talk to Dr. Frankl?"

"It must have been Saturday. Two days ago. Why?"

"Then you must know of his—condition?"

Long seemed puzzled. "Whatever do you mean?"

"He didn't mention it, then. The night before I flew out, Dr. Frankl went blind."

Long became visibly shaken, and Roger thought he saw Long's body sink into his wheelchair. "Oh, hell. I'm so sorry to hear that. It's so like him not to have mentioned it. My word, that's terrible. Reading and writing mean so much to him. And his writings mean so much to the world—even to people who've yet to discover him. This is awful. But he was typically upbeat when we talked. Just goes to show you the strength of this man's character."

Roger and Sherman helped Long outside, to a waiting airport shuttle equipped for wheelchairs.

"Would you mind," Long asked Roger just before he closed the door, "reaching into my satchel and getting one of my cards? I'd very much like to be of any assistance to you that I can."

As Roger did so, he thought about that last statement—an offer from a man without the use of his arms or legs to be of service to him. He thought Dr. Frankl was right again—that Jerry Long was, indeed, the embodiment of logotherapy.

◆   ◆   ◆

The bright yellow tint of what had to be a greeting card envelope greeted Roger as he sat down at his uncharacteristically clean newsroom desk. Before diving into it, though, he felt the desktop with his palms, then put his hands at his sides and grabbed the chair seat. It was old, torn and shabby, and it felt great. It was as if he were back in the driver's seat of the Chevy Impala he learned to drive on. It felt new, he felt new—until he remembered, and stroked the large bandage covering the stitches on his neck. He'd only been gone two weeks—but he'd never been gone that long before. Fact is, they'd always had to force him to take a week of vacation at a time. He loved his work, and he frankly didn't know what else to occupy his time with, other than 49ers' games, and those only came eight times a year.

Besides, a lot had happened to him in those two weeks. In a way, the old chair cushion felt more familiar than his own skin.

He picked up the envelope. He knew it was from Melody, and it made him smile. They hadn't been intimate since he got back, what with Luciana in the apartment and all, but he'd never felt closer to her.

"Friends?" Roger couldn't believe his eyes. The card was a poem about the value of friends. Was that all they were?

Suddenly, he understood: The signature was "S.M."—Sunny McHenry.

Roger smiled even broader this time. He'd actually turned their animosity into friendship, with one five-minute olive branch. And a baby grand piano in a box.

"Murphy!"

Ed Miller hadn't left his glass office, hadn't gotten up out of his seat—hadn't even looked up from his newspaper—but his voice carried throughout the news room.

"You rang, Chief?" Roger yapped as he hit the office threshold.

"Where the hell have you been?" He still didn't look up from his paper.

Roger had learned to expect the unexpected from Ed Miller, but this was just insane. "What do you mean, where have I been? You sent me! Practically under the threat of involuntary commitment."

Miller wrestled his paper to the desktop. "Oh, yeah. That." Clearly, Miller was screwing with Roger. "Tell me I didn't waste a thousand bucks, Murphy. Tell me you've got something."

Roger smiled. "I got something. I got a truckload of something."

Miller leaned back in his chair. "Well, Melody was on to something, then. You look good, Murph. Better. Except for that! What's up with the bandage?"

Roger had forgotten again, and put his hand to it. "Uh, infected hair."

"I hate it when that happens! So, ready to go to war?"

"Yeah."

"Well, this ain't ground zero. Get the hell outta here and get to work." Miller yanked his newspaper up with a crash and his face disappeared behind it. Roger just stood there. In a moment, Miller lowered the paper just enough to see over it. "What the hell?"

Roger smiled again. "Thanks, Chief."

Miller actually let a short smile escape his lips. He gave a small nod of the head and disappeared behind the headlines again.

Roger was just about to sit down when he heard, "And don't call me 'Chief'!"

Yep, he was home again.

◆   ◆   ◆

In the next few days, Roger, Melody and Luciana were nearly inseparable as they waited for word from the pathologist on Roger's cancer—and enjoyed as much of Luciana as they could before she would be taken by social services. As it turned out, she appeared headed for adoption rather than reunification with her troubled family. But, due to Luciana's unusually high adoptability for her age, due in no small part to her good nature, social workers were telling Melody to expect quick action—and not to get too attached to her.

The three of them were sitting down for dinner in Melody's apartment on the Friday night before a Monday doctor's visit in which Roger was likely to learn whether the cancer was isolated—or if he was in even greater danger. As the three ate silently—except for Luciana's slurping of spaghetti noodles—Roger stared at Melody without her realizing it. He pondered her predicament: She was sitting with two people she cared deeply about who, for all she knew, would not be around much longer. After all, she was in danger of losing Luciana to adoption and Roger to cancer. It amazed Roger that not once had she mentioned that, or complained or worried aloud. He put his hand on her arm and smiled; she looked at him as if to ask "What?" but left it alone when he simply started eating again.

After a while, he said, without looking up, "I've got some bad news. They cut my power again. I'll need to stay over."

Luciana smiled, as if she smelled a rat and didn't mind it. But Melody put her fork down. "You're kidding! Again?"

"Yep." He finished chewing a bite, then added, "I had to call them out and pay extra for them to cut it, but …"

Melody slapped his arm for having yanked her chain. "You don't have to be without electricity to stay here, you know."

"Yeah, I know."

Later, after Luciana was put to bed, and Roger and Melody were on the couch together watching *Casablanca* on television, Roger asked, "You love her, don't you?"

"Ingrid Bergman? Doesn't everybody?" Roger just frowned impatiently. "You mean Luciana? Yeah, I do."

"Have you thought about adopting her?"

"Of course I have, but …"

"But what?"

"I don't know if that would be fair to her—me being single and all."

Melody had been resting her head on Roger's shoulder, but lifted it when she felt him pulling back.

"Single? Tell me you're kidding," he complained.

"Do you see a ring?"

"I *know* you're single. But for Pete's sake, in 1990 I hope we're past the point of that being a problem."

Melody smiled. "Why, Roger Murphy, you're sounding positively liberal."

"I'll pretend I didn't hear that," he frowned. "Besides, you're assuming you'll always be single." Roger had said that without really thinking about what it might sound like, and it scared him as soon as he uttered it.

"Oh?" She folded her arms.

Roger shrugged his shoulders. "Well, don't look at me. I'm old enough to be—your older brother!"

"Wait a minute, Bub. You've gone on and on about how great the Frankls' marriage has been—and what's the age difference there? About the same, isn't it?"

"More, actually."

"There you go. You're 41, I'm 28. I'd say that's perfectly doable."

An awkward silence passed between these two friends, who were both shocked to be talking such talk.

"You love her, too, *don't* you?" Melody asked.

Roger looked toward the dark bedroom. "Yes." A few seconds later, he turned to Melody. "And I love you, too."

It dawned on Melody that those words hadn't yet passed between them. She reciprocated, and they kissed for what seemed half an hour.

"We're forgetting one thing." Roger pushed gently away. "We don't know what the future holds."

His euphemistic language didn't faze her. "I don't care what may come, Roger. In fact, I want to be there for you if the worst happens."

Try as he might, Roger couldn't get Melody to think of herself—of the possibility of being a widow just months after getting married. He finally gave up, and gave in.

"So does this mean we're engaged?" he finally asked.

"I don't know. You're the *oldest* here," she smiled. "*You* figure it out."

"Oh, so you're going to hold my age against me, eh?"

"Until you're senile and it's no fun anymore, yeah. I give it a couple years."

"Well," he said, glancing up at the movie just ending, "this looks like the start of a beautiful friendship."

"I was right all along," she cried. "You *are* a rank sentimentalist!"

Melody got up, closed the bedroom door and came back to the couch and Roger's waiting arms.

◆　　◆　　◆

Roger had never been hugged so hard in his life. Pat Mahoney nearly crushed him.

"If this is the way you treat the rest of your patients," he counseled the doctor, "I can think of a way to improve your mortality rate."

Roger couldn't believe he was making a joke at a time like this. He was about to find out whether he might be dying, or if he had been able to steal a few more years—perhaps even a lifetime. And the hug didn't help: Pat might be hugging him to give him the bad news, or to congratulate him.

When the doctor finally let go, Roger could see the answer in Pat's face.

◆　　◆　　◆

The moment the doctor's office door had shut behind him, and he'd smelled the cool afternoon bay air, Roger had somehow known instantly, without any forethought, where he wanted to go, what he needed to do.

"Murphy! Good lord, is that you?"

It was the same stern-faced state trooper as before—the not-on-my-shift jerk that had given Roger nightmares. Now, though, the officer sounded mildly concerned. After all, he now considered Roger an acquaintance—and here he was on the same Golden Gate Bridge ledge as before. Only this time, Roger was the potential suicide that had been reported.

"What the hell are you doing?" the officer demanded, still more concerned than angry. "Are you thinking about jumping—or was there someone else with you who jumped to save themselves from one of your diatribes?"

Roger smiled. "Neither, officer. I'm celebrating."

"You're what?"

"I'm celebrating. I just got a clean bill of health from my doctor—relatively speaking—and now I'm celebrating."

"By trying to kill yourself? You're crazier than I thought, you jackass!"

"I'm not trying to kill myself. Believe me, if that's what I wanted, you'd be all the inspiration I need."

"Very funny, ink stain. So what are you doing, which, I might add, whatever it is it's illegal."

"I'm treating myself."

"Treating yourself? Might I suggest treating yourself to ice cream instead and getting the hell off my bridge?"

"Not *that* kind of treating. I mean treating in a medical sense."

"I thought you said you had a clean bill of health," the officer pondered, scratching his head under his cap.

"I do, more or less—physically."

"Oh, I get it. You're nuts, just like I always tell my wife every time I read you."

Roger ignored the insult. He felt too good. "I'm treating my fear of heights with what's called 'paradoxical intention.'"

"I could have *told* you you were a paranoid SOB …"

"Not 'paranoid,' numbskull. 'Paradoxical.' I'm facing my fear of heights by—well, *facing* it. By *trying* to be afraid."

"Well, that *does* sound nuts." The officer took his cap completely off now and glanced behind him to make sure no one was listening to their nonsense. In a kind of shouted whisper, he couldn't help wondering, "Is it working?"

"I think so." Roger leaned forward over the edge, and yanked himself back. "It may take a couple more doses, though." He turned around and hurriedly climbed back over the railing.

"I oughta arrest you, Murphy," the officer snarled, poking Roger in the chest. "You scared some poor good Samaritan half outta her wits, and took me away from other police business."

Roger said not a word. He simply looked at the officer, thrust his wrists at him for handcuffing and gave the officer his best puppy-dog look. The officer fought a wisp of a smile, then demanded, "Get the hell out of here before I *do* run you in, you nutcase."

"Thanks, officer. It won't happen again, I promise." Roger turned and started off down the sidewalk.

"*Not on my shift*, it won't," he called after Roger, who looked back and smiled.

◆   ◆   ◆

The sun was finishing up its work, and the windsurfers were jumping out of their jeeps and vans for an after-work adventure on the bay as Roger sat along the marina and took it all in. On the sand and in the grass, children with brightly colored kites were feeding off the reliable bay breezes. Joggers and walkers and bicyclists crisscrossed each other on the footpath interstate running along the shore.

Roger Murphy watched it all with an outward calm, but inside he was frantic—a *good* kind of frantic, a morning-after Scrooge mania. If he could have thrown gold coins at the kids flying kites, ala Scrooge, he would have. Not the windsurfers, though—despite his newfound delirium, they still annoyed the hell out of him for some reason. Probably the Spandex.

He reflected on what Viktor Frankl had told him about the last of the human freedoms. And, looking back on the preceding days, Roger felt he indeed had done his best to choose his attitude in the face of possible death from cancer. He knew it wasn't over, either—that the cancer could rear its head again someday, and that, anyway, other, smaller, victories of attitude needed to be won every day. At least now he knew he had that power and freedom. And it changed how he saw everything.

Except the windsurfers.

"Well?"

Roger had been so caught up in his thoughts he hadn't even noticed that Melody had arrived a few minutes earlier than expected. He stood up and turned to face her.

"Hungry?" he asked.

"Roger!"

"Oh, right, you're probably wondering about that cancer thing. I'm clean, sweetie. Clean as I'm gonna get, anyhow."

She screeched and pounced on him with such force they went rolling in the sand. She was still screeching as they rolled to a stop. An elderly couple on a walk stopped to make sure the two were OK. "Help! We've fallen and we can't get up!" Roger cried. The woman shook her head and walked on, but the man tipped his cap and winked at the couple in the sand as he followed his wife.

"I guess you know this is a death sentence for *you* instead of me," Roger warned her. "You're the one who has to put up with me!"

"I can handle it. So what did he say?"

"It's the best-case scenario. The CT scan not only showed no spread, but the cancer hadn't worked its way toward the edges of the infected lymph node."

"What exactly does that mean?"

"It means for now I don't need any treatment. Just careful monitoring the next few months—periodic CT scans, blood tests, physical exams, and I have to keep a close watch on any intermittent fevers or unexplained weight loss—well, the rest of my life, really. But that's OK—I hope it means a *lot* of monitoring, cause that will mean a long life!"

"This calls for a celebration," Melody shrieked.

"Yes, let's go get Luciana and …"

"No, sweetie. I'll go get Luciana and we'll pick you up at your apartment. We've got something to deliver."

◆   ◆   ◆

Roger heard a commotion outside his apartment door, followed by someone scratching frantically at his door. He walked briskly over and looked through the peephole, but couldn't see a thing. He unlocked the deadbolt and turned the doorknob.

A black blob swung around the door and right into Roger's leg like a remote control car hitting a wall.

It was a black toy poodle puppy.

"Hey little guy!" Roger shouted as he bent down to pet it. "Where'd you…?"

Just then Melody and Luciana jumped out from behind the wall and yelled, "Surprise!"

"We had him picked out for several days," Melody explained. "But I didn't want to …" Roger somehow nodded to her while getting tackled and licked by a ferociously loving puppy.

Roger sat up, still fighting off his new love interest. "I love him! What shall we call him?"

"B-2," Melody proposed.

"You want to name him after a bomber?"

"Why not? He comes on like one, doesn't he? What I was thinking, really, was Bruno the second. B-2."

"Well, that sounds great." Roger added, fighting off the puppy's tongue, "but if we're going to call him B-2, he'll have to develop a little more stealth!"

20

It's really surreal. If you're on an assembly line, the only other person who knows when you've had a bad day may be the guy next to you in line. But when your work product hits people's driveways the next morning, everyone and their uncle has an opinion on whether you've had a good day at the office.

"Hey Roger! Great stuff today!"

"Thank you for saying what needs to be said, Mr. Murphy!"

"You stink, you fascist jerk!"

Well, it wasn't unanimous. But most San Franciscans seemed to agree: Roger Murphy was having a lot of good days these days. His column was the talk of the town again—this time not for its heartlessness, but for its heart.

He let them wonder why, enjoying their rampant speculation.

"What's up with Roger Murphy?" one letter to the editor asked. "Did they hook his defibrillator up to a Sears' Die Hard? Or straight to a nuclear power plant?"

Maybe it was his column on the desperate need for hope—in the inner city, in prisons, in the lives of those arrested. It certainly wasn't the let-them-eat-cake that his critics had come to expect.

"Look in the eyes of the people on our business pages," he wrote, "the ones who've gotten a new job or a promotion or attended some big-deal seminar or became president of a civic club. Then compare those beaming eyes to those lifeless, vacuous shark's eyes looking back at you from the mug shots of people arrested for crimes. You can see the difference in their eyes.

"The difference is having a meaning in life. The difference is hope. Hope is as essential to the human being as oxygen or water. Oxygen may fill the lungs, water may course the bloodstream. They feed the body. But hope fills the soul and nourishes the human heart.

"Nietzsche said 'He who has a 'why' to live for can bear with almost any 'how.' Hope provides the 'why' in life. In some cases it provides life itself: In the Nazi concentration camps, hopelessness was as deadly as typhus or starvation—maybe even deadlier. A friend of mine who survived four of those camps knew a man who dreamed he'd be liberated on a certain day; when that day passed without freedom, the man died. They didn't put 'hopelessness' down as the cause of death. But that's what he died from.

"In the same way, lives are withering on the vine here today—in our prisons and in inner cities, which still suffer the aftereffects of oppression and racism. There's a quiet holocaust of hopelessness going on under our very noses. My concentration camp friend, the great Dr. Viktor Frankl, called it an 'existential vacuum'—a fancy way of saying there's no meaning in your life. And, since nature abhors a vacuum, it gets filled with what nature naturally provides: animalistic tendencies. In particular, aggression, addiction to physical pleasures—and then the human response to all that vacuousness: depression.

"Now, I don't buy into mindless, blanket victimhood. Far from it. That woe-is-me stuff can keep you down more than any external forces. You have more power than you know to shape your life. In fact, Frankl is bigger on individual responsibility than anybody. Here's just part of what he wrote about that regarding life in the camps:

> 'We had to learn ourselves and, furthermore, we had to teach the despairing men, that *it did not really matter what we expected from life, but rather what life expected from us.* We needed to … think of ourselves as those who were being questioned by life—daily and hourly. Our answer must consist not in talk and meditation, but in right action and in right conduct. Life ultimately means taking the responsibility to find the right answer to its problems and to fulfill the tasks which it constantly sets for each individual.'

"Hear, hear! Yet, Frankl also knew that one of our greatest responsibilities we have is to each other—and that, in turn, helps us. Consider what he wrote about that:

> 'A man who becomes conscious of the responsibility he bears toward a human being who affectionately waits for him, or to an unfinished work, will never be able to throw away his life. He knows the 'why' for his existence, and will be able to bear almost any 'how.''

"So, I submit to you that while everyone has a responsibility to himself and to his future, we also have a responsibility to each other. In the case of our responsibility to the sons and daughters of those whom this country oppressed for so many years, and to others trapped in hopelessness, we owe them hope. We would owe it to them even absent past discrimination; it's simply a human obligation.

"Otherwise, it's the law of the jungle, isn't it? Every man for himself? Let's hope we're better than that.

"What I'm saying is that leaders, both public and private—but mostly private, such as, oh, the Chamber of Commerce—have a unique responsibility to provide hope to the hopeless. That doesn't mean free stuff. It doesn't mean giving them fish, or even a fishing pole. What it does mean is that everyone gets access to the same pond where the fish are biting. And, if necessary, maybe a little help getting to that pond.

"In a practical sense, what it means is that the business community needs to drill it into kids' heads that if they stay in school, mind their grades and stay off drugs, then the world will open up wide for them and opportunity will knock.

"Whether they're dressed and ready to go when the knock comes is up to them. You can't save people from themselves. Our obligation is simply to provide hope.

"But as obligations go, it's a solemn one."

Then again, there was his column on suffering—which he wrote after a particularly senseless and heinous crime shocked the sensibilities of the city. The old Roger surely would have railed against the perpetrator, dreaming up new and creative punishments for anyone so despicable. Instead, Roger tried to bring meaning to the situation.

"You know," he wrote, "I love it how, when a kid so much as falls and skins his knees on the school playground these days, they bring in grief counselors. As if the kids are sick when something bad happens. Good grief! They're not sick; they're suffering. There's a difference! And you know what? It's OK to suffer sometimes. And it may even be unhealthy to try to avoid it. In fact, suffering can be one of the most meaningful things we ever do. As Viktor Frankl wrote in *Man's Search for Meaning*:

> 'Someone looks down on each of us in difficult hours—a friend, a wife, somebody alive or dead, or a God—and he would not expect us to disappoint him. He would hope to find us suffering proudly—not miserably ...'"

His readers and colleagues saw all this as Roger moving toward the political center, or even the left. They wondered if it was his marriage to Melody, or his adoption of Luciana, that softened him. It also leaked out that he'd been battling cancer, and other media outlets were having a heyday with that. The more perceptive observers credited Viktor Frankl's influence. Whatever it was, though, Roger insisted his transformation wasn't about ideology, but humanity.

Regardless, they'd seen a side of Roger they not only had never seen, but never suspected was there. And that may have made them even more receptive to his column calling for the building of Frankl's "Statue of Responsibility." Indeed, in all his years he had never received so much feedback, so much praise, for anything he'd written.

He'd struck gold.

"The notion of individual responsibility certainly appeals to my conservative instincts," he admitted to readers. "After all, when masses of people are held not to be responsible for their own lives, their own destinies, you have a breeding ground for laziness, crime, divisiveness and take-from-others socialism. When no one's responsible for themselves, there's always someone else to blame. And a talk show host to cry to, or a lawyer to extract revenge.

"But the principle of responding to life's challenges like an adult, and being a good steward for the unique life God has granted you, is neither conservative nor liberal. Everyone along the political spectrum should recognize the importance of responsibility. Yet, for some reason we don't give it a second thought. All we think about is our rights. But that's only one side of the coin.

"I don't think we as a country have over-emphasized our rights so much as we've under-sold our responsibilities. Just look at the federal debt and entitlement spending: We're partying with our children's future paychecks! And then we're going to expect them to support us in our fat-butted old age? Come on!

"Again, that's not a conservative value—it's a moral value. What we're doing to our children by our insane overspending is immoral. It's irresponsible.

"When I met Viktor Frankl, a Holocaust survivor and maybe this century's greatest thinker, we had a dialogue about responsibility. Maybe that's what this country needs: one big-ass conversation about what it means to respond to what life throws at you. And about our responsibilities to each other.

"I can't think of anything that would get that conversation started quite like building the Statue of Responsibility on the West Coast that Frankl suggested as a bookend to the Statue of Liberty on the East Coast. What an incredible idea!

"Frankl knew that freedom without responsibility is worthless. They're two matching slices of bread, really—and if one is missing, you haven't got a sandwich. You've got a mess on your hands.

"That's what we've got on our hands in America today: a mess. We need that other slice of bread.

"It used to be that tradition and social norm and stigma—and a strong family—provided that slice of bread, that foundation of responsibility that freedom must be matched with. That's not true anymore. As traditional families have eroded, so have their traditions. As church attendance has gone down, so has the influence of religion. And let's face it: You don't feel free to correct your neighbor's kids the way adults did when you were young. Colin Powell talks about growing up in Brooklyn with so many adult relatives watching him—he says the Internet is nothing compared to the 'aunt-net'!

"For many of us, the 'aunt-net'—the family that used to keep us accountable—is disconnected. So who's teaching responsibility today? Freedom can be granted; heck, in America it's a birthright (though most kids today don't appreciate how it must be fought for and protected). In contrast, responsibility can't just appear out of nowhere; it can't be granted to you; it can't be a birthright protected by the Constitution or Bill of Rights. Responsibility must be taught.

"So, aside from liberty, I can't think of anything better to build a statue to than responsibility."

Except, Roger thought to himself, to Viktor Frankl.

21

Journalists, on the whole, don't pay much attention to their work spaces. People in other professions may decorate their cubicles and desks with all sorts of trinkets and photos and plants and the like, but few journalists either take the trouble or have the sentiment to have much around them except piles of newspapers and documents they'll never get to.

So when a journalist has a plant put on his desk, as Roger did on this day, it tends to stick out. Especially when it's a big-eared split-leaf philodendron.

He sat down and smiled, immediately suspecting who could have done this.

Before he could get to the card, though, the phone rang.

"Roger, my friend! How are you?"

It always shocked and humbled Roger to hear Dr. Frankl's crackly, long-distance voice—and in the three years since their first meeting, Roger had never grown accustomed to hearing this great man call him by his first name.

"I'm wonderful, doctor. How are you and Mrs. Frankl?"

"This is what I wish to talk to you about, my friend," Dr. Frankl pronounced ominously. "But first, we want to sincerely congratulate you and Melody on the birth of your son!"

"Thank you, doctor. I haven't opened the card yet. May I assume the plant is from you and Mrs. Frankl?"

"If it is the philodendron you speak of, yes. You may recall that we received such a plant upon the birth of our only child, Gabriele. This is the monstrosity that, as you know, to this day holds forth in an entire corner of our flat."

"How can I forget? It's the plant that nearly ate me whole!"

Dr. Frankl loved to laugh, and he did at that. "We trust all is well."

"Yes, sir. Melody is doing fine, and so is the baby. And Luciana, who's 11 now, just adores him. We named him after a very good friend of ours. Some guy named Viktor."

There were a couple seconds of silence. "This is a fine honor you have accorded me, my friend. A fine honor indeed. And, as a matter of coincidence, I am calling to tell you of another honor."

"Another honorary degree? Are you able to finish wallpapering your apartment with them?"

"Indeed, it *is* an honorary degree—but for Elly, not for me."

Roger's right eyebrow shot up as it always did when he was surprised. "Well, that *is* great news. What part of the world? What school?"

"It's in your country, in Chicago, at a place called North Park University, on May 22, 1993, this year. A very good friend of ours who teaches there, Haddon Klingberg, has arranged it. And we would be greatly honored if you would attend. I'm afraid Mrs. Frankl would insist on it!"

"I'll be there, thank you. I'll get the San Francisco Fire Department to water the plant while I'm gone."

◆   ◆   ◆

The tears could've watered all the philodendrons in Chicago when Eleonore Schwindt Frankl was conferred the doctor of laws degree at North Park University. She managed to hold back the tears through her introduction and the actual conferring of the degree—but she lost it, as did many others, when an essentially sightless Dr. Frankl rose up and shuffled without help toward her on the stage. As she cried, he held her face in his hands and kissed her tears away.

Roger watched with the pride of one privileged to be called friend by these two giants. It was that day, after all, that it occurred to Roger that she was nearly as much a giant as he. Since the days that Viktor Frankl's tears flowed upon his repatriation after the camps, she had typed his books, his notes, his letters. She had followed him to every inhabitable continent. She had risen early and retired late each day—and sometimes entertained her husband's eccentric middle-of-the-night intellectual flights of fancy—in order to keep his world turning neatly. And, in all this, she had absorbed and assimilated enough of the doctor's teachings to be able to share occasional bits of life-affirming wisdom with troubled friends and strangers on the streets and on the phone. She had sacrificed silently, stoically, even happily, in ways she will never tell—sharing her husband with an adoring, needful, pawing world, and giving completely of herself in the process.

In his research on Dr. Frankl, Roger had come across a 1979 book called *Austrians Who Belong to the World*. It named Viktor Frankl as one of them. Watching Mrs. Frankl be singled out for a high honor for her own contributions, he understood what Frankl friend Klingberg maintained about the Frankls: that they *both* belonged to the world.

The crowd at North Park that day was privileged—but truly had no idea how much—to see not only the light, but the warmth that accompanied it.

◆   ◆   ◆

Roger thought he'd seen it all in the early 1990s, and he wasn't alone. The world was shifting like the Marina District dirt. In retrospect, it can now be seen that the Soviet Union had been dying a slow death in the 1980s— for which Mikhail Gorbachev received the Nobel Peace Prize, which Roger wrote in a column was "like the Roman fire department giving Nero an award for valor." And who would have ever expected to see Nelson Mandela as president of South Africa?

But one thing Roger hadn't seen was the Frankls, except for the 1993 ceremony for Elly. So when an invitation to see them came up in October 1996, he jumped at the chance.

Especially the way the invitation was worded.

"This may be my last opportunity to see Dr. Frankl," his longtime stateside assistant Dr. Jay Levinson told Roger in a phone call from his home in Baltimore. "Perhaps yours, too. I'm going over this month to finish up a manuscript for his latest book, *Man's Search for Ultimate Meaning*. I've been very honored that he asked me to help put it together. But I have an ulterior motive for going to see him.

"I want to tell him thanks."

Roger felt like he'd had a knife stuck in his gut. His separation from the Frankls, one of both time and distance, now came into clear view. Friends don't cross the Atlantic every day—especially when one of them is in his 90s. But he didn't like the thought of losing Viktor.

"I know the Frankls think very highly of you," Levinson added. "And I have to imagine they are dear to you, because they sure are to me. He's like a father to me. Anyway, I thought you might like to fly over with me and my wife and—have a visit."

Roger appreciated Levinson's gentle use of words, but their impact wasn't lost on him. This was a chance for both of them to say goodbye. "I'd love to. I'll meet you at BWI."

As he hung up the phone, Roger looked at the philodendron next to his newsroom desk.

It was starting to take over the corner.

◆   ◆   ◆

Jay Levinson reminded Roger of a more slightly built Rob Reiner. He had a friendly, smart-looking face, with full cheeks, glasses and a short beard showing streaks of gray, with similarly short hair on the sides and back of his head. He was instantly friendly as Roger met him and his wife at the Baltimore/Washington airport. Levinson was a logotherapist in private practice who more or less specialized in grief and mourning—an irony considering the primary motivation for the trip.

Once they were settled in their plane seats for the overnight trip to Vienna, Roger was fascinated to know more about the bond between Levinson and Frankl, a bond he both respected and envied.

"I was a graduate student at U.S. International University in San Diego back in 1977," Levinson explained. "I was only a first-year student, but was lucky enough to be a graduate assistant for the dean, Dr. W. Ray Rucker. One day he called me into his office. He asked me if I knew that Dr. Frankl would be teaching a second-quarter course there. Well, he might as well have asked me if I knew my name! Everyone there knew of the great Viktor Frankl, and his yearly class was the most popular one there.

"Well, Dr. Rucker didn't happen to be teaching a second-quarter class, and out of the blue he asks me if I would like to work as an assistant to Dr. Frankl!"

Even now, Levinson was wide-eyed amazed at recalling the incredible turn his life was taking back then.

"I didn't deserve it; I knew that. But you don't turn down an opportunity like that. Of course, I said yes. I served as his graduate assistant for two years before earning my Ph.D. I was about to return to Baltimore for my internship when Dr. Frankl asked me if he could consider me an assistant to call on for various matters in the U.S. I said I would do that, and I always have—happily. I still do so today."

"That must be a thrill." Roger hoped his skin wasn't turning green.

Levinson didn't even have to answer the obvious question, except by expounding on it. "He has given me any number of errands and tasks, some exciting and some mundane. But when you work for someone as great as Dr. Frankl, no task and no gesture is trivial. Every one of them is monumental to me. The fact that he has asked me to edit and otherwise help with what may be his last book is a dream come true. And, frankly, I feel it means I've made the transition from lowly graduate assistant to colleague."

"May I?" They were in the air now, and the beverage cart had just rolled by. Roger had spirited a couple small bottles of red wine and glasses, and was playing steward to the Levinsons. His offering to Mrs. Levinson prompted her to join in on the conversation.

"From what I hear," she told Roger, "Jay never acted like a lowly graduate assistant. Tell Mr. Murphy about the incident at dinner."

Levinson smiled a wistful smile. "Don't get us wrong. I may have been naturally a little confident, shall we say, but I was always in awe of Dr. Frankl and very respectful to him."

"Except …" she prodded him.

"Well," he allowed, "there was one night I may have bordered on disrespectful.

"It was at the end of my second year as his assistant in San Diego. He took me and my first wife out to dinner. I was very curious and troubled by his absolute rejection of collective guilt—the notion that the German masses should be considered responsible for Nazi atrocities during World War II. I knew we'd be parting the next morning, so I took the opportunity to challenge him—relentlessly, and without much tact, as I was wont to do in those days.

"You have to understand, my father was a World War II veteran, and in his house we were not allowed to buy German or Japanese products. Even when I had my own money, and a Volkswagen Beetle was all I could afford, he forbade me to purchase it. That's the background I came from, you see. So I had a most difficult time understanding this attitude of Dr. Frankl's, coming as it did from a survivor of the death camps.

"I suppose I badgered him for two hours at dinner, and another two at the hotel afterward. He was eminently patient, though, and answered all my questions. Finally, I saw the gift he was trying to bestow on me: the gift of forgiveness. I have since learned that forgiveness is not a trait of the weak, but rather of the very strong.

"Anyway, my then-wife, my first wife, upbraided me, rightfully so, on the way home for being belligerent toward this great man, and I too, independent of what she thought, felt absolutely awful. So the next morning when I came to their hotel room for the trip to the airport, I apologized right out of the chute. It seems comical to think of the picture now: He stood there, looking at me across the hotel room's threshold like I had just spoken Martian to him. He turned to Elly, and she looked quizzically at him right back and shrugged her shoulders the cute way she does.

"He looked back at me, stepped toward me and gave me a big hug. He said I had made him feel more intellectually stimulated than he had been for years, and for me to never stop doing that. You can't imagine how relieved and humbled I felt. It sure showed me something. Here's the best, clearest thinker of the 20th century, and he welcomes an intellectual sparring match from an inferior like me. Unbelievable. What a man. What a human being."

"I don't get it," Roger abruptly challenged him.

Levinson looked stunned. "What don't you get?"

"Why is it that this guy's reputation isn't bigger?"

Levinson smiled and sipped his wine. "He saw himself in terms of Stekel's famous line: 'Even the dwarf standing on the shoulders of the giant can see farther.' He felt he was the dwarf standing on the shoulders of Freud and others who had come before him. He was not interested in being well-known, as odd as that may seem for a man so well-known! And well-traveled. He never had a public relations firm, a marketing manager or a publicist. No one even negotiated book and lecture fees for him. We'll never know how all this hurt him financially. He hated commercialism in general, but especially of logotherapy. When they started putting the 'logo' prefix on things—like when the Institute of Logotherapy staged a European 'Logo-Tour,' he recoiled. But ever the gentleman, he never complained.

"He was so retiring when it came to fame that he treasured those of us who had the privilege to 'protect' him on occasion. In fact, he once did a caricature of himself with an oversized drawing of me protecting him. I have it on my wall."

"Man," Roger shook his head. "What if he *had* been the least bit promotion-oriented?"

"My goodness, who knows? How much more popular might he and logotherapy be—if only he had put as much emphasis on disseminating his words as he did on forming them?"

As if toasting the thought, the three of them all took a drink.

◆   ◆   ◆

When their book-writing business was done in the afternoon, doctors Frankl and Levinson joined the others—Roger, Mrs. Frankl, Franz Vesely, his wife Gabriele, their daughter Katja, and Lori Levinson—in the living room of the Frankls' flat. Somehow, the group found enough places to sit; Roger didn't figure on the modest amount of furniture holding that many people.

The group quickly convinced Dr. Frankl to rest—and Jay Levinson saw his opportunity. He walked with Dr. and Mrs. Frankl to the doorway of the study, talking softly nearly right next to his ear. "Yes, of course!" the entire apartment could hear Dr. Frankl respond to Levinson.

Just before closing the door, Levinson looked over his shoulder and then over at Roger—motioning with his head to come join the small group in the study. Shocked at the invitation, Roger shook off his surprise and whisked in.

As Dr. Frankl settled in on his daybed to rest, three chairs were pulled up beside it. While Roger and Mrs. Frankl watched in respectful silence, Levinson addressed Dr. Frankl like a son clearing his conscience before a dying father. Except that Levinson wasn't expressing remorse or regret—only a timeless gratitude that seemed to rumble in the depths of his soul and erupt in a flow of words and tears.

"Dr. Frankl." Levinson eschewed the more informal "Viktor." "There have only been three truly important men in my life: my father, who taught me to be a man of integrity; my maternal grandfather, who taught me how to love; and you, my wonderful friend and mentor, who taught me how to be a professional and a human being at once."

Roger was amazed at how quickly the tears came to Levinson; obviously, these feelings that were now stirring had been simmering for years. Roger could not remember a time when he was so moved, and Mrs. Frankl, too, was dabbing at her eyes. Dr. Frankl just listened intently.

"I know the things of which I am speaking are not normally something you like to hear. I know how much you hate tributes. But this is not a tribute. This is simply overwhelming gratitude, from a man whose life you have helped make."

It was clearly awkward—raw emotions do not pass between men easily. But Levinson talked of his immeasurable love and respect for Dr. Frankl. How much he had learned from him—about psychology and philosophy, of course, but also about being a man. And about just being human.

"The most important thing I learned from you, Dr. Frankl, was that we, especially in the profession of psychology, must strive to remain human beings—and *humane* beings—whatever else we do in life. I've always marveled at your patience, and your uncomplaining nature—despite all you have endured. You *are* the living embodiment of logotherapy."

Levinson recounted how Dr. Frankl had shared in his joy at becoming a father—something Roger had experienced himself first-hand—and how Dr. Frankl had commiserated with Levinson in the difficulties of divorce as well as the hopeful joy of a new love and second marriage.

Taking off his glasses yet again to wipe his eyes, Levinson mumbled an apology for having imposed his emotional baggage on Dr. Frankl when he was tired and needed solitude.

Seconds after Levinson had finished, and some 20 minutes after he had begun, Dr. Frankl overcame the objections of both Levinson and Mrs. Frankl and got off his day bed to sit behind his desk. There, he grabbed a sheet of paper, knowing just where to place his hand, and wrote in the script of a man who could barely see. What the teacher wrote and handed to Levinson brought the former student to the brink of tears again.

Quickly composing himself, as Dr. Frankl made his way back to his bed, Levinson looked at Roger. "Dr. Frankl, I think perhaps I've not only imposed on you by unloading this way, but I've also monopolized the opportunity to do so. I think Mr. Murphy might have his own thoughts to add."

Roger was unprepared to have the ball thrown into his court. He looked at Dr. Frankl for signs of an objection, then at Mrs. Frankl, who smiled with her eyes and nodded encouragement.

"I confess to being more than a little jealous of the bond between you and Dr. Levinson, sir. I don't have near the history with you that he does. But I assure you, you have changed my life no less than you've changed his.

"When I came to you almost six years ago, I was ..." Roger struggled for the words. Self-exploration on the spur of the moment isn't easy. "I was self-absorbed, self-pitying and—well, something of a wretch. I frankly hadn't looked for meaning in life, and couldn't have found it if I had, because I was so focused inward.

"When it came right down to it, I was just plain sick."

"No!" barked Dr. Frankl, startling all three of them. "This is not sick! This is something that Freud maintained in a letter to Princess Bonaparte— that the moment a man begins to question his existence he is sick. As I have said before, it is a manifestation of being human. No other animal can question the meaning of its existence. It is man's privilege—a burden, perhaps, but a privilege primarily—that he cares about the meaning of his existence. Never forget that."

Roger smiled and nodded his head, not sure if Dr. Frankl even saw it. "Well, thanks to you, today I feel I am truly happy. And it's because I began looking outward rather than inward. I have a lovely wife, an adopted daughter, Luciana, whom I adore, and little Victor. I owe it all to you, Dr. Frankl. And who knows how much is owed to you by people you've never met—sad, desperate people who, in their moment of despair, reached out and touched your writings, which gave them hope and reason to go on."

Roger, like Levinson, began to feel guilt at having imposed himself. "I could say a lot more, Dr. Frankl. But really, all I want to say is thank you— from the bottom of my soul."

Dr. Frankl uttered not a word—he was tiring. He just reached for Roger's hand, which Roger helped him find. After a couple of squeezes, he let go, and the three closed the study doors behind them.

Lori Levinson stood up. Jay stuffed his handkerchief in his pocket and gave her a nod, and she nodded back.

◆   ◆   ◆

For two hours, Roger sat placidly in St. Stephen's cathedral while his mind raced through the decades, starting with the moments Viktor Frankl spent in this same place while wrestling with whether to leave Austria for his safety or stay for his parents. Roger searched his own past for any dilemma even close to that size. There was none. Then, thinking about what he'd be returning to—an uncertain career and an even more tenuous grasp on life—he remembered what Viktor would do.

Just then, Roger got on his knees and thanked God that nothing really bad had happened to him that day.

◆   ◆   ◆

At dinner with the Levinsons and the Frankl grandchildren that night, in a dimly lit authentic Italian restaurant in what Roger thought was west Vienna, he fell even deeper in love with Alexander and Katja. They were young adults now—Katja 26, and Alex 22. It was difficult not to be in love with Katja anyway—a beautiful, quick-to-smile curly-headed brunette with interests as wide as the world. But Roger was also quite enamored of both Alex's charm and intellect.

It didn't hurt, either, that Alex's cell phone played the theme from the original *Star Trek* when it rang—Roger was old enough to be one of the first "trekkers"—or that Alex, this brilliant young Austrian whose grandfather was one of the great men of the 20th century, thoroughly believed, as Roger did, that *The Simpsons* was the finest show in television history.

Roger and Alex were simply brothers in spirit.

"I'm glad you're pursuing film, like you said you would when you were a teenager," Roger told him.

"He's also being trained in opera," Katja broadcast proudly.

Alex's eyes sparkled just like his grandfather's. "I also want to be a logotherapist."

"Right," Roger concurred. "You don't have any other pursuits, apparently." Alex smiled his Hollywood smile.

"I'm extremely glad to hear you say that—that you want to be a logotherapist," Levinson spoke up. "You know, your grandfather, as much as he disdained marketing and promoting himself, has left it to the rest of us to carry the torch. How fitting that his grandchild would want to carry it."

Roger was intrigued. "What gave you that fever, Alex? So many kids resist the idea of carrying on their fathers' or grandfathers' work."

Alex thought for a moment. "Well, I've always admired grandfather's work. But I suppose the light really came on for me at the Ninth World Congress of Logotherapy in Toronto—that would have been, uh, 1993." He shot a questioning glance to Katja, who confirmed his recollection. "It was at that point that I really seriously read *Man's Search for Meaning*. And then, there was the Tenth Congress in Dallas last year …"

Katja picked up the story. "Of course, grandfather could not attend it because of his age and health, so Alex and I helped represent him. At the congress, there was a display of the uniform of one of the Texas soldiers who liberated grandfather from Turkheim. The soldier's widow and son, who had agreed to have it displayed, were there. It was very moving for both of us."

"When we told grandfather about this by phone," Alex continued, "he asked Katja and I to place a single rose from him on that soldier's uniform."

Roger, the only one at the table not there to see it, shook his head in deference to the moment.

"Alex and I knew our grandfather was special, even famous," Katja continued. "But I think those world congresses were really eye-openers for us. They showed us how deeply grandfather has touched so many around the world."

Dinner had ended, but Roger hadn't had enough of these two. "I'm not ready for the night to end. Is there maybe a nightclub we can go to and talk some more?"

"Sure," Alex glistened. "That'd be fun." Then, lapsing into his best Captain Kirk, he added, "We need to seek out new night life and new civilizations! We need to boldly go …"

"Beam me up, Scotty," Katja interjected, rolling her eyes.

◆   ◆   ◆

Roger and the Levinsons were sitting in the hotel lobby waiting for the shuttle to the airport when he looked at his watch.

"How long before the shuttle?" he asked.

Jay looked at his watch. "About 20 minutes. Why?"

Roger shot up. "I've got something I've gotta do." Running off, he yelled back, "I'll be back in time! Don't worry!"

Finally, he found the right place. He tested the employee to see if she knew English; no luck. He was just going to have to try to communicate what he wanted.

"What I want is, I think, a *schaumschnitten.*"

The woman instantly recognized it, and brought Roger one. And just in time. He paid, unconcerned if he overpaid, and ran out.

As the plane leveled off for the cruise home, Roger pulled it out and bit into it.

"He's absolutely right. Sinful."

"What?" Jay wondered.

"Dr. Frankl. He told he last time I was here that I needed to get one of these *schaumschnittens.* He was right. It's fabulous. I'm positively schaum-smitten."

"Well," Jay agreed, "Vienna *is* a bit of heaven on Earth. The architecture, the culture, the musical heritage—it all nurtures the soul. But the pastry—well, *that* nurtures the waistline. Believe me."

Jay went back to re-reading the note Dr. Frankl had written him. He saw Roger's interest in it. "Would you like to read what he wrote me?" Jay asked.

Roger nodded and took it from him. It said:

"Dear Jay,

"On some occasions, I have asked that anyone in the field of a helping profession, say, a psychologist like you, should set before himself a threefold goal: to become a psychologist; to be a good psychologist; and to remain a human being. Writing this down, for the first time, I become aware that is exactly what you have accomplished!

"In close friendship, Viktor"

"It's really not my accomplishment at all." Jay took the note back and put it in his breast pocket, next to his heart. "It's his."

22

The world was rocked and mortified when the fairy-tale princess of Wales, Diana, died, far too young, after a horrific car crash on a Paris street on Aug. 31, 1997. Before the mourning could even get into full swing, an even greater humanitarian—the legendary Mother Teresa—died at age 87 on Sept. 5, 1997.

In-between, on Sept. 2, and with quite a lot less fanfare, the world lost Viktor Frankl.

Not that his passing went unnoticed in Austria and other points around the globe. In fact, by the time Eleonore Frankl left his side and arrived back at the flat she had shared with her husband for some 50 years, the Austrian president was already on the radio lamenting the passing of a great countryman.

Elsewhere around the world, the initiated—those who knew Viktor Frankl, or those who merely knew of him—were deeply distraught at his passing. But far too many people *didn't* know of him, by Roger's reckoning. And sandwiched between the deaths of two of the best-known, best-loved women of the century, Viktor Frankl's death caused nowhere near the ripples that Roger thought it should have.

Fact is, he might not have known about it if Jay Levinson hadn't called him with the news immediately.

Roger grabbed a flight that very afternoon. With all the commotion of leaving, he hadn't had time to reflect on Viktor's passing. But by the time his connecting flight left the Philadelphia airport for the transatlantic journey, the dark blue had descended. Roger tried to buoy himself with the realization that it had been time. Jay Levinson had sensed it coming for the better part of a year. Certainly, Viktor had as well. Surely Viktor was quite prepared to die. He had had to prepare himself some 50 years before. And he had led a good second life, made good on his second chance. He had a life of the utmost meaning. He made the most of nearly every moment. He left the world an infinitely better place than he'd found it. While he viewed himself as a dwarf on others' shoulders, he had perhaps the broadest shoulders of his time, his thin earthly frame notwithstanding.

And that's just the part we could see, Roger thought. Truly there are unseen effects, unknown meanings, in all our lives. Roger couldn't help thinking about the lesson imparted by the guardian angel Clarence to George Bailey in the movie *It's a Wonderful Life*: Each life touches so many others; a man leaves an awful hole when he isn't around. Well, Roger thought, imagine the hole left by a man who touched as many people as Viktor Frankl did. It's likely the size of a crater that could swallow the Earth itself.

Roger had been thinking that his despair, and even his tears, had gone unnoticed—but suddenly a stewardess walking from the front of the plane to the back dropped a Kleenex and cup of water in his hand, not even breaking stride or stopping to acknowledge what she'd done. It was a simple act of kindness Roger would not soon forget.

◆   ◆   ◆

Roger didn't identify himself when he called the Frankl flat, and the voice on the phone was not one he recognized. The man's thick accent and brusque manner were not conducive to much explanation or exploration. So, when the man revealed that Dr. Frankl had already been memorialized and buried, Roger was both flabbergasted and devastated. He simply thanked the man and hung up, not knowing why he was even in Vienna at that point. He tried calling the Veselys, but to no avail. Moreover, he had made his plans in such haste that he had failed to find out where Dr. Levinson was staying.

Roger determined that he would visit the grave site and go home. But to do that, he had to first play journalist to find out where it might be, and explorer to get there without the use of any German.

After some asking around, he learned that the most likely grave site was in the city's Central Cemetery, which actually seemed to be in the southwest part of the city. It took some doing getting there—a subway ride, transfer to the wrong bus, a ride back to the right bus, and finally a bus stop close to the cemetery's entrance.

Roger stopped in to see the attendant, but the man didn't speak English, and no pronunciation of the word "Frankl" seemed to ring a bell. But Roger saw maps of the cemetery—and while Dr. Frankl's grave site wouldn't be shown on the maps, Roger had a sense from talking to someone that it would be on the other end of the cemetery.

It was an unusually warm day for September, so Roger saw no harm in setting out to cross the cemetery.

Until, after some amount of walking, he saw that the cemetery had no apparent end whatsoever. Ahead of him, seemingly forever, stretched a trail of crushed rock and trees and graves and trees and graves.

At one point, becoming a bit worried about dehydration, he stopped by a water crank. But a sign in both German and English warned him not to drink it. So he walked on.

Finally, he came upon two cemetery workers. They didn't speak English, and again no mention of Frankl helped. But one of the men, seeing Roger's camera and believing him a tourist, did his best, even drawing on his hand, to direct Roger toward the graves of such local luminaries as Beethoven and Brahms. The man seemed to indicate they would be on the far side of a huge green-copper domed church, a structure that a lot of countries might have been proud to use as a capitol. Roger hoped and figured Frankl's grave would be somewhere close.

Another long walk ensued, but this time with a payoff: Roger came upon a small group of tourists who had collected in an intimate garden-like enclave, and they were snapping photos of flashy, impressive graves. Beethoven and Brahms, as well as Schubert and others.

But no Frankl.

Roger took the obligatory photos of those monuments, and sat down to consider his increasingly precarious position. No way could he walk this cemetery from front to back, especially with no water. He made the only decision he could—a tactical retreat. He was sad that he wouldn't see Viktor's grave, but perhaps at another time.

Outside the gates, he found a small store selling drinks. As he finished a Sprite, he realized he had exited a different gate, one on the same side as the one he'd entered, but farther down. At this entrance there was more activity. He decided to see if anyone spoke English.

"The Jewish cemetery is on the other end," a stout woman named Helga boomed.

"That's too far to walk," Roger bemoaned.

"Ya, too far," she agreed. But seeing the disappointment in his face, she barked something in German to a man working with her. "Come, I will drive you."

Before they drove off, the man barked something back. She chortled and turned to Roger. "He told me to be careful with you in the car."

Considering her formidable build, Roger was wondering if *he* wasn't the one in peril.

At the other end of the cemetery, there was a phone booth-sized operation attended by a solitary man.

"This is the old Jewish cemetery," Helga explained. She appeared to ask the attendant where the Frankl grave site might be. "Over there," she translated for Roger, pointing out of the windshield into the trees.

"Can you wait?" Roger asked.

"A few minutes. Not many."

Roger navigated through the sea of gravestones and trees until he saw a group of men huddled around one. They appeared to be saying Jewish prayers. Roger hid behind a tree and got his camera out, putting the long-distance lens on it. Through it, he saw that this was, indeed, a service of some type for Viktor.

Tired and confused, he slid to the ground on the other side of the tree and put his camera away, so as not to be confused with paparazzi. It suddenly dawned on him that what the man at the Frankl flat told him on the phone was a ruse to discourage the curious and the press: Viktor Frankl hadn't been buried after all. It was going on right now.

Still sitting on the ground, Roger turned and leaned over to see around the tree, then turned back and looked at Helga sitting in the car down the way. He couldn't interrupt what appeared to be a solemn ceremony. On the other hand, Helga couldn't wait forever, either. And he sure as heck didn't want to be stranded.

All of a sudden he heard chattering and car doors shutting. He leaned around the tree again and saw the group leaving. There was one figure left. The man walked over to the gravestone and placed something on it. He backed away and stood for a moment, then turned and got in a car and left.

Roger couldn't believe his good fortune. He jumped up and race-walked nearer the grave site. And he couldn't believe what he saw.

Compared to the regal grave sites of Beethoven and his pals, Frankl's was a pauper's grave. It was an unbelievable contrast, and an unsettling one to Roger. The other graves were trimmed in gold, had busts and statues and magnificent sizes and shapes. They were in a well-tended garden of their own, and Beethoven's was even surrounded by an iron gate with flowers and wreaths and such. And in each case, the graves had but one name on them. Brahms. Or Beethoven. Or Franz Schubert.

In contrast, the Frankl gravestone was gray, modest in size and contained the names of various family members, including his parents, Gabriel and Elsa, and his brother Walter and his wife Else. There were also people with the last name Lion, who Roger assumed were Viktor's mother's relatives.

At the base of the tombstone, a simple, thin marker was placed with the name "Viktor Emil Frankl," along with his date of birth, March 26, 1905, and death, Sept. 2, 1997.

Nothing more. No bust. No statue. No ornate fencing or landscaping. No indications on the marker that here lies one of the great men of his time. Nothing about his fame, his acclaim. Not even the title "Dr." Just Viktor Emil Frankl.

It couldn't be much simpler, Roger thought.

In a way, Roger felt cheated. He expected more; wanted more. But he also realized the message being sent: Dr. Frankl didn't want to be remembered as someone famous or special. He had no PR man in life, and no wrought iron fence drawing attention to his death. He merely joined the family he'd entered the world with.

Before leaving, Roger whispered a prayer and, at the last second, realized what the solitary figure before him had placed on the grave: a stone. There were several there. An apparent tradition. Roger looked around, found a small rock on the ground, and put it on the grave. He thought it was an overly modest contribution—but he figured Viktor would have approved.

He brushed his hands off, wiped his eyes, turned and walked away.

◆   ◆   ◆

"Did you get what you wanted?" Helga asked as he got in the car.

"Yes, thank you." Roger put his seat belt on and realized how grateful he was to this woman who went so far out of her way to help a hapless foreigner. "That guy was right, you know," he told her. She looked at him puzzled. "You *do* have to watch out for me!"

Helga laughed and hit Roger in the shoulder. It hurt.

◆   ◆   ◆

The doorway to the Frankls' apartment building was jammed with reporters clamoring to get in. Roger had no hope of getting in, at least not without letting in a pack of wolves, he figured. He couldn't even call up on the intercom in front of all the other reporters. He understood their pursuit, and even appreciated it since he thought Dr. Frankl deserved the attention. Roger just wished they'd go away for a minute and let him in.

He noticed a young woman walking toward the crowd of journalists apprehensively. She stood for a moment watching them, then started squeezing through them. When she reached the door, Roger figured out she was a resident of another apartment in the building, just trying to get home through the madness.

Roger ran over and pushed his way to the woman just as she was opening the door.

"Darling!" Roger protested with a British accent, just for effect. "Where in the world have you been? You weren't going to leave me out here with these man-eating creatures, were you?" He put his arm around the befuddled young woman, who offered no resistance as Roger pushed her through the door and closed it behind them. She stood there looking at him as if he were insane. Besides the fact that she didn't know him from Adam, she didn't appear to speak English—and so she fully expected that he did, indeed, have some sort of business with her. She seemed willing to listen, even partly smiling when she realized what he'd done.

"Sorry about that, love," he said, keeping up the British pretense. "Just needed to get in. Hope you don't mind."

As he started to walk down the hall toward the stairs, she called out. He stopped. "Pardon?"

"Eight," she repeated in accented English, then went into apartment 8, closing the door slowly and smiling.

Roger smiled and turned up the stairs.

He was more than a little relieved to see the familiar face of Harald Mori answer the Frankl door. "Mr. Murphy, how nice to see you." Harald's pleasure quickly faded. "Come in, quickly."

"Sorry to arrive unannounced, but …"

"No, I completely understand. It's madness out there. Besides, it's a great pleasure to see that you have come. Mrs. Frankl will be so glad to see you."

She was. One of the world's great huggers, she practically carried him over to a seat with the other family members.

"I just wanted to come and express my condolences," Roger shared after all the hellos. "Let me apologize on behalf of my colleagues downstairs."

"Oh," Mrs. Frankl cried, waving her hand. "It's a terrible time, just a terrible time. I can't leave the apartment."

"I suppose that circus is why you were telling people that he was—well, that …"

"Buried? Yes, we told the reporters that right away, and everyone else, to get them to leave us alone and so he could have a private burial as he wished. Viktor didn't want anyone to know he was even dead before it was all over and done with. Of course, that didn't work, but we told people it was over and it wasn't true."

Roger looked for a bright spot. "Of course, it's a measure of his fame and the love people had for Dr. Frankl."

"Yes, undoubtedly," Mrs. Frankl allowed. "But for our family, it has been a terrible time. We were at our small apartment in the Vienna Woods—we have gone there often in the last few years, since Viktor became blind and we couldn't enjoy the mountains like we used to. But the press would look in the window. So I put down the blinds. Franz and Harald have been a big help. But journalists behind your back is a terrible thing, and in this situation, you are not really in the mood to discuss this with anyone."

Roger noticed some photographs on the coffee table. They seemed to be fairly new. "May I?"

"Of course," Mrs. Frankl offered, picking them up. "These were the last photographs taken of Viktor—last month, at the celebration of the marriage of Katja to Klaus Ratheiser. Doesn't he look happy?"

"Full of life."

"Yes, yes."

"He was quite brave," offered son-in-law Franz Vesely in his typical soft voice. "Before he was to have heart bypass surgery, he said, 'I see nothing tragic in these circumstances.'"

"He died well," Mrs. Frankl agreed, looking down and nodding her head. "He was ready. He even expressed concern about inconveniencing the medical staff and taking up their time." She shook her head, partly in amazement, partly in disagreement with him. "The good thing is that, even though his body failed him, his mind never did, even till the end. He had wished for this. He always wished, 'May God give me the opportunity to have my brain up to the last moment.' And this happened to him."

"He was also very lucky to have Elly," Harald added. "She was with him day and night, only coming here to the flat to sleep."

"He never regained consciousness after surgery," she jumped in, trying to change the subject from her own courage and steadfastness.

Roger laid the photos back on the table. "May I ask a rather personal question about him?" Mrs. Frankl shrugged in a neutral way, but Franz nodded slightly for Roger to proceed. "You mentioned God. Was he religious?"

Mrs. Frankl sighed, looking at Franz before answering. "This was very private to Viktor. He did not feel religion was his field, and that his patients had the right to their own private views on this. And he said religions were like languages—with people just using different ways to express the same things, to approach the same truths in vastly different ways. So he never talked much about it. But, yes, he was."

"Every day after the surgery," Harald chimed back in, "Elly would put earphones on Viktor's ears and play music by Mozart that Alexander had taped for him. The nurses couldn't believe her devotion—all day long, talking to him and playing that music. And before the surgery, she would take him his phylactery—the box containing the Hebrew prayers he would say each morning—and she would stand guard outside his hospital room so he could pray in private."

"He was a very private man," Mrs. Frankl added. "Very famous—but very private."

Franz nodded. "He said that there are three times when a human being should never be photographed: when he is loving, when he is praying and when he is dying. These are the most intensely private moments in a man's life."

That reminded Roger of the graveside service he spied on. "I have to admit, I was at the grave today."

Mrs. Frankl was shocked. "No!"

"I hid behind a tree. I didn't know about it, of course. I'm sorry if that was an intrusion."

"Of course I don't mind. I am touched you would come all this way for that."

"I don't mean to be disrespectful …" Roger stopped short.

"I can't imagine you would be," Mrs. Frankl said tenderly. "Speak."

"I was amazed at the differences between Dr. Frankl's grave and those of Beethoven, Brahms and the others. Why is that?"

Each member of the group seemed to look at each other and smile just a little. Franz took the lead in his quiet, confident way. "You may not know— because I suspect he did not tell you—that he was given the high award of honorary citizen of Vienna two years ago. As part of that honor, one is afforded a grave of honor, such as those you speak of. Viktor left precise instructions for that not to happen."

"He said," Mrs. Frankl added, "that he was born Viktor Frankl and that he would die Viktor Frankl—nothing more, nothing less. He always told me that both occasions are similar in that you should be surrounded only by family."

Roger smiled and shook his head. "What humility."

"Look around!" chirped Mrs. Frankl. "This is the home of a humble man. Do you see many material things? Do you know, he once bought a Rolex watch—but immediately regretted it. He had no use for such things, and neither do I."

"Spoken like a woman with two unused mink stoles." Roger coaxed a smile out of her.

"He would like to buy things for others, though," Franz gleamed. "If he saw a poor person longing for something in a store but unable to afford it, he would pay for it and leave it at the cashier as a gift.

"We were speaking of Mrs. Frankl's devotion to her husband," Franz continued. "You may know that after he became mostly blind, she read to him. Every day. For hours and hours and hours. Others of us would try to help, but he was so used to Mrs. Frankl …"

"It was very difficult, but what else should I do but that?" she explained. "He was my husband, and he needed me. At night, if I wasn't too tired, I would read some books to myself, things Viktor would never have listened to! But you know, he never complained about his blindness. Not once."

Suddenly, Katja had appeared, looking lovelier than ever, even in her grief. She spoke something in German. Seeing Roger, she greeted him. "I just told grandmother that the journalists seem to be gone now."

"It is time for us to be gone, too," Franz gently ordered. "Mrs. Frankl needs her rest."

The group said their goodbyes and the guests left. Roger lingered, putting his arms out to Mrs. Frankl for a hug. "This is permitted, yes?"

She recognized his imitation of her. "It is required," she directed.

◆   ◆   ◆

Elly Frankl was still too manic to rest after the others had left. Instead, she decided to dust.

In Dr. Frankl's silent study, she took each book down and wiped it, replacing it and taking another—until she found one out of place. It was a copy of Dr. Frankl's 1950 book *Homo Patiens*—"suffering man." On the dedication page was printed the usual one-word dedication: "Elly."

But in this copy, he had scrawled a fuller dedication—most likely sometime in the days or weeks before his death, if his handwriting was any indication. He had signed the book without telling her, knowing she would find it after his burial if it was left out of place.

Between the scrawling handwriting and the water in her eyes, she had a difficult time reading it. But she managed to. It read:

"For Elly,

Who succeeded in changing a suffering man into a loving man.

Viktor"

23

The phone rang. This time, Roger Murphy wasn't speechless or surprised.

He was ready to talk, and was trained and armed with the right words.

That's what you have to be when you're manning the phones at a suicide prevention hotline.

"My wife left me after 46 years, just like that," the man moaned. "I gave her no reason. She gave *me* no reason. What's it for? What a waste!"

"I understand."

"When will the pain stop? When will the loneliness stop?"

The man was asking rhetorical questions, Roger knew. And perhaps he only wanted to be listened to.

After deciding he'd been lazily hiding behind his journalistic "objectivity" all his working life, Roger several years ago had dived into civic work like a madman. And after four years of volunteering at the suicide prevention hotline—while juggling his schedule to help out at the Boys and Girls Club, the American Cancer Society and the homeless shelter—Roger had learned: For so many people, it's more important that you extend an ear than a hand.

But the fact that someone would call the hotline was a sure sign that they were looking for a life preserver.

As he had stood on the Golden Gate Bridge almost exactly eight years before, Roger Murphy had no idea where to find the life preserver for the troubled young man who'd turned to him. Since getting to know Viktor Frankl, he'd taken one with him wherever he went.

"Did you have a good marriage?" Roger asked.

"What?" The man was shocked by the question. "Well, yes—*I* thought so, anyway."

"Did your wife take that when she left?"

"What? What are you talking about? You're not making any sense!"

This is great, Roger thought. If he's barking at me, he's got some fire left.

"All those years you had together—there were some great things that happened, weren't there?"

"*I* sure thought so."

"And those things can't be changed now, can they—not even by her leaving. Right?"

The man seemed to be absorbing it. "I suppose not. But what's that …"

"All those things, great and good, that you did together, they're now safely tucked into the past. You created them and put them in the bank. They're in a safety deposit box, and only you have the key. No one else."

The man paused, and seemed to soften. "I suppose. But what about now? What about now? What have I got to live for?"

"Did you have children?"

"Yes, three of them."

"Where are they now?"

"Back east. All of them. Never see 'em. They never call. They've got their own lives."

"Would you like to? See them, I mean?"

"Of course I would. What the hell kind of question is that?"

Roger smiled. "How about grandchildren?"

"Five of them."

"Are you done seeing them?"

Now the man paused for the longest time. "No. Not as far as I'm concerned. But it's not that easy. Their parents …"

"How difficult can it be? Do you think they'll really turn you away? Is it that bad between you?"

Again a pause. "No. Maybe. I guess *I* don't think so."

"What are their other grandfathers like? Do you know them?"

"No. I mean, they're all deceased."

Roger had him now. "You mean *you're* their only grandfather?"

"Yes," he said. "I guess I hadn't thought of it that way. But yes."

"Did you know *your* grandfathers? Either one?"

"Yes. Both of them. We lived in a small inland town. They were actually good friends with each other, and used to take me fishing with them."

"You're probably not up to that anymore."

"What? Fishing? You better believe I am. You should see my den. I don't even have a third of my trophies up. Most of them are in the garage. Drove my wife nuts. May be why she left."

"Sounds to me like you're a pretty important guy. Those kids will never have another grandfather. They might get a nice grandfatherly neighbor if they're lucky, but it's not the same. I think you know that."

"Yeah, I know that."

"And we haven't even talked about all your friends and other relations. I have to imagine there are quite a few of them who depend on you for a laugh now and then, a card game, a fishing trip."

"I don't have that many friends."

"So you say."

"What's that mean?"

"Do you count *me* as a friend?"

"Of course not! You seem like a nice young man, but come on …"

"I appreciate the 'young' part, especially," Roger interrupted.

The man actually chuckled. "But we can't say we're friends, can we?"

"I suppose not," Roger allowed. "But your life has touched mine with just a phone call. I've enjoyed talking to you, and hearing about that rich, full life of yours—despite the pain you're going through right now. So, you see, you may not have me, or a thousand other people, on your list of so-called friends. But that doesn't mean we don't depend on you, don't appreciate what you add to our lives. And those people who *are* on your list of friends? You have no idea how much they need your friendship. Do you suppose any of them have been hurting lately like you?"

Roger wasn't sure the man was still there. There was no sound for a few moments. "Hello?" Roger finally probed. "Are you there?"

"Yes," the man admitted quietly. He appeared to be composing himself.

"Do you have any friends who you might be able to comfort?"

He thought for a moment. "There's a fellow in my Rotary Club who just lost his wife after 38 years."

"I guess you two have a lot you could give to each other."

A pause. "I've been thinking about calling him."

"I wish you would. And I'll tell you what. If you'd like to talk to someone else, someone more knowledgeable than me, I have the number of a good logotherapist I'd like to give you."

"I suppose that'd be all right," the man consented—an acceptance that Roger considered a huge victory. "A *what* again?"

"A logotherapist. It's a mental health professional who uses a thing called logotherapy."

"What is that exactly—logo … whatever?"

"Logotherapy. You'll find out. But one thing it'll do is help you through your pain."

"Will it make the pain go away?"

"No. Nothing will."

"Nothing?"

"Nothing. Not this phone call, not pills, not booze, not therapy."

"Then what's the point?"

"May I ask how old you are?"

"Sixty-eight."

"What's the point of having lived 68 years?"

"What the heck …?"

"You've had pain all your life, haven't you?"

"Of course! Everyone does!"

"But that didn't stop you from leading a rich, full life, did it?"

Another short pause. "I suppose not."

"In fact, I'll go one further: I'll venture to say that the pain in your life has made you a better person. You suppose?"

"I guess that's possible."

"And even better than that, I'd say that the pain you've experienced makes your life something to be proud of. If it had been easy, every one of these past 68 years, would you be as proud of yourself as you are now?"

"No. I see your point."

"I guess what I'm saying is, don't see your pain as something to be avoided all together. You know what I mean? Don't go out and cause yourself unnecessary pain; that's not what I'm saying. But you've just said that the pain in your past has actually helped enrich your life, right? This pain you're feeling now can do the same. It all depends on how you approach it."

"You say some pretty odd things, young fella. But I have to admit, you make an awful lot of sense."

"Well, I've learned from the best. I had a friend who told me a few years ago that the last of the human freedoms is the freedom to choose your own attitude, no matter what the circumstances. That was quite a gift he gave me. And I'd like to give it to you now."

Roger gave him the name and phone number of a logotherapist in the bay area.

"Now, I'd like to apologize," Roger said.

"Whatever for? You've been a Godsend."

"Well, I think I may have given you a lot of work! Between those grandchildren and your friends and the guy in Rotary—you've got a lot to do!"

Roger could almost feel the man's smile through the phone against his ear. "I guess you have. But it's good work, if you can get it."

"And it's work that no one but you can do. No one."

"It's been wonderful talking to you, son," the man said. "But I've got work to do."

As he hung up the phone, Roger mouthed a silent prayer for the man—and a prayer of thanks.

◆   ◆   ◆

It was no more than 15 seconds later that Roger's cell phone vibrated in his pants pocket.

"Roger! It's me, Sunny!" She was frantic.

"What's wrong, Sunny?"

"I can't talk. Just hang up the phone and wait. You'll be getting a call in just a second. I don't want to clog up the phone. Bye!"

Thirty seconds later, there it was.

"Hello? Yes, this is Roger Murphy. What?" Roger was skeptical now. "Yes, I'll hold." As he waited, he searched in his mental files for who might be behind this call. It had to be some nut at the *Chronicle.*

When the voice came on the line, though, Roger recognized it instantly, and realized this was no joke.

"Fine, sir. How are *you*, Mr. President?"

24

The cool wind stroked Roger Murphy and put his gray hair to dancing as he pulled his suit coat closed, but the sun was bright and tried to make up for it. Meanwhile, the crowd around him helped shield him from the cool bay breezes, and the warmth inside him could have sustained him no matter what the weather.

It was, after all, the biggest day of his life.

As soon as the band stopped playing, it was time.

"Ladies and gentlemen," the governor roared into the microphone, "it gives me great pleasure to introduce to you the president of the United States of America."

Roger was the first to stand and applaud as the president rose, looked over at Roger and winked, and strode to the lectern.

"Mr. Governor, Mr. Mayor, honored citizens and fellow Americans," the president began. "It was some 70 years ago that a still-young man, thin from deprivation and worn from the trauma of the Nazi death camps, poured out his feelings and observations for posterity—deep and profound words that shocked the senses and chronicled in very human terms man's capacity for inhumanity toward man.

"Dr. Viktor Frankl's book, *Man's Search for Meaning*—a book that Dr. Frankl initially wished to be anonymous—went on to become one of the great works and one of the most important and influential books of all time.

"In 1962, Dr. Frankl, by popular demand, expanded on his most famous work and added a section explaining his science of 'logotherapy'—a way of understanding and coping with life and finding unconditional meaning in it. It was a science that Dr. Frankl, himself, was forced to test on himself in order to survive the death camps.

"In that section, Dr. Frankl, an Austrian whose reputation has only grown since his death in 1997, took note of our country's inspirational Statue of Liberty. But he also wrote this:

> *'Freedom is only part of the story and half of the truth. Freedom is but the negative aspect of the whole phenomenon whose positive aspect is responsibleness. In fact, freedom is in danger of degenerating into mere arbitrariness unless it is lived in terms of responsibleness.'*

"For Dr. Frankl, it was largely responsibleness that gave life meaning. One's responsibility to others. One's responsibility to oneself. One's responsibility to life itself—to what life expects of one. And it is this sense of responsibility that not only counterbalances our freedom, but also separates us from the animals. No other living being can have a true, conscious sense of responsibility that rises above mere instinct. Only the human being.

"It is because of this that Dr. Frankl suggested, more than 50 years ago, that the Statue of Liberty on our East Coast be supplemented, balanced by, a Statue of Responsibility on our West Coast.

"Over two decades ago, this city's own Roger Murphy reminded us of Dr. Frankl's inspirational words and, in particular, his challenge to us to balance freedom with responsibility.

"Today, as a symbol to the world that America is living up to Dr. Frankl's challenge to be responsible to life, and to temper our great freedoms with even greater responsibility, we are deeply honored and privileged to unveil the Statue of Responsibility he envisioned so many years ago."

With that, National Park Service rangers cut the rope on a giant shroud enveloping the upper two-thirds of the statue behind the dais. Exactly according to plan, the white cloud slipped off the head of the statue toward the back, revealing Liberty's West-Coast sister, Responsibility.

She was gorgeous. Under a crowned head was a serious, but kind countenance of a woman. On the right arm was a shield, while the left arm cradled a thick tome that had all the look of a holy book. Perched on the left shoulder was a bald eagle, its wingspan and open mouth a fearsome sight.

The crowd gasped and burst into applause, as the U.S. Air Force Band broke into "God Bless America," inspiring the crowd to sing the words.

Now it was Roger's turn to speak, and as the governor introduced him, the crowd gave him the same standing ovation it had given the president. As the applause died down, Roger looked out over the crowd. To Melody, aglow in the midday sun. To Luciana—it was difficult for Roger to believe, but there she was, a beautiful, full-grown woman of some 30 years, with her own husband and child. To Roger's son, Victor, a strapping young man of 20. And behind them, Roger's friends Alex, Katja and Abdul.

As the applause died completely, and the crowd sat down, Abdul continued standing and whooping—drawing laughter from the crowd. Finally, Abdul found his seat, as the crowd broke into applause for his show of enthusiasm.

Roger shook his head in amazement, recalling the Paul Simon lyric, "Still crazy after all these years."

"Mr. President, Mr. Governor, Mr. Mayor, honored guests. I'll be brief," Roger's voice whipped through the crowd. "After all, someone once told me, if you want to be seen, stand up; if you want to be heard, speak up; if you want to be loved, sit down and shut up." The crowd both laughed and applauded.

"When I first met Dr. Viktor Frankl, I asked him the meaning of life. With the combination of a sharp rebuke—then days of patience in answering my many feeble questions—Dr. Frankl taught me that different meanings can be found in each life, and in each moment. But he said we shouldn't ask what we can expect from life—rather, what life expects of us.

"Many believe that this axiom of Dr. Frankl's was the inspiration for President John F. Kennedy's inaugural challenge to Americans—to ask not what our country can do for us, but what we can do for our country.

"This is the very essence of responsibility. Not to seek what we can get out of life, but what we can put *into* it. This is the essence of responsibility—and responsibility is the essence of a happy life, one worth living—and, if need be, worth dying for.

"This principle—and the statue that will stand forever as a beacon for a meaningful life—is Dr. Frankl's lesson and legacy."

With a "thank you," Roger stepped from the lectern and, as the crowd stood again and applauded, he walked back to the dignitaries' seating—and hugged Mrs. Frankl.

"It is permitted, yes!" he asked.

"It is permitted, yes!" she happily repeated.

Epilogue

Expert fingers grabbed at the earth from below and pulled the rest of the body up and over. Securing the rope immediately around a tree, then himself, the man sat in the dirt and called out a prearranged code. Within seconds he felt the unmistakable tug of a rock climber approaching.

"Congratulations, Victor Murphy!" exclaimed Abdul. "You are now a rock climber!"

Detaching himself from the line, and helping Abdul take up the slack, Victor Murphy stood and surveyed the vista as Abdul continued holding the line taut.

"I sure wish Dad were here to see this. It's unbelievable."

Within moments, Luciana appeared over the edge and pulled herself up with her stepbrother's help. Then Melody.

After an inordinate amount of time, Victor turned to Melody and pronounced, "Mother, do you think we lost him?"

"Fat chance!" called a voice over the edge. Finally, Roger Murphy crawled like a land-loving lizard over the cliff's edge.

"Welcome to the Hohe Wand, Roger Murphy," Abdul cried before bear hugging Roger on the ground and sending the two men rolling away from the edge. "You're 20 years late! I've been waiting for you up here!"

"Let go of me, you crazy Turk!" Roger cried with mock anger. "You'll get us both killed!"

Roger got up on his knees, put his glasses back on, coaxed his gray hair back and dusted himself off. Looking around, he thought his knees an appropriate place to be, for he felt he was on holy ground. He imagined Viktor Frankl here with his Aryan friend, Hubert. Roger felt a sense of loss, but a sense of connection to Viktor at the same time.

A bit overwhelmed by the unexpected flood of emotion, he sat back on his heels and lowered his head. Victor started toward his father out of concern, but Melody put her hand on Victor and nodded that he was OK.

Roger had expected some vertigo—but not the kind of emotional swirl that was about him. He recalled the last words of Viktor's original *Man's Search for Meaning*:

> *"The crowning experience of all, for the homecoming man, is the wonderful feeling that, after all he has suffered, there is nothing he need fear any more—except his God."*

Roger composed a silent prayer of thanks and rose up—having finally conquered his debilitating fear of heights, thanks to Viktor. Sensing the gravity of the moment for Roger, the others instantly enveloped him in a group hug.

Roger thought for a moment about Viktor's emotional climb here so long ago as his beloved Vienna was under siege. It is no longer Hitler's Austria, Roger thought—but Viktor Frankl's Austria. The best in mankind survives long after its worst instincts fall away.

When the group had settled in and was sitting in a circle, young Victor reached in his pocket.

"Dad, I have something here for you—it's a song I heard the other day that made me think of Dr. Frankl. I thought you'd like to listen to it up here."

Victor handed him a portable mini-CD player and headphones. Roger couldn't believe how compact they had become in the last 20 years. Putting the headphones on, Roger fumbled with the player. "How the heck do you turn this thing on?"

Victor reached over and showed him. "Just press here."

It was a beautiful song, an Italian song called *Canto Alla Vita*—"Song to Life." Roger always thought the Italian language was the most beautiful and melodic on Earth. And while he didn't speak Italian, he had studied other romance languages, so he could figure out most of the lyrics.

And he understood what drew his son to the song when he heard the words:

I sing to life
To all its beauty
To every wound of it
To every caress of it

I sing to life
To its tragic beauty
To pain and to strife
Let all that dance through me
The rise and the fall
I lived through it all

Roger took the headphones off, handed the player to his son and, as casually as he could, wiped his eyes. The song seemed to put music to the words so painfully but faithfully written by Viktor Emil Frankl.

"You're right, son. Viktor would have loved that song."

More than that, Roger thought, Viktor Frankl *lived* that song.

As Roger took Luciana in one arm and Victor in the other, he silently wished the same for them.

Michael F. Ryan is a journalist, speaker and editorial writer for *The Augusta (Ga.) Chronicle* and, prior to that, *The Topeka Capital-Journal*.

In researching *The Last Freedom*, he was granted rare access to Dr. Viktor Frankl's wonderful family, for which he is deeply appreciative.

Michael lives with his wife, Susan, daughter Amanda, son Kevin and wonder dog Choco in Augusta, Ga.

Breinigsville, PA USA
04 May 2010
237359BV00003B/1/P